PERFECTION UNLEASHED

A Double Helix Novel

JADE KERRION

Jade Kerrion's thrilling Double Helix novels

PERFECTION UNLEASHED
PERFECT BETRAYAL
PERFECT WEAPON
WHEN THE SILENCE ENDS
PERFECTION CHALLENGED

Other novels by Jade Kerrion

EARTH-SIM

ISBN: 1469980355
ISBN-13: 978-1469980355

PRAISE AND RECOGNITION FOR "PERFECTION UNLEASHED"

Second place winner, Science Fiction, Royal Palm Literary Awards, 2011

First place winner, Science Fiction, Reader Views Literary Awards, 2012

South-East Regional winner, Reader Views Literary Awards, 2012

Finalist, Science Fiction, Next Generation Indie Book Awards, 2012

Honorable Mention, Hollywood Book Festival, 2012

Gold Medal winner, Science Fiction, Readers Favorites 2013

"A breakout piece of science fiction"—Royal Palm Literary Award judge

DEDICATION

To Mark, for the joy, love, and life we share.

ACKNOWLEDGMENTS

My deepest thanks to my father-in-law, Doug Waters,
whose faith and financial support made this novel possible.

I would also like to thank my editor, Bobbie Christmas,
and my cover artist, Jason Alexander.

ONE

On another Friday night, she might have been out at a Georgetown bar, accepting drinks from attractive men and allowing them to delude themselves into imagining that they might be the lucky one to take her home.

Tonight, she had work to do.

The hem of the white lab coat brushed about her legs as she strode toward the double doors that barred entry to the western wing. No one paid her any attention. Scientists and lab technicians scurried past her, nodding at her with absent-minded politeness. On Friday evening, with the weekend beckoning, no one thought about security.

Where men faltered, technology kept going.

The corridor seemed endlessly long, and the security cameras that pivoted on their ceiling-mounted frames bore into her back. She knew that her image likely featured on one or more of the many monitors at the security desk, but a combination of training and nerves of steel steadied her. She resisted the urge to twitch or to hurry her pace.

Each step brought her closer to an ominously glowing red eye on the security panel beside the door. Undeterred, she waved her badge over the panel. Moments later, the security panel flashed to green and a heavy lock slid back. Another small triumph. It usually took a series of them to make a victory.

She lowered her head, ostensibly to look down at the tablet in her hand. Her long, dark hair fell forward, concealing the lower half of her face from the security camera as she walked through the open door. "Entering the western wing," she murmured, trusting the concealed microphone to pick up on her whisper.

"Good luck," Carlos's voice responded through the tiny earpiece inserted in her right ear. "All's clear out here."

"I'm really glad the security pass I programmed for you actually worked," Xin added, a whimsical tone in her voice.

Zara was glad, too. She had a solid plan. Two of her finest associates backed her up—Carlos Sanchez waiting in the car concealed off road outside Pioneer Labs, and Mu Xin poised in front of a computer in her Alexandria home—but she could come up with a list of a half-dozen things that could still go wrong.

"I've finished checking the employee log against the National Mutant Registry," Xin continued. "You've lucked out, Zara. Apparently Pioneer Labs isn't big into hiring mutants. You won't have to contend with any telepaths or telekinetics tonight."

Good. That was one thing she could strike off her list.

Another long hallway stretched in front of her, but the glass-enclosed research station on the left drew her attention. Two lab technicians huddled around a network of computers, their attention focused on the output pouring from the whirling terminals. Her gaze drifted over the lab technicians and focused on Roland Rakehell and Michael Cochran, the famous co-creators of "Galahad," the perfect human. The two scientists stood in contemplative discussion in front of a liquid-filled fiberglass chamber.

The man floating within the sensory deprivation tank, his head encased in a metallic hood and his face covered by breathing apparatus, writhed in agony. Wires monitoring heart rate and brain waves trailed from his naked body. Jagged edges leaped hysterically off the computer readouts as mind and body convulsed, shuddering with madness and pain.

One of the lab technicians spoke up, "Professor, his brain waves indicate that he is waking."

Roland Rakehell glanced at his watch. "Right on time," he noted, his voice tinged with disappointment. "I guess the miracles can't come thick and fast every single day."

"We made him human, not superhuman," Michael Cochran said. "Besides, we don't really have time to record a miracle today." He glanced at the two technicians. "Roland and I are meeting investors for dinner, and we have to leave now. Take Galahad back to his room. Make sure he gets something to eat."

Silently she pushed away from the viewing area and continued down the corridor. Her violet eyes betrayed the faintest flicker of confusion and consternation.

Galahad.

She would never have imagined it, but apparently the scientists had no qualms treating their prized creation like a common lab animal.

"Xin?" she murmured quietly.

"Right here," was the immediate response.

"Approaching the suite."

"I'm one step ahead of you," Xin said. "I've gotten through the security system and rerouted all the cameras in the suite to a static video feed. You're clear to enter."

The second door opened into a large suite pressed up against the western wall of the laboratory complex. No gentle ambient lighting there, just harsh pools of unforgiving white light blazing over the bed and table, leaving the rest of the large suite in muted shadows.

Was it through deliberate design or neglectful oversight that no attempt had been made to humanize Galahad's living quarters? Empty shelves lined the wall. The small metal table and matching chair were severe, the narrow bed unwelcoming. She had seen third-world hospital wards offer far more comfort to its occupants.

Footsteps echoed, drawing closer, and then paused outside the door. There was no time to waste. She strode across the room, slipping into the shadows that obscured the far side of the suite moments before the door slid open again.

The two technicians she had seen earlier half-dragged, half-carried Galahad into the room. It staggered with exhaustion, trying to stand on its own. The technicians hauled Galahad up and dumped it unceremoniously in a wet, shivering heap on the bed.

One of the technicians cast a backward glance at the unmoving figure on the bed. "Pete, are you sure he's going to be okay?" he asked the other.

"Eventually. It usually takes him a while to recover," Pete assured the younger man. He pulled out two sealed nutrient bars from his pocket and tossed them onto the table. "Let's go."

"I think we should at least get him a towel or put him under the sheets."

Pete snapped. "How many times do I have to say it? Let him be, Jack. He doesn't want to be helped, though God knows I've tried often enough. He wants to be able to do things for himself, at least here, in this room. It's the only dignity he has left; let's leave that to him."

"It was *bad* today."

The older man inhaled deeply, sparing a quick glance back. Galahad trembled so hard it seemed as if it would shatter. It curled into a fetal ball, perhaps to protect itself from further violation. "I know. And the best thing we can do for him right now is leave him alone," Pete said as he stepped out of the room and allowed the door to seal shut behind them.

The impact was thunderous—not audibly—but she felt it nonetheless. It was the sealing of a prison cell.

Zara had wondered what kind of luxuries and privileges the incomparable Galahad—the pinnacle of genetic perfection—enjoyed. Now she knew the answer.

She watched in silence as Galahad stirred, slowly standing and leaning on the wall for support as it staggered toward the bathroom. She had yet to get a good look at its face, but the blazing light did not leave much of its body to imagination. It was slender but well muscled, powerful and graceful, in spite of its obvious exhaustion—the promise of perfection come into fruition.

She waited through the sound of running water. Patience had never been easy for her, but she possessed the instincts of a hunter closing in on its quarry. Her patience was rewarded when it finally returned to the room, dressed simply in loose-fitting white cotton drawstring pants and a tunic of the same material. As it stepped into the blazing circle of light, her eyes narrowed briefly, and then a faint smile of easy appreciation curved her lips.

She had studied the surveillance video feed Xin had hacked from the central computers of Pioneer Labs the day before, but the wide-angle lenses had not captured anything approximating the full impact of Galahad's beauty. Its rare and lovely color—pale blond hair paired with dark eyes—stood out and attracted immediate attention, but the longer she looked, the more beauty she saw in its exquisitely chiseled features, as flawless as a Michelangelo masterpiece. Galahad was stunningly beautiful—would be stunningly beautiful, whatever the color of its hair or eyes. The scientists had certainly done well; more than well.

Galahad made its way over to a rattan chair, moving with greater ease. It was regaining its strength, though she did not think that it was anywhere near optimal form, not when it had almost collapsed with exhaustion on the way to the bathroom ten minutes earlier. It curled up in the chair and closed its eyes, looking oddly content, despite the fact that it did not fit very well into the chair. Within a minute, she realized from the even rise and fall of its chest with every breath, that it had fallen asleep.

It was time to get to work.

Galahad did not stir as she silently crossed the room. A*STAR had demanded fresh DNA samples obtained as directly from the source as possible. Hair or skin samples would be acceptable, and both were typically abundant in a bathroom. She pulled test tube and tweezers from the pocket of her lab coat and knelt to examine the bathroom counter.

Something flickered in the corner of her vision.

Instinct and trained reflexes took over. In a flash, her dagger was in her hand. She spun, the black serrated blade slicing outward.

Galahad reacted with uncanny speed. It dove to the side, dropping into a roll and coming up in a battle crouch. Her dagger slashed through the air where Galahad had been standing a moment before. Galahad's dark eyes narrowed as it assessed her. Its body shifted into motion, preparing to defend itself.

She too reassessed, readjusted. Her attack should not have missed. Galahad's battle instincts had been trained and polished to perfection. Apparently it was *more* than a common lab animal.

Her dagger lashed out once again in a graceful, snake-like motion, and Galahad evaded by dodging to one side. The blade sliced harmlessly through the air so close to Galahad that it must have felt the chill breath of the dagger's passing against its skin.

Galahad's silent and sinuously graceful movements were driven by so much speed and agility that strength—although abundant—was superfluous. It matched her, step for step, dodging each attack with a grace that made their deadly waltz seem choreographed. There was no doubt that Galahad was good, far better than anyone she had ever contended with. In spite of its obvious fatigue after a long and difficult day, Galahad possessed flawless timing and impeccable spatial precision, allowing it to escape injury by fractions of a second and a hairsbreadth. It had nerves of steel. It taunted her with its proximity and tempted the kiss of her blade, never straying too far as it sought an opening.

She saw the dark eyes glitter dangerously and knew that something in it had shifted, had changed. She thrust her blade at its face.

In less than a heartbeat, it was over.

With a swiftness that left her stunned, Galahad twisted its hand to catch her wrist in an iron grip. It sidestepped, yanked her forward, and drove its knee into her thigh. Her leg weakened and collapsed. Its superior weight drove her to the ground and kept her there without any visible effort.

A perfectly sequenced attack, executed with flawless precision and stunning speed.

Gritting her teeth against the pain, she recognized the inevitable outcome as it eased the dagger from between her nerveless fingers. She cursed soundlessly. She had underestimated its skill, perhaps to her folly. It suddenly released her, pulled her to her feet, and then stepped away from her. Some emotion she could not decipher rippled over its flawless features, and to her amazement, it flipped the dagger over in its hand and held it out, hilt first, to her. "I don't know why I'm fighting you. You came to kill me; I should thank you for your kindness."

She reached out and accepted the dagger from Galahad as her mind raced to understand the incomprehensible. Galahad held her gaze only for a moment before it lowered its eyes and looked away. She saw its throat work as it fought an internal battle to suppress its survival instincts, and then it turned its back on her deliberately and walked out of the bathroom.

She could have struck the fatal blow. Galahad was offering her the chance. She could pull Galahad's head back and apply the faintest pressure to the dagger's blade across its jugular. She could extract the tissue sample she had been sent to collect, and then leave, her mission completed.

She could not bring herself to do it. Oddly enough, something in her wanted it—wanted *him*—to live.

"Zara?" she heard Xin's voice softly inquiring in her ear, her tone concerned.

"I'm all right," she murmured. "Give me a minute." She paused by the bathroom door and watched him make his way toward the wide windows. He kept his back to her as he stared out at the manicured lawns around Pioneer Labs. Was he waiting for her to strike?

Well, she could play the waiting game too. She followed him and then turned, casually leaning against the window as she looked up at him, her gaze coolly challenging.

Several moments passed.

Finally he broke the silence. "Who sent you?" he asked quietly without looking at her.

She had expected the question, but not the calm, neutral tone in which it was asked. No anger. No hatred. No fear. Just a simple question, driven more by politeness than by any real need to know. "Does it matter?"

He inhaled deeply and released his breath in a soft sigh as she neatly evaded his inquiry. He tried another question. "Are you from around here?"

"Washington, D.C."

"I've seen media clips of that city. It's beautiful."

She offered a nonchalant shrug as a response to his statement. "It's pretty enough, I suppose. I take it you've never been there."

"I don't get out much, and the last time was a good while ago." He shrugged, a graceful motion that belied the bitterness in his voice. "I've seen media clips endorsed by Purest Humanity and other pro-humanist groups. There is no place for me in your world."

It was pointless to deny the obvious, but before she could open her mouth to toss out the retort on the edge of her tongue, an animal-like cry resonated through the complex. It was a ghastly sound, starting at a low pitch akin to the sound a lost puppy might make and then rising until it was a banshee's scream. "What was that?"

"It's an experiment in another part of the building."

"It doesn't sound like anything I recognize. What is it?"

He tossed her question back at her. "Does it matter?"

"Not if you don't care."

"It's been going on for as long as I can remember."

His matter-of-fact statement was like fuel to fire. Her eyes flashed. "And you feel nothing? No anger? No pity? You're inhuman."

"I thought you'd already decided that," was his mild rejoinder. "Isn't that why the pro-humanist groups want me killed?"

She hesitated. Somewhere along the way—she was not even sure when— she had stopped thinking of Galahad as an "it" and had started relating to it as a "he". She had attributed to him all the responsibilities of being human, but none of its rights or privileges, in effect placing him in the worst possible no-win situation. She recalled his anguished convulsions in the sensory deprivation chamber. How much pity did she expect him to dredge up for another creature in a position no different from his own? Very little. In fact, none at all.

She closed her eyes and inhaled deeply. The anger subsided. "Do they conduct experiments on you too?" she asked softly.

He stiffened. Without meeting her gaze, he answered the question, choosing his words with care. "I...yes, they do, sometimes."

"What did they do to you today?"

He averted his gaze and bit down hard on his lower lip. He shook his head, said nothing.

"You looked like hell when they brought you back. I want to know, please."

He was silent for so long she thought he was never going to answer the question, but then he spoke in a measured, neutral tone. "They gave me a highly concentrated sleeping pill and then injected a hallucinogen, to induce nightmares. They wanted to see if I could overcome the effects of the sleeping pill to wake up."

"Did you?"

Another long pause. His reply was a softly anguished whisper. "No."

"How long did the experiment last?"

"About eight hours, perhaps nine." He laughed, low and melodic, but it was a humorless sound. "I slept all day, and I'm exhausted."

"Why do they do that?"

"It's simple; because they can. Humans and their derivatives, the clones and in vitros, have rights. I'm considered non-human, in large part because of the successful lobbying of pro-humanist groups, and I don't have rights." Galahad released his breath in a soft sigh. Long eyelashes closed over dark, pain-filled orbs as he inhaled deeply. He opened his eyes and met her gaze directly, holding it for a long, silent moment. The corner of his lips tugged up again in a bittersweet half smile. "I'm tired. I need to lie down. You can do what you need to do whenever you want."

"Wait!" She grabbed his arm as he turned away from her. "You want me to kill you?"

"Isn't that what you came to do?"

"Do you actually *want* to die?"

He waved his hand to encompass the breadth and width of the impersonal and deliberately dehumanizing room. "I'm not sure this should count as living."

"But you're not human."

"No," he agreed, his voice even. "No, but I am alive...just like any other human. This isolation drives me crazy. I know this is not the way others live. This isn't living."

He looked away. His pain was real, his anger compelling. In spite of it, she had seen him smile a few times and wondered whether his twisted half-smile could ever be coaxed into becoming something more. In silence, she watched as he turned his back on her and walked to his rattan chair. He seemed tired, emotional weariness draining his physical strength. Slowly he settled into the chair, drawing his legs up and curling into a vaguely comfortable position. Apparently he had chosen to deliberately ignore her. He was tuning her out and was once again trying to find solace in the few things he had left, such as a worn chair and his own company, trying to get through each cheerless day and lonely night.

Outside, a rabbit, safe from predators in the falling dusk, emerged from its burrow and hopped across the small patch of grass in front of the large windows of the suite. Zara watched as a faint smile touched his face, briefly transforming it. His personality seemed wrapped around a core that was equal parts weary indifference and tightly controlled bitterness, but there was still enough left in him to savor the small crumbs that life saw fit to throw his way. If his quiet strength had amazed her, his enduring courage humbled her. As she watched him, she knew he had won the battle he had wanted, so badly, to lose. He had proved his right to live, even though there was no purpose in living in a place like this. He knew that fact intimately, and so did she.

Her eyes narrowed thoughtfully.

"Zara, we've got trouble." Carlos's voice cut through the silence of her thoughts, his habitual calmness edged with tension. "Lots of vehicles incoming. Purest Humanity logos. Could be a protest forming; they look seriously pissed."

She took a few steps away from Galahad. Annoyance disguised flickers of anxiety in her voice. "They're about two days too early. They've been gathering on Christmas Eve each year."

"Well, looks like someone had a change of plans. I'm estimating about forty...fifty cars, at least twice as many people."

"They won't get through the gate," Xin said. "It was designed to keep out APCs."

"Uh...The gate just opened...*Por dios*...They're driving in!"

"What?"

"No kidding, I swear to God." The tension in Carlos's voice escalated. "Someone must be screwing around with the security system."

Zara suppressed a hiss of irritation. "Find that person, Xin, and disable his access. I don't want to have to fight my way out of here."

"I'm on it, but I can't guarantee they won't get to you. If they're already through the gate, they'll be pounding on the front door in seconds. You don't have time; get moving. And Zara, if you don't take Galahad with you, he's as good as dead."

Zara's mind raced through the options available to her, the possibilities. She shrugged, dismissing the many logical reasons why she should not do what she was about to do, and took her first step down her path with a terse and coolly decisive order. "He's coming with me. I'll get us out of the building. Carlos, stand by for an extraction."

"Copy that."

She stepped toward Galahad. "You need to change into something else." The thin cotton tunic and pants he wore would not provide sufficient protection from the chilly night air. Besides, his clothes looked like something issued to long-term residents of mental hospitals. Something with fewer negative institutional implications would work better at keeping him as inconspicuous as possible.

He blinked in surprise, her voice jerking him back to reality, and he looked up at her. "There is nothing else to wear," he said. He released his breath in a soft sigh, his gaze drifting away from her to the rabbit outside the window.

Nothing else? A quick search of the suite confirmed his words. The only pieces of clothing in the suite's large and mostly empty walk-in closet were several pieces of identical white cotton tunics and pants, a subtle but highly effective dehumanizing strategy. "We're leaving anyway," she told him as she returned into the living area of the suite. "Get up. We're going."

He stared at her in bewilderment. "Going?"

Zara exercised exquisite politeness and reminded herself to be patient with him. "I'm getting you out of here."

A glimmer of understanding tinged with wary hope swirled through the confusion in his sin-black eyes, but he still did not move from the chair. "I thought you came to kill me."

Not precisely, but perhaps it wasn't a bad thing if he kept believing it, especially if it would make him more tractable. Things were complicated enough; an uncooperative captive would heighten the stakes and the danger of their situation. "I've changed my mind."

"Changed your mind?"

"It's a woman's prerogative," she told him, a wicked smile curving her lips. Her tone softened slightly. As huge as this step seemed for her, it must seem even larger for him. "I want to help you. Will you come with me?"

He met her gaze, held it for a long moment, and then finally smiled. "Yes."

The simplicity of his answer staggered her, to say nothing of the heart-stopping power of his smile. It was a smile that could melt iron. "You trust me," she said, "but you don't even know my name."

"It would be ungracious not to trust someone who has already passed up on several opportunities to kill me." He uncurled from his chair and stood. His manners were at least as exquisite as his looks. He made no mention of the fact that he had beaten her in a fair fight and then refused to follow up on his advantage.

Maybe he considered it irrelevant. The important point was that she did not. The fight she had lost had, after all, been the critical turning point. She smiled up at him, suddenly realizing that his dark, fathomless eyes did not seem nearly as distant and empty as they had several minutes earlier. "I'm Zara Itani."

He smiled faintly, the warmth from his smile briefly lighting up his eyes. "Zara, I'm Galahad."

TWO

Pete had seen a great deal in his fifteen years of employment with Pioneer Laboratories, the leading genetics research institute in the country, but nothing like this. Each year, right before Christmas, an irate crowd inevitably assembled at Pioneer Labs. Never mind that nearly two and a half decades had passed since Galahad's birth on that quiet Christmas Eve, the crowd still gathered as if its united voice would make a difference in the inevitable march of civilization toward increasingly sophisticated levels of genetic selection.

This year though, it was different. The crowd was significantly larger, more vocal, and *armed*. Leading them was a man who was familiar to most of the long-time employees of Pioneer Labs.

"Should we call the professor? Let him know his son is here?" Jack asked as he watched from behind the security desk.

Pete chewed on his lower lip. Outside, Jason Rakehell stirred the crowd into frenzy with a brilliant, though prejudiced, rhetoric against in vitros, clones, and most especially Galahad. Jason denounced his father, accused Roland Rakehell of playing God, of devaluing humanity, and stopped just short of declaring that his father was Satan's henchman.

Pete exchanged a long, worried look with Hank, who was in charge of the security detail for the night. They had not planned for this situation. The crowds, year after year, had faithfully gathered on Christmas Eve itself, and Pioneer Labs had planned for that occasion. Additional security teams had been hired, and the police force and other emergency personnel had been notified.

Two days before Christmas Eve however, only the standard security detail stood against a furious, armed crowd of pro-humanists gathered at the front door. "How did they even get through the gates?"

"Apparently it opened for them," Larry, another security guard said. He worked frantically at the computer terminal. "Someone's overriding our central security system. Nothing's responding to me. I can't lower the blast doors over the entrance." He looked up, fear racing through his eyes as he scanned the furious crowd. "I'm calling the cops." He picked up the phone, hanging up in frustration when he realized that the line was dead. He reached for his cell phone instead.

Pete listened to the first few moments of Larry's frantic communication with the 911 operator and then turned back to Hank. "Is everyone else out of the building?" Pete asked, peering over Hank's shoulder as the guard quickly scanned the personnel list.

"Just about," Hank confirmed. "Sherry Williams is still here, but everyone else is gone for the day."

"Sherry Williams?" Pete echoed, wondering who she was. He knew almost everyone in Pioneer Laboratories, but that name was unfamiliar to him. Any inquiry he might have made into the topic of Sherry Williams was cut off when the bright flare of a flame-thrower yanked his attention toward the glass doors that kept out the crowd.

Jason Rakehell turned to look at them. With a twisted sneer of his lip and a wave of his hand, he unleashed the madness of the mob upon the translucent piece of glass that separated those who would tear down humanity from those who would protect it.

"Oh, shit!" Pete stumbled back as the glass door shattered into a million fragments that glittered like icicles on the tiles. He turned and ran down the corridors leading into the heart of the laboratory, panic drying his throat. He could hardly breathe for the near-certainty of death licking at his heels.

"Stand your ground!" Hank ordered his four security guards as he whipped out his pistol. This was a fight he could not win. He barely managed to get off two or three shots before the mob reached him and pulled him down. He screamed once more, his voice ending in a gurgle of pain as his head was repeatedly smashed into the floor.

What to do...oh, God...What to do? Save Galahad. Seal off the eastern wing. Too much to do, and in opposite directions. "Go get Galahad," Pete threw the terse order over his shoulder at Jack, who raced behind him, pale-faced and wide-eyed with fear. "I'll manually seal the eastern wing."

The younger man nodded, skidding on the polished tiles as he darted down a side corridor that would take him to the western wing. Pete did not stop to watch if Jack obeyed him. Time, he realized, as he heard the roar of the mob closing in on him, was a luxury he did not have anymore.

~*~

Zara and Galahad had just stepped out of the suite when a sharp, rattling sound echoed through the corridors. Galahad jerked to a stop, his head angled as he tried to decipher the unfamiliar sound. "What is that?"

"Small-arms fire," Zara said. She pulled a dagger from its sheath hidden in her right boot, and handed it hilt first to Galahad. "Sounds like they've broken through the front door. Xin, I need alternate directions out of here."

The calm female voice responded in her ear: "There's no exit from the wing itself. You'll have to get back to the main corridor and then head south. Look for the kitchen; it'll be on your right, about halfway down the corridor. There's an exit on the far left of that room that will take you around the back of the building."

"All right. Carlos, you got that?"

"*Sí*, I'll bring the car around the back. That should be easy now that there's no longer a traffic jam trying to get into Pioneer Labs."

Zara shrugged off the white lab coat and lifted the hem of her skirt to briefly reveal slim, long legs. She pulled another dagger from the sheath strapped to her inner thigh. "Hate being unarmed," she said to Galahad, who watched without comment. "Let's move," she ordered, sprinting toward the large doors that separated the western wing from the rest of Pioneer Laboratories.

The doors slid apart silently as the pair neared, and the young lab technician—Jack—stumbled through. His panicked gaze flashed by her and locked on Galahad. If Jack was at all shocked at how Galahad had managed to get out of the suite, he got past it quickly enough. "We're...we've got to get out. The pro-humanists—"

"This way." She pushed past Jack. The sound of the approaching mob had escalated from a low murmur to something akin to the roar of a tidal wave about to crash on land. Zara heard the pounding of heavy feet several moments before a man, armed with a crowbar, charged around the corner. Prepared for him, she ducked beneath his raised arm to slide the dagger with merciless precision between his ribs and into his heart. The crowbar fell, slipping from his nerveless fingers into her waiting grasp. All it took then was a simple push to send the man to the ground.

His sightless eyes stared up at the ceiling.

Jack stared at her as if she had sprouted an extra head.

"South. To the kitchen," she said.

The lab technician blinked hard and then nodded. He scurried down the corridor. Zara and Galahad turned to follow, but harsh voices screaming curses against non-humans confirmed that the man's companions were not far behind.

"We'll have to fight our way there," Galahad said quietly as eight more men rounded the corner at breakneck pace. As one though, the men slowed to a cautious lope when they saw the body of their fallen comrade on the ground between them and their quarry.

Zara's feline smile was darkly predatory as she shifted her stance, ready for battle. The first man was overconfident. The half smile never left her lips as she deflected his clumsy attack with a flip of her wrist. She slipped around him before he had a chance to regain his balance and guided the edge of her blade across his jugular with just enough pressure to slice through skin and vein.

Blood sprayed. His scream died, frozen in his throat. Zara let him fall and moved on to her next target, all the while aware that Galahad was also on the move, easily taking on—and out—each opponent with graceful, economical motions. He was a pleasure to watch, and if she had the time, she might have stood on the sidelines and applauded.

As it was, they were in a bit of a rush. She cast a glance over her shoulder at the last man whose cowardice had finally overcome the rashness inspired by the madness of a mob. He backed away, his hands held in a defensive posture.

She spun a half circle and let her dagger fly. The black-bladed dagger raced through the air, spinning end over end, to sink deep into his chest. The man slumped to the ground, eyes wide with shock. "Fucking in vit," he gasped. His hands reached for the dagger, tightened on the hilt as if to pull it out, and then fell limply by his side as his eyes rolled up in his head.

Zara's eyes narrowed in a mixture of disgust and scorn. She stopped to retrieve her dagger and then met Galahad's dark, inscrutable gaze. "We're running out of time," she said.

Heat from surging flames inched down the hallway. Dark smoke wafted toward them. The mob was apparently burning as it went, and probably without the vaguest clue on how to get out of the building, short of going back through the flames.

Idiots. Zara gritted her teeth. Sometimes it was a wonder that humans hadn't yet driven themselves into extinction through sheer stupidity. She nodded toward the south. "Let's go."

~*~

Pete's hands, slick with sweat, fumbled at the computer that controlled access to the eastern wing of the laboratory. He scrambled to type in the commands that would drop the heavy steel blast doors across the eastern wing to seal it off.

Almost there, he thought. The computer awaited only his pass code and the final confirmation of his order. Almost safe.

"Trying to protect Galahad?" a mocking voice called out from behind him.

He spun around, gasped in shock, and then screamed as a long-bladed hunting knife sliced through his stomach. "No…no…" he choked, uncertain if he was begging for his life or for theirs. He dropped to his knees, his arms wrapped around his bleeding midsection. "Don't open the doors, please."

A man stepped over him, and with a contemptuous swing of his arm, sliced the blade across the side of Pete's neck and face. Pete could not scream. The pain took all his breath away, and the only relief he felt as the darkness pulled him under was that he would likely be dead when the doors to the eastern wing finally opened to reveal all the horrors concealed within.

The man who had killed Pete Danner looked down at the computer terminal, frowning at the waiting program as his companions, still jubilant over the death of the lab technician, gathered behind him. "Go on, open the doors," someone urged him.

He nodded, canceling Pete's order to seal the eastern wing, and then ordered the computer to open all the cell doors. He grinned in vicious anticipation. The moment was at hand. Galahad was close. In moments, the abomination would be completely at their mercy.

The double doors slid open to reveal a large circular foyer surrounded by open cells. It was quiet. He heard nothing over the wild pounding of his heart. Relishing the moment of his triumph, he brandished his hunting knife and charged in, his friends rallying close behind him.

He was the first to die, slain instantaneously by a single swipe of a malformed appendage that was more claw than hand. A sound that was part roar, part scream resonated in echoing waves around the chamber. It froze the mob in its tracks and shocked a resemblance of sanity and rationality back into the group. The twenty men and women in the room could only gape in horror as the darkness in the cells slid back to reveal creatures that had no possible claim on humanity.

There were only six, but even one would have been too many. Grossly deformed, they were twisted contortions of Galahad's physical perfection. Their eyes gleamed with raw hatred, and when they attacked, it was with superhuman strength and agility, fueled by inhuman fury that had simmered for three decades. The humans with their puny blades, and even their guns stood no chance at all.

The dying screams of the humans rent Pioneer Laboratories.

It was a massacre, a bloodbath. And it was only just beginning.

~*~

The spotlights in the kitchen were bright in comparison to the muted lighting in the hallway, but they were immensely welcome. Better still was the sight of Jack standing by the open door. He waved Zara and Galahad forward frantically. "The lab's on fire," he said, his voice thin and reedy, edged with panic.

"Get out!" Zara said. She estimated that they had all of a thirty-second head start before the rest of the psychotic mob realized that it had cut itself off from its exit and came scrambling down her way to find another.

A roar reverberated through the building. The new sound was the scream of a raging animal. Zara froze, her gaze seeking out Galahad's, searching for answers. She was stunned to see the first glimpses of horror pass over his flawless features. He shook his head, opened his mouth to speak, but fell silent as human screams began.

Screams of terror, of horror. Screams of the dying.

"What—"

"They're out," Galahad said quietly.

It was neither the right time or place to demand to know exactly what "they" were and she suspected she did not actually *want* to know, anyway. "We'll leave that up to the SWAT team. This way." She raced through the kitchen, sparing only a quick glance over her shoulder to confirm that Jack and Galahad followed her. *Almost safe,* she realized. Her BMW coupe was idling outside the kitchen door; Carlos at the driver's seat.

"Stop!" a voice, oddly familiar, shouted from behind them.

She didn't.

A single shot rang out. Jack jerked as the bullet ripped through his chest and tore through a lung. He stumbled forward a single step and then fell, spitting blood with his dying breath.

Zara did not stop as much as she stepped into a turn, spinning around to drop to one knee. She saw a man standing with a Glock held at ready twenty feet behind them. Her eyes widened in disbelief. "Jason?"

"Zara?" Jason Rakehell sounded equally surprised, but then he saw Galahad standing beside her. His incredulity twisted into an expression of all-consuming hatred. His finger tightened on the trigger.

Zara, without the merest flicker of hesitation, let her dagger fly.

Two shots rang out fractions of a second before the dagger plunged into Jason's right bicep, severing muscle and tendon, destroying any chances of a steady aim. Jason screamed an incoherent curse at Zara, but the damage was done.

Galahad twisted away from the path of the bullets quickly enough to avoid fatal injury, but not enough to avoid being hit. A bullet slammed into his stomach, another into his thigh. He staggered and choked back a gasp of pain.

Zara was beside him, warm and alive. "I've got you," she promised, her voice a low, assuring murmur. She rushed him out of the kitchen and toward the open back door of her car. "Stay with me; we're almost there."

She pushed him into the back seat and then slipped in after him. Carlos slammed his foot down on the accelerator even before she closed the door. As they pulled away, she glanced back. Jason Rakehell was screaming incoherently. His face, inscribed with hatred and murderous intent, was barely recognizable.

"Galahad?"

"I'm fine," he said softly, leaning back and closing his eyes. He breathed shallowly. Blood darkened his white cotton tunic and pants around his midsection and right thigh. He clearly needed medical attention, but it would be difficult to walk into an emergency room and ask for help. Galahad had no identification, which guaranteed no aid from hospitals. The free clinic was an option, but she would sooner abandon Galahad on the side of the road than take him to one of those under-funded clinics staffed by young, inadequately trained interns.

"Xin?"

The quiet, calm voice in her ear said, "I'm still here. Are you all right?"

"Yes, I'm fine. Galahad's hit; I don't think it's critical, but he needs attention as soon as possible. I want you to call Lucien—he's usually in D.C. for Christmas—and then meet me at his house."

"Lucien? Lucien Winter?"

"Yes, Lucien Winter. Call him, and tell him I need his help. I've absconded with the pinnacle of genetic perfection. There's a media circus in the making here, and I'm at the very heart of it. I'm in a boatload of trouble."

There was a brief silence and then a quietly amused chuckle. "'Boatload' doesn't adequately describe the amount of trouble you're in. It's more like an aircraft carrier," Xin said. "I'll call Lucien. See you there. Drive safe."

"Carlos, get us to McLean. I can give you directions to Lucien's house from there."

"Okay." The lean Hispanic man with a nervous tic under his left eye spared a quick glance through the rearview mirror. His mouth twitched with suppressed humor.

"What is it, Carlos?" Zara asked. They had worked together for almost five years, and in that time, Carlos had become her top spotter. He was as indispensible as Xin and could get away with smart-aleck comments she would not have entertained from her other employees.

"Couldn't just get a tissue sample, could you? Had to take the whole damn thing."

Zara smirked. "Well, here at the Three Fates, we believe in over-delivering on our contracts." She placed a hand gently over Galahad's. "We're going to a friend's house. You'll be safe there."

He nodded weakly. "Jason Rakehell knows you?" he asked. The quiet tone failed to conceal grinding pain.

Jason Rakehell was founder and president of Purest Humanity. Once though, he had been even more to her. The gleam in her eyes softened as other memories surfaced easily. They were just memories, she assured herself. Whatever they had once had together was long gone. "Jason Rakehell was once my fiancé."

~*~

The drive to McLean, Virginia, took a little more than an hour. Zara watched Galahad slip into unconsciousness shortly after leaving Pioneer Labs. He stirred occasionally when Carlos took a corner a little too recklessly, but did not wake. Consequently, Zara had an entire hour to ponder what she had done. Perhaps she had Jason Rakehell to thank for elevating her status from near-criminal to unexpected savior. Not that it particularly justified her theft of Galahad, but the attack on Pioneer Labs would certainly have resulted in Galahad's death.

She did not want to imagine the implications. Pioneer Labs destroyed, scores of people dead, and some laboratory *things* now presumably on the loose. Perhaps the fire at the laboratory killed them too, but if it hadn't, then what? The incidents of the evening would provide all kinds of fodder for delusional pro-humanist rhetoric.

"Crap," she muttered under her breath as they pulled into the circular driveway that led up to the entrance of Lucien's suburban home. It was cold comfort that most of the chaos was not entirely her fault, though she doubted Lucien would take that charitable a view of the situation.

The front door opened, and Xin, slim and svelte in black jeans and a black turtleneck sweater, stepped out with three of Lucien's staff members behind her. Apparently they had been briefed on the situation. With very little fanfare and no display of emotion, they opened the passenger door. Two of them maneuvered the unconscious Galahad out of the back seat and carried him carefully into the house.

"William will take your car to the garage," Xin announced as Lucien's third employee stepped into the driver's seat that Carlos had vacated. "Hi Carlos." She grinned at him before looking toward Zara. "Lucien wants to see you. He's in his study."

"Wait here for me, Carlos," Zara instructed. "How pissed is he?" she asked. Marble steps welcomed her into a vast foyer swirling with rich colors. Burgundy velvet curtains and black vases filled with burnished red roses were set against the white starkness of Italian marble files. Above her, a crystal chandelier shattered light into a thousand sparkles. "And how much did you tell him?"

Xin sighed, running elegant fingers through the silken fall of her black hair. "Pretty much all of it. He's already berated me for my part in helping you break into Pioneer Labs. 'Childish games' was the kindest thing he said, and it went rapidly downhill from there. I told him it was worth two million to you, but that's just pocket change to him, so he's not impressed. I suspect he's holding back and is saving some choice comments for you. I don't think he approves of what you do."

"He never did. Has he sent for a doctor?"

"Not yet. I gathered from your last communication that Galahad's situation isn't critical. Lucien wants to hear directly from you before he decides just how much of his personal reputation to put on the line to haul your ass out of the fire."

"Great." Zara inhaled deeply. She braced herself for a confrontation with one of her most trusted friends, and then pushed open the door to Lucien's study after a single, perfunctory knock.

"You're here." Lucien glanced up from where he had been brooding by an open window. Moving briskly, he went over to the liquor cabinet, poured fine whiskey into a crystal glass, and held it out to her. His face was unsmiling, but his deep blue eyes were concerned as he scanned her carefully. "Not hurt?"

"I'm fine, though I lost one of the daggers you gave me."

"I hope you didn't leave it buried in someone's heart."

"In Jason Rakehell's arm actually, but it was his fault. He started it," Zara protested, a smile toying at her lips.

"You're trying to charm me. It won't work, Zara. Did you and Xin wake up one morning and decide, just for the hell of it, to break into Pioneer Labs and kidnap Galahad?"

"Not precisely. The former was a fairly well put-together plan to break in, extract a tissue sample from Galahad, and sell it to A*STAR for two million dollars. The latter, however, was an improvisation on my part. A fortunate one, I might add, or he would be dead by now."

Lucien snarled, not at all amused by her flippancy. He ran a hand through his black hair as he sat on the edge of his desk. "Do you have any idea what you've done?" He waved his hand at the chaotic images flashing across the flat screen television mounted on the wall. "Breaking news...Pioneer Labs on fire. At least forty-five people believed killed. Galahad has not been located, but is believed to be dead. And hell, it's not even nine yet. The night's still young. What are you planning to do for an encore?"

She ignored his sarcasm. "Did they find those things yet?"

Lucien looked up at her. "What things?" he asked quietly.

"The things that got loose and are probably responsible for most of the body count." Zara tossed back her whiskey and set the empty glass down on the table. She took a moment to swallow, grimacing at the smoky taste of the whiskey, even though she knew the liquor was from Lucien's private collection, and consequently absurdly expensive. Some things, regardless of how much they cost, were acquired tastes.

"You didn't say anything about 'things,'" Xin said quietly. For the first time, a hint of worry crept into her brown eyes.

"There wasn't time, and I haven't actually seen anything. I don't know what it is, or rather what they are. I just heard them...once before the mob attacked the lab, and then again while we were trying to get out. The second time was followed by lots of human screams, which I suspect ended in a score of zero for the humans and one for the things."

"You're sure there's more than one?"

"I believe so. Galahad referred to them in the plural."

"Xin, can you call the police?" Lucien asked, "Let them know that something's out there." His voice faded into silence as the television crew cameras, filming the live breaking news at Pioneer Laboratories, zoomed in on six vaguely humanoid shapes emerging from the smoking ruins of the lab. The only commonality they shared was in their utter lack of anything that resembled normality.

"Somehow, I think the police already know," Xin said softly as the cops on the scene took up defensive positions around their cars, weapons drawn.

The creatures broke formation, and without hesitation threw themselves at the humans—cops, ambulance workers, news reporters—and savaged them, tearing and smashing. Screams shrilled through the open microphones, punctuated by scattered gunfire. Through it all, Zara heard the vicious growls and snarls of the abominations, a guttural series of moans that sounded like incoherent words.

It lasted no more than a minute, but the massacre seemed to extend forever into an eternal moment, until an abomination hurled the body of a cop directly into the camera. The screen went black. There was a brief flicker, and then the news anchor, comfortable and safe in the newsroom, reappeared on the screen. His face was pale, his speech stuttering as he tried to explain the madness captured by the final moments of his news crew.

Lucien muttered a curse under his breath. His hands clenched into fists, and a muscle worked tightly in his left cheek where a dimple typically resided. "Where's Galahad?" he asked finally, apparently having arrived at some kind of decision. "We need some answers out of him."

"Upstairs, in the Ivory Room," Xin said, pushing away from the wall in a sinuous motion. She led the way out of the study and upstairs toward the guest room, where Lucien's employees had brought Galahad.

One of Lucien's female employees had apparently been tasked to attend to him, and she jumped to her feet, blushing furiously as the three of them entered the room. "I've cleaned up the blood as best I can, sir." The words were released in a breathless rush.

Lucien dismissed her absently. "Fine, you can go." He strode toward the bed and took his first look at the young man who resided at the heart of the greatest genetic conflict facing mankind.

He froze. "But how…" Lucien's voice trailed into silence as he stared at Galahad's pale, beautiful face.

Xin and Zara exchanged startled glances. Lucien was by nature calm and collected, if a touch sarcastic, almost to the point of being unflappable. His reaction to Galahad wasn't right, wasn't normal. Finally, Xin's concerned voice and soft hand on his arm shook him out of his shocked state. "Lucien, are you all right?"

"Are you *sure* this is Galahad? There have never been any pictures of him. How do you know this is him?"

"This is Galahad," Zara insisted. "Roland Rakehell and Michael Cochran were at the lab experimenting on him. They called him Galahad. What the hell is wrong, Lucien?"

"I don't know." He shook his head, inhaled deeply, and then released his breath in a soft sigh. "Nothing, or maybe everything." He reached for the phone on the bedside table and dialed a number. "Phillip, I need you to send the plane to pick up Danyael from New York City. Yes, right now....Damn, I forgot my father took the plane to Europe. Do whatever you have to. Charter a plane, buy out the whole damn airline, I don't care. I just want Danyael here before midnight." He hung up the phone, took a final glance at Galahad and then turned resolutely away. "We'll figure this out, somehow," he said.

"And what exactly are we going to figure out?"

"You'll see," he promised Zara cryptically. His ironic smile did not bode well, though.

Zara, as a rule, hated surprises, but Lucien was doing her enough favors as it was, and she did not want to push her luck too hard, at least for now. "And what about a doctor?"

"Danyael's a doctor, and the best there is. In the meantime, I'll send one of the maids to sit with Galahad and watch him. Get some rest while you can. After Danyael gets here, we'll have lots of decisions to make." Lucien shook his head as he strode out of the room. "Damn it, Danyael," he said quietly. "What the hell have you gotten yourself into now?"

THREE

Jeremiah Smith watched Danyael Sabre set aside the medical notes. The doctor then smiled at him. Hope surged. Surely that had to be a good sign.

"You look better," Danyael said.

"I feel better, doc," Jeremiah said, a wide grin splitting his scarred face. Despite his enthusiasm, he tried not to lean into Danyael's personal space. He felt like a giant compared to the doctor. Danyael, at six feet, was hardly short, but Jeremiah was taller still, not to mention twice as wide and three times as heavy. "I gotta tell ya, man, I was freaked out by this AIDS thing, but you fixed me up real good, doc."

"Let me check your heartbeat and take your blood pressure for your records. You'll need to take care of yourself, Jerry," Danyael said, opening up a drawer to pull out a stethoscope. "You may feel better, but you need to be safe about what you do."

"Yeah, yeah, doc. I know now. No more stupid sex or sharing needles shit." Jeremiah leaned back in the chair. He winced as it squeaked in protest beneath him. Everything in this office was ancient, from the cracked linoleum tiles to the wooden desk with its peeling edges to the uncomfortable plastic chairs. Jeremiah chuckled softly. *Doc's probably the youngest thing in the room.* Danyael was a year or two shy of thirty, but easily the best doctor he had seen in the fifty-six years of his life. The doctor worked long hours at a free clinic with no help other than a receptionist who also served as a nurse's aide and practically no resources, thanks to state budget cuts, but accomplished near miracles with the little he had.

Absent-mindedly, Jeremiah picked at the slivers of wood on the table as he watched the doctor work with easy expertise. He prided himself on being a perceptive observer of situations and people. One did not become—or stay—the ruling mob boss of Crown Heights, Brooklyn, without accurately assessing and understanding underlings, friends and enemies. The whore who had stuck him with a HIV-tainted needle was a different matter entirely. He had been thinking with his *other* head. Besides, she was dead now, and her severed head had been delivered to the mob boss of East New York who had hired her to kill him.

He saw Danyael's eyes close as the doctor listened to the heartbeat through the stethoscope. Jeremiah saw something flicker beneath the closed lids. Those eyelashes were really absurdly long, he noted indifferently in passing. Likewise, he made no comment as Danyael asked him to roll up his sleeve for a blood pressure test. He saw the doctor stare blankly at the peeling paint on the far wall. A muscle in the smooth cheek twitched. The doctor closed his eyes slowly. Jaw muscles tightened as Danyael clenched his teeth. As the pressure of the blood pressure cuff around Jeremiah's bicep released gradually, he saw Danyael inhale and exhale deeply and then finally open his eyes.

Danyael looked at him and offered another faint smile. "You're all set, Jerry. I don't think you need to come back, but if you don't feel well, you're always welcome to stop by."

Jeremiah looked closely at the young man. He had not imagined the subtle hints of pain that he had seen in the doctor. He saw remnants of it still in those dark, fathomless eyes. He nodded, "Okay." He hesitated. There was something about Danyael that discouraged personal questions. In fact, it was hard even to feel like he should care enough to ask. It took a conscious act of the will to voice a simple question. "You okay, doc?"

He saw a flicker of surprise in Danyael's eyes. "I...I'm all right. It's just been a long day."

"Those people out from Brownsville ain't giving you any more shit?" Those mobsters from Brownsville had apparently decided that they would threaten the doctor with death and dismemberment unless he agreed to work at the free clinic at Brownsville instead. Jeremiah had not been happy to hear about it in the least. Nobody took his doctor away. Nobody.

A rare grin flashed. "No, they've backed off ever since you decided to station five of your biggest thugs outside the clinic."

"They be awful hurt to hear you call them thugs, doc." Jeremiah grinned, not in the least bit offended. "Besides, they're not the biggest. I have way bigger, but didn't want to scare all your patients away."

"I think they've scared enough of them away. The volume dipped a bit last week, and I don't think it was because the mob fights decreased. Could you ask them to stand across the street instead?"

"Sure can, doc." Jeremiah nodded vigorously. He pushed to his feet and stretched expansively. His extended arms almost touched the walls on opposite sides of the room. "You got a damn small place in here, doc."

"Go tell that to the New York City Department of Public Health," Danyael said, also rising to his feet. He held open the door of his office and ushered Jeremiah out before him. The two bodyguards lounging in the waiting room stood and flanked Jeremiah, who marched toward the door.

"You can call your team off for the night too, Jerry," Danyael called out. "We're wrapping up here."

"Sure thing. You take care, doc." Jeremiah strode out and waved an arm imperiously. The five thugs skulking outside the free clinic peeled off the brick wall and concrete sidewalk to tag along behind Jeremiah and his bodyguards.

Danyael chuckled softly as he watched them go. "We're done here," he told his nurse's aide who was seated behind the receptionist desk. "And it's late."

"It was that surgery that set us back," Marsha pointed out, a faint note of complaint in her voice.

The emergency surgery had saved the life of a three-year-old who had been in the wrong place at the wrong time and had been caught in the crossfire of a gang fight. Danyael considered that time well spent. Still, Marsha was tired and irritable. He might have tried to do something about her mood, except that he was exhausted too. Between saving the child's life and making sure that Jeremiah was fully healed, he felt drained. "Go on home."

"What about cleaning up here?" she challenged. Her voice rang with hostility.

"I'll take care of it."

"You gonna mop the floor?"

"Yes, and I'll wipe down all the surfaces too. Go home."

She hesitated, scowled. "Cleaning the damn place is my job."

"You're tired, Marsha. I'll take care of it today."

"The damn Department of Public Health doesn't pay you enough to clean the place."

"It doesn't pay either of us enough to do it," Danyael said with a weary smile. "I've got it covered today. It's all right." He did not have the energy to keep arguing with her and it was much easier to amplify her negative emotions. He glanced at her as his empathic mutant powers surged, subtle and controlled, yet as unstoppable as the tides. Instantly, Marsha huffed—a sharp, exasperated sound. She grabbed her purse and stormed out of the clinic without so much as a backward glance or a goodbye.

Danyael watched her leave. He slumped against the counter and pressed his closed fist against his forehead. *Just a little too warm.* Great, now he had a fever to accompany the pounding headache in his skull. He needed a break from the constant vigilance. More than anything, he needed to rest. One out of two wasn't bad, though. A faint half smile curved a corner of his mouth. He inhaled deeply, closed his eyes, and as he exhaled, he relaxed his psychic shields.

He waited for a moment longer, savoring the rare feeling of freedom, and then got to work. Fortunately, the clinic was tiny, consisting of a reception area, his office, a bathroom and an operating theater barely large enough to contain an operating bed and a metal drawer of instruments. With mop, paper towels and a bottle of antiseptic cleaner, he scrubbed down each room. He did not mind the physical labor, though he would have welcomed the opportunity to go to bed a half hour earlier. At least he was alone; there was not much more he could ask for, anyway.

Danyael worked thoroughly, and it was after ten o'clock when he put the cleaning supplies back behind the bathroom door. It was long past time to go home. His body screamed for rest. Closing his eyes, he leaned his head against the wall to brace himself physically as he pulled his psychic shields back in place. He hated the sensation—had never gotten fully comfortable, even though he had used psychic shields for more than sixteen years. They felt like steel bands clenching around mind and heart with a stranglehold that made it a strain just to breathe. Every time he grew resentful of those barriers though, he reminded himself to be thankful for them. They were better than the alternative.

Danyael shrugged on a black leather jacket, grabbed his backpack off the floor behind the reception counter, and stepped out of the clinic. He lifted his face to the night sky. Icy, stinging wind cut through his jacket. He sighed softly and rolled his shoulders in a futile attempt to dispel some of the tension that seemed permanently locked into his back muscles.

The sharp spike of a migraine pierced his skull as it had every night for a week. He winced and pressed a hand to his forehead as he ground his teeth against the pain. The pain did not bother him as much as the lingering exhaustion that would afflict him for weeks after the pain finally passed. The migraines he had suffered for decades had no apparent triggers, yet were consistent, taking place once every two months. This migraine was unusual, though. It was the first time a migraine had lasted for more than just a day or two.

Danyael released his breath in a sigh. The sooner he could get home, the better. With a little rest, he would be free of the migraine by morning, ready to face another long day at work.

As he turned the corner, brakes screeched, and a dark sedan pulled up alongside him. *Damn, not now.* Drive-by muggings were among the daily joys of working in one of the most crime-ridden neighborhoods in Brooklyn. He would deal with it and move on. He was not even sure he cared enough to be subtle about it this time.

Danyael took a step back from the pavement as four men, incongruously dressed in suits and looking even more out of place than he did as a white man in a predominantly black neighborhood, stepped out of the car and approached him with menacing auras.

"Danyael Sabre?" the one closest to him rumbled out.

Danyael tensed. This wasn't just a random mugging? He reached out with his empathic powers to probe for vulnerabilities, but could not penetrate their psychic shields. He did not recognize the energy signature, but there was enough power behind the shields to imply that an alpha telepath was at work. The men were protected. He could not touch them, could not affect them. They were prepared to go up against, and take down, an empath. He gritted his teeth. His mind raced, trying to work a way out of his predicament without hurting anyone else.

The man who had first spoken pulled out a SIG-Sauer P210 from his jacket, stepped behind Danyael, pulled off his backpack, and then jabbed the gun into the small of his back. "Get into the car."

Danyael did not move. The pressure against his spine increased, a warning.

"I said, get in."

Still he did not move, resisting the not-too-gentle shove against his back. He would not get another warning. From the corner of his eye, he could see the man's hand come up. Danyael tried to evade the blow, but there was no place to run. The butt of the gun smashed against the back of his skull. Stunned, he reeled, collapsing to his knees. His vision shifted in and out of focus. He could see the feet of the men surrounding him. Choking back the gasp of pain, he tried to push to his feet, but another blow slammed into the back of his neck. This time, he slumped to the ground as his world faded to black.

~*~

Danyael awoke slowly to the soft purr of an engine and a wretchedly painful headache. Was he on a boat? A plane? His eyes were blindfolded, his arms and legs bound to a cushioned surface that reclined almost all the way back. He tested the strength of his bonds and found them tight to the point of being painful. He hated being bound with a passion he could not even begin to put words to. He despised his vulnerability and loathed the memories torn from the past he had worked so hard to leave behind.

Focus, damn it. Focus.

No clues other than the sound of an engine, and a stale scent that typically plagued small closed places. He felt a small jolt. A plane perhaps, hitting an air pocket.

"Ah, you're awake, Danyael."

He turned his head in the direction of the nasal voice that was marked by a metallic undertone. The voice was disguised, artificially altered through a voice modulator.

"It's fortunate we took all the necessary precautions. I suggest you relax. We will reach our destination shortly, and until then, there is nothing you can do."

Danyael tensed as he felt the warmth of a body beside him. It was hard to focus through his headache but he forced his way through the pain. Fueled by the panicked terror of the child he had once been, his power surged, only to crash like a breaking wave against an impenetrable psychic shield.

The voice laughed. "You can't get away from me, Danyael. I know what you are. I know exactly how to disarm you. But you needn't worry for now. You're in no real danger."

Danyael tried to pull away. That was when he realized that both arms were completely immobilized, bound around his biceps and his wrists. Needles had been inserted into the tender vein at the joints of his arms.

A blood transfusion?

A *live* blood transfusion? Blood flowing directly between two parties? Nothing else would explain why the man was lying next to him or why he had needles in both arms. Was his blood flowing out of one arm to that man, and blood from that man to him through the other?

"What are you doing to me?" he demanded. Oh God, was that low, stricken whisper his voice? His hands clenched and unclenched helplessly. "You can't do this—"

"Why? Just because live blood transfusions have been banned? Why else do you think we're doing this in secret? We have been sharing blood for almost sixteen years, Danyael. Believe me, this isn't new for you, though it's a shame the off switch stopped working."

Shock expelled air from his lungs. The off switch? The piercing migraines that drove him to seek a dark, quiet place to rest? How often had the pain driven him to black out?

Far too often. This was the first time it had not.

"Relax. We're almost done. I'll see you again in two months, and if the off switch doesn't work any better then, I trust you won't put up as much resistance. It would be a shame to have to use other methods to subdue you, and believe me, I won't hesitate. I know you, Danyael. I know what you went through many times as a child, before you learned to control your empathic powers. It's been a while now, and you've grown strong. You may think the past is behind you, but it doesn't have to be. I know how to break you, make you weak again. I'd suggest you keep that in mind before you put up a fight the next time. Would you rather share just your blood, or your blood *and* your body?"

Danyael clenched his teeth and shook his head in denial. "I'd share neither."

"Ah." The man chuckled lowly. "I did forget to account for the strength of will that got you through your childhood."

There was movement around him. Hands expertly eased the needles out of his veins. Cool, alcohol-soaked pads pressed hard against the small wounds to clean them and stem the residual blood flow. He heard the rustle of sound beside him and the voice whispered in his ear. "How do you think Lucien would fare in your place?"

He tensed. *No, not Lucien.*

"Because that's what it's going to come down to, Danyael." The hand ran gently over the scar that marked the right side of his face. "Your choice."

Silence followed. A long, blessed silence filled with the purr of the plane gliding gently down to a smooth descent.

Breathe, just breathe.

He swallowed hard, tasted bile in his throat, and felt sick to the pit of his stomach. *I've gotten through this before. I've done this before. I can again. I know I can...I have to. Have no choice.*

Danyael braced himself for the landing, wondering what horrors would follow, even though his captor had implied that the torment was over, if only for the time being. He was surprised, unprepared for the hands that released the cuffs from around his wrists and ankles and pulled the blindfold from his eyes. The light in the plane, meager though it was, seemed bright in contrast. He squinted against the glare, raising a hand to shield his eyes.

"Your jacket and bag, sir." The man who had knocked him out hours earlier held out his belongings. Unsteadily, Danyael rose to his feet, gripping the armrest for balance. He tugged on the long sleeves of his shirt to conceal the small bandages on the insides of his arms. The four men who had taken him in New York watched him, one of them standing by the open door of the plane. Who was it? Had it been one of them or someone else? Their expressions were equally impassive, their emotions completely inaccessible. His mind racing with questions for which he had no answers, he wordlessly accepted his backpack and his jacket, and stepped out of the plane into the brisk cool night air.

A quick glance at the plane confirmed that it was a private charter. He committed the registration number to memory and then looked around for some hint as to where he was. A black limousine awaited him, and standing by the car was a tall, distinguished man in his late forties. It was a familiar face, the face of a friend. "It's good to see you again, Danyael." Phillip Evans stepped forward, a cordial smile curving his lips.

Danyael stared at him in disbelief, unable to reconcile the physical violation that had taken place with the realization that he was now completely safe, back among people he trusted. "Phillip? What...what are you doing here?"

Philip looked at him quizzically, as if puzzled that he would have to ask. "Lucien sent for you, of course. I know it was rather hurried, but Lucien insisted it was an emergency. I trust your flight was comfortable?"

Danyael turned his face away. He could not meet the concerned eyes of Lucien's trusted aide. What happened on the plane was a nightmare—a dissonance in an otherwise normal day. "I...Why did Lucien send for me?"

"He did not say. Just indicated that it was an emergency, and he wanted you here before midnight." Phillip glanced at his watch, a magnificent timepiece that cost more than what Danyael earned in a year. "We beat his deadline by about fifteen minutes. Let's get you back to McLean. Lucien wants to talk to you as soon as possible, and I'm sure you could use some rest."

The ride to McLean passed in awkward silence. Phillip made some attempt at small talk, but Danyael was too exhausted to maintain the façade of normality, and the conversation quickly lapsed into silence.

He felt drained. The deep weariness that dragged at him after each migraine was back, and he finally knew why. How much of his exhaustion came from the work he did at the free clinic, and how much from the live blood transfusions that he now knew he endured every two months?

And for *sixteen* years? How could he not have known? A violation so intimate, so consistent? How could he *never* have known?

As for the off switch, despair and disbelief warred for supremacy. He was an alpha mutant. Of course he had heard rumors of off switches, ranging from technology surgically inserted into the brain or triggers psychically embedded into the mind, but the Mutant Affairs Council had always categorically denied using them.

They had lied.

There was an off switch in him; he now knew without a shadow of doubt. The council had lied to him.

Had Lucien known?

Lucien had saved him. Lucien had brought him to the council. There he had learned to control his empathic powers, eventually clawing his way back into a semblance of a normal life.

What had Lucien known?

And just what else *didn't* Danyael know about his own life?

Doubt raked sharp claws through him. Betrayal coiled in the pit of his stomach. Danyael grimaced as his cursed mutant powers transformed emotional anguish into physical agony. He wrapped his arms around his midsection and clenched his teeth against the pain. Slowly, he raised his head and stared unseeingly out of the window, his eyes shadowed. He was unaware of how vulnerable and fragile he seemed, how alone he appeared to be.

What do I do? What can I do?

The answers were elusive, frustratingly out of reach.

He aroused himself out of his abstraction as the limousine pulled into the driveway of Lucien's home.

"Lucien's probably waiting for you in his study," Phillip said as Danyael stepped out of the car.

Danyael did not need directions to the study. He knew his way around Lucien's home; he had lived there for a good part of his life. The familiarity should have calmed him, but it did not. Still quivering between shock and fury, he chose fury. The anger allowed him to focus his energy, whatever little he had left, to deal with the situation.

Lucien was indeed waiting for him in the large, dark-paneled study. The furnishings—custom designed and handmade—were elegant, yet distinctly male. They exuded confidence and power, perfectly matched to the scion and heir to the Winter-Callahan financial empire. "Danyael." A warm grin split Lucien's face as he stepped forward from behind his desk to greet his friend, but then he froze, stunned by Danyael's eloquently clear "hands off" demeanor.

Danyael yanked his fingers through his pale blond hair. "Luce. Why did you send for me?" His words were terse, the tone clipped, almost hostile.

Lucien's eyes narrowed in bewilderment. "Danyael? What the hell is wrong?"

How could he even begin to explain? He could not. Lucien had been explicitly threatened. Lucien was for the most part perfectly capable of taking care of himself, but he would be completely outclassed by a mutant, most certainly by an alpha telepath. Danyael could not—would not—put his friend at risk. He gritted his teeth. Not even if Lucien had—

Trust. He had trusted Lucien all his life. He *had* to trust. Without Lucien, there was nothing else for Danyael.

Struggling to bring his rioting emotions under control, he fought for calm. *Breathe. It's over. I'm safe now. Safe again. Can't put him in danger.* He turned and walked toward the window. It was easier if he did not have to meet Lucien's gaze, a lot easier if he did not have to see the surprised hurt in those expressive blue eyes. "I'm sorry," he murmured, trying to start over. "I'm just tired. It's been a long day."

It was not a lie. They had been friends long enough. Danyael knew Lucien would recognize all the signs of exhaustion that bordered on fatigue. The psychic shields he used to protect others from his unchecked empathic powers took a heavy toll on him. He needed space. More importantly, he needed privacy and rest. Soon, desperately soon.

"Why did you send for me?" Danyael asked. His tone was deliberately neutral, once again calm.

"Have you seen the news tonight?"

"No."

"Pioneer Labs was attacked and burnt, and it's believed that the pro-humanist group, Purest Humanity, was behind it. Fortunately, one of my friends escaped with Galahad."

"And?"

"Galahad is here. He was injured in the escape, and I need you to help him."

Anger snapped up again, rearing its ugly head. Danyael spun around, dark eyes flashing. "You pulled me out of New York just because you needed a doctor? Couldn't you bribe someone in D.C. to take care of him?"

Lucien shook his head. "There's more," he said simply. "Come with me."

FOUR

Lucien flung open the door to the Ivory Room. There was a gleam in his sapphire blue eyes that Danyael recognized from years of close friendship. Lucien had found another cause to champion. Danyael suppressed a smile. Beneath Lucien's polished sophistication was a man who habitually picked up and nursed strays back to health, including stray people.

He had spent many years as Lucien's cause. It would be a relief to hand that baton off to someone else. Lucien gestured to someone behind him but Danyael did not look back. He stepped in and walked toward the motionless figure on the bed. The sooner he was done here, the sooner he could—

Galahad? His breath caught sharply. Shock clawed through him. Icy fingers seized his heart, squeezed hard.

Time slipped by, utterly unheeded. It could have been seconds, minutes. He simply stared.

"Danyael. Damn it, Danyael!"

He looked up and saw a young Chinese woman wrapped in Lucien's arms. She shuddered, her slim frame trembling, and would have fallen, if not for Lucien's support.

Guilt flared. His unchecked emotions had leaked past his psychic shields, barriers that faltered only when he was exhausted or deeply distressed. He clenched his teeth, and with conscious effort, reeled in his emotions, locking them once again beneath his meticulously constructed equilibrium. The air in the room cleared, save for a residual undercurrent of distress, mild enough to be ignored.

Lucien's grip gentled as the tension eased out of the woman's body. "Xin? Is it better now?"

Xin nodded, inhaling deeply as she straightened. "Yes. Didn't you feel it? It was…"

"No. I'm not affected by Danyael's emotions." Lucien held on to her for a moment longer, and then released her. She stepped away from him. Only then did he turn back to his friend. "Danyael? Are you all right?"

If he had energy to spare, he would have laughed at that question. How could he be possibly all right? Shock and disbelief entwined and wafted up, bubbling dangerously close to the surface, challenging the discipline he had cultivated through months of training, years of practice.

Name the emotion. Even if it's warranted, nine times out of ten, don't act on it.

Exquisite control masked stunned alarm. "This can't be," Danyael said quietly. His dark eyes never left Galahad's face.

"It can. You look like identical twins." Lucien moved to stand beside Danyael. "We've taken a blood sample from him and should have his full genetic code by tomorrow morning. We can run a comparative scan then. I'm sure it will confirm what we already suspect—what anyone with eyes can see. Someone stole your genetic code, Danyael. The real question is, did they take just parts of it, or did they take everything, including your mutant powers?" His mouth set into a grim line. "Imagine, your capabilities, combined with Galahad's other genetic advantages. If there's a disaster in the making, I want to be on top of it."

Danyael inhaled deeply and nodded. His mind reeled from what it would mean for Galahad and for him. Galahad would turn twenty-five on Christmas Eve. Danyael was twenty-eight, maybe twenty-nine. He did not know precisely how old he was, but precision was not needed at this point. They were two, perhaps three, years apart in age, the period of his life for which there were no public records on him, for which he had no memory to shed light on the mystery of his past.

But there was no time or luxury to dwell on himself. Even the events that had taken place on the plane ride into D.C. were irrelevant now in view of far more urgent and important matters. *Control...steady now...*He closed his eyes briefly. His angelically beautiful expression was one of ethereal calm as he extended his mutant powers without moving a muscle. He drove his emotions deep down and then opened his mind to absorb the waves of emotions emanating from others. He immediately sensed the deep pain and turmoil that laced through Galahad's emotional aura, screaming like an open, bleeding wound.

"May I?" he asked Lucien perfunctorily, but did not wait for an answer as he moved quickly to sit by Galahad. He gently turned back the covers, eyes narrowing as he assessed the bloodstained bandages. He placed his left hand on Galahad's forehead and his right hand across Galahad's bandaged abdomen, closed his eyes, and then allowed his secondary healing powers to surge. No need for props like stethoscopes and blood pressure cuffs to camouflage what he was doing. There was no need to hide his capabilities from Lucien, who knew everything about him. "The bullets passed through, which is fortunate, since I won't actually have to cut him open to remove them. One hit his liver though, and there's substantial internal bleeding."

"Can you fix it?"

"Yes. Give me a moment."

Galahad stirred, his dark, pain-filled eyes fluttering open weakly. He stared up in open bewilderment at Danyael's face, identical to his own. Danyael could sense the precise instant in which Galahad's bewilderment evolved into sharp panic. It was time to intervene. "It's all right," Danyael kept his voice low, calmly professional. All traces of his own personal hell were locked away as he released a gentle surge of peace, deep and tranquil, intoxicating. "My name is Danyael Sabre, and I'm a doctor. I'm here to help you. May I take a look at your injuries?"

An emotional transformation more powerful than a sedative flooded Galahad's mind and body. Galahad stared into Danyael's face for a moment longer and then nodded, lulled by a feeling of profound safety and well-being. Xin, privy to the same emotional transformation but far more mentally alert, stared at Danyael, her expression combining disbelief and awe.

"Everything will be all right," Danyael promised in the same reassuring tone as his deeper, stronger powers surged out, reaching deep into Galahad's broken body. "Go to sleep now. We'll sort it out when you wake."

Galahad resisted for a brief moment, but the depth of trust he felt for an absolute stranger won easily. His eyes closed again as sleep, now deeply anesthetic, claimed him. Unaware, he slept as his body healed. Deep internal injuries closed slowly; the bleeding halted. Open surface wounds knit together, forming scar tissue that gradually receded, replaced by new, healthy skin.

A minute of silence passed, but to Danyael, it felt far longer, as his powers penetrated into Galahad's body, repairing the damage before gently withdrawing. When he finally opened his eyes, the healing was complete. His face was pale. He pushed unsteadily to his feet, grateful when Lucien caught his arm, supporting him. "We should remove the bandages now," Danyael said. The quiet tone concealed weakness. "They're tight and constrict his breathing. They're no longer needed."

Xin slipped past Lucien to assist Danyael in unwrapping the bandages from around Galahad's chest and thigh. She ran her hand over the smooth, unmarred skin and flesh beneath the bloodstained white bandage and then stepped back as Danyael pulled the sheets over Galahad's naked body.

Lucien watched Danyael steadily. "You look like hell. Do you need to rest?"

Did he need to rest? Yes, he did. Desperately. He had extended his powers far beyond what he typically tried to do in a single day, surreptitiously healing a toddler while extracting the bullets from her body, eliminating the final traces of HIV from Jeremiah Smith's body, and now this. He pressed the back of his hand against his fevered brow as he struggled to control the deep chills that wracked his body from within, the price he paid for absorbing sickness and injuries. Still, he shook his head. "I'll be all right in a few hours," he said quietly, hating the fact that he sounded so sick. "I suspect you'd rather talk."

Lucien nodded. "I would. Xin, if Zara's awake, can you ask her to join us in my study?" He watched her leave the room.

Danyael caught Lucien's faint flicker of interest. He chuckled softly.

Lucien turned at the sound. "What?" he asked.

"Nothing important. Who is she?"

"I'll introduce you when we get back to the study. She's Mu Xin, the clone of Fu Hao."

"Fu Hao?"

"Twelve hundred BC queen, military general, and high priestess from ancient China."

"Busy woman," Danyael said as he walked slowly beside Lucien toward the study. "So what does she do these days?"

"Hacker." Lucien grinned. "She's one of the best cyber-warfare specialists I know, and I know—heck, I employ—many of them. She's on the payroll for the US government, but she does some part-time work for Zara."

"Zara. Zara Itani? You dated her once."

"A long while ago. She's more like a baby sister to me now. A very troublesome one, I might add. You were probably off at medical school when we were hailed as the most incongruous celebrity couple in Washington, D.C., but I know I've mentioned her."

"A little." Danyael had to wrack his memories for the few snippets of information Lucien had shared about Zara Itani over the years. A human, Lebanese and Venezuelan, with a distant infusion of Asian. A martial arts expert and owner of an agency of mercenaries that she kept staffed through her connections to resistance fighters in both Lebanon and Venezuela. "We've never met."

"No, you wouldn't have. She doesn't know you exist. You've always been careful to avoid meeting my friends, and I've gotten very good at self-censoring the most important friendship of my life entirely out of my communications with others." Lucien's tone was neutral, but Danyael winced, clenching his teeth as Lucien's emotions—quietly simmering resentment, hurt, even—slapped at him like the chill winter air.

"Not now, Luce. Please," he said quietly.

Lucien dropped the topic as they stepped into the study together. "Drink for you?"

"Just water, please." Danyael's stomach swirled with nausea that he barely kept under control. Eating and drinking would not be an option for several hours yet. With slow, deliberate movements, he lowered himself into an armchair by the smoldering fireplace. He did not think he could handle any swift motions; neither his sorely aching body nor crushing headache would permit it. He swallowed hard and winced at the taste of bile in his throat. God, he needed rest badly.

"Are you sure you're all right?"

Danyael did not look up at Lucien. He stared at his hands as he clenched and unclenched them slowly. He ran his thumbs over his numb fingers; he could not feel his fingertips. "I'll be all right. Eventually," he whispered, submitting without protest when Lucien reached for his hands.

"Shit, your hands are like ice." Lucien slammed the glass of water down on the side table and then squatted down in front of Danyael. He rubbed Danyael's hands briskly between his own, trying to warm them up. "When was the last time you ate?"

When? The clinic was so busy that he always worked through lunch, and his dinner plans had been sidelined when four thugs in business suits snatched him off the streets of New York. "Breakfast," he murmured. A half-cup of milk and an apple.

Lucien scowled. "I'm going to get you something from the kitchen."

"Can't eat right now."

"You're going to damn well try."

Danyael heard Lucien's departing footsteps. He closed his eyes and buried his face in his hands. Icy fingertips connected with his fevered brow. The emotional satisfaction he usually derived from helping someone in need was buried under layers of exhaustion. He needed to relax for a few minutes, but he required privacy for that, a fully enclosed room, sealed windows and doors, to contain the swell of emotions once he let down his guard. He did not have the time for that, not with so much at stake, and so many questions that demanded answers he did not have. *I can rest in a few hours. I can do this. Just need to take it slow, a few minutes at a time. Don't stare down the future. Just face the right direction and watch your feet move, one step at a time.*

The philosophy was hardly inspirational, but it had gotten him through some very difficult days and nights, and sometimes the outcome was even more than he could have hoped for. What his attitude said about the quality of his life, he did not know. Danyael swore under his breath and then laughed quietly, a bitter, self-mocking sound.

Quiet footsteps echoed down the corridor and paused by the open door of the study. "Galahad?" a soft female voice called out incredulously.

He looked up and saw a young woman standing beside Xin, gaping at him. It took a great deal of effort to think through the shafts of pain pulsing through his skull, even more to muster the energy respond to questions. "No, I'm Danyael. Danyael Sabre."

This was Danyael Sabre? Zara glared at Xin for failing to warn her of what to expect. Maybe Xin thought it would be funny to observe her unguarded reaction to the doctor Lucien had summoned so urgently from New York City, but Zara was not amused.

She stepped into the room and circled the chair to get a better look at him. He did not seem fazed by the close scrutiny; indeed he hardly seemed aware, or to care, that she was studying him.

Danyael Sabre was the perfect replica of Galahad's flawless beauty, but for a few minor differences: hair, the same rare shade of pale blond, cut shorter, and a thin white scar, almost invisible, that slashed across his right cheek, starting at the top of his cheekbone, close to his ear, and ending at the tip of his chin. One of his hands—his left hand—was subtly misshapen, as if the bones had been broken once and then badly reset. She estimated that Danyael and Galahad were about the same height, Danyael possibly a little thinner. He was dressed simply in a white shirt, faded denim jeans, and a well-worn pair of black sneakers. A black leather jacket that had seen far better days was draped over an equally well-used backpack.

The biggest observable, and critical, difference was in her reaction to him. Galahad had captured her imagination, and more importantly, her compassion, but Danyael stirred nothing in her. In fact, in spite of his staggering beauty, something about him repelled her. He was not physically repulsive; in fact, he was far from it. He had said nothing or done nothing to warrant that kind of reaction from her, but in spite of her marked curiosity over how both he and Galahad had come to share a face, she could not bring herself to care to know more about him as a person.

Her concern for Galahad drove her to talk to Danyael, though. "Lucien says you're a doctor. Where do you practice?"

"The free clinic at Crown Heights, Brooklyn." He did not even have enough social grace to look at her when responding.

The free clinic? The young doctors employed by free clinics were the ones who had barely passed their medical examinations and consequently could not find jobs at more reputable institutions. They were, as a rule, poorly trained and inadequate. She exchanged a dismayed glance with Xin, but her friend's expression was oddly sympathetic. What the hell? Was this really the best that Lucien could do with regard to finding a doctor?

She bit back a snarl of frustration. "Galahad was shot twice. I need you to see to him." She could not help the note of superiority that crept into her voice. This pathetic excuse for a doctor was not good enough for Galahad.

"I did. He's fine." He *still* did not look up at her.

He had the manners of a cretin. Snorting with disgust, she spun around and strode out the door, almost colliding with Lucien, who was returning with a bowl of soup and a small plate of crackers balanced on a tray. She gave him a furious, fulminating glare. "Your taste in friends is questionable, Lucien." She nodded toward Danyael, who sat hunched over in the chair.

Ignoring her sarcasm, Lucien grinned at her. "I always thought so too. Just look at you."

Zara's violet eyes shot daggers at him for the insult. Gritting her teeth, she walked out of the study.

Shrugging slightly, Lucien set the tray down on the side table. "Did you do that to her, Danyael?"

"No more so than usual."

"I wish you wouldn't always presume to know what's best for people to feel."

"I don't," Danyael protested simply, but did not have enough energy to argue his case any further. They had been through that same discussion too many times before. No need to rehash it in front of company.

"Have you two met?" Lucien glanced at Xin.

Danyael looked up at the petite Asian woman casually leaning against a bookcase filled with rare first editions. She was plain compared to Zara's flashy, exotic beauty. Her brown eyes were her most salient features, windows into a personality that was equal parts cool intelligence and calm competence. She was not beautiful, precisely, but there was something compelling about her that made her far more attractive than her looks warranted.

Lucien made the introductions. "Xin, this is Danyael Sabre. We've been friends for a long time. Danyael, Mu Xin. She works with Zara, among other things."

"It's a pleasure, Danyael. And thank you for healing Galahad."

Lucien's eyes narrowed. "Why aren't you biting off his head the way Zara did?"

"Psychic shields," she said. "I didn't have them on earlier, but after Danyael's emotions nearly knocked me off my feet, I thought it wouldn't hurt to put a few extra layers of protection in place."

"I'm sorry," Danyael murmured, looking up briefly at her. He winced when the motion—minor though it was—made his world spin.

"Don't worry about it; I know to be careful around you now. Why do you do it, Danyael?" Xin probed gently. "Zara does tend toward callousness, but her reaction to you was extreme, even for her. She's not immediately hostile or prejudiced toward someone she's meeting for the first time."

Danyael only shook his head. He did not reply.

Lucien stepped into the awkward silence. "How long before Galahad wakes?"

"Ah…" Danyael looked away, trying to work through a sharp ripple of pain as it sliced through him. He clenched his teeth and closed his eyes, inhaling deeply until it slowly passed. "He'll…he'll need at least a full night," he said finally.

"Good. We'll talk tomorrow. Your room has been prepared, by the way."

"Didn't you want to talk tonight?"

"Danyael, you can barely form a coherent thought, let alone complete a sentence. You're done. I've got it from here. I'm going to see how much of the pro-humanist media coverage I can subvert before they hit mainstream media. We don't need anyone else trying to add logs to this fire."

"What about Jason Rakehell?" Xin asked, "Zara told me that he knows she has Galahad."

Lucien's blue eyes narrowed. "I'll deal with Jason. He's a tiresome prick."

"Right." Amusement coiled through Xin's voice. "Is there anything you'd like me to do?"

Lucien glanced at Danyael. "Pull his records; anything you can find on him before the age of twelve, and focus on anything before the age of four. I want to know of any occasion when his genetic code might have been stolen. You need to tell us where to start digging. We don't have much time."

~*~

Zara had not believed Danyael Sabre when he said that Galahad was fine, but Galahad *was* fine. He was sleeping peacefully, his breathing deep and even. His injuries were gone, vanished as if they had never existed. No mere doctor could do such a thing. The answer was perfectly obvious to her. Danyael was a mutant healer perfectly disguised in the complementary profession of a doctor.

Arrogant bastard. Why couldn't he have taken the time and the courtesy to let her know what he was? Did he think that his mutant capabilities gave him the right to be a social retard and still command respect from people? Well, he was going to be deeply disappointed then; she was not planning on offering him any respect. It did not matter that he was Lucien's friend. In fact, it made perfect sense why Lucien had never spoken of Danyael to her before. Lucien's social etiquette was so polished that he practically glowed in the dark. And Danyael, so graceless and inept, must have been an embarrassment, someone you hide in a dark closet somewhere, dig out when you need him, and then toss him back, hoping no one else saw him.

It was such a pity Danyael had such a clear connection to Galahad. Obviously, Lucien thought that Danyael held the key to the secrets behind Galahad's creation. The sooner they found out, the better. They could then toss him back into the closet and move on with their lives.

Sighing softly, she pulled up a chair to sit by Galahad's bedside. It did not make sense. Nothing made sense. She had seen Galahad and had been impressed by his strength, his courage. She had seen Danyael and felt contemptuous indifference.

Tired and confused by the swirl of conflicting emotions, she curled her feet beneath her, content to stare at Galahad. She felt peace there, sitting by him, watching him, thinking, wondering. *How can you both look so perfectly alike, and yet bring out such different feelings in me?*

FIVE

Danyael awoke early, as was his habit. His throat was parched and his stomach reminded him that he had not eaten in nearly twenty-four hours, but otherwise he felt significantly better. A solid five hours of sleep had helped him work through the worst aftereffects of overextending his healing capabilities the previous day, apart from the lingering exhaustion and tension headache that no amount of rest or painkillers could alleviate.

A sudden chill deep within chased away the warmth as his mind groped for answers. The live blood transfusion: what were its effects on him other than the numbing weariness that lasted for weeks until his body purged the existing blood cells—both his and those from his donor—and eventually replenished them with fresh blood?

Given that he had apparently lived with that type of treatment for more than half his life, would he ever truly know what had actually come of it?

He gritted his teeth and fought down a growing sense of despair and helplessness. Live blood transfusions were banned precisely because more than just blood transferred between individuals. Decades earlier, Stanford University researchers had studied pairs of old and young mice sharing a circulatory system. As a result of the experiment, the brains of older mice were rejuvenated—the number of neurons increased as did synapse activity—but conversely, the brains of the younger mice deteriorated. The two mice had become a single, closed system seeking equilibrium.

How much of it was temporary? How much permanent?

Nobody knew.

The research promised tremendous medical implications for age-related brain disorders, but like the creation of the perfect human being, it was more than people could stomach ethically, and in response, the governments clamped down on live blood transfusions.

None of those old facts answered the single question that churned endlessly through his mind. How did he ever get sucked into that situation? If it had begun sixteen years before, it had to be related to the council somehow. There were few other explanations that would have made sense, but who could he talk to when he didn't know friend from foe?

I don't dare risk Lucien. What the hell do I do now?

For several minutes, he lay in bed, but not even the familiarity of his surroundings could reassure him. Solid wooden beams crisscrossed the ceiling. The walls were painted a warm shade of cream and decorated with black-and-white photographs of the great architectural wonders of the world. The room had been his since the first day he had been informally adopted into the Winter household. Even after he moved out, it was set aside for him, always available, should he choose to return. The room was his first, and very likely the only place he would ever call home. Here, he felt safe.

Almost.

He breathed in and out deeply, a calming ritual at the start of each day. The room reminded him that he owed everything—his sanity, even his life— to Lucien. He always knew that he would pay any price to repay his debt to Lucien. He often wondered if Lucien knew that too.

Was Lucien finally demanding payback?

He could not see any way for his desire for anonymity and privacy to survive the latest revelation, not when he shared a face with Galahad, the pivotal point in the genetic debate on the evolution of the human race. If rumors were true, Galahad had been coded with superior intelligence and health. The alterations made in his chromosomes through the extension of his telomeres ensured vitality and longevity. Current estimates ran that he could live anywhere from two hundred to three hundred years.

Galahad also apparently possessed genes from an alpha empath. With any luck, they would be only the genes that coded for physical appearance. Nevertheless, the complex interaction among genes was still something of a mystery. Nothing good could possibly come from possessing the genes—*any* gene—of an alpha empath.

Who knew what else had gone into those genes?

His teeth clenched against chill dread, Danyael glanced out of the window. It was still dark, though a rosy dawn tinted the distant horizon. He pushed the covers aside, inhaled deeply, and released his breath in a soft sigh. It was time to start his day.

Ten minutes later, he walked into the breakfast nook, his emotions locked beneath his psychic shields. The term "nook" was ludicrously applied to a room large enough to accommodate a circular oak table for eight and a sideboard on which a variety of breakfast choices had been placed. French windows, framed by white lace, opened out into a magnificent view of the patio and swimming pool.

A lean Hispanic man was already seated at the table with massive servings of eggs, sausages, and hash browns heaped high on his plate. He looked up, his jaw dropping at the sight of Danyael. "*Por dios!* You're out of bed already? Man, you were practically dying yesterday!"

Danyael's eyes narrowed, and then he relaxed into a faint smile at the obvious case of mistaken identity. "I'm not Galahad. My name is Danyael Sabre. I arrived late last night."

"Danyael? *El medico?* Zara said last night that Lucien had sent for you. But you look just like him! How can that be?" His voice echoed his bewilderment, the questions tumbling out of him. "Do you know that you look like him?"

"Yes, I do. I saw him and healed him last night."

"But did you know that before last night?"

"No, I didn't." Danyael stepped over to the sideboard to select an apple from the tray of fruit. "I'm Lucien's friend. Call it luck or serendipity that brought Zara and Galahad to his door."

The man blinked again, trying to absorb it all, and then he stood up, wiping his hand on his napkin before extending his hand to Danyael. "I'm Carlos Sanchez. I work for Zara Itani."

"It's a pleasure meeting you."

Carlos sat down, shaking his head again in good humor as he picked up his fork and dug into his scrambled eggs. "This is all pretty crazy, you know."

No kidding. Crazy, in Danyael's mind, was a heck of an understatement. He let the discussion drop, and the conversation faded into silence until Lucien and Xin joined them a few minutes later.

Lucien inclined his head by way of greeting. "We have a lot to talk about, but let's wait for Zara and Galahad before we debrief on the situation. The maid just informed me that they'll be coming along soon."

Danyael felt the low hum of hostility first. It set up a throbbing resonance that pulsed through his skull like a painful toothache, too minor to warrant intervention, yet too insistent to be ignored. Zara, he realized, as she walked through the entryway of the breakfast nook a moment later. She offered a warm smile to Lucien, Xin, and Carlos, who were already gathered around the table. She was too practiced to allow her smile to slip when her gaze passed over Danyael, but her emotions flashed into dislike, even disgust. A muscle in Danyael's smooth cheek twitched at the impact that was as real to him as a physical blow. He inhaled deeply, bracing himself against the continued onslaught, and then looked up as a fresh wave of emotions flowed into the room. He picked up on a strong current of uncertainty underscored by wary caution, and then a flash of intense shock from Galahad as two pairs of midnight black eyes met across the room. Apparently no one had seen fit to warn Galahad.

Shock turned into disbelief and then transformed into denial. Galahad took a single step toward him. "I don't understand. This isn't possible." Galahad glanced at Zara, perhaps waiting for an explanation, but when none appeared forthcoming, he closed the distance to Danyael and stared deeply into the face that was identical to his except for a faint scar that cut across the right cheek. Galahad's dark eyes narrowed. "I didn't just imagine your face last night."

"No, you didn't. I'm Danyael Sabre. How do you feel this morning?"

"I feel fine." Distrust and suspicion flashed through Galahad's emotional spectrum. "I remember last night. You healed me. But how?" he demanded, his tone sharp, almost brittle.

Danyael winced. His psychic shields were designed to contain his emotions, not block out the emotions of others. Indifference he could easily handle, but negative emotions directly targeted at him hurt like hell. Galahad's emotions sliced deeply, and Danyael had to drop his gaze to hide the flicker of pain. "I'm a mutant," he explained simply.

A sudden burst of enmity from Zara slammed into him like a blow between his eyes. He inhaled sharply and gritted his teeth against it. He had felt that reaction often enough from others. She hated mutants. Welcome to the club, he thought. He was far too accustomed to that kind of reaction to be bitter about it anymore.

"A mutant?" Galahad asked. "What's your connection with Pioneer Labs, and with me?"

"That's what we're trying to find out, Galahad," Lucien interjected. "I'm Lucien Winter." He stood up and extended his hand. "And this is Mu Xin. I believe you met Carlos last night, and of course Danyael. Have a seat, please. Join us for breakfast."

Galahad looked at Lucien, assessed him, and then inhaled deeply, a studied calm once again flowing across his demeanor. "I know of you from the media the professors allowed me to read."

Lucien grinned in response. "I hope you read the good things."

"You are the only child of Damien Winter and Madge Callahan, household names in the world of international finance. The Winter-Callahan Corporation is a privately held diversified financial services company, with significant assets in Brazil, India, China, and Russia. You are, by reputation, open-minded and tolerant of the genetic revolution, even if your parents are not."

"My closest friend is a mutant. It would be hard not to be open-minded about the genetic revolution. And as for my parents, they frequently forget that I'm technically an in vitro. They wanted only one child, so they hired the leading geneticists in the country to optimize the combination of their gene pool. Rest assured, you're in the company of people who are sympathetic to you, Galahad. I'm an in vitro. Xin is a clone, and Danyael, of course, is a mutant."

"Human-born or derivative?"

"We don't know. His past is a bit murky."

"And does that have anything to do with why we look alike?"

"Possibly," Lucien conceded, taking his seat. "Grab some breakfast, and then we can talk."

Galahad followed Lucien's gesture toward the sideboard, and his dark eyes widened. The heaping platters offered a bewildering variety of food that must have seemed like a kingly feast.

Zara cast Galahad a casual sideway glance and made the first move toward filling her plate, making it easy for him to follow her lead. "Bacon, ham, sausages, scrambled eggs, hard-boiled eggs, sautéed mushrooms, roasted potatoes, hash browns, gravy, and the most amazing selection of freshly baked bread and pastries." A smile of appreciation curved her lips. "Were you trying to feed an army, Lucien?"

Lucien Winter, raised from birth in the lap of luxury, shrugged, "It's just standard fare. Pancakes, French toast, waffles, and omelets are made to order, if you want them." He cast a quick glance at Danyael's plate, empty but for a slice of toast and a partly eaten apple. His eyes narrowed. "Do you want Henri to prepare something for you?"

Danyael demurred. "No, I'm fine."

Galahad took the seat across from him. Tension rippled through Galahad's lithe frame, exquisitely controlled, but Danyael, who could see with eyes and heart, caught the flicker of suppressed emotion. He watched Galahad closely. Galahad was observing others around the table, taking cues from their actions and then blending in swiftly and subtly. Keen mental dexterity and highly developed social intelligence facilitated Galahad's early steps into the real world, yet Galahad made the process appear effortless. Danyael considered himself warned: Galahad was not someone to be underestimated.

"Let's get started, even if at the risk of ruining our digestion," Lucien began the moment everyone was seated. "The situation is deteriorating by the second, and it's probably just a matter of time before someone realizes that we're sitting at the heart of it all and it goes completely downhill. The six things that escaped from the lab were apparently responsible for slaughtering most of the people who attacked the laboratory. They then killed the emergency and news crews. By the time the second set of cops arrived, the creatures had vanished. No confirmed sightings yet, but lots of clues—dead bodies and the like—that suggest that they're moving south, generally avoiding detection by staying out of highly populated areas."

Xin took up the debriefing seamlessly when Lucien paused. "That tactic isn't going to work once they hit D.C., of course. Regardless, the world now knows that they're out there. It has resulted in a massive media backlash against Pioneer Labs and anything that even remotely hints of genetic selection, including in vitros and clones. Public fighting started in the streets of D.C. an hour ago. Humans are mobbing and killing in vitros and clones, and of course the derivatives aren't exactly sitting back and allowing themselves to get killed. Unfortunately, the cops are taking sides. There are rumors that the president will declare a state of emergency and bring in the military, but there's a good chance the military will take sides too, which is causing him to hesitate. At this point, just *not* adding to the chaos is a win."

"And the mutants?" Danyael asked.

"They're staying out of it, thank God," Xin picked up a tablet computer, selected a media clip and handed it to Danyael to peruse. "I downloaded this clip fifteen minutes ago. The director general of the Mutant Advisory Council has issued an injunction to all mutants to *not* get involved. In fact, all mutants within a hundred miles of D.C. have been ordered to report to the council office, where they will remain in custody until further notice."

"They're locking down the mutants?"

"They can't afford to have mutants involved," Lucien said reasonably. "It'd escalate from knives and guns to telepathic and telekinetic battles. If I thought all the mutants would come down on one side, I wouldn't actually oppose it, but some mutants are human-born, others are derivatives. We're back to a stalemate."

"Mutant fights are never stalemates," Danyael said, putting down the tablet. "But you're right in that it's probably better not to escalate it beyond knives and guns." He inhaled deeply and then released his breath in a soft sigh, resisting the need to massage his aching temples or roll his shoulders in an attempt to dispel the tension Zara's active dislike was triggering in him.

The source of his headache leaned forward in her seat. "Any news on Galahad?"

"They know he's alive but they don't know where," Xin told Zara. "The lab was searched by rescuers. The western wing was found sealed, undamaged by fire. They're looking for him now. No photos have been released yet, but in my opinion, that's just a matter of time."

Danyael shook his head. "So where does that leave us? I think we need to get Galahad out of the country."

"What would you propose?"

"Brazil, maybe even Singapore. There are countries that accept, even embrace, genetic superiority, but America isn't one of them. He will never be safe here."

"Why?" Galahad asked.

Danyael did not take offense at Galahad's tone or the strident demand. "The national approach toward genetic superiority is typically an extension of the majority opinion. Some countries embrace genetic superiority because they've been breeding for it for centuries, long before the launch of the genetic revolution. Culturally, they've always instinctively believed that power, wealth, and influence accrue to the strong, and make no apologies for that belief. Matches are made, children born, with the intention of ensuring that the next generation is stronger."

"Why wouldn't that be the natural, obvious thing to do?"

"Because deliberate genetic selection takes time and effort. It costs money. Today, in countries where wealth is a great deal more evenly dispersed, or where the government is wealthy, genetic superiority is an accepted way of life. In vitro testing and selection is actually mandated and paid for by the Singaporean government. But in America..." Danyael shrugged. "And I apologize in advance, for there's no way I can say this without sounding like an embittered mutant, our nation's inability to wholeheartedly embrace the genetic revolution in large part derives from our founding beliefs in equality."

"How can equality be at odds with success? Isn't the former a requirement for the latter?"

"That's one point of view," Danyael said. "Another point of view suggests that even though most of us silently acknowledge that natural ability has a great deal to do with how far a person goes in life, it's not politically correct to say that out loud. We apparently marry for love, not because our selected partner has genes that will complement ours in order to create a stronger next generation. So far, we've depended on government policies to balance out weaknesses in the gene pool, but our government does not have the kind of money to pay for everyone to be superior, so most of the country isn't. Most people live in deadly envy of those who are superior, which includes many historic clones like Xin, most in vitros, all mutants, and most especially you, the embodiment of genetic perfection. While there very well may be a place for you somewhere in the world, America is probably not it."

Lucien shook his head. "Getting Galahad out of the country is a perfectly viable option, but I think other things have taken precedence. If we can figure out why you two share a face, we could use that information to diffuse the tension. The party has started before us, but I don't think the plan has changed, just the timelines. Xin, what do you have on Danyael and Galahad?"

Xin picked up the tablet, flicked through a few screens and commands, and handed the instrument to Danyael who looked over it in silence for a few moments before passing it to Galahad.

Xin summarized the report Galahad was reviewing. "Perfect physical genetic match but you're not genetically identical. The majority of your genes, such as those that determine intelligence and personality, are different. However, small portions of the genes that are believed to contribute to Danyael's empathic powers are also present in Galahad. Their combined effect is unknown."

"Mutations are complex," Galahad said, quietly at first, but gaining confidence quickly. A warm, natural charisma eased out from beneath his initial wariness as he relaxed. "At the lab, I spent years studying genetics, among other things. The expressions of genes are usually best understood in comparison to something else—in this case, perhaps Danyael's genetic code. What exactly are you trying to prove, Lucien?" he asked.

"I'm trying to understand how you and Danyael are related. What do you know about how your genetic code came about?"

"I was always told it was created directly from nucleotide base pairing. No one ever mentioned templates, but of course it's logical to assume that there would have been templates. Anything short of using templates would be trying to replicate evolution all over again." He paused briefly, set the tablet aside, and looked at everyone gathered around the table. His gaze was strong and direct, his dark eyes compelling. "It's obvious that Danyael's genetic code was used as a template, but it's not as simple as taking two chromosomes from Danyael and the rest from others and then inserting them into a cell. The genes that code for physical appearance are scattered across all forty-six chromosomes. Rakehell and Cochran would have known exactly which ones, of course. The human genome was mapped long before I was created. Still, it's not a simple task, even with a template, or templates, to copy."

Danyael leaned back in his chair, his dark eyes distant. It was easier to think coherently, easier to endure the barrage of Zara's emotions, now that he no longer had to deal with Galahad's emotions simultaneously. "Could they have cloned my cells, used restriction enzymes to cut out the sections they needed, and then combined them with genetic fragments from others?"

"Yes, but that's leaving a great deal to chance. There would have been a high recombine error rate—"

"Which could have resulted in the creation of those other things at the lab," Danyael said quietly.

Galahad arched a brow. "Yes, that's right."

"Do you know how those things came about?" Lucien asked.

"No." Galahad shook his head, "No one ever discussed them with me. I have my suspicions, and they are as Danyael has suggested, that they were created in the process of creating me. Failed experiments, essentially."

"Will their records be at the lab, or perhaps stored in a back-up drive somewhere?" Xin asked. "And more importantly, will they be of any use whatsoever in solving this?"

"Perhaps. You have Danyael's full genetic code, and if we can locate theirs, we can match portions of their code to incorrectly combined sections of Danyael's. That would be strong enough evidence that they share Danyael's genes."

Lucien frowned. "We need to move on that quickly. If they have empathic powers, I want to know immediately."

"All right, that's something I can work on. I'll see if I can locate their codes remotely; otherwise we might have to break back into the lab and find them." Xin glanced at Lucien and hesitated briefly before plunging on. "That could answer the 'how,' of course, but not the 'why.' Why did Rakehell and Cochran use Danyael's genes to begin with? Someone out there must know."

Danyael clenched his hands into fists; he had known this question was coming. He averted his gaze. "It's not a good idea, Luce. You know that."

Lucien sighed softly. "You are approximately three years older than Galahad, and there is no information about you prior to that age. Maybe that's not a coincidence."

"You have a police report." Nothing in his voice betrayed the hollow ache he still felt at the mention of his past. "What more do you need?"

"What happened before the police report."

"There's nothing before the police report. The Mutant Advisory Council tried to figure out where I came from. They found nothing."

"They didn't know about your connection with Galahad. This is a definite link—"

Zara scowled. "You're wasting time."

Danyael winced as disgust fueled Zara's irritation, transforming it into shards of anger, brittle and deadly.

She continued, "If you haven't noticed, we have a crisis here. There is open fighting in the streets of D.C. People are dying, and we're just *sitting* here trying to convince you to do the right thing."

Her scorn sliced deeply into him.

"We don't need you," she said. "If we have to, we'll stop this madness, without you."

"Zara!" Lucien's rebuke was sharp, but Danyael held out a hand to stop him.

"You're right," Danyael conceded simply. His voice was even, but it took a great deal of effort to keep it as steady as it sounded. He met Zara's hard, unrelenting gaze for a brief second and then looked away. His contact with most people was usually brief enough that he could endure their distaste for him without too much sustained effort. Zara, though, was another matter entirely. Her reaction to him was deeply negative and stunningly visceral. For reasons he could not understand, they cut right through his formidable emotional defenses and left him reeling from the effort of trying to process her emotions. "What do you want to know? How can I tell you what I don't remember?"

"Let me see that report," Galahad said. "A set of fresh eyes usually helps."

"Here." Xin picked up a folder at least an inch thick. "This is every publicly available report—and even some not-so-publicly available reports— on the first twelve years of Danyael's life." She pushed her plate away, her breakfast barely touched. "Lucien, I'm going to use the computers in your study. It's time to hack into Pioneer Labs off-location records."

"Sure, go ahead," Lucien said. "I'll clear out too, give you two some privacy to talk." He rose and followed Xin from the breakfast nook. Carlos looked around the rapidly emptying room, shrugged, and then stood up as well, taking his full plate with him as he sought another place to finish his meal.

Zara was the last to leave, but she paused by the door before departing. She looked at Galahad, not even dignifying Danyael with a glance. "I appreciate your attempt to get to the bottom of this, Galahad, but don't waste too much time on him. I know his type. He's like Jason Rakehell, too trapped in the past to face the present, let alone the future. He's dragging us down with him." She departed, leaving Galahad staring speechlessly after her.

Galahad's stunned gaze shifted over to Danyael. "She's not like that," he insisted, rising to Zara's defense. "What are you doing to her?"

Danyael gritted his teeth against the surge of suspicion he felt from Galahad, suspicion that bordered on defensive hostility and threatened to unravel the fragile rapport they had briefly shared moments earlier. He closed his eyes, a gesture of weariness, as he tried to explain. "I use psychic shields…barriers…to contain my empathic powers, and one of their natural side effects is that they repel people, encourage them to overlook me, to ignore me."

"Why?"

"You were raised in a lab, Galahad." Danyael met his gaze squarely. "Here in the real world, looks like ours is more curse than blessing. All in all, I'd rather deal with apathy and indifference than suffer the attentions of others."

"But why does she dislike you so intensely, when this barrier of yours doesn't affect the rest of us?"

"Because first impressions matter, and they either amplify or counterbalance the repellant effect of the psychic shield. Your first impression of me was somewhat positive, Zara's much less so." A wry half smile tugged at his lips. "And who's to say you're not susceptible to the shield's effects? Zara verbally attacked me, I said nothing, and yet you came to her defense."

Galahad's eyes widened, surprise chased by the faintest flickers of guilt.

Danyael shook his head dismissively. "Don't worry about it. I tend to bring out the worst in people. It's rarely their fault, and in this case, it's most certainly not yours." He paused briefly and then asked pointedly, "Are you planning to read that report?"

Galahad turned his attention to the police report dated almost twenty-six years earlier, written by Jacob Johnson, police officer for the town of Franklin, West Virginia.

Subject admitted to the ER at 10:54 p.m. is a two- or three-year old male child, predominantly Caucasian. Subject does not speak and appears to be severely developmentally delayed. Significant evidence of abuse, including malnourishment, recently fractured right femur, and multiple partly healed fractures in the bones of the left hand. Eyewitness accounts report that a car stopped on a bridge at Mill Run River, and a person—likely female—emerged from the car at around 9:45 p.m., removed the child from the back seat, and threw him into the river before driving away.'

Mill Run River was a tributary stream of the South Branch Potomac River, and Franklin was a three-hour drive from Pioneer Labs in Boonsboro, Maryland, just an easy car ride away. Galahad was not convinced, though. "This doesn't make sense. My life at the lab wasn't easy. I spent hours every day studying or in physical training. And then there were experiments, a few of them horrific, but I've never suffered that kind of pointless abuse—not for a single day in my nearly twenty-five years at the lab. Whatever your association with Pioneer Labs, it was not as a subject there."

Danyael's response was a thin, humorless smile. "Just keep reading."

In the folio was page after page of police and welfare officer reports, capturing the essence of Danyael's life from the point where he had been found up until around the age of twelve. Almost an hour later, Galahad reached the last page in the folio and set it down with a troubled expression on his face. "You're an alpha mutant," he said.

"Yes," Danyael said, his voice very quiet. "There are only two ways to attain that classification. One is to have some truly devastating abilities. The other is to be born with the abilities, as opposed to having them manifest at puberty, as is usual with most mutants. I'm classified as an alpha mutant on both counts. The evidence, as you can see, is fairly convincing." Actually, the evidence was damning. In the file was an entire series of interviews with people who seemed to be normal, decent people, people who claimed they had no idea what had come over them when they were found physically, emotionally, or mentally abusing a helpless, friendless child.

"How could it have taken them so long to figure out that you were a mutant?" Galahad asked, looking up at Danyael, who was standing by the French windows, staring out at the patio and the manicured lawn beyond.

"No one around me could think or feel clearly long enough to reach that conclusion until Lucien found me," Danyael explained, his voice dispassionate. He glanced back over his shoulder and then turned around fully and rejoined Galahad at the table. His beautiful face was stoic, though his dark eyes glittered with ancient pain. "For reasons we've never been able to figure out, Lucien is immune to my primary empathic powers, which allowed him to react with his natural compassion. He was only fifteen then, but he was able to protect me from any further attacks. When I was finally diagnosed as an alpha empath, the Mutant Advisory Council assigned a telepath to work with me until I learned how to control my empathic powers."

"How long did that take?"

"Years."

Galahad slipped the reports back into the folder and shut it. "What is it like, being a mutant?"

"I can't say. I've never had the privilege of being anything else. For now, I live in New York City. You can't throw a stone without hitting a mutant. For the most part, I can keep a low profile there."

"Why? You're an alpha empath. According to the report, you're among the most powerful in the world. Why do you hide?"

How could he explain, when he didn't even know the answer himself? Habit? Training? Post traumatic stress disorder? Some of those, perhaps even all of those. He shrugged, offered the simplest answer, because it was also the most truthful. "There's nothing wrong with wanting to be normal."

"Except when you're not."

Danyael acknowledged Galahad's rebuke with a half smile and a slight incline of his head. Time to move on; there was nothing to be gained by examining his many personality flaws in exacting detail. Deflecting attention was what he did best, and he did it so easily and smoothly that Galahad did not even notice. The surge of his empathic powers was subtle, a reinforcing of Galahad's ego, just enough to tug Galahad's attention back onto himself.

Galahad tapped lightly on the folder to focus their attention back on the task at hand, the task that would shed light on his own past. "Let's start with the lab. Have Xin pull the records of all female employees who worked there at that time, and you can look them over, see if any of them sparks something in you."

"I don't remember those years."

"You're an empath. You should know—better than most—how memories imprint permanently into the emotional psyche. If you see a face and something in you reacts to it, you may have found a lead worth investigating."

Danyael hesitated, the fierce internal struggle reflected in his dark eyes. "All right," he said after several long moments, "We'll give it a try."

They found Xin in Lucien's study. She glanced up from the three computer screens in front of her and smiled distractedly, her mind focused on her work. Still, her politeness was innate. "What can I do for you gentlemen?"

She listened as Galahad summarized their plan. "It sounds simple enough, and it could work," she agreed. "Pull up a chair, boys. I'm already in their system; it shouldn't take too long to find the relevant employment records." Her fingers flew over the keys, accessing records and files that were— theoretically, at least—protected behind firewalls. Five minutes passed in silence. "And here they are…just twelve female employees." She leaned back in her chair. "Not big on equal opportunity employment, at least back then. Here, Danyael, check them out."

Danyael held his breath, anticipating something—anything—each time he saw a new face pop up on the computer monitor, but nothing happened. He shook his head at the twelfth photograph. "It's not any of them."

Xin shrugged. "I'd have been surprised if it was. I'm not usually that lucky the first time out of the gate. I'll run a background check on each of them anyway, see if there are missing children in there somewhere. Any other ideas?"

"I know you don't have clear memories of your childhood, but you must have something, Danyael," Galahad insisted. He leaned forward, resting his arms, fingers interlinked, on the desk. His eyes were intent, searching. "What do you feel when you think about the past?"

What did he feel? For a fraction of a second, the emotional shields wavered, and myriad feelings instantly flooded through the room like a tidal wave. Emotions so tangible as to be like tastes to the tongue swamped through the silent observers. Confusion and bewilderment; aching, hollow loneliness; quiet, hopeless longing; a desperate, denied need to be held, to be loved; the silence, the emptiness punctuated by sharp bursts of pain, followed by pulses of throbbing agony. And then screaming terror, the rending shock of abandonment, a wound so visceral that not even time could soothe away.

Distantly, he heard Xin's sharp gasp and knew that the torrent of emotions had to be pushing hard against her psychic shields. Her shields would have muted the impact and absorbed a portion of his empathic energy, but not nearly enough. He saw tears spill unchecked from her brown eyes. She was not crying for him. She was crying for herself. His pain—the heartache of an unshielded alpha empath—had transformed into *her* pain.

As suddenly as the emotions had flashed through the room, they were gone.

Danyael yanked them all back in a stunning demonstration of skill, control, and willpower. Psychic shields clamped down so hard he had to fight to breathe. Without a word, he pushed to his feet and walked across the length of the room, as far away as he could get from Xin and Galahad. He pressed his forehead against the cool glass window, his body shuddering as he fought to contain the pain he always carried deep within. "I'm so sorry," he murmured. He curled his fingers into fists. How could he have allowed the pain to leak through? So careless. So stupid. He should have known better. He couldn't make mistakes like that. People had gotten hurt—people had *died* before when his mental and emotional shields collapsed. He could not let it happen again.

"His mother," he heard Galahad say softly. "His mother threw him into the river."

His mother. He had always wondered, but could not bring himself to believe. Galahad, who had handled his pain without the benefit of psychic shields, must have somehow seen to the heart of the matter. Perhaps Galahad suspected, as he knew, that there could be no other explanation for the depths of his heartache. Something within him remembered, even though he did not have any conscious memories of those early years.

Danyael closed his eyes. He inhaled shakily. Perhaps it was time to accept the fragile fiction of his life for exactly what it was—fiction.

He turned and walked out of the room without a word to either of them.

But nothing silenced the word that rang again and again in the vaults of his mind. *Mother*—

SIX

Alex Saunders looked up when he heard the quiet knock on the door. "Come in," he called out, and then nodded a greeting to the young woman who entered his expansive office. "Miriya. All done?"

"Almost," she confirmed. The heels of her boots clicked sharply against the hardwood floors as she approached his desk. "Everyone has checked in. The alpha mutants have been relocated to our North Carolina installation, per your orders, and everyone else is comfortably ensconced in guest suites here or in the Baltimore office."

"Then what's the problem?" he asked, anticipating the "but" in her sentence.

"We just caught the power signature of an alpha mutant who has not checked in. Actually, we saw it once last night, just after midnight, but for a variety of reasons, thought it might have been just an error in the readings. And then it flashed again, just a few minutes ago."

"Who is it?"

"Danyael Sabre."

Alex's eyes narrowed immediately. "Danyael? What is he doing here? He's based in New York City. When did you say he came down?"

"Likely last night. I went back through our records here and in New York and searched his energy signatures. There's strong evidence that he was in New York City until late yesterday evening. The machines recorded strong traces of his secondary power signature in Brooklyn, at the free clinic where he works. But after midnight, his primary power signature showed up here, in McLean, followed by a secondary flash. We thought it might have been a mistake with the machines—they do screw up every now and again."

"Not with an alpha, though. Their signatures are too powerful to be a machine glitch."

Miriya acknowledged the implicit rebuke with a graceful incline of her head. "And then his primary flashed this morning, once again in McLean."

"Damn." Alex leaned back in his seat. All in all, the expletive was a mild one considering the potential for absolute disaster implicit in Danyael's presence in an area already riding high on a host of irrational emotions. "What could he be doing here?" he mused aloud, not expecting an answer to his rhetorical question.

Miriya offered none. "I've contacted his controller in New York, who is understandably in a bit of a panic that Danyael had somehow managed to get out of New York without her knowing. She insists that Danyael has been historically easy to manage and very responsive to the requests of the council."

"He is," Alex confirmed. His relationship—if anyone could have been said to have a relationship with the painfully reclusive young man—went back some sixteen years, when Danyael had been first identified as an alpha mutant at the age of twelve. The child, beaten but not broken by a lifetime of horrendous abuse, had been grateful, thankful for the training that allowed him to control his powers and attain some semblance of a normal life. Danyael had never balked at the "big brother" oversight of the Mutant Advisory Council the way many other mutants did, but if Danyael was rebelling now, he had certainly chosen the worst time for it. With D.C. in an uproar, his emphatic abilities would amplify the chaos and heighten the madness to unprecedented levels.

Alex leaned back in his chair, damning the fact that he had no good choices available to him. He liked and trusted Danyael, but he could not afford to have an alpha empath loose in Washington D.C. in the midst of the crisis. "Find him, Miriya, and bring him in."

"Or put him down?" she asked explicitly.

Alex winced. How could it even have come to that? An execution order on Danyael Sabre? He hesitated, mulled over it for several long seconds, and then for the sake of the country, he finally nodded. "Only if there are no other options available to you."

Miriya nodded in acknowledgement. Her green eyes gleamed in her sharp-featured face. "Do you have any advice for me?"

He reassessed everything he knew about Danyael's strengths and weaknesses. "Just be careful, Miriya, and don't get overconfident. There are depths to Danyael's power that he doesn't typically draw from, but they're available to him. If you need to take him down, do it fast, because if he actually cuts loose, he'll most certainly drive hundreds of unprotected minds to suicide."

He saw her blink in surprise, perhaps re-evaluating just how difficult the mission could actually be, but Miriya—supremely talented and immensely confident in her abilities as one of the most powerful telepaths in the country—said nothing. She merely nodded thoughtfully, then turned on her heel and strode out of the office. Alex watched her leave, and then sighed. He swiveled his chair around to stare out his windows at the sweeping view overlooking the Potomac. *Danyael.* He sighed again. *Please don't let this be what I think this could be. For God's sake, remember your training.*

If he did not, Alex Saunders knew that there would be absolute hell to pay.

~*~

Jason Rakehell awoke hungry and in pain. For a moment, he stared up at the ceiling and waited for his head to clear. His right arm throbbed, reminding him that he needed medical attention. He ground his teeth. How could it have gone so wrong? The previous night was supposed to be his night of triumph. That morning, he should have woken with the glorious feeling that the greatest insult on humanity was dead, slaughtered by his hand.

Instead, all he had to show for it were soot-blackened clothes and a throwing dagger. *She attacked me…she fucking attacked me…and then she took it…saved it.*

And I was once engaged to her. Bitch.

His cell phone shrilled. His handsome face etched in a scowl, he rolled out of bed and fumbled for the cell phone on his bedside table. The call came from a number he did not recognize. He did not bother. Tossing the cell phone back negligently onto the crumpled sheets, he walked into the bathroom. Dumped carelessly in the sink were the bandages and bottle of antiseptic he had used to treat his wound the day before. He ignored them, though his arm screamed for attention, and headed straight to the shower.

Showering took a long time with his damaged arm hampering even the most basic movement. He probably needed to get it checked. Cautiously, he sniffed at the wet, bloodstained bandage as he dried himself with a bath towel he had picked up off the tiled floor. The injury had the metallic scent of blood, but did not smell putrid

The phone rang again. Frowning, he strode over to the bed. Five missed calls. The cell phone had probably been ringing incessantly while he took a shower, though whoever was so desperate to reach him had left no voicemail messages. Driven by curiosity, he accepted the call. "Yes?"

"Jason?" It was a painfully familiar voice, yet one he had not heard in a long time.

"Well, well." His scornful drawl barely concealed the surging anger. "To what do I owe this pleasure, *Father?*"

"I just read the police reports. You and your damned fanatics were behind the attack that resulted in millions of dollars of property damage and sixty-seven people dead, six of whom were *my* employees."

"Don't forget the extreme damage to your reputation when the cameras captured those monsters coming out of the lab and killing innocent emergency personnel and bystanders," Jason mocked. "Have you found them yet, Father?"

"*You're* the monster!" Roland Rakehell's voice trembled. "Intolerant bigoted bastard!"

"Fuck you."

"Is this how you repay me? I gave you everything!"

"Except a father. You're more of a father to that damned monster you created twenty-five years ago."

Roland never heard the soft whimper of a neglected child beneath the harsh edge of Jason's voice. "That doesn't excuse what you've done. You tossed away the sixty or more lives trying to get to Galahad. Where is he?"

"Consider it dead," Jason returned sardonically. "Oh, and thanks for calling." He hung up the phone, and just to keep the cell phone from ringing again, pulled out the battery.

Dressing slowly, he considered his options and tried to keep his thoughts focused on Galahad instead of dwelling on his father. He had to find Galahad and Zara. Her condo in Georgetown would be the first, the most obvious place to start. If he did not find her there, he would have to expand his search to the list of her friends who might have been willing to harbor her and Galahad. Jason's upper lip twisted at the thought. He would find her. He would flush her out, and when he did, he would kill Galahad, just as he had always planned to do.

~*~

Hungry...

Thirsty...

They slipped through the lightly wooded forests that bordered magnificent estates. The scent of blood and reek of death accompanied them. A dog caught their scent. It started barking in a frenzy. The bark ended in a whimper of pain. "Stupid animal! Shut the hell up!"

Humans...cruel...

Hurt it, kill it...

As one, they turned from their destination, ignoring the instinct that pulsed within them like a hurting, open wound, drawing them closer to the one they sought so desperately. With surprising silence and grace, they loped out of the woods. The human, so secure in his world, so unaware that the rules of his world were changing all around him, was both blind and deaf to them as they approached from behind. He kicked the dog cowering at his feet. "Dumb mutt! You're waking everyone up!"

The dog, afraid of its owner, yet even more afraid of the six grotesque forms that had slipped out of the darkness of the woods behind the house, crouched into a snarl, its teeth pulled back, exposing fangs. The man aimed another kick at the dog's ribs. "What are you growling about, you dumb mutt! I said shut up!"

The first blow lifted the man off the ground, flinging him into the air to land heavily on his back. Stunned by the fall, he stared in disbelief as they closed in on him. He had no time to scream. Claws and fangs tore into him, ripping and shredding. Blood spurted, sprayed.

The dog lunged forward, sinking fangs into flesh. The monster turned, picked up the animal, and snarled, exposing fangs that dripped blood. The monster raised a clawed appendage, too deformed to call a hand and prepared to rip the small terrier to pieces. *Kill...*

No...let live...

It obeyed the eldest without hesitation. Indifferently, it flung the dog away. The terrier landed in the bushes with a yelp of surprise and then tumbled, unhurt, to the ground.

Their grisly work done, they turned, and as one, loped with the grace of hunters, predators, back into the woods. The corpse, mutilated almost beyond recognition, they left on the ground as they resumed their journey. They were near. They could feel his presence drawing them closer like the stars draw weary sailors home.

Find him...find him...

So close now...almost there...

SEVEN

Danyael sensed Galahad's presence long before he heard the quiet footsteps stop beside him. Galahad's emotional aura was laced with curiosity instead of concern. Good; he didn't want Galahad's pity. Any emotion outside of neutral—whether positive or negative—tended to backfire on him one way or another.

He caught the brief flicker of uncertainty, slivers the color of mercury piercing Galahad's vivid emotional spectrum, before misting away like fog under spotlights. In the visible world, Galahad scarcely seemed to hesitate before joining him on the bench in the sun-flooded solarium. "Very pretty," Galahad said, a faint smile passing over his lips as he took in the wonder of the indoor garden in a single sweeping glance.

Danyael nodded. The garden was lush with tropical plants that did not have a chance of surviving outside, even in the mild Virginian winters. The artful display of nature apparently growing wild had taken teams of skilled gardeners hours of work to attain. It was beautiful, and it was one of his favorite haunts at Lucien's house, the place he went to be alone. He inhaled deeply of the earth-scented air as he braced himself for the inevitable questions.

"Are you all right?"

"I don't think I've ever been," Danyael said. He looked up, staring unseeingly at the tangle of plants in front of him.

"Did you know it was your mother?"

Danyael was silent for a long while. Conflict roiled through him. "Maybe," he conceded, the words reluctantly torn from him. "I suspected, but didn't want to believe." A soundless sigh. "I guess it's time to take those blinders off."

"Things could have changed. It's been a long time. She could have had a change of heart."

"Unlikely."

"You don't think so?"

Danyael shook his head slightly. "No one ever came back to look for me," he said quietly, stating the one key fact that Galahad had somehow missed when reviewing the records of Danyael's life.

"How can you say that so easily?"

Danyael looked away. He knew his dark eyes reflected anguish; he had never been able to keep his eyes from betraying him, but nothing crept past his iron control. "Practice," he said simply.

"I expected an empath to be overly emotional, a victim of heightened sensitivity. I did not think I would find the polar opposite, powerful emotions carefully reined, exquisitely controlled." Galahad paused. "Are you ready to see her again?"

"I don't know what I can say to apologize."

"Apologize?"

"Maternal instinct is an extremely well documented mammalian behavior. For my mother to have behaved so wildly out of the norm, she was likely driven to it by an alpha empath."

"You think this is your fault?"

"Everything else after that is; you saw my file. Why wouldn't the first tragedy in my life also be my fault?"

"You were only three years old."

"So it took her three years to get around to trying to get rid of me. That speaks more for her emotional resilience than anything else."

Danyael's empathic awareness flashed a warning as something deep and dark stirred in Galahad.

Galahad shot to his feet. "Do you really believe you're personally and completely responsible for everything in your file?"

Danyael raised his head and met Galahad's gaze squarely. "You've seen what I can do to your emotions," he said, his quiet, controlled voice standing out in contrast to the dangerous glitter of his black eyes. "Did you think that there's no dark side to that?"

"That's not the point," Galahad retorted. "You didn't ask for your genes. You didn't ask to be a mutant. How can you be responsible for something you had no choice in…no control over? That's not the way the world works."

"You were raised in a lab. What the hell do you know about the way the world works?"

Galahad's hands clenched into fists. His dark eyes flashed, glittering with fury fueled by twenty-five years of injustice. "That's not the way the world *should* work. If I accepted your point of view, I'd have to hold myself personally and completely responsible for the years of isolation and misery I suffered at the lab. The scientists who ran experiments on me are not absolved of their responsibility just because I was born with the supposedly perfect genetic code. None of us had any say in the genes that were inserted, either naturally or by design, into our cells. But instead of treasuring the diversity, the superiority we bring to the gene pool, we're treated like social pariahs, or worse, lab animals."

It was not just anger and fury that arced like lightning through Galahad. It was resentment, dark and towering, a jagged spike that sliced through his composure like a blade through paper.

It caught Danyael off-guard. Galahad's emotions seared through him, a blast of intense heat that scorched and burned and ignited mirroring emotions in him. *Galahad's empathic* was Danyael's first startled thought. Xin had cautioned as much based on a comparison of their genetic codes, but now he had evidence to support her suspicions. Galahad was not powerful enough to trigger the monitors that tracked the energy signatures of mutants, but he was easily on par with some of the most charismatic human leaders who inspired with and led by the sheer force of their personality.

Danyael deliberately quenched the backlash of Galahad's emotions and then pushed to his feet. Controlled anger surged through his eyes. Black locked on black, both sets glittering. "The difference between your situation and mine, Galahad, is subtle but profound," he said quietly. What happened to you at the lab was cruel, and it wasn't your fault. What happened to me…that *was* my fault, because I didn't control it."

"You were a child."

"Age doesn't acquit me. I screwed them up. I unbalanced the emotions of perfectly normal, decent people to the point where they lashed out at me. Of course I'm responsible."

Galahad shook his head. "And what about the adults? Aren't they responsible too?"

Danyael chuckled, a bitter sound. "You really are an innocent. There is nothing special, nothing heart-rending about my story, because it's as common as dirt. It's been repeated for generations, across cultures. Every day, in millions of homes, children are abused, and probably not a single one of them is an alpha empath. Those children aren't responsible. They don't deserve it, but it happens anyway."

"Why?"

It was another one of those questions for which he had no answers. He looked away, said nothing.

"Humans are cruel."

The quiet certainty in Galahad's voice sent a fissure of alarm racing down Danyael's spine. Danyael shook his head, the gesture a habitual denial of the truth. "We're human too," he said quietly and then turned and walked away. His fists were clenched, the subtlest physical betrayal of the excruciatingly tight bonds he had wrapped around his heart to contain his emotions. He swallowed hard, struggling to pull together the threads of calmness and peace that hung in tattered shreds before him. *I'm not ready, and I have no answers that make sense anymore.*

~*~

Trespassing on private property was one of those things that was ridiculously easy to do if you were a telepath. Miriya ran a mental sweep of the Spanish-revival home that presided over three acres of prime real estate in McLean. She found Danyael Sabre's energy signature easily, a low-frequency hum that suggested that he was keeping it well under wraps, likely beneath psychic shields.

She encountered a few psychic shields besides Danyael's, but far fewer than she had expected, and none of them shimmered with the undercurrent of extraordinary power the way Danyael's did. Her task would be easy. Walk in, talk to Danyael, and either walk out with Danyael or cart him away in a body bag. The choice was his.

Following the low pulse of his energy around the side of the house, she strolled through the gardens, easily deterring the curious or the watchful with a carefully placed mental suggestion that she belonged there. As luck would have it, as she was walking along the far side of the swimming pool, she saw the patio doors open, and the low-frequency hum shot up a few notches. Danyael himself.

If the empath had seen her, he gave no indication of it. In fact, as she crouched down by the bushes to watch him, she was convinced he had not noticed her. How very careless of him. She smirked. Cocking her head to one side, she observed him in silence as he prowled the length of the patio beside the curved edges of the swimming pool. He was disturbed, even distressed. She did not need any empathic or even telepathic skills to figure that out. Anyone with eyes would have noticed it from his restive motions; from the tension in his slender, muscular frame; and from the way he clenched and unclenched his fists as he tried to work through his anxiety and stress.

Up close, the edges of his energy signature were jagged, though nothing slipped past his iron-clad control. He was beautiful, she mused, allowing herself an appreciative smile. That observation was an understatement. Danyael's beauty was of the sort made for blood feuds, his profile so flawlessly perfect that it could have driven angels to tears of envy. She noticed that he was doing his damnedest to hide it. He probably did not make very many friends with his ingeniously designed psychic shield that continuously emitted emotional cues to deflect interest away from him.

She inhaled sharply, bracing herself to make the initial contact with him, but halted when the patio door opened again and another man, *inconceivably Danyael's twin*, stepped out. Miriya gaped, stunned into inaction for several precious seconds, before reaching out with her mind, desperately probing the other man's unshielded mind for answers.

A flurry of confused images pounded through her mind, but a single answer screamed through loud and clear. *Galahad.* The destruction of Pioneer Labs and the disappearance of Galahad started the entire mess. Danyael was behind it all. There was no point in talking or even hoping that he would come in quietly, no point in giving away the advantage of surprise.

Alex Saunders's words echoed in her mind: Take him down; do it fast.

She did not hesitate. Rallying her powers, she spiked an attack into Danyael's mind to shatter his shields, and then followed up with a blast that should have splintered his conscious mind into fragments. In disbelief, she watched as Danyael screamed in anguish and reeled to one knee, clutching his head in both hands in agony, but his shields did not collapse. *Shit.* She had taken out other alpha telepaths with the same attack. How could a mere empath withstand it? He was stronger—far stronger—than she had expected. She gritted her teeth and braced herself for a battle that was going to be a great deal messier than she feared.

Galahad raced forward as Danyael collapsed. "Danyael!" he cried with alarm, leaning over the mutant, supporting him through the wracking shudders.

"Telepath..." The warning was forced past clenched teeth.

She saw Galahad tense. He straightened, his dark eyes scanning the area.

She had considered herself fairly well concealed, but she knew the instant he saw her.

For a split second, his dark gaze darted past her before locking back on her. "Zara! Lucien!" His cry set off panicked alarm in the house.

Miriya tensed as Galahad sprinted toward her. No need for secrecy now. She pushed to her feet, prepared to send a psychic blast into Galahad's mind, but froze as she was stricken by fear. Some distant part of her mind, still rational, screamed at her that Danyael, who was struggling to rise to his feet, was actually fighting back. He had latched on to the psychic trail left by her attack and followed it back to her mind, snaking insidiously past the psychic barriers that would otherwise have kept him out, before unleashing his own particular brand of hell.

Galahad reached her, but inexplicably, he grabbed her and in a smooth motion, pushed her toward Danyael, toward the house. She stumbled, falling beside Danyael as two people—a young man and a young woman—ran out of the house and raced past her to join Galahad. As she looked past them, she saw what Galahad had seen—six grotesque, vaguely humanoid forms loping rapidly across the lawn toward the house.

She pulled away in panic, when Danyael tightly gripped her wrist. "Help me," he said. His dark eyes were vast pools of pain. He broke off his attack on her emotions as swiftly and cleanly as he had launched it. She gasped as her emotions cleared, freeing her mind and body to act. "Link us," he said tersely. "All of us."

Miriya searched his face. Her eyes narrowed as she grasped his plan. "You're crazy! You *can't* absorb all their injuries."

"I have to." He forced the words through another hiss of barely suppressed agony. "Those creatures tore through an entire police contingent, and will tear through my friends unless I can keep them alive long enough to win the fight."

His plan went against all of her better instincts, but Galahad and his companions were out of time. She closed her eyes. Her powers surged out like rippling tentacles to latch onto the unshielded minds of Danyael's three companions. She then glanced over at Danyael and felt his psychic shields drop, permitting her entry. She reached in, latched on, and met Danyael's gaze with new respect. It was an act of extreme courage, of stunning vulnerability. He had freely opened his mind to her, giving her full access to help his friends, even if it meant that she could easily destroy him.

We have found him...Brothers...Kill humans...kill humans.

Miriya shook her head sharply, her blond hair swaying as she braced against the flurry of incoherent images and maddened thoughts coming from the creatures. Scarcely ten feet away, Galahad, Lucien, and Zara fought, back to back, against the creatures that came at them from all sides. The three humans were power and grace personified, trained elegance and precision of the finest martial arts training pitted against brute strength and inhuman speed. The odds were stacked against the humans, but Miriya could sense the unnatural calmness that flowed from Danyael to the humans through her, reinforcing their ability to face the creatures with absence of fear.

Danyael tensed and then shuddered. One of the creatures had broken through Lucien's defenses. A massive claw, stained with dried blood, had raked across Lucien's abdomen, tearing through skin and flesh, yet it was not Lucien who cried out, but Danyael who whimpered softly in pain. Crouched beside him, she felt his secondary powers—his empathic healing ability—surge out through her and into Lucien, absorbing both the pain and the effects of the injury, sealing Lucien's wounds even before blood had a chance to spill.

Miriya stood at the heart of it all, the central link between Danyael and his friends. His primary and secondary powers flowed effortlessly through her, reinforcing their courage, whisking away pain and injury, offering healing and succor.

The fight dragged on interminably, though in reality less than three minutes had passed. Time had a way of slowing down when lives were in danger of being crushed in each second. They would lose, slowly but inevitably, Miriya realized, as Danyael grew progressively weaker. She had lost track of how many near-death experiences he had absorbed. She hovered protectively over him as he curled into a fetal ball, shaking so hard that it seemed he might shatter. He could not even cry out each time one of his companions took the brunt of an attack that washed through the psychic chain directly into him. All his energy seemed focused on dragging another gasp of air into his lungs.

The other people in the house were rallying, rushing outside, trying to figure out how best to help, although in view of the close-contact fighting, guns would have been too dangerous to bring to bear. Nevertheless, a young woman on the balcony braced a large handgun against the railing, took careful aim, and then fired a single, precise shot.

One of the creatures roared in pain as the bullet slammed into its forehead. Breaking away from the core of the fighting around Galahad, Lucien, and Zara, it clawed through an older man and then began to scale the wall, trying to reach the young woman. Someone in the house shrieked a warning. With a sudden surge of desperate strength, Danyael pushed to his feet and lunged after the creature, grabbing onto the bottom of its leg just as it leapt for the balcony. It snarled in rage as Danyael's weight threw it off balance. It lost its grip and fell to the ground.

Miriya cursed as the creature collapsed on top of Danyael, and then clambered laboriously to its feet. Beneath it, Danyael stirred weakly, and then convulsed, coughing blood, as another brutal attack—this one sustained by Zara—surged through the psychic chain. Danyael was unresisting as the creature hauled him up by his white shirt and lifted him off the ground with no visible effort. Danyael's head fell limply back. He was barely conscious, as the creature pulled a clawed appendage back, poised to rip out his throat.

Kill humans...kill humans.

Miriya did the only thing she had time left to do, blasting a psychic jolt with surgical precision into Danyael's brain, straight into the primitive limbic system, into his subconscious where his innate instincts and innermost emotions resided. It screamed out a single, terse order: *Fight!*

Danyael gasped, shuddering back into full awareness from her direct mental contact. His eyes opened, and he looked without fear into gaping jaws that dripped saliva and blood. He reached forward, grabbed onto the creature's shoulder with one hand to brace himself, and then drove the heel of his other hand with all his strength into its temple. The blow was insignificant, nothing at all compared to the bullet that had not even managed to slow it, but the physical contact was merely a channel for the true attack he intended.

Shields up! Break the link!

Miriya reacted instinctively to his order, tearing her mind away from his and severing the psychic chain fractions of a second before his shields yanked back up. His mind and emotions were once again fully protected behind exquisitely perfected barriers when he pulled the plug on the dam that kept his most destructive emotions walled away. The physical contact was all he needed to direct his pain, and he wielded it with deadly precision as he drove it into the creature.

The creature froze, its mouth open in mid-roar. The sound died in its throat. Its hands flexed, dropping Danyael to the ground. He scrambled back from it, but it scarcely noticed. It started to move again, first slowly, as its mouth opened wider to release a heart-rending wail of misery, and then with increasing speed as it tore into itself. Bloodied nails raked furrows into its hideously deformed face, clawing out its own eyes. The hands moved quickly, frantically, across its own body as it ripped through its own chest cavity, all the time uttering a wrenching moan of desperate sorrow, the kind of sorrow that could end only in suicide. With inhuman strength, it used two hands to pull apart its ribs, breaking them, and then reached in to yank out its still-beating heart. It stared at the organ with an expression of pitiful relief, and then dropped, first to its knees, before crumpling to the ground. The bloody, malformed heart rolled out of its hand to stop at Danyael's feet.

With a loud gasp, Miriya released the breath she had been holding.

The other creatures halted their attack, staring in a combination of shock and horror. *Brother...Brother.* The wail began, an aching howl that echoed among the creatures. *Humans kill...Kill humans...Kill humans now...No, leave now.*

She did not know which one of the creatures issued the order, but as one, they all turned and loped away, cutting across the lawn and vanishing into shadows as they neared the tree line. As suddenly as the attack had begun, it was over.

Only Danyael's pained, harsh breathing punctuated the silence that had fallen over everyone.

Lucien sprang into action. He looked up at the young woman on the balcony who had fired the weapon. "Xin. Call the police; tell them what happened and that those things are on the loose somewhere in this neighborhood. Under no circumstances are the police permitted inside the house." He pushed past Miriya, and knelt down by Danyael, supporting the mutant as he slowly tried to rise. "Danyael."

Miriya could see the near panic in Lucien's blue eyes.

Lucien wrapped his arm around Danyael's back, helping him to his feet, and then grimaced as Danyael coughed up blood with such force that the mutant staggered and would have fallen if not for Lucien's grip on him. "Damn," Lucien cursed aloud. "Help me get him to his room." He threw the order at the people pouring out of the house.

"No, wait. Carlos..." Danyael looked over his shoulder at the older man who had been torn apart by the creature and was curled up in a rapidly growing pool of blood.

"Someone else will have to get to him."

"Not enough time," Danyael insisted.

Zara raced past them and knelt down to gather the dying man in her arms. "Hang in there." She pressed her hand against Carlos's torn chest and glanced back over her shoulder at Danyael. "Help him!"

Danyael dropped to his knees beside Carlos, his face pale, his breathing labored. Miriya did not want to imagine how much damage he had sustained and was still planning to take on, damage that he would then have to work through on his own, without help from anyone.

She felt him release his powers once again, and her eyes widened immediately with concern. The psychic glow of his empathic healing powers was weak, faint. It spluttered, rising and falling with every pained breath. It flowed out of him ungrudgingly, but it was a mere trickle now compared to the powerful surge that had kept his friends alive through the fight. His healing capability was limited only by how much he could endure, and he could not absorb any more. His body had been pushed past all limits of human endurance. Any more, and his own life would be at risk.

Carlos gasped, choking on the blood that was rapidly filling his lungs. He reached out, grasping Zara's hands desperately, clinging on to her like a lifeline. The rapid gush of blood slowed but did not stop, as Danyael's powers trickled through the ravaged body. The open, raw wounds did not close. Carlos's breath rattled in his throat, a weak, dying gurgle.

Zara glared at Danyael. "Why aren't you healing him?"

"I…can't anymore," Danyael whispered in quiet defeat. He slumped back into Lucien's supporting arms, shuddering as he turned his face away. A cough racked his body and he convulsed, coughing blood—dark and viscous—into his hand.

"That's not good enough." Zara grabbed his shirt with two hands and shook him hard until Lucien intervened by pushing her back. Her anger snaked out, lashing like a whip. "You cower, you hide through the entire fight, and now when he needs your help, you can't come through for him?"

Danyael reeled from the blistering emotional attack. He paused and looked at Zara. Quiet heartache filled his dark eyes before he squeezed them shut. His teeth gritted against the waves of scorn and loathing that swamped him, battering with hurricane force at emotional barriers that were already stretched near to breaking. Guilt racked him, and he reached out to Carlos once more.

Lucien held him back. "Enough," he said.

Zara held Carlos's hand tightly. "He is dying!"

Lucien pulled Danyael away. "I'm not going to let Danyael kill himself trying to save Carlos. He's done here. Galahad, give me a hand."

Galahad moved to Danyael's other side, and together, the two men helped Danyael into the house.

Carlos died in Zara's arms. Miriya watched in silence as Zara choked back a sob. She leaned over her friend's body and gently closed his eyes. The virulence of her thoughts, targeted against Danyael, caused Miriya to recoil. *He's pathetic, weak,* Zara's mental voice spiked with fury. *He let Carlos die.*

Ungrateful bitch! Miriya spun on her heel, ready to knock some sense into Zara but was halted by Danyael's voice speaking quietly in her mind.

Not her fault. Mine. With those weary words, Danyael's mental voice trailed into exhausted silence.

Miriya looked at Zara through narrowed green eyes, and then with her usual lack of good manners, reached straight into Zara's mind without permission, flicking quickly through images captured forever in her memories. She saw Danyael as Zara had seen him, huddled on the patio, shaking as she, Lucien and Galahad fought off the creatures.

The distinction of whether Danyael was shaking in fear or shuddering in pain seemed not to have occurred to her. She saw him as weak, incompetent, a failure. She did not seem to know or care that the reason she was standing tall, arrogant, and proud instead of crawling on the ground trying to stuff her entrails back into her stomach was because Danyael had protected and healed her through the battle at nearly unthinkable cost to himself. How could Zara be so blind?

The reason was perfectly obvious: Zara had been tampered with. Her behavior had all the trademarks of it: she was single-mindedly irrational to the point of interpreting all new information in precisely the same vein. No one—not even a prejudiced human—was actually capable of being *that* clueless. Danyael's psychic shield was clearly doing exactly what it had been designed to do, exacerbating a negative opinion into heightened dislike.

On the other hand, Miriya could not conveniently blame Danyael's psychic shield for her own lapse into female oblivion. She had attacked him without provocation, and now, it was apparent, without any basis either. Whatever was happening there, it was clear that Galahad was not a reluctant captive. He obviously considered himself among friends.

Miriya's cell phone shrilled. She took a few steps away from the small crowd gawking like curious children at the corpse of the creature. "Yes, I'm still alive," she announced preemptively into the phone.

On the other end, Alex Saunders released an explosive sigh of relief. "Thank God! The machines picked up what I assume were your initial attack and Danyael's counterattack. And then the machines went completely crazy for about five minutes, tracking your power signature and Danyael's in perfect resonance, almost as if you were amplifying his, like two waves cresting to create an even greater wave. We've never seen his secondary healing powers spike that high before."

"I'd be surprised if you had." The corner of her mouth twisted in an ironic smile.

"And then he cut loose, didn't he?" Alex finished, his tone quiet. "It happened once, when he was much younger, and didn't have as fine a control over his powers. You probably won't believe the power readings we recorded here. What happened, Miriya, and why are you still alive?" he asked bluntly.

"Probably because he wasn't targeting me." She shook her hair back from her face and then glanced over at the corpse lying on the patio floor, beside the swimming pool. "The abominations—the ones that escaped from the lab—showed up just seconds after I attacked Danyael. He concluded that 'surviving' needed to be part of our revised agenda for the day, so we decided to work together, just for novelty's sake."

"And the abominations?"

"One's dead. Danyael drove it to suicide when he 'cut loose,' as you call it. It wasn't pretty. The others fled. And Alex." She hesitated briefly. "There are other things going on around here."

"Spill it, Miriya. You know I hate secrets."

"Yes, me too. It appears you left out quite a bit when you debriefed me on Danyael's capabilities."

"What do you mean?"

"His shields are insanely strong."

"He's a defense-class alpha empath, and he's double-shielded. What were you expecting?"

"I've broken through defense-class alpha telepaths with far less effort. But that's the least of it. Danyael followed my telepathic attack back to my mind. Since when could empaths do things like that?"

"They can't," Alex said firmly. "Danyael is an alpha empath. He has no telepathic capabilities."

"Well, then you need to consider rewriting the alpha empath playbook, because not only did he manage to sneak past my shields but we also linked telepathically, seamlessly, and he psychically healed his friends through me. I've never seen an empath pull off such a clean, perfect telepathic link before."

"Danyael's very capable."

Nevertheless, she heard doubt and decided to push her case a bit harder. "Telepathic-level capable?"

"No, he is not telepathic. Trust me. We ran all those tests on him when he was first identified as a mutant. And there is no alpha empath playbook. There are far too few of them to make any generalizations on what they're capable of doing."

"I know what I saw," Miriya said. "I think Danyael is overdue for another review. An alpha empath with secondary healing abilities and minor telepathic capabilities? That kind of mutant would be just a little too capable and too dangerous to leave out there. We can't run the risk of someone snatching him up."

"You are blowing things out of proportion, Miriya. I know the results of Danyael's tests. He's not telepathic, and we're not going to yank him out of whatever normal life he's managed to make for himself."

"I'd say 'normal' is about to go 'poof' for him. Galahad, Pioneer Lab's missing pet project, is here, and he looks *just* like Danyael."

"What do you mean he looks just like Danyael?"

She shrugged. "They look like twins—*identical twins*. It's far more complicated than we'd originally envisioned. I need to stay around, see it through."

"I don't want mutants involved in this."

"It's too late for that, Alex. Danyael *is* inextricably involved in this. And if you're going to have an alpha empath running loose during this crisis, it may not hurt to have a telepath around to reinforce his shields, if it gets to the point where he can no longer sustain them."

Alex inhaled sharply and was silent for a while. "How badly hurt was he?"

"He'll probably want to stay in bed for a month, though I doubt he has the luxury." She chuckled softly. "Alex, just how strong is he?"

"He's stronger than people expect," Alex Saunders said without any hesitation whatsoever. "And he is stronger than he himself knows. Take good care of him, Miriya."

~*~

"We're here."

Lucien's words echoed raucously through Danyael's spinning head, and he might have winced except that he was not even sure he had the strength for it. Without adrenaline fueling his body, his strength faded so quickly that Lucien and Galahad had to carry him the final few steps toward the bed. Hovering on the edge of blackout, Danyael allowed Lucien and Galahad to lower him onto the cool silk sheets. He closed his eyes, grateful to block out the world that was now painted in garish shades of yellow and brown.

"He's burning up," Galahad said quietly. "What can we do?"

"Nothing except wait. The pain's just all in his head, as they say." Lucien laughed, a bitter sound.

"He saved my life."

"He saved all our lives. Several times over, as a matter of fact." Lucien hesitated, staring down at Danyael's clothes, splattered with the blood and flesh fragments of the creature that had torn itself apart in front of him. The stench of death lingered on him. "Danyael, I'm going to get your clothes off, all right?"

Quickly and efficiently, they stripped off his clothes and then pulled the covers over him. With the ruined clothes bundled in his arms, Lucien headed for the door. He paused to look back at his best friend lying pale and still beneath the sheets. "Danyael, we're leaving now. Do you need anything else?"

He stirred weakly, turning his head on the pillow to look at them. "Can't keep shields up...don't let anyone in..."

Lucien pulled the door shut behind him. Outside the room, his façade of strength collapsed, and he sagged against the closed door. He muttered an incoherent curse under his breath.

"How bad is it?" Galahad asked.

"It's the worst I've ever seen, and I've seen Danyael go through some really rough patches in the past." Lucien cursed again. "I don't know where he got his imbecilic idea of healing us through the fight. It probably saved all our lives, but still—"

"How long will it take him to recover?"

Lucien inhaled deeply and then released his breath in a soft sigh. "I don't know. We're in completely new territory here." He turned his head and assessed Galahad carefully. "Could they have followed you here?"

"I don't know," Galahad said, "but I don't really believe in coincidences. I never did."

"I don't either."

"The telepath's arrival was timely, though for a while, I wasn't sure which side she was on."

Lucien's eyes narrowed. "What telepath?"

"The young woman who telepathically linked us to Danyael. Didn't you feel it when her mind connected with yours?"

"Not particularly," Lucien confessed. "I was a bit distracted then."

"She attacked Danyael without warning. That's when I shouted for you and Zara. I was about to go for her, when I saw the abominations."

A muscle twitched in Lucien's cheek. "Let's go down and talk to her. I want to know who the hell she is and what she's doing here."

The telepath was still outside, waiting by the pool as Lucien's staff began the arduous task of scrubbing blood off the patio tiles. Carlos's body had been removed, and Zara was nowhere in sight. The telepath seemed to expect them, although given her mutant capabilities, Lucien would have been surprised if she hadn't.

She introduced herself with a faint smile. "I'm Miriya." She was surprisingly petite, scarcely over five feet tall, though she carried herself with such confidence that it was easy to forget how small she was. Her blond hair was cut in an attractive bob that framed her wide green eyes, pointed chin, and sharp features. All in all, she looked like an adorable kitten, albeit one with very dangerous claws. "I'm from the government and I'm here to help." She smiled a little wickedly at her clichéd introduction. "Actually, I represent the Mutant Advisory Council, and you may be aware that we've issued a recall on all mutants in the D.C. area."

"Recall?" Lucien echoed. "Why do you refer to your own kind as if they're defective products?"

"Many people consider us defective products," Miriya countered, "but I digress. When Danyael did not respond to the recall, I was sent to investigate and bring him in."

"Dead or alive?" Lucien asked.

"Alive, preferably, but dead was an option for me too." She waved her hand toward the corpse of the abomination. "I realize now that the situation is more complex than we had originally anticipated. I have now been assigned to assist in any way I can to resolve this."

"Resolve *what*, exactly?" Lucien yanked his fingers through his dark hair. "There's a gene war breaking out in D.C., monsters are roaming my neighborhood, and my best friend shares a face with the most wanted man in the world. Which one of those problems did you want to tackle first?"

Miriya laughed out loud, a rich, husky sound. "Why don't you fill me in on what happened?"

"Why don't you just pick through my mind for the details?" Lucien challenged.

She tilted her head to one side, assessing him. "You don't like what I did to Danyael. I acknowledge that I was wrong and hasty, and I will apologize to him. I am a telepath, and I won't apologize for using short cuts that are available to me. Power is power, whether it comes from the genetic lottery or from extreme wealth. Like it or not, you and I are more alike than you would prefer to admit." Miriya smiled, serene and lovely. "It is indeed a pleasure to meet you, Lucien Winter."

EIGHT

Ten minutes later, Zara, Lucien, Xin, Miriya and Galahad regrouped at Lucien's study. Miriya, slouched in a large chair, looked around the room. They could not possibly have been a more diverse mix of people—a naturally born human, an in vitro, a clone, a mutant, and someone who was in a category of his own.

Xin, the woman who had fired the gun from the balcony, was the only one whose mind was protected behind a psychic shield, unreadable, inaccessible. The others were open books to Miriya. Zara, in particular, seethed like an open cauldron bubbling over a fire. The young woman jerked away from Lucien when he laid a hand gently upon her shoulder and said, "I'm sorry about Carlos."

Zara turned shimmering violet eyes up at Lucien. "He let Carlos die," she said harshly.

Lucien shook his head. "You know it's not as simple as that."

"Couldn't he just heal Carlos? How could that be too much to ask?"

"After keeping the rest of us alive? Do you even know what he did for us?" He stared at her, searching her face for a long silent moment, and then shook his head in disbelief. "You have no clue, do you? Either that, or your dislike of him is coloring your perspective." He turned away from her. "Keep hating his guts if you want, but at least hate him for the right reasons. We'd all be dead if not for him." Stepping past her, he sat down behind his desk. "This is Miriya. Miriya, Xin, Zara, and Galahad. Miriya's a telepath; she's been assigned by the council to help out."

"A mutant." Zara's eyes narrowed.

"Considering a mutant saved your life, you could be a bit more grateful," Miriya retorted.

Zara shot to her feet. "Grateful? You've unbalanced our world. You use your mutant capabilities to create advantages for yourself that no one else has, and then play God. You choose who succeeds and who fails, who lives or dies. You and your kind are the reasons the economy and the financial markets have been teetering on the brink of chaos for almost a decade now. You've derailed international relations and diplomatic negotiations. You have no respect for secrets or for the rules."

"That's right," Miriya said. "What you consider diplomacy and intrigue, we consider bullshit and a general waste of everyone's time. And while you're enumerating all the wonderful things we've done for the world, don't forget to include the fact that mutants eliminated the Islamic terrorist threat once and for all and are largely credited with checking China's ascendency. If not for us, you'd all be speaking Mandarin right now. Or Arabic."

Xin chuckled softly and turned it into a cough when Zara spun around to glare at her.

"But let's get to the heart of the matter," Miriya said. "You're not actually the bigot you appear to be." She looked meaningfully toward Galahad. "You hire clones, date in vitros. You even have friends who are mutants. You acknowledge that we're occasionally a pain in the butt if we're not on your side, but you've found ways to work around us, and you're fairly effective at doing so. More importantly, you know as well as I do that this is not really about humans versus derivatives. It's about the haves versus the have-nots. And in spite of your human heritage, you're actually among the 'haves.' You're beautiful, intelligent, extremely skilled, and are probably mistaken for an in vitro most of the time. You have the best of both worlds—the access most mutants are denied and the ability to succeed, which most humans don't have. Your issue isn't with mutants. It's just Danyael you can't stand, so don't waste your time taking it out on me."

Miriya paused briefly, scanning through Zara's tumultuous thoughts. When Miriya spoke again, she said softly. "I am sorry about Carlos. I know you considered him a good friend."

Zara inhaled, the sound a jagged, breathless half sob. Her eyes were moist as she met Miriya's knowing, penetrating gaze for a brief moment and then looked away.

Lucien sighed. His thoughts whispered through Miriya's mind. *Great, now I feel like a bastard for coming down so hard on her. She counted on Danyael to save Carlos. Of course she would be furious with Danyael.* "Did you want to take a few minutes, Zara?"

Zara waved him on. "No, go on. We don't have much time."

Miriya saw Zara shudder as she deliberately set Carlos out of her mind and focused on the problems at hand. So cleanly and swiftly did she cut him off, it was almost as if Carlos had never existed. Her ability to segment her life was amazing, Miriya concluded, though likely necessary, given her work as a mercenary.

"How much background information will you need, Miriya?" Lucien asked.

"Almost none at all." She smiled sweetly at Lucien. "I'll just pick it out of your minds as you talk. If I'm confused, I'll ask."

Lucien took charge of the meeting easily. "All right, let's prioritize here. Any progress on Danyael's past?"

"We've more or less concluded that Danyael's mother threw him into the river," Xin said.

"His mother?" Lucien looked stricken. "Damn, that had to hurt."

"It did," Xin confirmed. "Anyway, we had Danyael look at photographs of all female employees at the lab at that time. None triggered any emotional feedback," she reported. "I'm running background checks now on all employees, males included, to see if there are reports of missing children some twenty-five years ago. It'll take a little longer." She leaned over in her chair to peer at her computer that was rapidly churning through information. "Nothing so far. If that fails to turn up something interesting, then I'll expand the search to areas around Mill Run River. We'll get there, eventually."

"All right. And what do we do about the things from the lab? Hunt them down?"

Xin arched an eyebrow. "With what, exactly? The shot I fired had practically no impact on it. You'll note that none of us did any real or lasting damage to any of them, and the one that died killed itself." She pushed to her feet and walked around the table, picked up a tablet computer, and then handed it to Lucien. "I found their genetic records and compared them to both Galahad and Danyael. There are trace similarities to Galahad in a few scattered places though not consistently across all six of them. One thing is consistent in all seven DNAs though…a fully sequenced tracker gene."

"They put a tracker gene in me? Where?" Galahad asked.

Lucien handed the tablet over to Galahad. "According to this, chromosome four, in the telomere."

Galahad scanned the report. "There are sections called telomeres located at the ends of chromosomes. They are a series of repetitive DNA intended to protect the chromosome from deterioration as a result of the shortening of chromosome ends, which necessarily occurs during chromosome replication. Telomeres are believed to control the aging process indirectly, and if they malfunction, they're responsible for many types of cancers. Tracker genes are occasionally placed in the telomeres of clones and in vitros, almost like a trademark, indicating which laboratory they came from."

"You didn't know you had one in you?"

"No. It's hard to tell unless there's some kind of comparison to the DNA of others with similar codes."

Lucien inhaled deeply. "Could the tracker gene somehow be facilitating those creatures' ability to find you?"

"That's never been the purpose or functionality of the tracker gene, but that's not to say it can't be done. I don't think we can assume that the physical and scientific laws governing humans also apply to those creatures."

"Let's assume that the tracker gene works," Lucien said, "and that they could show up wherever we are. It'll be just one more thing to keep this game interesting." His voice was calm as he accepted the information, adjusted, and kept moving. "What about Danyael? Anything on his genetic sequence?"

"Ah…" Xin hesitated. "Nothing definitive."

"But…?" Lucien asked.

"Danyael has several genetic mutations, the combination of which has made him who he is, and—"

"*Several* mutations?" Zara snorted. "Just how messed up is Danyael anyway?"

"Power like his doesn't come through a single mutation," Miriya interjected coolly. "It takes quite a bit of luck and chance to create an alpha empath. Go on, Xin."

"There's a single sequences on all those creatures that is an eighty…ninety percent match to his."

"I see what you mean." Galahad's dark eyes scanned the DNA sequence flowing across the screen tablet. He was silent for a while. When he finally spoke, it was quietly, contemplatively. "This gene is one of many that control the rate of recuperation, the ability of the body to heal over time. The effects of a single mutation aren't always obvious or easy to explain, especially in Danyael's case, where there are several mutations working in conjunction, but we know he's able to accelerate the healing in others. Mutated further in these creatures, perhaps—and I'm speculating here—the result is accelerated self-healing. That would explain why we couldn't hurt them, why bullets didn't stop them."

"But why would just one of Danyael's mutated genetic sequences show up in them but not in you?"

"I don't know. Maybe it wasn't from Danyael; it could have been copied from another mutant, perhaps one with a known capacity for accelerated self-healing. Let's not dismiss the possibility of coincidence here."

"I thought you didn't believe in coincidence," Lucien said.

Galahad shook his head. "I don't, but mutant genes are notoriously hard to work with. Most scientific communities steer clear of them for fear of creating something they can't predict or control. Despite all the advances we've made in our understanding of genetics, no one has ever fully explained how combinations of human genes interact with each other to create the vast spectrum of phenotypes. Mutant genes add several layers of complexity to that equation. To take a mutated gene and mutate it further in the hopes of enhancing it would be downright foolhardy."

"And trying to create a human being a base pair at a time isn't?" Zara asked.

Galahad conceded the point with an incline of his head and a faint smile. "I think we'd all agree that the scientists from Pioneer Labs aren't the sort to be deterred by the limited odds of success. But I don't think the data is sufficient to conclude that Danyael's genetic sequence had anything to do with the creation of those creatures from the lab. More than likely, they were created before the scientists decided to use Danyael as a template."

"So it's a dead end," Lucien said.

"Why don't we just ask Rakehell and Cochran?" Zara asked. "This beating around the bush is ridiculous. There is an easier way, and that is to take both Galahad and Danyael to them and demand to know what happened. And with your telepath here..." She waved a hand toward Miriya. "She can pick the truth out of their minds, even if they decide not to talk."

Miriya shrugged as she considered the idea and then nodded. Zara preferred the most direct route to whatever she wanted, come hell or high water. No wonder Danyael's reluctance to stir up the past annoyed her. It likely would have anyway, though the repellant effect of Danyael's emotional barriers exacerbated the situation and heightened her dislike to the point that she could not see any good in him anymore even if it smacked her in the face.

Zara's cell phone rang. "It's Jason Rakehell," she said tersely before accepting the call. "Jason darling," she practically purred into the phone. It was a startling change from the brusque, strictly business approach she had utilized thus far. Her voice was now purely feminine, coyly mocking, and could aim a punch straight into a man's gut.

"Don't fuck with me, Zara." Jason shouted so loudly into the phone that everyone in the room could hear him even without the benefit of a speakerphone.

She winced at the phone and held it away from her ear. "I wouldn't do that, Jason. I couldn't anyway." Her tone remained silky smooth. "You weren't that much into it, if I recall."

"You know why!"

"Yes, but I still don't understand. You claimed to love me, but you couldn't—or didn't want to—put aside your obsession with the past to look toward the future. It does nothing for my ego to know that you'd rather cuddle up to your thoughts of vengeance against your father than hold me. I deserve better, Jason, and you're just not it."

Lucien caught a glimpse of Miriya's smirk, and he winced. *I've always appreciated her frankness, but I can certainly see how or why someone else wouldn't. I don't know how she maintains that warmly feminine purr while viciously emasculating a man.*

Practice, I bet, Miriya replied with a soft laugh.

"Where is Galahad?" Jason's voice shouted through the phone.

"Oh, he's safe and warm with me." She winked at Galahad, a mischievous gleam in her eyes. "He's beautiful, too, stunningly beautiful. In all your rants against him and your father, you never mentioned how breathtakingly gorgeous he is. It's probably a good thing, or I might have broken into Pioneer Labs earlier to steal him."

"I want him, Zara."

"I don't think he's interested. He's not really that way inclined." Zara laughed softly. She looked at the piece of paper Xin held out to her. *His cell phone signal is coming from Georgetown.* "And by the way, Jason, send the cleaning crew to pick up my place after you're done trashing it."

"You've got that psycho clone with you again, haven't you?" Jason snarled into the phone.

"He just called you a psycho," she mouthed at Xin with a grin.

Xin shrugged, chuckling silently.

"Jason, Xin has a bigger claim to fame in her current life than you do in yours. Your blanket hatred of anything that isn't a naturally born human is growing tiresome."

"If you knew—"

She cut him off. "I do know." The purr vanished from her voice. Her tone was clipped, terse, and vibrated with annoyance. "I've heard it often enough. You're a neglected child; your father was obsessed with his pet project and left you home alone. What you've always failed to mention is that you were left at home with all the luxuries money could buy and in the company of devoted nannies. If you think your life was so miserable and you can't get over how deprived you were, maybe you could consider switching places with Galahad. Would you prefer to be experimented on all day, only to be locked up at night in a dehumanizing cell? You are a tiresome, self-centered prick, Jason. If you want Galahad, come and get him, only, you'll have to get through me, and we both know I can beat you in any fight, any day of the week."

"That's telling him." Xin laughed as Zara hung up on Jason.

"No, it's not." Zara wore an expression of disgust. "He can't be told, or he would have regained his senses long before it came down to the burning of Pioneer Labs."

"Lucien called him a tiresome prick too, yesterday."

"Yeah, well, Lucien's usually right about people," Zara conceded with a grin at her friend. "Let's add Jason to the list of complications. He's dangerous; he commands a host of paranoid pro-humanists. The world would be better off without them, but I could have trouble explaining that to the police."

"I could wreck him financially," Lucien offered solicitously.

Zara smiled. "Tempting. Very tempting."

Miriya spoke aloud for the first time. "We should at least remove him and his pro-humanist buddies from the equation. He's muddying the waters, and we don't need that."

Galahad looked over at Lucien. "Are people truly so bloodthirsty?"

Lucien shrugged. "Only the females of our species," he assured Galahad, and then ducked the pen that Xin threw at his head. "And you object, Xin? Weren't you a military general in a former life?"

"That was a long time ago." She smiled at him. "I could have changed, you know. It's been three thousand years after all, give or take a century or two."

"I vote for taking Jason out. We don't have to kill him, just check him into a hospital for two weeks or so. I need to get my dagger back anyway," Zara said.

"Your dagger?" Xin looked at Zara quizzically.

"The one I left stuck in his arm after he fired that gun at Galahad last night. Let's go."

"Danyael's not ready to move," Miriya pointed out.

"So?" Zara tensed at the mere mention of his name.

"We don't go without him."

"We don't need to take him. This isn't a group outing."

"Were you planning on taking me along?" the telepath asked.

"Of course."

Miriya shrugged then. "I'm not going anywhere without Danyael. Understand this. I'm here to help you, but more importantly, I'm here to make sure that Danyael's shields do not collapse, or that I'm around to shield him if they do collapse. An empath of Danyael's caliber *without* shields could make what's happening in D.C. right now look like a Sunday school picnic."

Zara opened her mouth to retort, but there was a knock on the door.

A young housemaid peeked in. "Excuse me, sir." She looked at Lucien. "The police have arrived, and they want to speak to you."

Lucien pushed to his feet. "I'll take care of this. Galahad, stay out of sight. I know there aren't any pictures of you out there yet, but let's not take any chances."

Galahad nodded.

"Do we just wait?" Zara asked, a little testily.

"You're welcome to hunt down those things from the lab, but I wouldn't recommend it," Lucien shot back. He walked out of the study, closing the door behind him.

Scowling at his back, Zara sank into her comfortable leather chair by the unlit fireplace. "Surely there must be something we can do," she said to no one in particular.

Patient waiting was clearly not part of Zara's skill set. Miriya could identify with Zara's sentiment, but after that near fiasco when she attacked Danyael without waiting to fully assess the situation, she was a great deal more willing to take things a little more slowly. "Tell me about yourself, Galahad."

He smiled faintly. "I'm not sure there's much to tell."

"You've lived a very different life from the most of us. That's interesting in and of itself. Will you relax, Zara?" Miriya directed her question at the other woman without actually looking at her. "It's not your fault. What happened to Carlos isn't your fault. And just to be clear, it's not Danyael's fault either."

Zara froze for an instant and then recovered quickly, glaring at Miriya. "Stay out of my head."

"That's really hard. You're projecting very loudly." Miriya looked at her now, her green eyes intent. "We've got enough issues as it is, and there's really no time for you to take a guilt trip on how you might be even partially responsible for what's happening out there."

Their gazes locked challengingly on each other, flashing violet against icy green.

From behind her computer monitors, Xin looked up idly. "Play nicely now, children," was all she said. "Danyael's resting and doesn't have the time or energy to heal anyone."

Zara stalked from the room. Galahad inhaled deeply, released his breath in a soft sigh, and then headed out after her. Miriya chuckled softly the moment the door closed behind them. "About time."

"You did that on purpose?"

"They needed to talk," Miriya said and then seemed content to leave Xin to her work while she perused a book from Lucien's extensive collection.

Xin shook her head, bemused. "Sometimes I think mutants are even weirder than clones. And humans are by far the weirdest of all."

~*~

Zara heard footsteps behind her but did not turn away from her perch by the window.

"You think you're somehow responsible for this?" Galahad asked quietly.

She did not answer immediately. Her bedroom window overlooked the patio where the gruesome corpse was surrounded by cops and other emergency personnel who were probably debating what to do with it. She did notice that everyone was distinctly nervous, constantly looking around to see if the creatures were coming back. Lucien was out there too, the only one who looked like he was in control of the situation, cool and collected as he always was in public.

"I did have a hand in it from the beginning." Zara pulled the heavy velvet drapes across the window. She walked past Galahad and closed the bedroom door that he left open when he followed her into her room. Conversations like these were best held in private.

"Who sent you to kill me? I can't believe it was Purest Humanity." Considering her obvious disdain for her former fiancé, it was clear that she would not have been running any errands for him.

Zara chuckled softly, a rich, warm sound. "I wasn't there to kill you. I just came for a blood or tissue sample. The professors have the central computers at Pioneer Labs stuffed full with false genetic codes to deter hackers. Your full genetic code was one of the best kept secrets in the world, at least until yesterday."

"You got a whole lot more than you'd bargained for."

"My day is usually not complete unless I get myself into trouble. I get bonus points for getting my friends into trouble too, so as you can imagine, yesterday was a whopper of a day. In my defense, Xin was an active conspirator." She pulled out her Pioneer Laboratories security card, imprinted with her photograph, and tapped it against the palm of her other hand. "She did this for me."

"Xin did this?"

"She has access to some truly scary technology in her work with the government, and every now and again, she'll commandeer them for a pet project."

"Is that allowed?"

"Not really, but she's too hard to replace, so they just look the other way." Zara relinquished the security card as Galahad took it out of her hand to take a closer look at her photograph.

He smiled, a slow, private smile that was like the sun peeking out from behind a cloud. "May I have this?" he asked.

"Sure, and would you like my autograph too?"

He laughed, slipping the security card into his pocket, a memento of the occasion and potentially an escape route, if he was ever recaptured. "How did you meet Xin?"

"I was looking for a top-notch hacker with flexible morals who might be willing to take on some part-time jobs for my agency. I asked around and it didn't take long for her name to rise to the top. She's not just top notch, she's world class. Her morals aren't nearly as flexible as I'd like, but nobody's perfect. We've been associates for almost three years now. For the most part, we get along beautifully, as long as she turns a blind eye to some of the people I hire and most of the work I do."

"And what do you do, Zara?"

"I own the Three Fates."

"Clotho, Lachesis and Atropos?"

A dazzling smile flashed. "You know your Greek mythology. You really do have a vast repertoire of random knowledge," she noted approvingly. "The Three Fates provides free agents for hire."

"Mercenaries?"

She looked unapologetic. "Technically, yes. Let's be clear though: we haven't done any completely illegal work yet."

"There's a difference between completely illegal and partly illegal?"

Her laughter was wicked and shimmered like silver bells. "You're starting to sound like Xin. There's a pretty big difference between completely illegal and partly illegal. The size of the difference is controlled by the quantity and quality of the lawyers you hire. Legal fees constitute thirty percent of my expenses; it's high, but that's just the cost of doing business."

"Would breaking into Pioneer Labs fall under the completely illegal or partly illegal category?"

"Neither." She laughed again. "That was just light-hearted mischief, until, of course, I absconded with you."

"How did you get into this line of work?"

"That's not important," she said, casually dismissive. Her tumultuous childhood, the many wars that had eventually ripped the heart and soul out of the Mediterranean paradise of Lebanon, the years spent in the squalid conditions of a refugee camp, the harrowing journey to America—to the one land that still held out the promise of freedom to any who came to its shores—none of that mattered any more.

The actual events of the past, she had reasoned with brutal clarity of hindsight, were not important. Only the outcomes mattered. She had survived, become strong, and then worked tirelessly night and day to ensure that what she had could never be taken from her again.

If in the process, she had lost a bit of herself, she considered it well worth the price. The bright-eyed, sunny-faced child who had once danced with artless innocence in the courtyard of a Lebanese home and counted everyone a friend would never have made it in a world brimming with brutal realities, anyway.

Life didn't work like that.

With very little effort, she put aside the flashing memories of her past and focused on the conversation at hand. "All that's relevant is that it took a long time and a great deal of hard work to get to this point. Miriya talks about having natural advantages as if it actually counts for something. The fact is nothing counts for anything until you put your back into it to make something of it. The world is shaped only by people who dare."

"People like you," he murmured quietly. "Thank you."

She met his gaze directly. He had expressive eyes and they shimmered with emotions that pierced her heart and warmed her. "What for?"

"For taking me with you. You freed me, Zara."

She could clearly hear the ring of heartfelt gratitude in his melodic tenor.

"You've always been free, and it's hard to express how much what you did—even if on a whim—means to someone who has never been free."

After several silent moments, she said, "I couldn't leave you behind. Not after I saw what they were doing to you." The memory of the compassion she felt tickled uncomfortably against her spine. Compassion got people into trouble. The absolute certainty of that single fact caused her to stiffen. She tried to push past him, but stopped when he reached out to catch her hand in his. His hand was dry and warm, his skin soft. She looked down at her hand clasped loosely in his. They fit well together.

She gazed up at his face, which was a huge mistake. If she had taken a step back, she would have seen his staggering beauty, so flawlessly perfect as to be intimidating, but standing so close to him that she could feel his breath against her skin, she could see only the strength in his dark eyes and the gentleness in his smile.

She leaned in and breathed a faint kiss against his lips. For a moment, he did not react. She was the first person who had ever kissed him, she realized, as she drew back and found him looking at her with an expression that swirled tenderness and vulnerability into a potently intoxicating mixture. "Just relax," she murmured as she rested her cheek against his briefly. "Trust yourself."

He hesitated, torn between the demands of his body that craved the intimacy that had always been denied him and the equally strong desire to maintain the simplicity and innocence of their growing friendship.

She waited for a long silent moment until he finally whispered his quiet assent, the words of ultimate surrender wrenching his soul.

With a faint smile of triumph, she raised her lips to his. His kiss was tentative at first, scarcely a flutter of breath, but she pressed hard against him, demanding more, as her slim hands glided gently down his back in a teasing caress. She felt it the moment he gave in. She closed her eyes, sighed as she allowed him to capture her mouth in a lingering kiss, savoring the sweet taste of him and reveling in the strength of the arms that held her up and carried her to the bed.

They shed their clothes. The first contact of skin against skin had him closing his eyes in delight. She could sense his wonder, his amazement at the trusting surrender of her body. She felt the urgency of his need and the iron-clad control that kept him focused. He was inexperienced, but she could sense his eagerness to learn, his responsiveness to her lead as she guided his hands over her body.

He was a blank slate. He was hers to shape and mold.

A smile, gleaming with anticipation, curved her lips as she twisted out from under him. She leaned into him, easing him back onto the sheets. "Relax," she whispered again as she smoothed her fingertips across his chest. "Let me show you…"

~*~

Lucien glanced at his watch. How much longer would the interview take?

"What I still don't understand is why it killed itself," the detective said.

"We've been through all this several times, officer." The patience in Lucien's voice was wearing thin. "For the past two hours, no less. Who knows how mutants do what they do? I don't know what Danyael did either."

"I need to speak to him."

"And I've told you before, that's not an option. He's resting, and unless you want to end up like that creature there, we'd do well to leave him entirely and thoroughly alone until he's recovered." Lucien ground his teeth, but managed to keep his voice even. *Miriya?*

What is it, Lucien?

We could use some of your opinion-altering capabilities out here.

The detective refused to give ground. "He's a mutant. All mutants are dangerous. We're taking him in."

"That's far outside your realm of authority, officer." Lucien had refined stubbornness to an art form. It was the only way he had been able to win the trust and loyalty of an abused child years earlier. "You know the mutants fall under the jurisdiction of the Mutant Advisory Council."

"Well, there's no one here now from the council, is there?" The detective sneered at Lucien. "We're bringing him in. Tell us where he is, or do we need to obtain a warrant to search your house?"

Lucien made a mental note of the officer's name and badge number. Once this crisis was over, the officer was going to find himself out of a job.

Miriya walked through the open patio doors and headed straight for Lucien and the detective. "Actually, I'm a representative of the Mutant Advisory Council. Danyael Sabre is under my watch."

"You?" The detective snorted. "You're just a little girl."

"I really do abhor it when people assume that age or height, neither of which I have in abundance, are somehow correlated to skill or authority," Miriya said. The gleam in her eyes flashed and the detective dropped to the ground, screaming, his hands clutching the sides of his head in agony.

The other policemen stared in shock and horror. Some of them rushed toward Miriya, drawing their weapons, but were felled by a single precise telepathic blast straight into their minds. As they lay groaning on the ground in pain, Miriya pulled out the badge that identified her as an enforcer in the Mutant Advisory Council. The black badge, slashed through with streaks of silver, was rarely seen, only because there were so few enforcers. They were the most capable, most trusted mutants and were granted extensive authority, to the point that they could commandeer local police and federal resources if necessary.

"The next time," Miriya said to the humiliated detective, "just ask for my identification. You're relieved of duty, officer." She turned to the other policemen who were staring at her with reluctant awe and no small degree of sullenness. "Who's the most senior officer here?"

A baby-faced officer stepped forward. "I'm Sergeant Brooks, ma'am."

Miriya smiled warmly at him. "You're in charge now, *Lieutenant*. Please coordinate with Lucien's chief of security to deploy your men to protect the house. If there are any issues, I'd like to hear about them right away."

"Yes, ma'am," he responded with a great deal more enthusiasm than he had previously displayed.

"Battlefield promotions—tried and tested tactic," Lucien said as they watched the young officer give orders to his men. The detective was skulking back toward his car. He appeared shrunken, his shoulders hunched. "I take it 'How to make friends and influence people' wasn't part of your enforcer training."

"I was absent from class that day," Miriya said with a flippant smile.

"I thought that those telepathic abilities would have allowed you to be a bit more subtle."

"Oh, you mean like the Jedi mind trick? I could have, of course, but then what would have been the fun of it? Ordinarily, I don't go out of my way to hit people over the head with my power or authority, but he had it coming. He's slime. I wouldn't hire him to babysit kids any time soon."

"Are you serious?" Lucien glanced over his shoulder at the detective. "Should we report him?"

"Just for thinking nasty thoughts about what he'd like to do to children? We can't, Lucien. He hasn't actually done anything illegal. Yet."

"Zara would say that the point of having power is to prevent those things from happening in the first place."

"It's a good philosophy, but she's not accounting for willpower. I've learned not to underestimate it. That officer is a jerk and his mind is a sewer, but willpower has kept him on the straight and narrow so far. Willpower is what got Danyael through that fight—well, that and an incredible tolerance for pain. More to the point..." She looked directly at Lucien. "Is what you would say."

"Why is what I believe important?"

"Because you've appointed yourself Danyael's protector. Many—likely including Zara—would conclude that the best and safest option is to lock Danyael up, because he is a huge threat, even though he has not done anything wrong. Ten mutant containment facilities have been built in the United States in the past three years, and they're all overcrowded. The population grows daily. The council is doing everything it can to minimize the appearance of mutants as a threat, but paranoia is making the rounds here. Mutants—and most certainly Galahad—are first in the line of fire. Clones and in vitros won't be far behind."

"I won't let anything like that happen to Danyael," Lucien said.

"That's good to hear. I hope you're up to the task of protecting him, because he will likely need it. There's just no way sharing a face with Galahad could be anything but profoundly bad news."

"Lucien!"

He looked up at Xin's voice and saw her waving at him from the balcony of his study. "She's found something," he said and quickly returned to the house, Miriya beside him. He stepped into the study and closed the doors. "Anything interesting?"

"We may want to accelerate our plans to 'take care' of Jason Rakehell." Xin waved a slim hand at the computer monitoring the news frequencies used by pro-humanist groups, including Purest Humanity. "He's just issued a call to arms, and has apparently figured out that you're harboring Zara and Galahad. He doesn't mention Galahad per se, but the coordinates he's delivered to his members are right here in McLean, just a mile down the road. Either he picked the wrong house, which is unlikely, since he's not actually that stupid, or he's using that place as a meeting point prior to converging on this house."

"I'll let the cops know," Lucien said after scanning the Purest Humanity news feed. "Xin, find out where Jason is right now. It'll take his mobs a while to gather, and in the meantime, we're going to take the fight to him. Where's Zara and Galahad?"

"In her bedroom," Miriya responded, her voice deceptively sweet. She did not elaborate. She did not have to.

Lucien hesitated. Miriya chuckled at the image that went through his mind. Dark against light, the contrast startling, beautiful. Zara, slim and lovely, her skin the color of golden dusk, coiled around Danyael—no, Galahad—Lucien corrected mentally. The image did not change though. *Damn, I'll have trouble getting that picture out of my head now.* "I'll get them after I debrief the cops. Miriya, you've probably got the strongest shields. Can you wake Danyael?"

Miriya left the study and headed unerringly toward Danyael's room, having picked the location out of Lucien's head. She knocked on the door, not really expecting a response, and then with her strongest shields locked around her mind, she quickly opened the door, slipped in, and then shut it behind her.

She could feel the waves of unrestrained, uncensored emotions push against her shields, but they were not entirely what she had expected out of Danyael, in view of his background. She had anticipated a great deal of anger and bitterness, the kind of emotions powerful enough to drive others to suicide, but he had locked the pain and terror of his childhood away so deeply that conscious effort was required to access those emotions. Instead, she felt his quiet loneliness, and to her surprise, emotions that were startlingly close to pleasure, gratitude, and hope. He was lonely, but he enjoyed his work and found simple contentment, even within the limited boundaries of his life. He did not have many friends, but cherished the ones he had. He had no plans for the future, no expectations for a marriage or a family, but he was immeasurably grateful for the semblance of normality that he did have. He focused on getting through one day at a time, always with the hope that someday he would look up, look back, and be surprised by how far he had managed to come.

"Danyael." She shook him gently. Three hours of sleep would not have made any dent in his exhaustion, but it was all he could afford just then.

It took a long time to wake him, a long time to coax his conscious mind to awareness, but she felt it the moment he was awake enough to draw the emotional and mental barriers back around him. The pressure against her psychic shields vanished as if all the emotions that had hung so heavily in the room just moments before had been sucked up by a vacuum cleaner. His dark eyes—the pain locked deep within—flickered open and focused on her.

"I know we haven't been officially introduced," she said gently. "First, I'd like to apologize for attacking you earlier today. I was impatient and acted in ignorance. I'd like a chance to start over. I'm Miriya, and I'm with the Mutant Advisory Council."

He averted his gaze. She did not need access to his thoughts to know what he was thinking. He did not trust her. No, it was more than just her. He did not trust the council. Well, no surprises there. There were some days when she did not particularly trust the council either.

Danyael. It was easier to think than speak just then. *Good...to meet you.*

"We have a bit of a crisis, and we need you to join us. How soon do you feel up to getting out of bed?"

She heard the frank answers fly like nervous, fluttering sparrows through his mind. Eavesdropping unapologetically on his internal mental debate, she winced at the exhaustion evident even in his thoughts. *Next week...five days at least...maybe three. Don't have that kind of time. One day, perhaps just overnight or a few more hours. I can do this...Just take it an hour at a time.* She was not surprised when he finally mustered the strength to respond out loud to her question. "I'll be down in ten minutes."

~*~

Miriya was in the study when Zara and Galahad arrived together. She kept her face straight and held back a smug smile as she pried into their thoughts. They were well-matched. Zara respected inner strength, and Galahad had it in abundance. Who knew how the crisis would end, but their now-deeper ties to each other would help them both through it.

Xin was psychically shielded, protected from Danyael's empathic powers and from her telepathic nosiness. Miriya was polite enough not to probe too deeply. Besides, it was not necessary. Xin's life was largely on public record. Her successful cloning from three-thousand-year-old genes had been one of the most celebrated events in the genetic revolution twenty-eight years earlier. She had been carefully raised and inserted into her current role with the government. Clones of historical personalities were closely tracked. Xin was no exception.

Lucien, seated behind his desk, was the very image of wealth and power, exquisitely polished into incandescence. Miriya doubted Lucien knew how powerful he truly was. He knew he had the influence that wealth and his family name could command, and he had never had any qualms about using them to further his ends, or the ambitions of those he considered friends. What he did not seem to realize was that he also commanded the undying gratitude and absolute loyalty of one of the world's most powerful empaths. The combination of Lucien's wealth and Danyael's empathic abilities could have easily created crises on the scale of national disasters. It was a wonder it hadn't yet. She was grateful that the pair was at least on the right side of the crisis. She would not have wanted to go up against both Lucien and Danyael and the resources they had at their command.

Danyael arrived, finally. Lucien pushed to his feet and met him at the door. "Are you all right?"

Danyael nodded tiredly, saying nothing. He had felt the flash of intense annoyance from Zara the moment he entered the room. She was standing on the far side of the room, talking quietly to Galahad. The changes in their emotions, in their relationship, were obvious to him.

A smile of genuine delight spread across Danyael's face.

"Do you see in him what your life could have been if it'd been different for you?" Lucien asked quietly. "A relationship with a woman. Physical intimacy. A chance at affection, even love?"

Danyael's mouth twisted at the suggestion of physical intimacy, and he shook his head. "We're not the same person, Lucien. We look alike physically, but the genes that code for appearance are just a small portion of the total genetic code. My childhood was difficult, but I've had sixteen years of a normal life. Galahad, on the other hand…his life has been brutal, and he deserves a chance at whatever passes for normal these days."

"I wouldn't have typically included Zara in my definition of normal. Her world view is hardly conventional, and he's somewhat impressionable at this point."

"Not entirely. I'd…be careful around him."

Lucien looked at his friend. "Is he dangerous?"

Danyael was silent, and then he shrugged. "I think he deserves a chance."

"You didn't answer my question."

"Of course he's dangerous, but so is Zara. So are you. And so am I." He glanced away, turmoil surging through the dark eyes, and then he looked back at Lucien. "Only, he's perfect," he said simply, as if it explained everything.

"Right. Perfect for what?" Lucien completed the thought Danyael did not give voice to. They had been friends for the better part of their lives. They understood each other. *Perfect for what?* What did the blueprints of Galahad's double helix contain? Just what exactly had Galahad been created to do?

"Perfect frightens me," Danyael said slowly, almost reluctantly.

"Yeah, me too."

They stood together in united silence for a moment. The left side of Danyael's mouth slowly tugged into a crooked smile. "But I still think he deserves a chance."

"You would." Lucien's blue eyes warmed with affection for his friend. He glanced over at Zara, who was standing next to Galahad. "She doesn't like you."

It was an understatement. The active dislike that she had felt for him in the beginning had evolved quickly over several hours into disgust and loathing. Danyael was caught off guard by the intensity of her feelings. If he had been more aware of their progression, he would have checked their downward slide earlier, but it was too late then. "My psychic shield and Zara obviously don't get along very well together."

"That's not funny, Danyael. I know her feelings toward you couldn't have eroded this quickly without some expert assistance from an alpha empath."

"I don't do this deliberately or consciously, Luce," Danyael replied, his tone carefully mild. They had been through the same discussion time and time again, always with Lucien accusing him of deliberately pushing people away, intentionally keeping them at bay.

"You need to stop doing it. Period." Lucien's emotions shot sparks of exasperation, even irritation. "It's emotional manipulation. I fail to see how engendering intense dislike of you even remotely enriches their emotional wellbeing."

"This isn't about their emotional well-being, and I'm not interested in winning a popularity contest. Maybe it's selfish, but you know why I use those shields. That's not up for negotiation. Ever."

Lucien shook his head in disgust. "Can you change how she feels about you?"

"Not without appreciable effort," Danyael said. "Besides, it doesn't matter. As long as it doesn't affect her ability to think clearly about other things, there's no need to interfere. I do owe her an apology though, for Carlos."

"I don't necessarily agree, but that's your decision." He stepped away from Danyael and informally called the meeting to order by raising his voice to provide a quick debrief of the situation. "Any updates, Xin?" he asked.

"Only that Jason's cell phone signal is coming from Bethesda."

"He's likely at his house," Zara said. "I know the way. Let's go."

NINE

Danyael joined Lucien, Zara, Galahad, and Miriya in Lucien's armored BMW for the twenty-minute drive from McLean to Bethesda. Xin opted to stay back to monitor the situation; she was most useful behind a computer, anyway. The dark gray SUV cruised through the silent, empty streets. Though the open fighting was taking place mostly in D.C. itself, apparently no one in the suburbs was taking any chances. Huddling at home was on the agenda for the day. The suburbs appeared desolate, stripped of any signs of life.

So empty, like my life, Danyael's traitorous mind whispered.

A muscle in his smooth cheek twitched as the self-pitying thought caught him off guard. *I'm thankful; there's so much to be thankful for.*

The familiar mantra did very little for him that time.

A tension headache pounded through his skull, keeping merciless rhythm with the beating of his heart. *Or maybe I'm just too tired.*

Fatigued, Danyael leaned his head back against the seat and gently massaged the back of his neck with his left hand. It was the only hint he betrayed of physical discomfort. The soft purr of the car engine was almost comforting, a low hum that—if he focused on it intently enough—helped him function in spite of the incessant assault of Zara's emotions.

He needed to put some distance between them, allow physical space to dull the impact. He glanced briefly at her and saw the sunlight catch the dangerous gleam in her violet eyes as she turned to return his gaze. He broke eye contact, but only because an odd thought occurred to him. *Pretty.* He smiled ironically. *She's not for me, though.*

A stray memory flashed through his mind. He had been in his senior year in college, but instead of spending his evening alone studying in his dorm room, he was slouched in his favorite armchair in the comfortably shabby living room of Lucien's Cambridge townhouse and watching with subtle concern as Lucien downed his seventh shot of whiskey before slamming the crystal shot glass down on the hand-carved oaken table.

No point in asking if Lucien was okay. He could not affect Lucien's emotions, but he could sense them. His friend was a long way from okay. Lucien looked up at him and scowled. "Women are nothing but trouble."

"Trouble's usually inevitable." Danyael shrugged. "If it's not a woman, it'll be something else. The real question is whether the woman's worth it."

"This one wasn't."

Danyael agreed with him. It was unusual for Lucien to have fallen so hard and so fast, but somehow he had, and then she had broken his heart. Danyael reached over and pulled the bottle out of Lucien's hand before he filled the shot glass again. "You're done," Danyael said firmly.

"I'm not nearly drunk enough."

"You're going to regret it tomorrow."

"I wish you could do something about it."

"No, you don't. Your emotions are real; nothing's worth trading them for a falsehood."

"Bullshit. You'd let me believe a lie if you thought it would be easier for me to live with."

Danyael's eyes narrowed. "Where the hell is this coming from, Luce?"

Lucien dismissed it with a frown. "Forget I said anything." He looked over at Danyael, his blue-eyed gaze slightly unfocused. "Are you still dating that journalism major?"

Danyael shook his head. "No, she's not for me."

"You say that about everyone you date. Do you even know what you're looking for?"

"I've narrowed it down to alpha telepaths." Danyael's faint smile was humorless. "That way I don't have to worry about accidentally killing her if my shields drop when I fall asleep. Other than that, I'm not really that picky."

Lucien considered it for a moment. "I thought I had it bad, never knowing if she's just a bloodsucker after my money, but maybe your situation does suck worse than mine." He leaned over, pulled the Glenfiddich whiskey bottle out of Danyael's hand, and filled two shot glasses. The golden liquid sloshed over the edge of one of the glasses. "Let's drink to us." The dimple flashed again. "There's no one I'd rather be drinking with."

Danyael chuckled. "You say that only because you know you'll get to drink my share." He raised the shot glass to his lips, wetting them, and then set it down. He leaned back in his chair, watching as Lucien tossed back the whiskey from both shot glasses. Comfortable in their unchanging friendship, they talked about inconsequential things as the flames burned low in the fireplace.

When Lucien finally fell asleep on the sofa, Danyael covered his friend with a cashmere throw and then retired for the night in the bedroom that Lucien had set aside permanently for his use. There was no point in going back to his dorm room. He wanted to be nearby in the morning when Lucien woke with a killer hangover. Danyael could not do anything about Lucien's emotional heartache, but he could alleviate the physical cost of overindulging in expensive whiskey.

Even back then, Danyael had dabbled in healing. Nevertheless, his college years were among the best years of his life, before medical school and his subsequent career as a doctor ensured that he would always pay the price for healing someone else.

He knew why the memory had returned. At first glance, it seemed as if Chloe Larson, the journalism major from Harvard University, a year his junior, had nothing in common with Zara Itani. How could anyone compete with Zara's stunning coloring—her golden-honey skin, violet eyes, ebony hair—and exotic good looks? Still, Chloe had a certain flash of something—perhaps spirit, strength of will—that resonated with striking clarity through Zara too.

Against his will, he found his attention drawn back to Zara.

This time, she did not even bother to conceal the scorn in her eyes

And like Chloe, he reminded himself wryly, Zara was not for him.

The hostile surge of her emotions subsided momentarily as her attention shifted. "That's his house; the third on the left. Pull over here," Zara instructed Lucien.

Lucien pulled his SUV into a neighboring driveway three doors down. He peered out of the window and then reached for his cell phone. "Xin, is his cell signal still in Bethesda?"

"Hasn't moved, and it's actively being used," Xin reported.

"Great." Zara released the seat belt. "I vote for holding a dagger to his throat until he calls off his minions."

"We can be a great deal more subtle than that," Miriya said. "As long as we can get in, we can handle this without messing up the carpet. Do we have to find a broken window to crawl through?"

"We don't have to." Zara pulled a keychain out of her pocket, dangled it from a fingertip, and let it jangle slightly. Her violet eyes glittered with amusement. "After we broke our engagement, he never asked for his house keys back. I'm betting he never got the locks changed."

Zara was right, the locks had not been changed. She pushed the door open, and the five of them stepped into the foyer. They could hear Jason's voice in another part of the house, issuing orders into his cell phone. Her eyes glinting dangerously, Zara pulled out a dagger from the sheath in her boot and strode toward his voice.

"Luce," Danyael cautioned quietly as he sensed Zara's deadly intent.

Lucien shrugged. "I don't entirely approve of Zara's casual attitude toward killing, but then again, I don't particularly approve of people organizing mobs to assault my home, either."

Lucien's non-interference was all the approval Zara needed. She moved in for the kill. Her shadow shifted in Jason's peripheral vision. He looked up with a startled cry, grabbed the gun from the table and fired without aiming. Zara's dagger flew through the air and sank deep into his stomach, painful but not fatal.

Jason snarled as Zara, sleek and predatory, walked into his study. The bullet had grazed her arm before slamming into the doorframe, but she paid no attention to the injury. "Your aim sucks," she purred at him. "Did you get your arm seen to yet?"

"Bitch!" Jason tried to stand, but she pushed him into his chair with little effort. His eyes widened when Galahad entered the room. "I shot you!" Adrenaline surging through his veins, he lunged past Zara and threw himself at Galahad, who merely stepped aside. Jason's momentum took him to the ground, the impact causing him to grunt in pain as he rolled to the side and glared up at Galahad.

Galahad smiled faintly in response.

Outside the door, Danyael paused, struggling to discern the tantalizing nuances of Galahad's subtly changing emotions in the wake of Jason's emotional maelstrom. The process was especially difficult if only because Galahad's emotions were foreign to him. Empathy was far less precise than telepathy. All of his conclusions were opinions. How many of those opinions were dead wrong? He had to be careful. He could not condemn Galahad on the basis of an opinion.

Even so, Galahad's emotions troubled him. *Absolute certainty, confidence that borders on newfound arrogance.*

Dangerous emotions for the perfect human being.

Not enough to act on, Danyael decided. He had to give Galahad the benefit of the doubt.

Danyael stepped into the study, his eyes narrowing as he braced against the fury and hatred that flowed out of Jason Rakehell, swamping everything in sight. Jason froze, anger transforming into shock and disbelief. He stared wordlessly at Danyael.

Zara knelt down behind Jason and yanked his head back, prepared to draw the edge of a second dagger across his jugular, but Danyael shook his head. "Zara, no. Not in cold blood."

"This has nothing to do with you."

Danyael gritted his teeth against the slap of her anger, but he did not back down. "We need him alive to call off his pro-humanists."

"I won't call them off." Jason's furious gaze alternated between Galahad and Danyael. Zara's blade was snugly nestled against his neck; he did not move when Danyael knelt down beside him and placed a hand over the wound. "Who the hell are you?" Jason spat out.

"My name is Danyael Sabre." He closed his dark eyes and inhaled deeply as he channeled his mutant powers toward assessing Jason's physical and emotional state. He winced, a muscle twitching in his smooth cheek as he worked through the painful blast of Jason's wild, intense emotions, probing for the truth that lay beneath.

Jason's body throbbed with pain. The injuries themselves were not serious, though left untreated, they would likely become a problem. The bigger challenge was Jason's emotional state. It unfolded before Danyael like a tapestry, woven throughout with brilliant color, a testament to a personality that was both vivid and bold. The patterns were complex, beautifully intricate, but the tapestry was torn, rent as if by sharp claws in many places, ruining the effect of the whole. There was no easy fix, not even for an alpha empath highly skilled in the art and science of emotional manipulation. Jason's emotional damage was far too extensive, much too intensive.

"How bad is it, Danyael?" Lucien asked quietly.

"The physical part is easy to fix; the emotional part a great deal harder. It's fully embedded into his psyche." Danyael removed his hand as he opened his eyes and sat back on his heels. "I'd have to absorb it, and given how much he hates someone who is my exact physical mirror image, that's probably not a good idea."

Lucien glanced over at the other young woman. "Miriya?"

"Obsession is a very good defense against a telepath, and he's taken the definition of obsession to entirely new heights. I can change his mind, but it'll take a while."

"So it's back down to my option." Zara's voice had a decidedly dangerous edge to it.

Danyael shook his head. "Put that dagger away. I won't let you murder someone in cold blood." Inhaling deeply as he braced against the onslaught of her disgust, he deliberately opened both heart and mind to her. Changing her feelings toward him demanded energy he did not consider worth spending, but a more generalized emotional transformation was eminently viable. His primary empathic powers surged, potent enough to ease subtly past her emotional defenses, carefully teasing and coaxing out the compassion she had worked hard to bury under hardened layers of cool, indifferent professionalism, the very same compassion that the day before had driven a seasoned mercenary to an act of impulsive, selfless kindness.

A silent second passed, then two.

He felt when something in her shifted—subtle but significant—like tectonic plates underground shifting against each other, reducing the pressure on the entire system. A hazy image grew fractionally clearer as he gently eased back one of the many thin layers obscuring a truer vision of her.

He was startled to find her almost likeable.

To everyone's surprise but Danyael's, Zara complied after a brief hesitation, and the dagger retracted.

Jason grabbed Danyael's shirt and shook him. "Who the hell are you? Why do you look like *it*?"

"That's what we've been trying to figure out," Lucien said. "How much do you know of your father's work?"

"More than I ever wanted to. It's all he ever talked about, if he was even home to begin with." Jason's words came out in a hiss of pain.

Lucien looked down at Jason, working through the options available to him, and then finally glanced over at Danyael. "Heal him."

"Heal him?" Zara echoed incredulously.

"We've tried violence, and it's not working," Lucien pointed out. "Maybe it's time to try talking instead. Danyael?"

Danyael nodded. Jason watched in silence as Danyael placed his hand on the wound. It took several moments to focus his exhausted energies, but the healing surge, when it came, was strong enough to make a difference. Danyael felt warmth emanating from the contact—the first hint that the healing had begun—and then he yanked the dagger out in a swift, smooth motion. Jason hissed, more in surprise than pain, as flesh twitched beneath Danyael's touch, the torn muscles knitting together.

The contact lasted no more than a minute until Danyael inhaled deeply and slowly withdrew his hand. His eyes fluttered open, the dark depths glittering with flickers of pain. Jason stared down at his flat stomach, the smooth expanse of skin. There was no evidence of any injury beneath his bloodstained shirt.

"All right," Danyael said, his voice unsteady, laced with tightly controlled pain. "Let's take a look at your arm." He unwrapped the bandage from around Jason's right bicep and caught the familiar scent of antiseptic as he placed his hand over the injury. He inhaled deeply once again, and his emotions settled into a deep calm, allowing his healing powers to flow freely, ungrudgingly out of him. For a brief moment, nothing seemed to happen, and then the healing began all at once as muscle, tendon, and flesh knitted together beneath his touch in the space of seconds rather than weeks or months.

Done. Danyael released his breath in a shaky sigh as he finally broke contact.

Lucien stepped forward and offered Danyael the support he needed to rise to his feet. "You okay?"

Danyael nodded slowly, his teeth clenched against the pain, the wracking chills. "I'll be all right." The emotional satisfaction he derived from healing was never enough to offset the physical discomfort, but every little bit helped counterbalance the indifferent and negative attitudes of others toward him.

Some days—like today—he needed that positive boost more than other days, just to keep going.

Jason flexed his arm, testing its strength.

"No sudden moves," Zara warned. "The next time I strike, the dagger will land in your heart, and not even Danyael will be able to save you then. Now move," she ordered with a jerk of her head toward the living room.

Jason pushed to his feet and walked slowly toward the living room. Sitting down on the couch, he stared at Galahad, quiet madness in his dark eyes. Zara blocked his view, directly standing between him and Galahad. It was both a warning and a threat.

Miriya followed Jason into the living room and curled up comfortably in a large chair, pulling up her feet and folding them beneath her. She was the only one in the room who looked relaxed.

Danyael remained by the doorway that separated the living room from the study. Pale and exhausted, he slid slowly down the length of the wall to sit on the hardwood floors, resting his head against the wall. His eyes were closed, but his heart was open and receptive to emotions as they surged across the room, weaving a tangled web of hatred and betrayal.

He flinched from the impact when Jason's anger and resentment toward Galahad flared. The hatred that Jason had spent decades nursing lashed out, indifferently including him in the line of fire. He swallowed hard, painfully, his breathing jagged and unsteady as he tried to work through the damage he had absorbed.

Lucien took the seat directly across from Jason. Lucien's blue eyes were hard and cold. "Look at me, Jason, and leave Danyael alone. He's not the one you're mad at. Start talking."

"There's nothing to talk about. My father, together with Michael Cochran, created it, a base pair at a time, just like they said."

"Then why do Galahad and Danyael look alike?"

"They used templates. They tried to do it without templates, but those experiments didn't work, so they switched to templates instead."

"Exactly what do you mean by templates?"

"Exactly what it looks like," Jason waved a hand at Danyael. "They took various people, selected them for their looks or their intelligence or personality, and then used the exact same genetic sequence that coded for what they were trying to copy."

"Why Danyael?"

"I have no fucking clue why Danyael. I don't know how my father chose his templates." Jason ground his teeth. "You think he talks to me? Even when he does, the only thing he talks about is that damn thing."

"What about to your mother? He must have said something to her."

"She died when I was seven. He wasn't around before she died; he sure as hell wasn't around after that. In fact, he spent even more time at the lab. Less than a year later, it was born."

Danyael shuddered as Jason's emotions buffeted him like chill winter winds. They matched the words he spit out, sin black and bitter. They were so intense and overpowering that he almost missed the subtle change in Galahad's emotions as they overlaid with open curiosity.

"You said you lost your mother about a year before I was born. How did she die?" Galahad asked.

When it was clear that Jason was not going to deign Galahad with a response, Lucien ordered, "Answer the question."

Jason glared, first at Galahad, and then at Lucien. He chose to keep looking at Lucien. "In a car accident."

"When and where did it happen?"

"At night, near the border of West Virginia. No one knows why she was out there. She'd taken my brother, gone out for a drive, and she never came back."

The emotions swirling through the room like wind sprites suddenly coalesced into a frozen lump in the middle of his throat. Danyael's eyes flashed open. *No!*

"Brother?" Zara tensed. Her gaze flickered briefly across the hall and held Danyael's gaze for a split second before returning to Jason. "I didn't know you had a brother."

"He was never relevant. He's long gone."

Danyael pushed slowly back to his feet, staring hard at Jason, an expression of disbelief misting slowly across his dark eyes. Miriya bit down on her lower lip; she stood and walked over to Danyael. She slipped an arm around his waist and slid her hand into his. Her green eyes were wary, preternaturally alert for the first hints that Danyael's shields might not hold.

The expression in Lucien's blue eyes changed rapidly from concerned to anguished. He glanced over at Danyael, who was bracing against what Jason might or might not say. Jason, ignorant of Danyael's history, was too caught up in his own pain to notice.

"What do you mean 'gone?' Did he die in the accident?" Galahad asked in the same quiet tone.

"Probably," Jason sighed. His anger subsided as the gentler memories of his mother took precedence. "The car went over an embankment and the gas tank exploded. The rescue workers found my mother's body, but not his. They think he died too."

"How old was he then?"

Jason frowned, trying to remember. "Two years old. Almost three."

Danyael inhaled sharply and then squeezed his eyes shut. He could feel the subtle pressure of Miriya's shields locking around his mind, reinforcing his barriers, but otherwise, he could not think, could not feel, over the vast roaring in his mind and the searing pain of an old emotional wound torn open. "No," he breathed. "No, it can't be." He kept his eyes closed, embraced the darkness, and clung desperately to the lifeline that was Miriya's hand in his. It wasn't possible.

"Do you have him covered?" Lucien asked tersely. Miriya nodded. Only then did Lucien reach for his phone. "Xin, I need you to run a genetic analysis. Danyael and Jason Rakehell."

"You're not serious!" Xin's stunned response mirrored what all of them were feeling.

"I know you have Danyael's genetic records from the Mutant Advisory Council. Do you think you can find Jason's somewhere?"

"That's easier done than said. I know Zara took a cellular sample from him when they were engaged. His genetic record is stored at the Three Fates genetic registry."

"How long is the analysis going to take?"

"Just a few minutes. Stay on the line," she instructed.

Jason looked around, suddenly aware of the tension and of the fact that everyone in the room knew something he did not. "What the hell is going on?"

Lucien held up a hand, indicating that he needed to wait. The room was deathly silent for several minutes, punctuated only by the sound of Danyael's harsh breathing, almost as if he were choking back silent sobs. Lucien cast Miriya a look of concern. She nodded, assuring him. "The shields will hold."

Xin's voice finally came back over the line. "Lucien, there's a seventy-two percent probability that Danyael and Jason are siblings. You'll never get better odds than that without the concurrent genetic analysis of at least one parent. It's effectively a match. Please tell Danyael I'm sorry."

"I will. Thanks, Xin." Lucien hung up the phone, pushed to his feet, and walked over to Danyael. There was nothing he could say. Nothing would be able to assuage the wound of abandonment that had underscored Danyael's entire life, that had hurt so deeply, so badly, that the only way Danyael had been able to handle it was to lock it deep down. "Danyael? Do you want me to ask Jason for a picture of her to confirm the results of the analysis?"

Danyael opened his eyes, the motion slow, pained. His dark, fathomless eyes were vast pools of heartache, but they were—through sheer force of will—dry. The tears were locked away, but they choked him, made it nearly impossible to breathe, to speak. He shook his head as he glanced over at Jason Rakehell. His *brother*. Danyael whispered, his voice heavy with irony, "Welcome home."

TEN

Jason Rakehell lunged out of his chair and threw himself at Danyael, slamming him back against the wall. "No fucking way!" He roared into Danyael's face. "What is this? Some kind of sick cosmic joke?"

Lucien yanked him away from Danyael. "You touch him again, and I'll let Zara kill you," he promised.

Jason's strength was fueled by anger. He twisted out of Lucien's grip, grabbed Danyael's chin in his hand, and turned it so that he could see the right side of Danyael's face. Jason saw the thin white scar, almost invisible with age, which started from the top of Danyael's cheekbone, cutting across his cheek to end at the chin. Jason's eyes widened with shock, then narrowed with recognition.

Miriya shook her head slightly, keeping Lucien in check, when he would have pulled Jason back again. From across the room, Zara and Galahad watched the reunion in silence; Galahad's dark eyes reflecting curiosity, Zara's violet eyes determinedly impassive but for a flicker of something deep within that almost seemed like empathy.

Jason shook his head roughly, not with disbelief, but with refusal to accept the evidence before him.

Danyael did not resist when Jason roughly grabbed his left hand, the bones subtly misshapen from an unremembered injury that had not healed correctly. He could not read his brother's thoughts, but he could sense Jason's emotions as disbelief gave way to towering anger and hatred. *At this point, I think it's a toss-up as to whether he hates me or Galahad more.*

Miriya smiled thinly, not amused. *This isn't funny, Danyael.*

It's laugh or cry, Miriya. What does he remember?

He remembers when your mother struck you, and her ring tore the gash in your cheek. He remembers when your mother used a pestle to smash your hand after you'd reached for one of his toys. She obviously failed parenting class. I wouldn't have trusted her with a goldfish, let alone a child.

"You're a mutant, you fucking monster!" The rage that swelled up and burst out of Jason stunned Danyael with its intensity, as powerful, as real to him as a physical blow. "You drove her mad. You killed her!"

Lucien intercepted the blow that Jason hurled at Danyael and then dragged him back. With Galahad's help, Lucien wrestled Jason down into the couch. "Zara," Lucien ordered.

With an anticipatory gleam, she leaned forward to caress the edge of her dagger against Jason's jugular.

The touch of cold steel against Jason's throat forced him to keep still, but he glared at Danyael, ancient rivers of anger and hatred undammed by the revelation that his brother was alive.

Lucien glanced at the telepath. "Miriya, any chance you can translate his thoughts into a language the rest of us would understand, preferably without the curse words?"

She nodded, summarizing all that she had gleaned from Jason's memories and thoughts, and then piecing those scattered memories together with what she knew of Danyael's past. "Their mother suffered from post-natal depression after Danyael's birth. Danyael's empathic powers likely didn't help the situation at all. Over time, she became increasingly obsessed with trying to hurt Danyael, to the point where she began neglecting Jason. The rest we know and can easily fill in the blanks. She finally snapped, took Danyael with her, and tossed him over a bridge. On the way back home, she was killed in a car accident." Miriya paused, carefully choosing her next words. "In short, Jason believes that Danyael took his mother from him, and Galahad took his father."

With the two of them sharing just *one* face, Jason would never be able to see them as separate individuals, not that it particularly mattered, since he hated both of them for similar reasons.

Danyael pulled away his hand away from Miriya's. His thoughts churned, his heart breaking for his brother and for himself. Guilt gnawed at him and consumed him, mixing self-hatred with the waves of virulent hatred that Jason unleashed, creating a cacophony that made it nearly impossible to think clearly. "I'm sorry," he murmured, his voice breaking slightly.

"You're sorry?" Jason snarled. He lunged at Danyael again, but Lucien and Galahad pulled him down before he reached Danyael. He slumped down on the couch, blood pouring from shallow wound Zara's dagger had sliced in his throat in his maddened attack. "You drive my mother mad, you take her from me…you *kill* her, and all you can say is you're sorry?"

"There is nothing else I can say." Danyael closed the distance to his brother, his dark eyes glistening. He had long since stopped crying for himself, but he could still weep for others. Jason's emotional trauma screamed at him, an open, bleeding wound that spewed anger and hatred over the quiet cry of a motherless, abandoned boy. Only Danyael heard his brother's heartbroken sobs. Jason was crying the tears he had once cried for himself. *My fault. I killed her, forced my mother to abandon my brother the same way she'd abandoned me. I tore my own family apart.*

Danyael closed his eyes as he placed his hand gently over Jason's bleeding neck and drove his healing powers in the face of the brutal emotional hurricane that battered at him. When the wound was repaired, he withdrew his hand and stepped back.

"This changes nothing!" Jason's dark eyes flashed unrestrained fury.

"I'm not expecting it to," Danyael said quietly.

"This explains a great deal, doesn't it?" Miriya stepped forward to stare searchingly into Jason's face. "You're an empath too. You're charismatic and powerfully persuasive when you choose. You can turn crowds into mobs with a single impassioned speech."

"I'm not a fucking mutant."

"Of course you're not, but you should know that being classified as a mutant isn't a binary sort of thing. There's a lot of gray here, especially for empaths. All of us are empaths—our emotions affect others both positively and negatively—and we all fall along a scale. I think someone arbitrarily draws a vertical line across the bell curve and decides that anything on the other side is outside the bounds of normal." Her smile had a distinctly bitter twist. "Based on my observations, the precise location of the line is usually decided by the most prejudiced people, and it can vary, depending on how much influence the 'mutant' possesses. There are some extremely 'capable' people out there who aren't classified as mutants, because they're too rich and powerful, and have the ability to crush anyone who would even dare suggest that they're a mutant."

"You can't deny that he's a mutant! He killed my mother!"

Miriya shrugged. "Of course Danyael is a mutant. There are few alpha empaths who can match what he does with such flawless ease, and combined with his secondary healing capabilities, he is simply too powerful to fly under the radar. But before you hold him entirely and solely responsible, consider for a moment the possibility that your minor empathic abilities might also have contributed to your mother's depression and her eventual insanity." Her smile was cool, almost chilling, as she patted Jason's cheek gently.

Danyael spoke directly to Miriya's mind. *You know that's not true.*

And you don't know that it's not. Empathy stacks. I don't doubt that you were the primary factor, but Jason's not entirely blameless.

And that's supposed to make me feel less responsible for the fact that I killed my mother?

I can't change what you feel, Danyael. I'm just a telepath, remember? I'm pointing out the facts. Whether or not you accept them is up to you.

Lucien's cell phone rang. He glanced briefly at the caller ID before accepting the call. "Xin, what is it?"

"You'll need to hire more security personnel," Xin said over the speakerphone. Her voice was edged with tension. "And there's a good chance the McLean PD will need a new marketing campaign for its next recruitment drive."

"Purest Humanity?" Lucien asked.

"They've broken through the security cordon and are combing through the house now. I've backed up your computer files remotely and purged the drives."

"Get out of the house, Xin."

"I don't think there's enough time for that. The good news is that they're not burning as they go, but for a group of people supposedly driven by the noblest intentions of protecting the inherent sanctity of humanity, they're giving in a great deal to their base instincts to loot and steal."

"It's all insured," Lucien said dismissively. "Get out."

"Give me the phone, Lucien." Miriya reached for it. "Xin? It's Miriya. Drop your shields. I'm going to link to you, and I'll be able to trace you anywhere." She closed her eyes for a brief moment. "All set," she said briskly. "Now, stay out of trouble until we can get to you."

"I'll try. I don't have Zara's compulsion to make trouble, so I should be fine. I'll try not to piss anyone off. I guess that means I probably shouldn't shoot any of them." With a click, Xin disconnected the call.

Lucien turned on Jason, his blue eyes flashing anger. "Call off your mob, Jason."

"He can't do that," Miriya said. "Mobs like Purest Humanity can't be controlled. Jason turned them loose, and now they'll have to run their course. Let's just get back to Xin as quickly as we can."

"What should we do with him?" Zara asked, her hand tightening on the blade. "Kill him?"

"No." The quiet, firm answer was Danyael's.

Lucien glanced over at Danyael. "I know that as a doctor and healer, you tend not to approve of casual violence, but if you were ever going to make an exception, I would have thought that it would be for Jason Rakehell."

Danyael dropped his gaze. "He's my brother," he said simply, his dark eyes anguished, but his voice once again steady.

"We can't take him with us," Zara pointed out testily.

"She's right, and Danyael's right too," Miriya interjected. She glanced dismissively at Jason. Her mutant powers surged, and he unexpectedly keeled over sideways on the couch, his eyes rolling upwards in his head. "That will hold him for awhile. Load him up. Let's go."

~*~

Lucien could not get to McLean quickly enough, pushing the SUV well beyond the speed limit on the empty highways. *I should never have let Xin stay behind.*

Miriya kept her eyes on the road ahead. Nothing in her impassive face suggested that she was having a silent conversation with Lucien. *Stop that self-flagellation, Lucien. It's very unattractive, not to mention tedious. You've been repeating yourself for ten minutes now.*

I should have insisted she come along.

And do what? Twiddle her thumbs in the car while we went down to beat Jason up? She's happiest behind her computers, and I'd like to remind you that she's also an adult. She made her decision.

So now she has to live with it?

No. So now we go save her ass and you can have the pleasure of saying to her "I told you so."

Lucien chuckled. *That's something I can look forward to. How is Danyael doing?*

Everything considered, surprisingly well. The attack I blasted into his mind this morning would have felled an alpha telepath, but not only did my attack not manage to get past his shields, he followed the path back to my mind, past my shields, in order to strike back. He's exhausted from keeping you, Galahad, and Zara alive through the fight with those lab creatures, but somehow, he's still going. And when the truth came out, his shields barely flickered.

Barely?

They did waver, Lucien. It would be insane to imagine that something like this wouldn't have rocked the tenuously constructed foundations of his world. But he regained control so quickly that I barely even felt the pressure against the shields I used to reinforce his. That's not to say he isn't hurting, Lucien. I'm sure he is, and badly, but he's still hanging in there.

I don't know if the truth was worth this, Miriya.

A bit late for that now. Of course, one could do a whole lot better than having a hate-filled, revenge-driven psycho for a brother, but it beats never knowing.

I don't know if Danyael would agree with that.

He's subscribes to the ostrich philosophy of life. Bury your head in the sand, and perhaps, life will pass you by.

That's not fair, Miriya.

No, it's not. I do understand why he chooses not to dwell on his past. There wasn't anything pretty in there, and we've got a vivid example in Jason Rakehell as to why dwelling overmuch on your past is never a good idea. But unless Danyael comes to terms with his past, he'll never really be able to face the future.

Danyael's doing well.

He's surviving, not living, Miriya countered. *Considering his past, I'd say he's more than merely functional. In fact, he's extremely well adjusted. But he lives without hope, without any expectations or plans for his future.*

You're describing eighty percent of the world's population.

True, but that's a dangerous frame of mind for an empath of Danyael's caliber. His only ties of loyalty are to you, Lucien. That makes you especially pivotal.

Lucien tore his gaze off the road for a brief second to throw her an incredulous glance. *Me? You're grossly overestimating the influence I have on him.*

You don't know what's in his head or behind his shields. I do. She paused briefly. *What's in this for you? Why are you Danyael's friend?*

He was startled. *The answer should be obvious to you. He's the closest thing I have to a brother. We were raised together from the day he saved my life. I was fifteen; he was twelve. He even moved to our Cambridge townhouse to be with me when I went to Harvard, first for college and then for my MBA. Six years ago he finally decided to break out on his own. I think that's why he accepted the offer from Johns Hopkins instead of Harvard for medical school, and then chose to work in New York instead of returning to D.C. He's not just a friend anymore. He's family.*

But before he became family, why did you care? He had nothing to offer you then.

Lucien's eyes narrowed with irritation. *I didn't realize I came across as a shallow-hearted mercenary. Do people need to offer me something for me to care? He needed help, but didn't know how to expect kindness from anyone anymore, so I gave it to him. It was no hardship for me to protect him, and in return...* His mental voice trailed into silence.

And what did you get in return, she prompted when he remained quiet.

Lucien grinned. *It was the best damned trade I ever made. I got the most loyal friendship of my life—a friend who wants nothing from me except friendship. He won't take money. Getting him to accept a gift that's even fractionally more than a mere token is worse than trying to pull teeth with pliers. Ever since he turned eighteen, he's insisted on paying his own way, even if it meant going massively in debt to pay for college and medical school.* Lucien shook his head sharply. *My friendships have always been...complicated. I've never really managed to figure out if people were friends with me for my own sake or because of my family's name, wealth, and influence. Except for Danyael. I know that all he sees when he looks at me is a friend.* His grin gentled into a smile, tender and warm. *He restores my faith in people.*

Miriya smiled too. It was very nearly impossible to lie to a telepath, and Lucien's words rang with so much sincerity that she knew the friendship meant as much to Lucien as it did to Danyael. A rare thing indeed, that friendship. She might have said more, but suddenly she spoke aloud, more for the benefit of the others in the car. "She's on the move."

"Where?" Zara demanded, leaning forward to talk to Miriya.

"East...into D.C."

Zara gritted her teeth. "Damn. At least we know she's alive. They wouldn't bother to move a corpse."

"Exactly." Miriya smiled thinly.

Lucien swung the SUV around and drove it over the divider on the highway. "How good is that GPS in your head?"

"I've tracked people halfway around the world, and I can get within ten feet of her."

"Good enough," Zara said. "We should expect a fight. My guess is that they're taking her to the Purest Humanity headquarters on K Street."

"You've been there," Lucien said. It wasn't a question.

"Jason gave me the grand tour once before."

Galahad glanced thoughtfully at Jason Rakehell, bound and unconscious in the back row of the SUV. "Do you think they'll agree to a hostage exchange?"

"If they were rational, sure, but I think rationality is at a bit of a premium within their circles. Let's just assume we'd have to fight our way to her and then fight our way out," Zara said.

"May I take a look at your arm?" Danyael asked.

"What?" Zara looked at Danyael with annoyance flashing in her violet eyes.

"The bullet wound on your arm."

"It's just a graze," she said, a clear ring of finality in her dismissal.

Danyael's faint half smile was self-mocking, and he dropped the topic. "Is there a plan, or are we just going to make it up as we go along?" he asked.

Galahad chuckled softly and then had the grace to conceal it behind a cough as Zara shot him a slanted glare. "You have to admit, you do have a tendency to…improvise."

"How much resistance can we expect, Zara?" Lucien asked. He did not take his eyes off the road. He seemed calm, but the grim set of his jaw gave him away.

"Usually just about enough to make it fun. What they lack in skill, they make up for with sheer force of numbers."

"Watch out," Miriya warned sharply. "It's getting crowded."

Danyael turned his head to look out the window. At the edge of the city, they had seen insignificant fights involving small numbers of people shoving at each other, but those fights had escalated into full-blown riots by the time the SUV entered the central business district. The brawls spilled out of buildings and into the streets. Fists, knives, and guns were employed. The police were noticeably absent. Fortunately most people ignored the SUV as it raced past, not that bullets would have done much against the armor-plated vehicle.

"I'd put my money on the in vitros and clones," Miriya murmured as she observed an altercation end in a fatality. "They're a bit more motivated and generally in better shape."

"Which way, Miriya?" Lucien demanded. "We're just about out of time here."

"Straight down. I think it's coming from the eight-story building with the glass façade."

"Purest Humanity's headquarters," Zara confirmed. "And there's a welcoming committee coming straight toward us," she observed, tossing a quick glance over her shoulder.

"Human or derivative?" Lucien demanded, circling the building as he tried to find a safe place to park his SUV.

"They're too attractive to be human. Derivatives, probably. My guess is they are converging on Purest Humanity's headquarters. A bit of generalized fighting wouldn't necessarily be a bad thing, you know."

"They'll also get in our way. I was hoping to sneak through."

"Seriously?" Zara looked at Lucien in disbelief. "Sometimes your unbridled optimism gets the better of you. We can't possibly pass unnoticed with these two pretty boys here."

Lucien spotted a sign leading to an underground garage. It was close enough to be accessible if they needed a quick getaway, but out of sight and consequently not an obvious target. The SUV lurched as he drove it down the ramp at a speed that would have been considered seriously unsafe. "I wasn't planning to take Galahad with us, and Danyael's relatively good at discouraging any interest in himself."

Zara bristled immediately. "You can't leave Galahad here."

Lucien cut the engine and then turned around in his seat. "Zara. The pro-humanists would sell their first-born child for an opportunity to kill him. We can't just deliver him into their hands."

"Lucien," Zara replied with the same exaggerated patience. "There are just five of us against a building full of fanatics frothing at the mouth. We leave Galahad, we lose twenty percent of our strength...more, since some of us can't fight worth a crap." She did not quite look at Danyael, but there was very little doubt as to whom she was referring.

"He'll be safer with us, Luce," Danyael confirmed quietly. "Miriya, how long do we have before Jason wakes up?"

"At least an hour."

If we're not out in an hour, we're probably all dead anyway. Lucien stared thoughtfully at Danyael, and then at Galahad. "All right, you and Miriya keep him safe. Let's go."

What the hell. Zara scowled as she slipped out of the SUV. *You treat me like an idiot child when I say we need to bring Galahad along, but you play along the moment Danyael says the same.*

Miriya's eyes narrowed as she eavesdropped on Zara's inner voice. She hurled a thought at Danyael. *She's becoming a problem.*

Zara?

Is there any other she *in the group?* Even Miriya's mental voice was loaded with sarcasm. *What the hell did you do to her?*

I don't know exactly. I don't think I did anything to her beyond my usual barriers, though I was sick from healing Galahad when we first met. Maybe she just doesn't like me. It happens sometimes.

She hates you, Danyael.

She despises me, Danyael corrected meticulously. *She's still a few degrees away from hatred.*

I don't see how you can laugh at this.

I told you before, Miriya. It's laugh or cry. I think we should just agree that I suck at relationships.

You need to stop pushing people away.

Have you been talking to Luce? You sound almost exactly like him.

Zara likes to believe she controls her own life, her own destiny.

She's entitled to be delusional.

Miriya chuckled and then continued. *She's going to be furious if she ever discovers you've been emotionally manipulating her.*

I'm not doing this deliberately or consciously, Miriya. Even Danyael's mental voice was laden with the patiently weary tone of someone tired of repeating himself.

I don't think the distinction will matter to her. She's going to carve out your guts with a dull butter knife when she finds out.

Oh, now I'm terrified.

Danyael—

He shook his head sharply. *She won't find out. The facts about me won't matter to her now or ever. I'm too good at what I do—consciously or not. It'd take the equivalent of an emotional hurricane to divert her from her path now. I'm not even sure I could do it, short of absorbing it from her.*

If you're okay with people disliking you, you clearly have an intimacy problem.

That's something of an understatement, and I don't think I have enough cash on hand to pay you to be my shrink. I understand my mental and emotional state, Miriya. I know it's not the best, but it's a great deal better than it used to be before Lucien found me. And maybe one day, years from now, it'll be even better. I'll just take it a day at a time.

That's a depressing outlook.

Considering we may not live past the next hour, taking it a day at a time is about as visionary as I can feel right now.

Miriya laughed out loud, wondering why Danyael's understated, wry sense of humor emerged only in his mental voice, and almost never out loud. Lucien looked at her quizzically. "Just talking to Danyael," she explained airily. "I'm sorry, I must ask again. Is there a plan?"

Galahad walked up the ramp that led out of the garage to take a quick scan of the area. "The mob arrived, and they're definitely derivatives—in vitros and clones," he reported. "They're trying to break down Purest Humanity's front door."

"How many?" Danyael asked.

"Hard to say. Forty, maybe fifty."

Danyael inhaled deeply and then looked over at Lucien. "What do you want them to do?"

"What can you make them do?"

"I can make them leave, or I can make them very, very determined to get through that door."

Miriya's green eyes narrowed. "I don't think that's a good idea."

"It's not a good idea, I know," Danyael agreed, "but it is an option. A mob would be a great distraction, but there's a chance we'd have to fight them and the humans at the same time. I wouldn't recommend it. Still, I can keep Purest Humanity's attention riveted on the front door so that you can enter through the back."

Lucien stared at Danyael, amazed that they had not even considered that option before Danyael spoke. *I need to stop hanging around people like Zara who don't use anything other than the front door.* He heard Miriya's warm chuckle of amusement in his head. "That sounds like a plan. Let's find a back door. Danyael, can you keep the derivatives more or less under control and then disperse them once we're in the building?" Lucien asked.

"Of course." Danyael stepped out of the garage and walked toward the howling mob of people outside the building.

"Will he be safe?" Galahad asked quietly. "Does he need to get that close?"

"Of course, he will." Miriya shrugged gracefully, "And yes to the second question too. Emotions are a type of energy, or at least they behave like energy. They need a medium through which to travel, and for Danyael, it's line of sight. Obstructions—even windows—tend to get in the way. Osmosis works too, but line of sight is a great deal more effective."

"This way." Zara led the way around to the back of the building. It was located on a narrower, less traveled street with a separate security-protected entrance. "Fewer people, but we're still on the wrong side of the door."

"Not for long." Miriya tossed a casual glance at the two security guards behind the glass door. Their attention was focused on the screens behind their security desk, likely providing live feed from the cameras monitoring the mob outside the front door. Her green eyes gleamed brightly for a moment, and then without the faintest glimmer of confusion, one of the security guards walked over, unlocked the door, and ushered them in as if they were long-lost friends.

"So you can be subtle," Lucien murmured, quietly amused.

"Only occasionally," Miriya said with a faint smile. *Danyael, we're in. We're moving on ahead. I'll instruct the guard to leave the door open for you.*

The old Jedi mind trick? Danyael's voice whispered softly through her mind, carrying the same tone of quiet amusement.

Works every time.

I'll be right there.

"Danyael's on his way." Miriya kept her voice pitched low as they strode through past the security desk and down the corridors.

"We won't even have to fight if you can keep pulling this stunt."

"It worked on the guards because they were so busy watching what was happening up front that they weren't focused on their jobs. Besides, they're just employees, as opposed to rabid pro-humanists. They are largely indifferent to the mission of this organization. We won't be so lucky with the rest; as I think I've said once before, obsession is a really good defense against a telepath." Miriya paused, hesitating at the foot of the stairs. She reached out with her telepathic senses and felt the pulse that tugged her unerringly toward Xin. "Upstairs, I think." She inhaled deeply and then released her breath in a soft sigh. "And get ready for a fight."

~*~

Brother...brother...

The creatures moaned as one, grieving the brother that was dead and the brother that was lost to them. Indifferent to the need to stay concealed as they had through the night, they now moved openly.

There was no need to hide anymore. No one challenged them. Those humans who looked alike in their dull blue cloth coverings, who wielded metallic weapons that flashed and spit out particles, were pitiful. They lacked courage unless their pack stood with them. Only a few humans, back at the battle where their brother had been killed, had demonstrated the strength, courage, and the skill to fight back.

One of them had even demonstrated the ability to kill.

Follow...close now. They lumbered through the streets of Washington, D.C. with surprising agility and grace, in spite of their deformed bulk. The humans who clustered in their pitiful squabbles gave way to them as they passed. No time for petty battles now. An occasional flea-brained human chose to attack, but those fools were torn and killed in seconds, their skin and flesh shredded, bones broken. The corpse was left where it fell, a grim marker to the way they had come.

They did not question the instinct that led them into a forest of metal and glass. The instinct had not failed them. It had led them to the one they sought though that meeting that tragically ended in the death of their brother. They knew now. They knew of whom to be wary, of the one who could use pain to turn their strength against them. *The human will be with him. The human guards and protects him.*

The human must be the first to die.

~*~

109

"Take a left here!"

Michael Cochran twisted the steering wheel and swung the car out of the lane as he negotiated a sudden turn. What were two elderly scientists doing in the midst of this madness, he wondered.

That they were responsible for this madness was of course the obvious answer. Jason Rakehell had destroyed the lab and allowed the creatures to break out of their holding cells, but Michael and Roland had created the creatures in an all-consuming pursuit of genetic perfection. To compound their mistake, they had chosen not to euthanize the creatures even when they realized that those creatures were monstrous, dark reflections of humanity twisted beyond comprehension.

"That is the Purest Humanity headquarters, right there in that building." Roland leaned forward in his seat to peer up at the triangular building constructed of glass and steel. It was reminiscent of a pyramid—a symbol of eternal life. He considered it especially ironic. Humanity had aspired toward godhood. He had given the world Galahad, the closest thing humans had for a god, the embodiment of humanity's absolute perfection. Inconceivably, the world had balked at it.

A crowd was gathered outside the building, and judging by how they were riding the razor-thin edge of open hostility, Roland assumed that they were derivatives—in vitros and clones. "There's a parking garage around the back. It's probably a bit quieter there too."

Michael Cochran nodded. It was insane what they were doing, or planning to do. The Purest Humanity headquarters was unquestionably the only place where Jason would have taken Galahad. What they were going to do to get into the building and find Galahad had not exactly been defined yet. What they were going to do to get out once they actually found Galahad was even less clear.

Realistically, Michael did not think much of their chances, but Roland seemed determined to try. What could possibly go wrong? It was as simple as driving into an anarchic city where there was open fighting on the streets and the authorities seemed determined to stay out of sight, break into a well-protected building filled with pro-humanists who considered them the greatest criminal masterminds and corruptors of the sanctity of human life, find Galahad, and then walk out, perfectly unharmed, not a hair out of place.

Not hard at all.

Michael took another right turn and then slammed his foot down on the brakes.

Roland jerked forward in his seat. His seatbelt saved him from going through the glass. He threw an annoyed glance at his partner. "The garage is in the next building. The white brick one."

"Look…" Michael breathed, pointing a trembling finger at a figure standing against the building adjacent to Purest Humanity.

Roland looked over and inhaled sharply. He saw a young man, tall and leanly muscular. The man was dressed in a white shirt, blue jeans, and a black leather jacket that had seen better days, yet no amount of dressing down could conceal that heartbreaking, rare beauty

Galahad.

Danyael lingered within the shadows cast by the adjacent building, trying to be as unobtrusive as possible. He could easily deflect attention if it came down to that, but there was no point in overextending his powers until there was a real need for it. Carefully he assessed the mood of the crowd. As a descriptor, *furious* would have been a mild understatement. The derivatives were livid at the way they were routinely treated, the years of pent-up anger over their legal discrimination finally boiling over. It would not have taken much to push them over the edge into *rabid.*

That was hardly his intent. He needed to control the crowd, needed to keep it from breaking into the building. Closing his eyes, he took a deep breath to calm and focus his thoughts and emotions. He reinforced his internal shields, the ones that kept his worst memories and their associated emotions locked away, and then deliberately dropped his external shields.

He called vast power to him without moving a muscle.

For a moment it seemed as if the world held its breath, just waiting. His emphatic power finally whispered out, softly seductive, wickedly insidious. It wove its way through the mob, leeching into each person there, manipulating emotions the way a skilled musician coaxes the violin to sing.

The crowd surged as his power urged them into a crescendo, and then fell back as he issued a softer note, sent out a gentle surge of cool rationality to take the edge off the heat of their emotions. He kept them teetering between calmness and fury, kept them shouting angrily and pounding on the doors of Purest Humanity without breaking the doors down.

Miriya's voice echoed with its rich, vibrant timbre through his mind. *Danyael, we're in. We're moving on ahead. I'll instruct the guard to leave the door open for you.*

His angelically beautiful face, usually serious and unsmiling, eased into a rare, unchecked smile. *The old Jedi mind trick?*

Miriya's response was flippant. *Works every time.*

I'll be right there.

It was time to send them home. His concentration and focus were so intertwined in guiding and shaping the emotional flow of the crowd that he was oblivious to the aches of his weary body. He knew he would feel them acutely once he was able to relax again, but it did not seem that relaxing would be an option in his immediate future. Danyael inhaled deeply and then released his breath slowly. He felt his heartbeat slow in response, his mind calm in preparation for the release.

He felt a surge of panic sweep through the crowd, fear that hovered tenuously on the verge of terror. Startled, he glanced up sharply and saw the five grotesque shapes of the abominations from the laboratory prowl down the street, looking neither to the left nor right. They headed straight for Purest Humanity. Danyael pressed back against the wall as they passed within twenty feet of him. His heartbeat accelerated. His fear—a natural one of the creatures that were so much faster and stronger than humans—surged and spilled unchecked past his lowered barriers.

His fear washed into the crowd to whom he was emotionally linked. Their fear, amplified by an alpha empath, transformed into terror, the kind that spurred stampedes and left people crushed, dead on the ground, as their companions trampled over them in unthinking panic.

Within seconds, the steps leading up to Purest Humanity were cleared of anyone who could still move. Only the dead and critically injured were left behind.

Horrified by the carnage that his fear and his mistake had inspired, Danyael's heart wrenched with guilt. Still concealed within the shadows, he watched in silence as the creatures lumbered up the steps and walked right through the reinforced glass that had kept out a furious mob. He could hear the terrified screams of the people within as they ran for safety or gathered, with the misplaced courage that only the truly misguided could summon, to fight off the abominations.

Danyael was about to shout out a mental warning to Miriya, when he felt her telepathic powers connect with his mind, creating a conduit, a channel for his empathic healing powers to pass through her and into Galahad, Zara, and Lucien. His friends were bracing for a fight. Not the abominations; they couldn't have seen them yet. The pro-humanists, most likely.

He cursed softly under his breath. Not exactly what they had bargained for. To suggest that the abominations would complicate things tremendously would have been a heck of an understatement. He had to get to his friends quickly.

Pain drove him to his knees. His head ringing from the blow, his skull feeling like it would split, he twisted around to see Jason Rakehell standing over him with a brick in his hand.

A thin sneer curved Jason's lips. "Well, well, hello my little piece-of-shit brother." His grip tightened on the brick as he hefted it in his hand. He grinned maniacally at Danyael's grimace of pain.

Jason Rakehell raised his hand, prepared to bring the brick down again on Danyael's unprotected head. "You should have died years ago. I'll make sure of it now."

ELEVEN

"I'll take point. Ladies first and all that," Zara insisted when she saw that Lucien was about to protest. "If you went first and got shot, your dad would be pissed at me, and it's a bad idea to piss off someone who can afford to buy all of Hong Kong, most of London, and at least half of New York."

"Maybe just a third of New York," Lucien corrected with a tight grin, but waved her ahead. "I'll admit you probably have faster reflexes anyway." He and Galahad followed her, and Miriya brought up the rear with a final glance back over her shoulder. Lucien asked, "Everything all right, Miriya?"

"So far," she said, though she sounded uneasy. "I think I'm just the paranoid type. It's been going well so far; it's probably about time for something to go wrong." She reached out with her mind, tendrils of her psychic power snaking into Zara, Lucien, and Galahad, and then reinforced them, including her link with Xin. They would be practically invulnerable, as long as Danyael was able to sustain them.

The second floor opened out into an expansive landing with artwork lining the brilliantly white walls. The foyer was dominated by a curved desk constructed of burnished copper plates in a distinctly artsy form of questionable stability, occupied by a single receptionist.

Zara smiled at her. "They told me to come and cover for you if you want to catch a glimpse of the action downstairs."

The receptionist's eyes lit up. "Oh, thank you!" she gushed as she pushed back from her desk. "Thank you so much!" She dashed toward the stairs, squeezing past the others who were on their way up. She even threw a flirty grin at Galahad as she skipped past him.

"Do they have any idea how pissed off that mob is?" Lucien wondered, his voice pitched low.

"Obviously not. Prudence is in very short supply here. It's all fun and games until someone gets hurt."

"People are getting hurt," Galahad pointed out.

"Just not them, and not yet. Which way, Miriya?"

Miriya nodded toward the north, down a corridor that led to a reinforced steel door. The good news was that the door was open. The bad news was that they had arrived during a change in shift, and instead of four guards, there were eight. The guards took a single look at Zara's distinctly predatory expression and instinctively reached for their guns. She hardly broke her stride, dropping down into a crouch and swinging her leg in a wide circle, sweeping two of the closest guards off their feet.

"We've got it covered here," Lucien ordered her as he and Galahad moved to attack. "You keep moving. Find her."

Zara nodded, pausing long enough to slam one of the guard's heads back into the ground, knocking him out. She yanked the guard's security pass off his shirt pocket, before scrambling gracefully to her feet and sprinting down the hallway. *Her signal's coming from the end of the corridor,* Miriya's voice murmured straight into her mind.

"Okay."

Just think it, no need to say it out loud too. You're echoing.

Zara did not bother to reply. She paused by the last door, listening, but heard nothing. Only one way to find out. She swiped the security card over the security panel and the bolt slid back noiselessly. Pressing two slender fingers against the door, she eased it open. Voices, a male voice, slow, ponderous, a female voice, vibrant, irritated.

Zara allowed herself a faint smile. *Found her.*

"Will you just look at my driver's license?" Xin demanded of the pro-humanist interrogator who stood in front of her with her driver's license in one hand and a pugnacious look on his face. Incredulity infused her voice. How could anyone be that dumb? The human race was headed for the rocks. "Does it say Zara Itani on that anywhere? That's because I'm not Zara Itani."

"IDs can be faked," he intoned.

"Right. And I'd go to all that trouble to fake everything else, right? Including credit cards and my government ID that clearly identifies my security clearance."

"Maybe you're just a meticulous, detail-oriented person."

"Or maybe I'm just not Zara Itani. You have no clue who you're looking for."

"We do," the interrogator protested, sounding hurt. "Rakehell said to look for a woman with dark hair."

Xin rolled her eyes. She might have smacked her forehead if her hands were not cuffed tightly behind her back. "All you got from Jason Rakehell is a description that would fit hundreds of millions of people in the United States. Didn't you think to ask for more information, or better yet, a picture?"

"We know what we're doing, *Zara*." He backhanded her across her face. "Now, where is Galahad? Where did you hide him?"

Xin jerked her head back to glare at him. "Did you look between your ears?" she responded sweetly. "There's so much empty space in between, he could be hiding there, and you wouldn't know it."

The interrogator hesitated for a moment, his wide blue eyes drawing together in momentary confusion. Xin's jaw dropped. Was it even possible for anyone to be that stupid? Maybe it was long past time for the derivatives to rule the world, especially considering the evolutionary path—or rather the de-evolutionary path—of the naturally born humans.

Or maybe it was just a pro-humanist thing. Fanaticism tended to soften the brain cells, since none were required to process even an iota of original thought.

Xin tasted blood when he struck her across the face again. That one was going to need some pretty serious make-up to cover up. Unexpectedly, she felt the open cut in her mouth close smoothly, the flesh twitching only slightly as the edges pulled together and sealed seamlessly. The only evidence that remained was the faint taste of blood. Puzzled, she ran her tongue over the smooth inside of her cheek. Danyael? It had to be. Was he doing now to her what he had done with the others earlier that morning, healing through Miriya's telepathic link?

There weren't any other explanations that would have made sense. That meant that he and the others were close. Relieved, Xin lowered her eyes to hide her jubilation.

Her interrogator however took her action to mean that his methods of interrogation had succeeded in breaking her spirit. He grinned triumphantly. "So where is Galahad?" he asked.

Xin looked up, her brown eyes innocently wide. "Right behind you," she suggested.

He turned and a booted heel slammed into his midsection, knocking him back. He saw a flash of long, dark hair as another kick, this one straight into his chest, cracked ribs under the impact. He slammed back into the wall and then slid to the ground with a heavy whoosh of air.

Blearily he looked up at the young woman who stood over him. Long, wavy dark hair framed features that were more exotically mixed than purely Asian. "Didn't your mother ever tell you it's rude to hit women who weigh about eighty percent less than you do?" Zara asked, her voice a feline purr more frequently attached to porn stars than to martial arts experts.

"He insisted I was you," Xin said as she jiggled her handcuffs hopefully. "I told him I was prettier and smarter than you were, but he didn't believe me."

"I hope she also told you that I'm the more dangerous one." Zara did not bother to wait for an answer. She took his head between her hands, and with a single, sharp jerk, snapped his neck. She searched his pocket for the keys and had just freed Xin when Lucien rushed into the cell, Galahad not far behind him.

"Thank God you're all right." Lucien seized Xin in a tight hug that made her wince.

"I'm fine, really." She patted his back carefully when he did not let go after several long seconds. "Lucien? Are you okay?"

"I'm fine." He released her, his practiced aura of calm momentarily displaced. "I thought we'd lost you when the pro-humanists got through the police barricade."

"They wanted answers out of me more than they wanted me dead." Xin shrugged, rubbing her sore wrists absentmindedly.

"Are we done with the reunion?" Miriya looked into the cell, her tone sharp, even irritable. Blond hair swaying, she shook her head, trying to process the inexplicable flash of chaotic images she had received from Danyael. The derivatives screaming, fleeing, a stampede, people dying. They were all the more terrifying because those images were seared with Danyael's sudden fear and near panic. He had lost control of the mob. "We need to go. Now."

"We're doing fine, Miriya," Zara said silkily. "There wasn't even any opposition worth mentioning."

Screams of terror and pain clamored through the building.

"I hate it when we jinx ourselves," Lucien muttered. "The derivatives must have broken through."

"No, not the derivatives," Miriya murmured, her blood turning to ice in her veins as more images were transmitted to her through Danyael's eyes. Grotesque, humanoid forms lumbering up the steps, shattering the reinforced glass doors of Purest Humanity with virtually no effort at all. The inhuman snarls and moans that played bass to the terrifying soprano of human screams confirmed those images. "The abominations. They're here."

~*~

Danyael did not have years of martial arts training to fall back on, but his sense of survival had been exquisitely honed and was surpassed only by his tolerance for pain. As the brick descended, he dropped down on his back, reached up with two hands to grip Jason's hand, and then yanked forward hard, slamming Jason's head into the wall behind them.

As Jason crumpled in pain, Danyael rolled to the side and back onto his feet. He barely had time to regain his balance when Jason lunged at him, tackling him with arms wrapped around his midsection and wrestling him to the ground. Jason had the advantage of superior weight, and his strength was fueled by furious hatred for Danyael and for Galahad. It hardly even mattered who he was fighting, when he hated them both, and they looked so alike.

He pinned Danyael to the ground, grabbed Danyael's head between his hands and pounded it repeatedly into the concrete. Danyael gasped, his senses reeling, stunned more by Jason's vivid anger and the open emotional wounds than by the physical impact of the attack. Barely able to think coherently, he clawed for survival, an inch at a time, dragging his emotional shields back up to protect himself.

He sighed with relief when the external shields locked into place, a thin buffer against the storm of Jason's emotions. His head clearing, he struggled to dislodge Jason, knowing that he was desperately short on workable alternatives. He could not drop his internal shields. He could not channel his deepest, darkest emotions, not with his mind actively linked to his friends through Miriya's telepathic power. The emotions would flow through their joint minds and drive his friends to suicide.

But even if he had been free to act, he could not bring himself to unleash the full extent of his powers against his brother. Danyael stared up into his brother's hate-twisted features and saw no resemblance, but he did not need to. It wasn't training that held his hand. It was guilt born from a familial bond that both time and distance had failed to cleave.

He could not do it.

He's a victim, and I drove him to this when I took his mother from him.

Entirely out of options, Danyael reached out with his empathic powers, seized Jason's emotions, and twisted them. The irony tore at Danyael. He would have given almost anything to take his brother's hatred away, to purchase a second chance for the both of them. Instead, he was intensifying it, to buy himself a fleeting chance at survival.

Hatred took on the viscosity of quicksand, anger the edge of a sharpened sword. It wasn't enough then for Jason to smash his brother's brains out on the concrete. Jason needed something else, needed to make Danyael acknowledge him, needed to make Danyael scream in pain. Caught up in the powerful empathic backlash, Jason released Danyael and reached for the brick.

In that moment, Danyael struck back, seizing Jason's shirt in one hand and driving his other fist into Jason's jaw. Jason staggered back as Danyael scrambled to his feet. Jason was so furious, he could barely see clearly. He swung out, clumsy, graceless, as his body struggled to accommodate the overwhelming surge of norepinephrine. The heightened anger made him stronger, faster, but less accurate, and far more likely to overextend, to make mistakes.

It was the only advantage afforded to Danyael, and he seized it. Survival came down to a desperate battle, strength against precision. He evaded Jason's clumsy attacks and managed to throw a few punches that sent Jason reeling back, winded, even momentarily stunned. *Now.* Danyael fisted his hands together, prepared to bring them down on the back of Jason's neck to knock him out.

Danyael screamed in agony as pain, sharper than a thousand blades, surged through the telepathic link and sliced into him. *Zara.* The attack she had sustained would have eviscerated her, killed her slowly and with exquisite pain. Dropping to his knees, he wrapped his arms around his stomach and braced against the phantom injury as his potent healing powers surged.

Danyael shuddered, from the pain and from the staggering effort of focusing his healing powers through it. He was vaguely aware that Jason had managed to catch his breath. He saw the shadow his brother cast on the ground as Jason stood over him with a crowbar in hand, but he could not find the strength to escape the inevitable blow. The empath trembled, coughing blood as his exhausted body rebelled, begging for relief from the unending pain. He gritted his teeth when Jason's shadow moved. Danyael braced for the attack, for more pain.

The crowbar fell harmlessly to the ground.

Jason toppled gracelessly to his knees, blood staining his blue shirt.

Danyael had not heard the single bullet shot ring out. He looked up. Through his pain-glazed vision, he saw two men race from a car parked across the street. He was dimly aware that they knelt beside him. He did not resist when gentle hands tilted his face up.

"Who are you? *What* are you?"

He heard their disbelieving questions, but did not have the strength to answer.

He could not think beyond the pain that kept flowing through the telepathic link to sear his mind and ravage his body. *God, please be merciful.* When would it end?

TWELVE

Chaos descended quickly, utterly on Purest Humanity. Bullets and blades had no apparent effect on the abominations, and the question about killing them soon became irrelevant. The critical issue boiled down to whether anyone would survive their attack, and it was quickly evident that the odds were not stacked in favor of the humans.

It was a massacre, a bloodbath as the abominations rampaged with abandon, killing everything that moved, as if they knew they were among their worst enemies.

One found its way into the kitchen, hunting with relish the humans who crawled between tables and tried to hide behind shelves, sobbing with fear. It found them all and slaughtered them all, tearing bodies apart with the efficiency of a skilled butcher. It grabbed one quivering human, snapped its neck, and indifferently tossed it onto the lit gas burners, before lumbering out. Behind it, the kitchen started to burn, the flames consuming first the corpse on the burner before spreading to the polished wood countertops and cabinets.

On the other side of the building, four people fled down the service corridor. "In here!" one of them gasped, pushing open the door to the storage room. "There's a lock here." The others pushed past him, and together they slammed the door shut, sliding the deadbolt in place.

"God, oh, God, save us." One of them fumbled, trying to light a cigarette, his fingers clicking over and over again on the lighter.

The others pressed their ears to the door and heard the ponderous footsteps of an abomination stop outside the door. It made a strange sound, like that of a puppy sniffing for its owner's scent.

The lighter flickered into flame.

The door caved in. The abomination threw its weight against the door and it crumpled like paper. Inside, four people shrieked in panic as death entered.

Death lumbered out a minute later, leaving four bodies smashed against collapsed metal storage racks. Supplies spilled out on the floor. Safety cans filled with gasoline and diesel were perforated by claws and then smashed underfoot. The heady smell of gasoline wafted from the room as the clear liquid pooled around the bodies, around the pale blue flame of the lighter that had fallen to the ground.

The abomination did not look back when the room exploded, the red and orange tongues of fire licking at its heels.

~*~

"Only three," Zara murmured, stepping back from the stairs as the abominations clambered up into the large circular reception area on the second floor and fanned out to meet them.

"That's already about three too many, in my opinion," Lucien countered. *This is going to be bad for Danyael.*

Twice in a day is bad, Miriya agreed. *Here they come.*

She took several steps back, dragging Xin with her, as the three abominations charged. One-on-one were better odds than Lucien, Zara and Galahad had enjoyed that morning, but without Danyael, they had little chance of bringing any of the creatures down. Where was he, damn it?

Miriya winced when she saw an abomination rip through Zara's midsection. That injury should have killed her. Miriya could only imagine how it must have felt to Danyael.

"We need Danyael, don't we?" Xin asked quietly, her brown eyes locked on Lucien as he ducked under a vicious swipe of an abomination's arm, narrowly escaping injury. "We can't win this without him. Where is he?"

"Outside, I think."

"I can get him."

"You can't get past them," Miriya cautioned her. Miriya and Xin were pressed up against the far wall. While Galahad, Lucien, and Zara did their best to draw the battle away from the two women, the abominations sometimes came distressingly close. Miriya winced again as another creature broke through Galahad's defenses, briefly drawing blood before Danyael's empathic healing power whisked the injury away.

A sound—shockingly loud—blasted through the building.

Miriya glanced up sharply.

Xin listened too. She turned to meet Miriya's gaze. "An explosion?"

Miriya nodded, a cold ball of dread taking shape in the pit of her stomach. "Not a weapon, though. Sounded like a gas tank or something exploding." Deliberately she lowered her psychic shields, trying to catch the whispers of passing minds.

A fading human whisper. *Help me please. So much blood. Oh, God, I can't die, not yet. Please help.*

The mournful moan of an abomination, *Brother, brother, why fight?*

A panicked human scream. *Fire! It's on fire! I can't get out!*

"Something's burning," Miriya said. She looked toward the staircase but could not see any signs of smoke. "I can't tell how bad it is."

Xin knelt down and placed a hand against the floor. She looked up at Miriya, her fear seeping through the cracks in her naturally calm personality. "I can feel the heat. It's not just warm, it's hot. The fire's likely right below us, and it's weakening the physical structure of the building."

Disengage! Miriya screamed the order out through the telepathic links. *The building's on fire. It's going to collapse.*

The order came several seconds too late. With a deep, rumbling moan, the building convulsed. Foundation pillars melted, weakened by the heat from the petrochemical fire, and crumpled slowly under the weight of the upper floors. The floor vanished, marble tiles falling away to shatter on the ground floor.

The five of them fell, landing gracelessly among the rubble. The ground floor was in ruins. The injured huddled next to the dead under the fallen ceiling. Thick black smoke rapidly filled the room, and the heat from the flames was becoming unbearable.

Xin pushed to her feet, feeling the minor cuts and bruises from her fall heal rapidly through Danyael's empathic link. She pulled Miriya up. "We have to get out. Now! Zara! Where are you?"

"Here." Several feet away, a slim shadow moved toward them, and moments later, Zara, her face sooty but otherwise unscathed, appeared out of the smoke. "Where the hell are the creatures? They just vanished on me."

"I don't know, and I don't care. Lucien! Galahad!"

"Right here." Lucien appeared from behind her, Galahad with him. He cupped his hand over his nose and mouth, trying to breathe shallowly. "That way." He pointed toward the approximate direction of the exit.

Carefully but swiftly, they clambered over the rubble. They were twenty feet away from the front door, sunlight gleaming through its broken glass, when another sharp sound cracked overhead.

Lucien looked up, alarm ringing through his voice. "The next floor! It's coming down!"

They ran. Small grains of cement rained down on them, a prelude to the storm. Seconds later, the larger pieces broke away. Xin cried out in pain as one piece struck her on the shoulder, but Lucien pulled her close, shielding her with his own body as he raced toward the exit.

"Zara!"

Zara heard Galahad shout. A violent shove sent her sprawling several feet forward, and then she heard him scream in agony. She threw a quick glance back over her shoulder, and her heart skipped a single terrified beat. Galahad was trapped beneath the rubble that would have crushed her, had he not saved her.

Scrambling to her feet, she ran back to his side. "Galahad!"

His breath fluttered faintly against her skin. It was enough to give her hope. "Help me here!" she cried out to the others. She strained to lift the massive piece of lumber that had crushed Galahad's back and legs, pinning him to the ground. "We'll get you out, Galahad. Damn it, do you hear me? Stay with me; we'll get you out."

Galahad could not respond. The pain stole his breath, robbed him of his ability to speak, to think. He had endured a great deal in his years at the laboratory, but nothing had ever felt like that. The pain was excruciating, even overwhelming, and then miraculously, it eased away with breathtaking speed.

Danyael.

Empathic healing powers alleviated the shattering pain of multiple fractures, carefully aligning bone fragments in the crushed legs and spine before accelerating the production of chondroblasts and osteoblasts to produce the hyaline cartilage and woven bone needed to hold the fractured bone fragments pieces together. Galahad could feel the healing process as bone fragments moved, then locked into place and strengthened, once again perfectly aligned.

He inhaled deeply as Lucien, Xin, Zara, and Miriya struggled—without success—to move the lumber. The weight against his back and legs was uncomfortable, but not unbearable, now that they no longer ground against broken bones.

"We're so close," Lucien said, glancing at the exit that taunted with its inaccessible nearness. "On my count, one, two, three!"

The heavy piece of wood did not even budge.

"Lucien!" Xin's voice was a quiet whisper, but the urgency in it demanded that he look up. Something moved in the smoke in front of them. Something massive.

Lucien cursed under his breath. "Again!"

The four friends struggled and strained, muscles tensing against the effort, but the lumber mocked their every effort to free Galahad.

The smoke parted, giving way to the five massive, misshapen forms of the abominations, grotesquely hideous, completely inhuman. Their clawed hands dripped blood as the monsters deliberately and slowly lumbered forward. *Kill, kill. Brother.*

Galahad met their amber-eyed stares without flinching and then inhaled deeply before releasing his breath in a soft sigh. "Go," he said simply.

"What?" Zara seized his hand in hers and held tight. "No!"

The sincerity in her voice warmed him immeasurably; she had meant it. "You're out of time!" He had to shout to be heard above the cacophony all around them. The flames crackled furiously and the moans and wails of the dying echoed off the shattered walls. The building groaned, its structural integrity severely compromised. "Go, now!"

A sharp, cracking sound ricocheted overhead and set up an echo as other foundational structures snapped under the pressure. Lucien grabbed Xin's wrist and pulled her along as he raced out of the building and onto the street. Miriya was just a step behind him, and Zara was the last to leave. "I won't forget," she promised as she tore away from Galahad, taking a single step back, her violet eyes never leaving his face as if trying to imprint into memory.

"I know." He breathed the words too quietly for her to hear and then saw her turn to run. He looked up stoically as the abominations closed in around him. His last glimpse of his friends was taken from him as their massive forms encircled him.

Outside the building, Lucien ground his teeth together, his eyes betraying his anguish over the decision he was about to make. "Cut the link, Miriya."

"What?"

"Cut the telepathic link, or Danyael will die too."

Miriya glanced sharply at him and then severed all their telepathic ties to Danyael. "Get back; it's coming down!"

They fled across the street and watched in horror as the structural frame of the building crumpled. The top five floors collapsed all at once, imploding. Lucien, Zara, Xin and Miriya ducked behind parked cars to protect themselves from the spray of debris, but they were still covered in fine gray dust. It took ten minutes for the rubble to finally settle, and when it was over, nothing moved. Galahad and the abominations were buried in the ruins of Purest Humanity.

Miriya clenched her hands into fists, not at all amused by the symbolism. She ached a hollow sense of loss over someone she was beginning to consider a friend. Galahad had been at the very heart of the genetic crisis, but he was—more than anyone else—a true victim of circumstances. The injustice of his having to pay the highest price galled her.

Tense and angry, feeling desperately cheated, Miriya strode around the ruins of the building toward the corner where they had left Danyael. She stopped short, staring in disbelief at the empty street. Danyael was nowhere to be found.

Far more alarming, Jason Rakehell was gone too.

THIRTEEN

Roland twisted around to look over his shoulder. The moment was surreal. Nothing could have prepared him to see his two adult sons slumped in the backseat of his car. Jason was unconscious and bleeding, but stable. His younger son—Luke, he recalled vaguely—was barely clinging to consciousness, fighting for every labored breath, in the grip of some kind of vicious pain for which there was no basis in reality.

Roland and Michael had both been crouching beside Luke on the sidewalk, watching him shudder in agony, debating what to do when they heard the first of many loud explosions inside Purest Humanity. Michael looked up sharply. "The building! I think it's coming down."

Roland shot to his feet and turned to race into the burning building.

Michael grabbed his hand. "You can't! It's suicide. You don't even know if Galahad is in there. Getting killed accomplishes nothing! We can't leave Jason and this man here. They could get killed by debris."

Roland hesitated.

Michael's eyes widened. "God, man, you can't be serious. I know Jason has been a pain in the ass, but he is your son and he's hurt. I still can't believe you *shot* him."

"He was going to kill...him."

Michael shook his head with an expression that married disbelief and relief. "It's a damned good thing you don't actually know how to aim that gun. Jason may actually make it through this. And this young man, he looks like he could be one of the templates for Galahad."

"He's not. He can't be," Roland insisted, striving to control his panic. *He* had selected the genetic templates on his own. Michael did not know the truth. Michael could *not* find out the truth.

Michael shrugged. Perhaps the truth seemed irrelevant in view of the fact that the building in whose shadow they were standing seemed determined to crumble to pieces. "You have to help me get them into the car."

They moved Jason first, maneuvering his dead weight into the car with some difficulty, and then they ducked instinctively when another explosion rocked the building. On the pavement, the young man suddenly screamed, his dark eyes wide with shock, blind with pain. Every muscle tensed against excruciating agony. For the space of two seconds, he was utterly still, but then, unexpectedly, he inhaled shakily, dragging air into his lungs. His dark eyes then closed, his shoulders sagging in exhaustion.

Maybe it was safe to move him, though Roland would have been the first to admit that he was completely out of his depth. He had worked at the cutting edges of science for most of his life, but had never witnessed anything like that. He exchanged a worried glance with Michael, and then together, they lifted him off the ground and carried him to the car.

"Go, go, go!" Roland shouted as Michael slammed his foot on the accelerator. A massive rumble consumed the building, and it came crashing down with a thunderous roar. Just in time, he realized. They left just in time.

But what now, he wondered, looking back at his sons. He could not let Michael find out that he had used his own dead son, or so he had believed at that time, as the physical template for Galahad. The decision he made had violated the boundaries of acceptable personal distance in science. It had impaired his ability to assess Galahad objectively. If Michael knew, if anyone else knew, it would place doubt on everything he had done with Galahad and call into question his reputation as one of the leading minds in genetic manipulation. They could never know. No one could ever know.

"Roland!" Michael called sharply. From the faintly irritable tone, he knew that Michael must have been calling his name for a while. Michael took his attention off the road briefly to look at him. "Where should we take them?"

Where? Roland Rakehell suppressed the laughter that bubbled up at the obvious answer. "Why, back to Pioneer Labs, of course."

~*~

Alex Saunders had been very kind, and did not call Miriya any of the names she knew she deserved. *Imbecile* was probably the mildest term she would have used for herself. She had *multiple* telepathic links to Danyael's mind, and then dropped them *all*. Yes, Lucien had given the order, but she should have known better. She first broke the cardinal rule of leaving Danyael unprotected while he was channeling his healing powers far beyond what he could have endured. The fresh blood spilled on the sidewalk indicated that there had been a fight, and it could not have gone well for Danyael. And then she voluntarily gave up any means of locating him when she severed all the telepathic links.

"We'll monitor all the channels," Alex promised. "Danyael isn't dead; that much I can promise you. Both his internal and external shields will drop before he dies. It will be very significant and very nasty for everyone in the vicinity, but we haven't picked up that pulse of energy on any of our monitors. Sooner or later, he'll exercise his powers, and we'll be able to get a lock on his location. It won't be as precise as your telepathic link, but it'll get you within fifty square miles of him."

"Call me as soon as you know anything."

"Of course. Now, go get some rest," Alex said kindly. "You've had a long day."

Miriya sighed soundlessly as she hung up her cell phone.

"You okay?" Lucien asked from behind her.

"Stop being so kind." Miriya groaned. She turned to face him. Behind her, the moonlight cast its silver, ethereal glow over the grounds of Lucien's estate.

"Someone once told me that self-flagellation is both unattractive and tedious. We screwed up, Miriya. No need for you to take all the blame."

"Yeah, with protectors like us, Danyael doesn't even need any enemies. Aren't you worried for him?"

"Yes, but he's incredibly resilient. If there's any way at all to survive whatever situation he's in and return home, he'll find it."

"You have faith in him."

"He's proven himself, time and time again. He'll be all right."

Still, Miriya shook her head, disgusted with herself. "You're human. You're entitled to be..." She searched for a word that would not be completely offensive. "Clueless, when it comes to managing the nuances of mutant powers. I should have known better, though. Leaving Danyael unprotected was a big no-no. What if the pain had been too much for him? If he died, his shields would have collapsed. I didn't even consider that." She managed an ironic half-smile. "Apparently I still have quite a bit of growing up to do."

Lucien shook his head. "Will you be joining us for dinner, or would you like a tray in your room?"

She almost opted for the latter, but paused, asking, "What are you doing?"

"Dinner with Xin and Zara. Zara wasn't really in the mood for it, but at times like these, you need to be with others. Come join us."

Miriya contemplated the offer, nearly turned it down, but then Lucien held out his hand in invitation, a half-smile curving his lips, and waited.

She inhaled deeply and released her breath in a soft sigh. "All right, I'll come," she said simply, extending her hand to him. Smiling up at him, she said, "Thank you."

She filed a mental note that Lucien's charm and warmth, his natural kindness and sincerity were weapons far more potent than all the power and influence his wealth could command.

~*~

Michael steered the car into the empty lot adjacent to the building and looked out at the blackened husk of Pioneer Labs. The building cast a long, ominous shadow over the moonlit lawns. A day earlier, the laboratory had been vibrant and thriving, the heart of the most brilliant and profound work ever done in genetics. Within a mere span of twenty-four hours, Pioneer Labs, the scene of a fire and a massacre, had become a monument to human arrogance and human failure.

Michael cut the engine and leaned forward on the steering wheel. He stared at the building with an odd sort of melancholy. "I don't think this is a good idea, Roland."

"It's the safest place," Roland insisted. "The fire destroyed only the northern and eastern wings. The western wing is still completely self-sufficient and secure, and the backup generators will be able to supply all the power we need. Let me go ahead and see if I can get the generator going in the western wing. I'll be back in a bit."

Roland stepped out of the car, his footsteps tapping rhythmically on the pavement as he jogged the short distance to the front entrance of the lab. Climbing over the yellow police tape, he winced at the sound of the broken glass crunching underfoot. He felt like an intruder, as he walked down smoke-charred corridors. The laboratories where he had spent almost every hour of every day no longer seemed familiar to him. It was like seeing a former lover scarred beyond recognition.

Dismissing the nostalgia with an ironic, self-mocking smirk, he made his way toward the back of the laboratory and used his keys to unlock the utility room, where the backup generator was stored. There was enough fuel in the generator to run the entire laboratory for two weeks; surely it would be able to keep just the western wing going for a lot longer than that.

Using a flashlight by the door, he studied the instructions pasted on the wall, and after he flicked a few switches to ensure that power was routed only to the western wing, the generator hummed to life. *Done.* He made his way over to the western wing, but saw the heavy steel double doors blocking his way. *Damn.* He had forgotten to account for the security system, but nevertheless, he swiped his badge across the security console.

He was surprised when the heavy steel door slid open soundlessly in response to his security identification card. The central computers *were* located in the western wing, he recalled belatedly. How fortunate. The western wing was indeed completely self-sufficient, and the fire had not damaged it. They might as well use it.

Moving quickly through the wing, he turned on the lights and the central heating and checked each suite to be sure it was empty; no abominations or trespassing humans hid anywhere.

Finally relaxing, he returned to the car and gave Michael an affirmative nod. "Let's get them down." They moved Jason first, awkwardly and slowly, pausing several times to rest, but finally managed to install him in one of the small guest suites adjacent to Galahad's master suite. The other man was placed, without any previous discussion, in Galahad's suite.

As the young man lay on the narrow bed drifting in and out of consciousness, Roland had to remind himself constantly that the young man was the template, and not Galahad. The resemblance was so perfect, so uncanny that it would have been the most natural thing in the world to mix them up.

"Let's see out who he is." Roland searched the young man's pockets and pulled out a wallet. He read the name off a New York driver's license. "Danyael Sabre. Listed address in Brooklyn, New York. There's not much else in here. Looks like an ATM card. No credit cards. Little cash." He tossed the leather wallet down on the table. "What now?" he asked, looking up at his partner. "What do we do?" The question was rhetorical; Roland had a tendency to ask questions even when he had already made up his mind as Michael knew from their long years of association.

"We wait till he wakes, I guess."

"You know he wasn't outside Purest Humanity by accident," Roland said. "Coincidences like that don't just happen. We need to figure out what he knows about Galahad without giving any information about ourselves away."

"What exactly are you trying to say, Roland?"

"He may not know who we are. When he wakes, he probably won't know where he is, and there's no need to tell him. We need information out of him, and if he knows we're the creators of Galahad, he may not be willing to provide that information."

Michael nodded, too tired to argue for long. "Fine, Roland. We'll play it your way and see if he talks. Let's check on Jason. I'm sure we can get him through one night, but he'll probably need professional medical care by tomorrow."

"Maybe." Roland shrugged. "We'll see."

FOURTEEN

Danyael awoke as he almost always did, with a violent start, the layers of sleep ripping away—the result of an infinitely troubled childhood. He sat upright in the bed. The sheets pooled around his narrow hips, and he looked wildly around at his surroundings, clamping down on the instinctive panic he always felt when waking in unfamiliar places.

He sat on a narrow bed, on a mattress so thin he could feel the metal frame beneath him. The largeness of the room was accentuated by the sparseness of the furniture—a small table, a single chair, and shelves stripped bare. White-washed walls were devoid of decoration. In contrast, the rattan chair by the windows seemed out of place—the only element of warmth in a room that would have redefined the word *sterile*.

Imprisoned? But why? Where was he? He cursed under his breath, shoved the thin sheets aside, and pushed to his feet. The world spun crazily around him. He reached for the metal rail on the bed, but missed and fell to his hands and knees.

Not ready yet. He did not know how long he had been asleep, but obviously, his body was not anywhere near fully recovered. Weakness dragged at his limbs as he slowly pulled himself up, holding on to the bed for support.

The door to the room slid open. He looked up sharply and studied the gray haired man who entered the room. The alarm in Danyael's dark eyes gave way to confusion when he sensed a genuine concern and curiosity. No psychic shields, no malicious intent. The man's emotions surprised him because they were so far from the reactions his psychic shields typically elicited.

The man indicated the monitor on the table. "I heard a sound. Are you all right? Did you fall?"

"I…where am I? Who are you?"

"I'm Michael." The man stepped forward, closing the distance, yet staying far away enough to allow Danyael not to feel threatened. "I work here."

"Where is here? How did I get here?" Danyael straightened slowly, fighting a losing battle against the vertigo that assaulted his senses. He needed to sit down, to close his eyes, but he could not afford to display any vulnerability in so uncertain a situation.

"What do you remember?" the man asked.

If Danyael had been more alert, he might have caught the obvious omission, but with all of his efforts focused on trying to hold himself together physically, he was in no condition to engage in a battle of wits. "I...remember Jason." Flashes of images danced through his mind. He saw his brother's face, angry and hateful, looming above him. He remembered manipulating his brother's emotions, deepening his anger, darkening his hatred, betting it all on the off chance that it would impair his brother's ability to fight long enough for Danyael to win.

And then pain. Searing. Intense. Unbearable.

Unending.

"The young man you were fighting." It was not exactly a question.

Danyael nodded slowly. Speaking was difficult, took too much effort. "Is he all right?"

"Uh, Jason is here too. He's resting in another room. He was shot, but he's stable."

His brother, still alive. Danyael's hesitation was barely perceptible. "May I see him please?"

"This way. Can you walk?"

Danyael nodded again, once, slowly. Michael swiped his card over the security panel to unlock the door and then ushered Danyael out before him. A man stood in the corridor, apparently on his way to the suite. He paused with a startled jerk as Michael and Danyael walked out, and then he stepped back without introducing himself, allowing them to pass.

Michael led the way into a suite several feet down the corridor. The suite was far smaller, but decorated with warm earth tones, a large bed, and furnishings designed to provide both utility and comfort. The room was a world apart from the large, sterile suite he had occupied, but Danyael scarcely noticed the differences in decor as his gaze locked on his brother. He sat on the edge of the bed and carefully touched the edges of the bandage wrapped around Jason's chest. His empathic powers surged; he assessed the damage, estimating—and wincing at—the energy required to heal Jason.

He knew that not healing Jason was a perfectly viable option, but his mind could not wrap around that possibility. This was his *brother*. If he could not bring himself to heal his own brother, what kind of monster would that make him? "He's stable, but the bullet is still inside and needs to be removed. Do you have operating tools? Scalpel, tweezers, a place where I can work?"

The two older men exchanged cautious glances. "There's a research station down the hall. You can use the table there. We do have some surgical instruments, but there's no anesthesia or even antiseptic."

"It's fine. I won't need it."

Neither voiced any other objection. Danyael had taken charge with cool, confident competence, and they deferred to him. At his request, the men carried Jason into one of the research stations and laid him on the stainless steel table.

Jason stirred as they placed him on the operating table. Hastily, they stepped out of sight, and it was only Danyael Jason saw when his eyes fully opened. They narrowed instantly. Jason, his face twisting with the pain of his injury, raised himself off the table with a great deal of effort to spit into Danyael's face. "I *hate* you."

"I know," Danyael said simply. His dark, fathomless eyes—the only feature he shared with his brother—were regretful, but his expression gave nothing else away. "Rest now," he said quietly. His empathic powers rippled out like a wave, gentle but irresistible, easing past Jason's barriers of virulent hatred, channeling an intense peace and calm to lure his brother into a sleep so deep that it was almost a coma. Jason's head fell back onto the table, his eyes fluttered closed and within moments, his breathing became deep and even.

Danyael swallowed hard, painfully, and then got started. The two men watched in silence as he worked with easy, swift expertise. He had done that before, many, many times. He used no anesthesia, no antiseptic. He skipped steps, broke rules, and yet worked with the sureness of someone who knew exactly what he was doing.

Distantly, he was aware of Michael's growing curiosity, curiosity that bordered on confusion.

"You're a doctor," Michael surmised quietly, more to himself than to Danyael.

Danyael nodded once in brief acknowledgement as he used tweezers to extract the bullet. It clattered, a tiny sound when he dropped it on the tray, and then he set his surgical instruments down.

He did not sew Jason back up, did not use needle or surgical thread to seal the incision he had made in Jason's chest to extract the bullet. Danyael simply placed his hand on Jason's chest and closed his eyes. It took a moment to focus his exhausted powers and brace himself for the additional cost and burden of bearing Jason's injury, but his mutant powers surged easily, ungrudgingly out of him and into Jason, healing from within, cleansing the wound and repairing the injury. The two men watched in slack-jawed amazement as the open incision slowly closed before their disbelieving eyes and new skin sealed over the cut, leaving nothing, not even a scar, to mark its location.

"What *are* you?" Michael asked softly.

Danyael's eyes opened slowly, pain flashing through the dark depths. He turned his face in Michael's direction to acknowledge the question, but did not look up. "I'm a mutant," he explained, his eyes still downcast. He said nothing else. He waited for the condemnation he knew would follow.

It was not his fault; he had no control over it, but it did not matter. The condemnation was inevitable. Fortunately, he had been trained to deal with it. Don't brace for it; it makes the blow, when it does come, that much harder to take. Open your heart, let it wash over you, through you.

Then let it go.

His breathing was jagged and uneven as he inhaled through spikes of pain. His hands clenched and unclenched reflexively through each spasm. *Finish this. Just say what's in your heart. I can take it. I'll be all right.* It was just that....

He clenched his teeth. It was just that it would be too hard to take on top of the physical pain.

"You look like you need to rest," Michael said, his voice quiet.

A muscle twitched in Danyael's smooth cheek. His jaw tensed. Slowly, he nodded.

"Will you let me help you?"

Surprised, Danyael looked up at Michael, meeting his gaze steadily for the first time. "Yes, thank you," Danyael whispered. Nausea swirled in the pit of his stomach, blackness at the edge of his vision. He had been petrified at the thought of moving, afraid that he would collapse and pass out and that his psychic shields would fall. With help from Michael, he stumbled toward the door of the research station, flinching from the icy blast of the other man's disgust and loathing as they moved past him.

He did not understand Michael's kindness any more than he understood the other man's disdain for him, but he did not have the energy or even the desire to alter it. In the grand scheme of things, he supposed it did not matter what people felt about him. He could not pretend he did not care. He was an empath; he felt intensely—perhaps too intensely—but he had learned to accept the fact that his feelings meant little to others, and that there was no reason to take their indifference to heart.

It was a struggle, even with Michael's help, to make it back to the suite, but they managed slowly, and without incident. Danyael was relieved when Michael lowered him to the bed, grateful that he could stretch out on the thin mattress and close his eyes against the world that spun around him.

"Are you all right? Can I get you anything? Food? Drink?" Michael's voice sounded far away.

Danyael shook his head weakly, his shoulders hunched and tensed against the cold that consumed him from within. He was only dimly aware that Michael had pulled the sheets up to his shoulders and hurried away before returning several minutes later with a heavier blanket that he wrapped tightly around him. "Thank you," Danyael breathed so quietly that it was almost inaudible.

"You're welcome, Danyael," Michael responded, watching as the mutant drifted into restless sleep. Michael stood by Danyael's bedside for a long, silent moment before he left the suite, locking it behind him. He found Roland in the large lounge, seated in a chair by the window. "Should we get Jason back to his suite?" he asked.

Roland shrugged. He seemed unusually dejected, even morose. "He's a mutant," he muttered, his voice laced with profound disgust.

"I don't see how that was his fault, Roland," Michael said, his tone level and reasonable. "Maybe we should count ourselves lucky we used him merely as the physical template for Galahad and somehow managed to avoid creating a mutant in the process."

Roland hesitated. "Did he say anything about Jason, why Jason hated him?"

Michael chuckled under his breath. "Say anything? It took all his energy just to say 'thank you.' No, he didn't say anything about Jason, though it's obvious, isn't it? Jason hates Galahad and hates Danyael because they look alike."

"So you think Danyael knows about Galahad?"

Michael recalled how simply Danyael had accepted Jason's hatred. "That's almost a certainty. By the way, the central computer just completed its analysis of Danyael's blood sample. He's a perfect match for Galahad's physical genetic code. How could that have happened, Roland?" he asked pointedly.

Roland merely grunted and then turned away to stare out of the window. "We could keep him, you know." The words were quietly uttered

"Keep who?"

"Danyael. If Galahad is dead, we could keep Danyael. No one would ever know. They would think Galahad was still in our custody."

Michael stared at him aghast. "You mean pretend that Danyael is Galahad? That's not right, Roland. I'm sure he's got friends and family waiting for him. We can't keep him imprisoned here and tell the world that he's Galahad, just to save whatever's left of our reputations."

Michael paused and stared at his partner. They had worked together for a long time. Michael recognized the sullen, stubborn set of the jaw and knew that Roland was unconvinced. Michael could not believe he even needed to convince Roland that the proposal was blatantly, obviously wrong on so many fronts. Michael shook his head, exasperated with Roland's flexible sense of morality and ethics.

"We could lose everything, Michael," Roland said, his voice quiet, almost sad. "Everything we've worked for these past twenty-five years, our entire professional career, is tied up in Galahad."

Michael understood where Roland was coming from, but he did not fully understand *why*. Maybe the problem was not with Roland's morals. It was with Roland's overwhelming focus and dedication to his life's ambition. That ambition had been realized with the birth of Galahad, and now that it was threatened, Roland would have done anything—even sacrifice his firstborn—to cling to that dream. Sacrificing the freedom of a mere stranger would not have registered as even a blip on that scale. What could he say? He shook his head and placed a gentle hand on Roland's shoulder. "Hang in there for a while longer, will you?" His voice was kind, reassuring. "We don't know anything for certain about Galahad yet. Maybe he's all right. Maybe this will all work out somehow."

And maybe the moon is made of blue cheese, Roland thought sourly as Michael walked away, leaving him alone with his thoughts. *A mutant.* He scowled as his thoughts turned to Luke, to Danyael. *Damned shame. What a bloody waste of a life.*

~*~

Miriya was awakened by the ringing of her cell phone. She glanced at the clock on her bedside table, 5:49 a.m. Still pitch black outside. She came instantly awake when she saw the phone number. "What is it, Alex?"

"The monitors just picked up Danyael's primary and secondary power signatures."

"Great!" She tossed the sheets aside and climbed out of bed. "Where is it?"

"Boonsboro, Maryland."

"How far is it?"

"About an hour out from McLean."

"We'll be there. Wait." She froze as Alex's words fully sank in. "Did you say *Boonsboro, Maryland*?"

"Yes, I did. Quiet, rural neighborhood. Wide fields and rolling horse pastures. The octagonal structure of Pioneer Laboratories is out of place amid all the farm houses. Quite an eyesore, actually."

Miriya's eyes narrowed as she fought down a combination of confusion and fear. "What would Danyael be doing back at Pioneer Laboratories?"

"Use your imagination, Miriya. He's probably with Jason Rakehell. What do you think Jason would do to someone who looks like Galahad?"

Miriya's blood ran cold. "Faked media event. Public execution at the place of his 'birth.' Then Jason can claim he's the hero of humanity—he's killed Galahad. Crap, we have to get to him."

"That's the most likely theory. There could be others, Miriya, because that theory wouldn't necessarily explain why we picked up Danyael's power signatures. Just get out there as quickly as you can. I'm sending a team in as backup as well. They'll likely rendezvous with you by the time you get to Pioneer Labs."

"I thought you said you didn't want the mutants involved."

"I'd like to keep Danyael alive," Alex conceded. "And if I have to get another enforcer or two out of bed early to see to it, it'd still be a good investment in a life worth saving."

"I'm surprised you never made Danyael an enforcer."

"He turned down the offer four times, maybe five. Go get him, Miriya. Bring him home safe."

She hung up the phone and then dressed quickly. Five minutes later, she was pounding on Lucien's door. He opened it within moments, his eyes alert. "You found him?"

Nodding grimly, she said, "He's at Boonsboro, Maryland."

Obviously Lucien was a great deal more awake than she had been when first told. *"Pioneer Labs?"* She could tell from the anguish in his eyes that he was mentally racing over the same possibilities. She did not miss the resolute gleam in his blue eyes as he started to close the door on her. "Wake Zara and Xin, will you? We're leaving in ten minutes."

Why would the lights be on?

Galahad crouched at the edge of the clearing and stared at the husk of Pioneer Labs. The pale light of the early dawn spread over the complex. Soot darkened the northern and eastern walls of the building, the extensive damage clearly evident from the outside, but the western wing was intact. Lights gleamed softly through the windows.

Just one car in the parking lot, he noted, as he crept around the perimeter of the building toward the western wing, moving soundlessly over the damp grass. He could not imagine why anyone would even be there. There was nothing left at the laboratories, but clearly someone else thought otherwise.

Galahad had a destination in mind, the large suite at the furthest western edge of the octagonal complex. He kept his head low, crouching to keep beneath the height of the windowpanes. He could not risk being seen, being identified. The pace was agonizingly slow, but the caution was necessary. As a result, his clothes were damp with dew by the time he arrived at his destination.

He had no clear expectation of what he would see through the window of the western suite, but his list of possibilities had certainly not included a beautiful young man fast asleep on the single narrow bed, curled beneath layers of heavy blankets. He breathed softly. "Danyael."

But how, and why?

It did not matter. He sank back, out of sight, as his mind churned through the new information. Danyael was asleep on the bed that had been his, imprisoned in the room that had been his prison. It was surreal, like looking at himself through a distorted mirror, looking into a world where reality had been displaced.

If somehow Danyael had been mistaken for him, that meant that he could be free. He could be free to embrace the fullness of life, while Danyael took his place.

He could almost taste the sweetness of it on his tongue as he basked in the thrill of that possibility. No one would know. The scientists would, but protecting the secret meant even more to them than his freedom to him. Their reputations, their lives' work were at stake. Danyael would know, but who would believe him? He would have no contact with the outside world, no way to get the word out. Danyael would languish in there, as Galahad once had.

The sweetness then curdled, souring the pit of his stomach. He clenched his teeth against the hollow ache. He had tasted freedom. He wanted it, needed it, craved it with every fiber of his being, but he could not walk away from Danyael.

Pioneer Labs was his personal hell. He had spent twenty-five years in it. It was not Danyael's to endure, but nor would it be his, never again. He would never return to his prison as a captive, but he had no intention of being caught. His hours-long journey from Washington, D.C. back to Pioneer Labs had driven home one single fact: He could not make his way in the world alone. Not yet. He knew too little. He had too little.

He desperately needed allies. Danyael had proven a willing ally and a powerful one. More importantly, Danyael was the key to securing Lucien's aid.

All in all, Danyael was a risk well worth taking.

Moving as quickly as he could, Galahad returned the way he had come. He paused by the broken front doors of Pioneer Laboratories, hesitating before taking the final step that would commit him to what he had come to do. It struck him as singularly ironic that he was trying to break into the laboratory, instead of making good his escape.

He inhaled deeply and then crossed the threshold.

He had rarely been permitted outside the confines of the western wing in the twenty-five years he had spent at the laboratories, but it was not hard to navigate around an octagon that had only two directions in which to go, forward or backward. A security door blocked off his access to the western wing, but without hesitation, he pulled out the access card Zara had given him and held it against the panel. The red light flashed to green and the door slid silently back.

He knew where he was. It was home, cold, sterile, and unwelcoming, and he knew his way around. There was no sign of anyone, but he was not going out of his way to tempt fate either by searching all the rooms. He headed straight toward the double doors that barred the way to his suite. Another swipe of the access card opened the door. *Bless you, Xin,* he thought as he slid the card back into his pocket and raced toward the bed.

"Danyael?" Galahad whispered, shaking him gently. Danyael stirred slightly, his brow furrowing into a crease of pain, but he did not wake. Galahad swept sweat-soaked locks from Danyael's fevered brow. The mutant was shivering hard under those heavy blankets, yet burning with fever. "Danyael, please." Galahad shook Danyael with greater urgency. "We have to go."

FIFTEEN

For several seconds, Jason Rakehell stared blankly up at the blindingly bright florescent lights as they wavered into focus.

Where the hell was he?

He sat up slowly, pushed aside the bloodstained sheets covering his body, and ran a hand over his chest. There was no evidence of injury, yet he remembered the staggering impact of the bullet as it pierced him, remembered looking up with stunned disbelief into his father's dark eyes and expressionless face, and then down at the gun his father held. He remembered Michael Cochran, his father's partner, running toward him, toward Danyael.

He possessed just enough memory and context to offer up a very good guess as to where he was.

Pioneer Laboratories.

Danyael was here too; he had no doubt of that. He picked up the bloodied bullet from the small tray beside the operating table. He had not imagined getting hit by the bullet. Danyael must have removed the bullet and then healed him.

It would not change anything.

Danyael was a fool if he thought that a single moment of kindness would make up for the fact that he had driven his mother to madness and deprived his brother of her love and care. A single right did not make up for a lifetime of wrongs.

Yes, Danyael was here. He had to be here somewhere. His father too.

He had never had an opportunity like this: a single chance to set everything right.

Jason picked up his shirt, which had been carelessly discarded on the floor beside the operating table, and put it on. His jaw set, his eyes gleaming with hatred and glittering with anticipation, he stepped out of the research station. He knew that a series of guest suites lined the hallways, with Galahad's suite at one end and the lounge at the other. Avoiding Galahad's suite, he searched each of the other suites, finding them empty, but chancing upon his father's weapon of choice, a Glock, in the suite his father had selected for his own use. A quick check confirmed that he had bullets enough to spare, one for his brother, one for his father, and even a few extras, just to be sure the job was thoroughly completed.

As he stepped out into the hallway, he heard the low murmur of voices from the lounge. He recognized his father's voice and Michael Cochran's. Just as well. It was long past time to finish the nightmare that began with Galahad's creation.

Stepping into the lounge, he brought his weapon up to aim it at his father's face. "Good morning, gentlemen. Am I in time for breakfast? Stay seated," he warned Michael, who had started to rise from his seat by the window.

Michael froze, and then slowly, carefully lowered himself into the chair.

"Jason, what are you doing?" Roland demanded irritably. "Put the damn gun down."

"Oh, I will eventually, after I kill Danyael."

"Jason, there's no reason to do that," Michael spoke quietly, his voice calm, though his dark eyes were alert, darting anxiously from side to side.

"I take it you've met him. What do you think of him?"

"I know you're angry with Galahad, but this isn't Danyael's fault. He's just the template."

"He's not *just* the fucking template."

Michael's expression of genuine confusion did not change.

Jason's gaze darted from Michael Cochran back to his father. A grin dawned over Jason's face. "He doesn't know, does he?"

"Know what?" Michael demanded, turning to look at Roland.

"Keeping secrets from your partner now? Does he know where you got your templates from, father?"

"He knows I got them from the genetic IDs of dead people, Jason," Roland said. His hands clenched into the armrests of the sofa so tightly that the veins stood out on his arms.

"Well, it's too bad one of them didn't want to stay dead."

Michael shook his head. "That's not necessarily a bad thing, Jason. Danyael is the closest thing Galahad has to a brother right now."

Jason burst out laughing hysterically. "A *brother*? That's perfect. That makes us all brothers. Should we call him Luke again?" He did not take his eyes off his father. He did not need to look at Michael to know that Michael finally understood what had happened years before.

Michael's jaw dropped in disbelief. "Luke? Your son who died in the car accident with your wife? You used Luke's DNA as the physical template for Galahad?"

"He was dead! And his genetic code was already stored in our registry. He didn't need it anymore!"

"He was your son. He was out of bounds! Who else did you use? Are there any other 'dead' relatives or friends living through Galahad that I should know about?"

"I did what I felt was the right thing at that time. None of this would have ever come to light anyway, if that damn mutant had just stayed dead!"

"How is *any* of this Danyael's fault?"

"Stop defending him!" Jason snarled at Michael. "You know *nothing* about him. He drove my mother to madness until she finally snapped and tried to kill him. If she had not gotten into an accident on the way home, she'd be alive and well now."

Michael shook his head. "Danyael was just a child when all this happened!"

"Danyael is a fucking alpha mutant!"

"I don't care if he's an alpha mutant or the devil himself!" Michael shot to his feet, too angry to care about the gun in Jason's hand. "How old was he, two years old? Three years old? For God's sake, it's time *humans* started taking responsibility for their actions instead of blaming a three-year-old *mutant*. If she had sought help, someone would have figured out pretty damn quickly that Danyael was a mutant and then taken the right corrective measures that you would for a young alpha."

"You're protecting him? Why are you defending him? What about me? I was only seven when my mother was stolen from me, and my father was too damned obsessed with my brother's physical twin to come home from work at night!"

"You're doing such a great job watching out for yourself," Roland interjected, his tone scornful. "You don't need anyone doing it for you."

"I know exactly how to watch out for myself, and it'll start by ending this nightmare that you started, Father, twenty-five years ago, when you created Galahad. When it's dead, maybe you'll remember that you actually have a *real* family."

"Where is he? Where is Galahad?"

"Danyael will know. He and his friends have been protecting it. Now, get up and move," Jason gestured with his gun, stepping aside from the door. He paused, glancing at the monitor on the table when it crackled.

A familiar voice came though softly. "Danyael? Danyael, please, we have to go."

Galahad.

Jason stared at the monitor in disbelief. Galahad? Here? But how, and why? Why would Galahad have returned to his prison? How had he even known that Danyael was there?

The answers, Jason concluded, were irrelevant. They would certainly be, if he had his way. Galahad would be dead, and all would once again be right with the world.

He smiled slowly, his lethal intent clear. "It's time for a long overdue family reunion."

~*~

Danyael's eyes flickered open briefly and then shut again, a pitiful defense against the blinding spotlights overhead. Shafts of pain pulsed through his skull, and he whispered a protest, a weak moan that he could scarcely believe was his own voice.

"Danyael." Galahad sounded relieved. "Can you stand? I need to get you out of here."

Galahad's anxiety battered at his psychic shields. He opened his eyes, though he kept them narrowed in a feeble attempt to keep out most of the light. Galahad's face shifted in and out of focus in front of him. "What... doing here?"

"Trying to get you out." Galahad's mouth tugged up into a smile. "Here, let me help." He slipped an arm around Danyael's shoulders, but Danyael resisted, pulling away from him, cringing from the physical contact even in, or perhaps because of, his weakened state.

"Just need a moment," Danyael whispered. He rolled onto his stomach and let his head hang over the side of the bed while he struggled against the nausea that swirled in his stomach. The nausea threatened to bring up the meager remnants of his last meal, which seemed like a lifetime ago.

Several moments passed before he inhaled deeply, grateful when his stomach did not lurch and his head did not spin. "I think I can manage." He swung his feet over the side of the bed and stood up. Willpower kept him going, willpower and a general inability to know when to quit. "What time is it?"

"About seven in the morning."

"The next day?" Danyael had lost track of several days once before when he overextended his healing powers and slipped into a near coma for nearly sixty-five hours.

"Yes, the next day. Can you walk? We have to go."

He nodded, just a step behind Galahad, as Galahad led the way back toward the door. "Where are we?"

Galahad looked back sharply over his shoulder. "You don't know? You're at Pioneer Labs. This used to be my room."

Shock flashed through Danyael, barely reined in by exquisitely cultivated equilibrium. He looked around the bare, stark room; he had seen county prison cells with more furniture and personalization. It was a wonder Galahad

had not gone stark raving mad while imprisoned in there. "How did I get here?"

"You don't know that either?"

He shook his head slowly. "No, I...there was so much pain." He lowered his eyes; *that* memory was vivid. He did not think he would survive it. "I just don't remember. Jason...Jason's here too. He was shot; I removed the bullet and healed him."

Galahad's eyes narrowed in disbelief and disgust. "We're going to have a long talk one day about your proclivities for keeping alive people who want you dead. If that's not suicidal, I don't know what is."

"He's my brother."

"He'd kill you if he had a chance. You need to be smarter about things like that if you intend to make it to the ripe old age of thirty." Galahad reached for his access card, but before he could hold it over the security panel, the door slid open soundlessly. He looked up at the two figures standing outside the door and froze.

Roland Rakehell and Michael Cochran.

Behind Galahad, Danyael stopped short as well. The faintest flicker of anguish seeped through Danyael's emotional shields as the mutant looked upon his father and recognized him for the first time.

"Step back slowly, Galahad. You too, Danyael," Jason's voice came from behind the two scientists. "Don't crowd the doorway. We have a lot to talk about."

Galahad backed away slowly, his eyes locked on the gun in Jason's right hand. Danyael stepped back too, and Jason pushed Roland and Michael ahead of him into the suite.

Jason was the last to enter the suite. He locked the door behind him before turning to survey the four people who stood in a semi-circle in front of him. "I know what you're capable of, Danyael." His voice was a harsh snarl. "If I even so much as think you're fucking with my emotions, I'll shoot Galahad through the heart, and not even your healing powers will be able to bring him back. Do you understand?"

Danyael nodded slowly, wordlessly. It took all his energy to maintain his emotional shields against the hurricane force of Jason's maelstrom of fury and hatred—a maelstrom he had personally agitated. He could not alter the path of Jason's emotions anymore, not without significant effort, not without the kind of energy that he could no longer spare.

"Do you understand?" Jason roared, striding forward. With a single, swift motion, he drove the side of his fist, clad around the pistol grip, into Danyael's right cheek. The mutant staggered, but he caught himself before he fell and straightened slowly. "Answer me!" Jason shouted into Danyael's face. "I said, do you understand?"

A single word: "Yes."

Two sets of dark eyes locked, black hatred in one set, quiet pain in the other. It was Jason who first looked away as he took a few steps back. "I'm being remiss. You haven't seen our father in a long time, Danyael. Perhaps some introductions are in order?"

"That won't be necessary, Jason," Roland said tersely. "What are you doing?"

Jason smiled. "How often does one get to be in the same room with the son he neglected, the son he believed was dead, and the son he created? We're not going to waste this opportunity. I want you to choose, Father," he said flatly, all traces of mocking humor disappearing from his voice. He waved his hand toward Galahad and Danyael. "If you could have only one, who would you choose?"

Danyael knew the answer.

No words were needed when he could sense his father's scorn. Waves of disgust and loathing flowed out of his father, washing against Danyael's psychic shields, wearing them down with their intensity and persistency.

He did not understand why. Perhaps it was because he was a mutant. Perhaps it was because—despite the similarity in their appearance—he was a shadow of Galahad's perfection. Perhaps it was because his life was still a wreck, despite how far he thought he had managed to come.

The exact reason or reasons did not matter. His father did not want him. His mother had not wanted him either. He looked up at Jason and stared down at the barrel of the gun pointed at him. His brother wanted him dead. His family, the last line of defense for most people, was resolutely set against him. Maybe they were all completely dysfunctional.

Or maybe he was. After all, he was the single common factor in all those ruined relationships, those ruined lives.

My fault, he acknowledged silently. He could not change the past. He had ruined the collective lives of his family, the ones for whom he should have been the last line of defense.

He had killed his own mother.

There was nothing he could do, not in an entire lifetime, to make up for what he had done to them, nothing he could do to earn their forgiveness.

Nothing at all.

Galahad knew the answer.

Roland Rakehell looked steadily at him. He did not even spare a glance at Danyael. He did not even pretend to consider. Glancing over at Danyael, Galahad saw the exact moment when Danyael's heart broke. Anguish swirled in to mix with the quiet loneliness that seemed permanently etched into Danyael's eyes. He saw the long eyelashes lower over the dark eyes to conceal the pain, saw Danyael's jaw tense, his hands clench into fists. He had learned to read Danyael's reactions over the course of only one day in his company. Danyael was bracing himself, reinforcing his shields, trying to keep his emotions, his heartache from breaking through.

Danyael was still trying to protect the people who hated him.

Galahad did not understand it, could *never* understand it, but he was starting to understand friendship, its risks and costs. And perhaps a little about its rewards.

He had never done before what he was attempting to do now, but there was nothing to be lost in trying. He reached out with his mind, casting his thoughts toward the copse of trees on the far southern side of the laboratory grounds. *Help me.*

In the shadow of the trees, something monstrous stirred.

Jason knew the answer. He knew the answer long before his father gave voice to his decision. His father cared nothing for him. He would care even less for a son he had believed dead for more than twenty years. Luke—Danyael—had served his purpose as the physical template for Galahad. There was no use for him anymore.

In fact, Danyael was worth more dead than alive. With the original template destroyed, Galahad's supremacy could not be challenged. His beauty would once again have no equal. With the original physical template destroyed, no one could challenge Roland Rakehell's claim on creating the only perfect being in the world.

A slow grin spread over Jason's face when his father made the pronouncement he had expected. "I choose Galahad."

"Well, well, Danyael." Jason looked into the dark eyes of his hated brother and saw quiet acceptance swirl in the depths. "It looks like you've lost." He braced himself to feel something, anything. He had expected his brother to pull a crazy mutant stunt to save his own miserable life, but he felt nothing, nothing at all.

Apparently Danyael had chosen not to risk Galahad's life by exercising his empathic abilities to save his own. He wondered why. "Fucking grow a spine, baby brother." He spit the words out like a curse. "They stole your genetic ID to create him. If you wanted revenge, you would be more than justified. You're pitiful. Sickeningly pitiful." His lips curled in disgust. "Our father doesn't want you, so you're going to die. But don't worry. You won't be alone for long. There are enough bullets here for all of us, for Galahad, for our beloved father, even for me. One happy family." Insanity gleamed in the dark eyes. "We'll be together forever."

His finger tightened deliberately on the trigger.

~*~

"Danyael's here," Miriya announced the moment she stepped out of the car. She could sense the low hum of his power signature, shimmering beneath his shields, as she did a quick mental sweep of the area. Her jaw dropped, her green eyes wide with confusion and unexpected delight. "And Galahad!"

"Galahad?" Zara turned on her, the initial bewilderment giving way to incautious hope. "He's alive? He's here?"

Miriya nodded. "This way!" She raced toward the western wing, following Danyael's power signature like a homing beacon. Zara and Lucien easily kept pace beside her, and within seconds, they were standing outside the reinforced windows of Galahad's suite, looking in with growing horror at the tableau unfolding within.

Zara's violet eyes sought out and locked on Galahad. Lucien sought out Danyael. It was Miriya whose telepathic ability picked up on the low, inhuman moan first.

Brother...brother....

She spun around and saw five massive, hideous shapes amble straight toward them out of the surroundings woods.

"Lucien!" she shouted.

There was a flash of light from the Glock. Danyael lurched and dropped to his knees, a hand pressed against his chest. He lowered his head to stare at the blood seeping out from between his trembling fingers.

Lucien's mind went blank with shock. "Danyael! No!"

The Glock spit out a single bullet, and Danyael jerked from the shocking impact, his dark eyes suddenly wide and ablaze with pain. The world inched into slow motion as adrenaline raced through his system, trying to stimulate a flight-or-fight response. Reflexively, his left hand went to his chest, to press against the wound that the bullet had torn through his flesh. His legs trembled and gave out beneath him. He slowly crumpled to his knees.

Strong arms caught him as he fell. Michael Cochran, Danyael realized dimly. There was a flurry of motion on the other side of the room. Galahad had launched himself at Jason the moment Jason had fired the gun, and in seconds, had both disarmed and disabled him. He pushed Jason face first into the carpet and then jammed his knee into his back to keep him there.

Roland Rakehell rushed like an anxious mother hen to Galahad, examining him for nonexistent injuries while blind to the son who lay bleeding several feet away. "You know why I choose you! You're perfect. We made you perfect."

"To hell with perfect. Danyael's your *son!*" Galahad snarled, pushing Roland away. His voice reflected anger and disgust. "Your own flesh and blood. How could you *not* choose him?"

"He's nothing to me. He never was."

Danyael closed his eyes at his father's words and allowed the heartache to wash over him. *Almost over now. It'll be all right. It's almost over.*

Every breath was agony, like a knife running through his lungs. He could feel the blood gushing out between his fingers, keeping pace with the beating of his heart. The bullet had pierced his vena cava. Unconsciousness was less than thirty seconds away, death less than two minutes.

"Hang in there." Michael pressed his hand over Danyael's. "We'll get help; just hang in there."

Not enough time. His field of vision blurred as he slipped into hypovolemic shock from his rapidly dropping blood volume. *I need to finish this….*

The pale morning light washing in through the open windows disappeared suddenly as massive shadows moved to block the sun. Galahad glanced toward the window as the five abominations closed in on Pioneer Laboratories. Outside, Lucien, Zara and Miriya turned to face the creatures in a battle they had no chance of winning, but the abominations lumbered past them, disinterested, and crashed through the reinforced glass window. *Brother.*

Brothers. Galahad acknowledged the five creatures that had fought and killed scores of people in an attempt to reach him, to save him from the humans who were known for their cruelty.

Kill. Their eyes glittered with anticipation as their gazes shuttled back and forth between Roland Rakehell and Michael Cochran.

*No, wait…*Galahad instructed, looking up at Lucien, Zara, and Miriya as they clambered in through the broken window. Lucien rushed to Danyael's side, and Zara to Galahad's. Miriya knelt down beside Danyael, her green eyes abstracted as she reached out with her mind and searched rapidly through Danyael's fading consciousness, grasping the severity of his injury. She pulled out a cell phone and hit the speed dial. "Danyael's got a minute to live. Where the bloody hell is the team? We need a healer here, now!"

Danyael whispered into Miriya's mind. *Jason, father, touch them.*

She hung up the phone and looked up sharply. "Bring Jason here. His father too."

Galahad wrested an unwilling Jason Rakehell to his feet and dragged him over to Danyael. Roland Rakehell cast a single glance at the cool menace in Zara's eyes and complied without a struggle.

Need to touch them.

"Closer," Miriya ordered. "Here, Danyael," she said, her tone gentler as she placed Danyael's bloodied, misshapen left hand on Jason's wrist and his right hand on his father's.

"What is he doing?"

Miriya looked up at Lucien. "Killing them, I hope," she said simply.

Danyael's inner shields—the emotional barricade sheltering the painful memories that fueled his most lethal powers—never dropped. They never even faltered. When he unleashed his empathic powers, it was with agonizing slowness. With exquisite precision, he sieved through their emotions, balancing the ones he could adjust, absorbing the ones he could not.

Miriya was the first to gasp in surprise and horror, as her mind, linked with Danyael's, understood his intent. "Danyael," she breathed, tears filling her eyes. "What are you doing?" *You can't do this. They hate each other, and you. The emotions you absorb from them will turn into self-hatred. You can't live with that in you. You can't live like that. No one can.*

It doesn't matter; I'm dying, Miriya. This—all this—is my fault. If I can give them back each other...

"You stupid, stupid man," Miriya whispered. *They don't deserve this.*

Everyone deserves a second chance. Luce gave me mine. I can give them theirs.

He arched in pain, throwing his head back as his powers— dangerously unstable—surged through the emotional connection he had created between his father and his brother. He stood at the nexus, filtering and absorbing all the twisted emotions that had defined their relationship with each other. Each emotion he pulled into himself wrenched and tore through him in ways that made the physical injury he had suffered, the injury that would actually kill him, seem trivial in comparison. *Just a bit more. Almost there.* He drew in a strangled gasp of air and his eyes opened, glassy with anguish. A silent, agonized scream caught in his throat.

"What's going on?" Lucien demanded. He yanked Danyael's hands away from Jason and Roland. The physical and emotional connection broken, Danyael slumped over in Michael's arms. His dark eyes fluttered closed. His breathing was rapid, shallow. Blood pumped out of the bullet wound, keeping pace with the beat of his faltering heart.

Miriya slipped her hand into his limp hand. She reinforced her connection to him, wrapping her most formidable psychic shields around Danyael's mind, bracing for the moment when he died, when all his shields dropped. Her shields were going to be the only thing standing between everyone in the vicinity and mass suicide.

She looked up at Lucien, tears in her eyes. She did not need words. Lucien knew the end was near too. His eyes seared with the anticipated loss of his closest friend as he slipped his hand into Danyael's other hand and lowered his forehead gently to touch Danyael's forehead in a final gesture of friendship, of farewell.

Danyael's skin was cold, clammy. He did not even have the strength to shiver any more.

"Luce," he whispered, his breath rattling in his throat. His eyes were closed, but for a single moment, a smile lingered on his lips before fading slowly as he stopped fighting the irresistible riptide of darkness and finally allowed it to carry him away.

SIXTEEN

Miriya winced. Danyael's shields were collapsing, disintegrating, at first slowly and then with increasing speed. The pressure against her mind mounted. She closed her eyes, reached for Lucien's hands, and then held on to him desperately, trying to draw strength from him. If she faltered, they were all dead.

Miriya, open the goddamned door!

"Get the door!" she ordered tersely and then bit down on her lower lip as the pressure pounded through her mind. She sensed a flurry of motion. Someone must have unlocked and opened the door of the suite, because the suite was suddenly flooded with a host of very familiar power signatures. The pressure around her mind lightened noticeably as another telepath linked to her, reinforcing her shields and sharing the burden of protecting Danyael's mind.

Her eyes flashed open. The room was suddenly very crowded. She recognized Alex Saunders first and sighed with relief. He had come, and brought with him Jake Hansen, one of her closest friends and a fellow enforcer, an alpha telepath and telekinetic.

Thank God you're here. Your timing was perfect. I owe you.

Jake Hansen's voice chucked softly into her mind. *Yes, you do. I was having such a great dream when Alex hauled my ass out of bed and told me to hop into the car. If you're really serious about owing me, you can give us our first-born son.*

You'll have a long wait coming, Miriya pointed out, a smile in her voice now that she knew the crisis was marginally under control again.

Strong little bastard. Jake winced at the crushing weight of Danyael's emotions as the empath's shields collapsed entirely. *The next time I make fun of an empath, remind me about today, will you?*

Remind you? Hell, no. As far as I'm concerned, no one is ever going to hear of this absolutely mortifying moment. Not that anyone will ever believe that it took two alpha telepaths to contain an empath.

An alpha empath. At this point, the words alpha empath are the only words salvaging what's left of my dignity and pride. Bloody hell. He's so damned unhappy. How does he get through each day without slicing his wrists?

By locking all those memories and their associated emotions behind those shields and pretending they don't exist. He's got denial down to an art form. How long do we have to keep the shields up?

Until Mrs. Crenshaw saves his life. Jake looked up and nodded as an older woman, dressed in a bright pink and purple floral blouse and matching ankle-length skirt, scurried in through the open door. The woman was out of breath and panting from the effort of keeping up with Alex and Jake as they had raced through the corridors of Pioneer Labs. She looked like someone's grandmother. Wavy gray hair framed a round, cheerful face. The sparkle in her brown eyes became grimly determined as she knelt down beside Danyael and placed both hands on his chest.

She's not an empathic healer, is she? Miriya asked, slightly alarmed.

No, fortunately not. Empathic healers absorb the injury, which is why they usually have trouble working with brain and heart injuries. In her file, she claims that she aligns the frequency of the body with the core frequency of the earth.

Miriya summarized it in four words: *New age mumbo jumbo.*

It sure beats saying 'How the hell do I know,' which is what most mutants say when asked to explain the basis of their powers. At least she's stabilizing him.

Miriya could sense it too. She did not know exactly what Mrs. Crenshaw's healing powers were doing to Danyael, but whatever it was, they worked. Danyael's heart started beating again, falteringly at first, and then with increasing steadiness. The flow of blood reduced to a trickle and then halted. His skin was still cool to the touch, and he had lost a great deal of blood, which no amount of mutant healing powers could fix, but with a bit of care, he would make it.

Danyael. Miriya sent a quick mental jolt into his mind, hoping for a response.

Jake frowned at her. *Will you just let him rest, Miriya? He's had a crappy day.*

Too late for that. He's waking.

Danyael stirred, not fully regaining consciousness, but the jolt had been enough to kick his limbic system back into full gear. Slowly and painfully, he flawlessly pulled his psyche back together; his internal psychic shields reformed and strengthened until he was once again carrying the full burden of shielding his own darkest emotions. His external shields, which required conscious effort to maintain, would remain lowered until he fully recovered, but it was no burden for a skilled telepath to shield him as long as he or she did not have to simultaneously support his internal shields.

Alex nodded approvingly. His face was expressionless, but his eyes betrayed his relief. "Nice work, everyone. Lucien Winter?" He extended his hand toward Lucien. "I'm Alex Saunders, director general of the Mutant

Advisory Council. With your permission, I'd like to take Danyael back to the council headquarters in D.C. We have a team standing by to care for him until he fully recovers."

Lucien glanced over at Jason and Roland Rakehell and then looked back at Alex. "Danyael's not all right, is he?"

"That's what we'll have to ascertain, and it'll be a lot safer for everyone, including Danyael, if he's surrounded by people who understand his abilities and his limitations."

"It'll be fine, Lucien," Miriya promised. "I'll watch over him, and I'll let you know when he wakes and asks for you."

"We're leaving now, unless you think you'd need some help with that." Alex looked over meaningfully at the five abominations that waited patiently in the corner of the suite, looking like a pack of well-behaved monsters.

"They're not a problem; they're with me," Galahad confirmed, glancing at them. The abominations returned his gaze, looking as innocent as it was possible for anything with massive fangs and claws to appear.

Alex looked over at him, a faint smile passing over his face. "Ah, Galahad." He extended his hand. "It's a pleasure to finally meet you. You have some excellent genes in you. Take good care of them." Alex nodded toward Jake. "Let's go."

Jake's formidable telekinetic powers lifted Danyael easily from Michael's arms and then carried him as if on an invisible stretcher, easily maneuvering him through the shattered window. "It'll be easier not to have to go down corridors," he explained with a quirky grin.

Mrs. Crenshaw frowned at the jagged edges of broken glass framing the windowpane. "I'll take the conventional route and meet you at the car, if you don't mind," she said primly as she headed toward the door.

Zara chuckled softly. "She brings a dying man back to life, and she's nervous about cutting herself on broken glass?"

Miriya smiled thinly. "Healing others isn't in the same class of mutant powers as accelerated self-regeneration. Most healers can't heal themselves. Danyael can't. Neither can Mrs. Crenshaw, though I suspect the reason she doesn't want to climb over broken glass is because she's worried about snagging her pantyhose." Miriya gracefully clambered over the broken window. She glanced over her shoulder at Lucien. "Stay in touch," was all she said as she shot him a winsome smile.

The moment the mutants were gone, Lucien pulled Jason Rakehell up from the ground. "You're going to tell me what the hell happened. What did Danyael do to you?"

"I...I don't know." Jason looked over at his father, genuine confusion in his eyes, and then back at Lucien. "I don't feel it anymore."

"Feel what anymore?" Lucien demanded.

"Feel anything," Jason struggled to sort through what he could only sense but could not explain. Confusion reigned. His scattered emotions slowly drifted through the odd emptiness he felt somewhere in the deepest recesses of his mind and his heart. Every attempt he made to forcibly wring some sense out of them only tossed the emotions up again like autumn leaves to the wind. They fluttered, disassociated from context, from memory. He knew why he had been angry. He remembered why he had hated his father and Galahad, but those reasons no longer summoned the anger and hatred he had lived with all his life.

"And Danyael. What do you feel about Danyael?"

Jason's brow furrowed as he concentrated. "Nothing," he said finally, "I don't feel anything."

Lucien sighed, releasing Jason and turning away. "I guess that's something to be grateful for anyway." Suddenly weary, he slumped into the rattan chair, leaned over to rest his elbows on his thighs, and then buried his face in his hands.

Jason persisted, following Lucien. "What did Danyael do to me?"

"I don't know for sure," Lucien admitted, dropping his hands away from his face. He looked up at Jason. "I'm guessing he absorbed your emotions. It's just the kind of stupid thing he would do if he thought he was going to die."

"And he wouldn't have done that if he thought he would survive?"

"Probably not. It's easier to live with someone hating you than you hating yourself. Danyael tried to explain it to me once before. If the emotions are too deep-seated, he can't change them, and the only way to get rid of them is to absorb them from the other person. That means that everything you and your father once felt for him, he now feels for himself. If that doesn't completely screw him up, I don't know what else will." Lucien looked over at Galahad, his smile faint, but relieved. "What are you doing here? We thought we lost you when the ceiling caved in at Purest Humanity."

Jason gaped. "The ceiling caved in?"

Zara smiled viciously. "Right. You didn't stick around to see it, but yes, Purest Humanity is now a big pile of rubble. I'm guessing your insurers aren't going to be pleased."

"What happened?"

"The abominations showed up, killed a couple of people, started a fire, and then the building came down," Lucien summarized, an undercurrent of irritation in his voice. "It's the hottest news story since the burning of Pioneer Laboratories. Ironically, many people consider it due justice." He shot a quick glance at the abominations. "You took away their building, they take away your building." His gaze shifted back to Galahad. "How did you survive?"

Galahad gestured toward the abominations. "They gathered around me, sheltering me from the debris as the building came down and then dug me out. I concluded then that they weren't trying to hurt me, so I brought them back here, hoping to search the lab's computers for information about them."

"You managed to get all the way back here unnoticed?"

"Well, not precisely unnoticed," Galahad hedged carefully. "Let's just say we weren't reported."

"Right." Lucien smiled ironically.

"And that's when I saw Danyael. I came in to get him out, but my escape plan from Pioneer Labs was obviously less well formulated than Zara's."

"I'm just grateful you tried."

"What do we do now?" Zara asked quietly as she looked around the room. Technically Galahad was the property of Pioneer Labs, but with the abominations standing behind him, she did not think anyone was going to enforce property laws just then. Roland Rakehell and Michael Cochran appeared flabbergasted by how easily Galahad seemed to keep the abominations in check. Perhaps it was time to renegotiate a change in the terms of their relationship with Galahad.

"We could wait out in the car, give Galahad a couple of minutes to finish up here, and then he can join us at the parking lot," Lucien said indifferently as he pushed easily to his feet.

Jason's jaw dropped. "You're going to let him kill us?"

Lucien's temper, usually perfectly controlled, flared into white rage. He grabbed Jason by his shirt and hauled him close, staring him down. "You started this bull crap when you and your mob of fanatics burned down Pioneer Labs. Scores of people are dead because of you. Just to round out your list of accomplishments, you shot my best friend, and you would have killed him, if his mutant friends didn't show up in time to save his life. And now, he's got to live with all the shit he absorbed from you and your equally screwed up father. All in all, I'd say that if the only thing that happened here is that Galahad turned his abominations loose on you, you'd have gotten off way too easy."

Zara interjected, "In fact, I'll give you a choice." She glanced toward the abominations. "The painful way or my way, which I promise will be fast and as painless as humanly possible."

"Zara, we were engaged." Jason's voice mirrored his incredulity.

"That's why I'm offering you an option out of consideration for our past relationship. What will it be?"

"No, wait," Lucien said sharply. "Danyael can put them back."

Zara glanced at him. "Put what back?"

"The emotions he absorbed from Jason and Roland. Danyael can transfer them back."

"Are you sure?"

"He's an empath; it's what he does. I can convince him to transfer the emotions back. I have to." He shook his head, disbelief still echoing in his voice. "He just can't live with that kind of self-hatred."

"So what do you want me to do here?"

"No fatal accidents, Zara." The instruction was curt, pointed. "But as long as they're alive enough for Danyael to undo what he did, I don't really care what else happens here. I just want to get back to Danyael and make sure he's all right."

"We're not going to be able to resolve this within the next five minutes," Zara said reasonably. "And you need to get to Danyael. Why don't you go? I've got my own car; you don't have to wait around for me."

Lucien inhaled deeply and then nodded. "Fine, if you're sure you're going to be okay here."

"Absolutely." She placed a hand lightly flat against his chest, a very lover-like gesture. "How much of your money can I spend, Lucien?"

When violence isn't an option, try bribery.

He understood her question immediately. He might have resented it, except that he had expected it from her. Former girlfriends who evolved into token kid sisters could get expensive to maintain, and Zara Itani tended to be more expensive than most. "Try to keep it to quarter of my net worth. He's more than worth it." Lucien stepped over to Galahad and extended a hand of friendship. "You came back for Danyael, and for that, I'm eternally in your debt. Thank you."

"It was the least I could do," Galahad said quietly.

"I hope you realize that you'll always have a friend in me." Lucien's affirmation of support was not intended just for Galahad. It was not-so-subtly directed to all listeners present—a very public declaration that if anyone decided to mess with Galahad, he would have to take on Lucien too.

Got to give him credit, Zara concealed a smirk. *He's got style.* She waited until Lucien left and then sat down in the rattan chair Lucien had vacated. Her voice shifted from cool and businesslike to a warm, feline purr. She wore a smile to match, but her eyes were icy violet, coolly assessing, and dangerous. "I think we have a great deal to talk about, don't we, gentlemen?"

~*~

Despite his stated urgency to get to Danyael, Lucien sat in the parking lot at Pioneer Labs for a long time, leaning his hands on the steering wheel and staring moodily out the windshield. He would have cursed, but there were no curse words adequate to the task of describing how he felt.

He had dragged Danyael into this nightmare, against Danyael's will and better judgment, and Danyael had been right. His past would have been better left buried, undisturbed. What had he gained? The added heartache of knowing how much his family despised and hated him, and the added burden of carrying their absorbed emotions.

Lucien clenched his hands tightly on the steering wheel until his knuckles were white. He owed Danyael an apology; hell, he owed Danyael a whole lot more than that, but Danyael never called in the favors owed to him anyway.

What could he do now? What could he possibly say to tell Danyael just how wrong he was?

He released a pained sigh and reached for the key in the ignition, but then stopped short when his breath caught on a choked sob in his throat. Almost incapacitated by remorse, he reached for his cell phone, stared at it for a brief second, and then punched in a now-familiar number.

Xin picked up on the other end even before the phone completed its first ring. "What happened? Is everything all right?"

She must have been going crazy waiting at his home for someone to call with the latest news, but her voice was calm despite the urgency inherent in her question. Her voice was an instant balm to his soul. He inhaled deeply and for the first time since he witnessed the horror of Danyael being shot, he felt like he was breathing clean air. "Everyone's alive, including Galahad, who appears to be on excellent terms with the five abominations. Somehow they all survived the collapse of Purest Humanity."

"That's good."

"Yeah, that's just about all the good news we have. Danyael was shot. I think he's going to be okay, but for a while, we didn't think he'd make it."

"Is he all right? Are you all right?"

Odd that she would think to ask about him as well. "He's fine…well, he'll survive," Lucien amended. "Fine is still debatable at this point." Sighing softly, he started at the beginning, relating the bare facts of everything that had happened.

Xin listened in silence, and when he finished, she spoke again, her voice soft with compassion. "I'm sure Danyael is in good hands now. How are you doing?"

He shook his head in confusion. "Why are you asking about me?"

"Well, Danyael is one of your closest friends. Seeing him get shot and almost die must have been a huge shock for you. I know you well enough to suspect that it is tearing you up inside. Do you want to talk about it, or do you just want someone to be with you when you visit Danyael at the council headquarters?"

She amazed him and humbled him. "I can be there in about an hour."

"I'll see you there, Lucien. Drive safe."

Lucien turned the key in the ignition and pulled his BMW smoothly out of the parking lot. He was about five miles down the state road when he saw the first in a long series of military vehicles, including some of the latest APCs that were more tank than truck.

He bit back several choice curse words, grabbed his cell phone and dialed Zara's number. "Get out of there," he ordered tersely the moment she picked up the phone. "The game is up; a military convoy is on its way to the lab. You've got five minutes to make a run for it."

"Got it."

"Get to Leesburg Executive Airport. I'll have a private jet standing by."

"Will do." She hung up on him.

He made one more call to Phillip Evans with instructions for the private jet. Downshifting, he accelerated, driving at near reckless speeds through the winding country roads that would take him from rural Boonsboro to the urban jungle of Washington, D.C. He had to get to Danyael.

The equation had changed completely, and he did not know how the game would play out anymore.

SEVENTEEN

Zara's negotiations did not start out well.

Roland Rakehell planted his feet in a wide, openly aggressive stance. "Who the hell is she, and what is she doing here?" he demanded, pointing at Zara.

"My name is Zara Itani, and I was once engaged to your son, Jason. However, that has nothing to do with why I'm here today. Let's just say I've appointed myself Galahad's representative in this matter to ensure that his rights are appropriately protected."

"Galahad's non-human," Roland retorted flatly. "He has no rights."

Galahad's dark eyes flashed, and he took a single step forward, but Zara placed a hand gently on his arm, holding him back. Her eyes iced over, but her smile never faltered. "In that case then, you'll be negotiating directly with me, since I am Galahad's current owner."

"What?" Roland's jaw dropped with shock at her audacity.

"I freed him from the laboratory two nights ago, just before Jason's goons burned the place down."

"All that makes you is a thief. Galahad is still my rightful property."

"Wrong," Zara said flatly, toying carelessly with the edge of her dagger. "To the victor go the spoils of war. Galahad is mine. I didn't steal the abominations, but since they seem attached to him, I guess I'm, by extension, their new owner too."

"You have no legal claim to him. We'll get him back in a court of law."

"There's only one problem with that. The person with the most expensive lawyers wins—which would make it Lucien. I would have thought you'd be eager to settle it out of court, if only to avoid all that career-destroying publicity. I want you to relinquish all claims to Galahad. What's your price?"

"There is no damned price!" Roland burst out. "That's completely out of the bounds of responsible research. He is a created lab animal; setting him free would be like creating a pathogen that has never before existed and releasing it into the atmosphere just to see what it does to decimate the human race."

Michael rolled his eyes. "You're overreacting, Roland."

"No, I'm not! The only difference between him and the abominations is in the genes we used. The process that created them was absolutely identical. There is no place for him out there, just like there's no place for the abominations out there."

"He is not an abomination. The scientific process was the same, but the genes make all the difference. We've spent our entire lives working with the premise that genes do matter. We spent twenty-five years testing Galahad, only to conclude each and every day that Galahad is a superb specimen of a human being. It's time for us to let go. It's done, Roland. Finished," Michael concluded with absolute finality.

"No, it's not!"

"Yes, it is!" Michael roared, stalking over to Roland. He seized Roland's shirt and shook him hard. "I just saw your son shoot his own brother in cold blood because you chose your pet science project over your own flesh and blood. I've seen the three lives you've wrecked because you couldn't see past your obsession with Galahad. Go find something else to be obsessed over, because we're done here."

Zara arched an eyebrow and almost applauded. She had never met Michael Cochran before, but she was officially impressed. He was the voice of calm reason to Roland's single-minded obsession.

Roland was not done. Flustered with anger, he pulled out of Michael's grip. "I won't let everything we've worked for our entire lives mean nothing! Galahad isn't any less perfect just because we used templates. Our work isn't any less groundbreaking. If you're going to insist on turning Galahad free, then I want to ensure that our reputation at least remains perfectly intact."

"Not much chance of it now that the abominations made the evening news," Michael remarked dryly.

"No one knows yet that we used templates. I want that part buried. Forever."

Michael shrugged and then looked over at Zara.

She shrugged too and said, "Not many people know, and those who do are good at keeping secrets. There's nothing to be gained from revealing the truth anyway, especially once Galahad's freedom is ensured. I'm sure that can be arranged."

"The only person with anything to gain is Luke," Roland said.

"Luke?" Zara asked. "Who's Luke?"

"Danyael," Jason corrected quietly.

"Why would Danyael want news like this made public?"

"You mean besides the fact that he could file a multimillion-dollar lawsuit against Pioneer Laboratories for using his genetic code without his consent?"

Jason asked. "I can't imagine why else. He wouldn't need to work for another day in his life."

"Danyael doesn't want or need money," Galahad said.

"Right, Lucien would be happy to let Danyael sponge off him for the rest of his life," Zara agreed.

"It's not the money," Roland insisted. He looked like a dog with a bone. "He could use the information to blackmail us into accepting him back into the family."

Zara burst out laughing. She knew it bordered on rude, but the hilarity exploded unchecked. Had Roland looked into a mirror recently? Did he realize that he was an obsessed sociopath and that his elder son wasn't a significant improvement on him? Who would want to join a family like that? But then again, Danyael wasn't much of a prize either, so perhaps he did belong with them.

Galahad assessed Roland. "Danyael touched you too. He managed to change something in Jason, but what changed in you?"

"I don't see what that has to do with this," Roland retorted.

"It has everything to do with this. Answer the question."

Roland glared angrily at Galahad before biting off the answer. "Nothing. Nothing changed."

Zara glanced at Galahad. "What does that mean? That Danyael's not as powerful as everyone thinks?"

"Or maybe there wasn't anything to change," Galahad said. "Jason clearly hated Danyael and me. On the other hand, Roland was an indifferent father, because he had other priorities. If there aren't any inherent emotions to alter, there would have been nothing for Danyael to work with."

Roland apparently did not care for a technical discussion of the mutant's empathic capabilities. "I want to be sure that Luke will never reveal that he's the template for Galahad."

"Fine. I'll talk to him, or Lucien will talk to him," Zara promised.

"Not good enough." Roland folded his arms. "In exchange for letting Galahad go, I need a hundred percent guarantee that Luke will never speak of this."

Zara's cell phone rang, interrupting the conversation. She glanced at it briefly. "Just a moment." She accepted the call and after a cryptic conversation, hung up less than thirty seconds later. "We're leaving. Now," Zara announced brusquely.

"Why?"

"Let's go, Galahad."

"Not unless you explain," he insisted. "We've got our best chance here to negotiate the terms of my freedom."

"Not anymore. There are military vehicles on their way here, and the last time I checked, they're not big into negotiation." She paused as she caught a flicker of recognition and alarm on Roland's face. Awareness dawned in an instant, followed by a burst of shock. She closed the distance to Roland in three long strides. "What is Galahad's connection with the military?"

"I don't know what you're talking about."

"You're lying." Violet eyes narrowed dangerously.

Roland arched his head back nervously as the black blade of her dagger slid against his throat, a hairsbreadth from his skin.

"Start talking; I don't have much time."

Roland said nothing. It was Michael who spoke. "Initially, nothing. Galahad was created independently of any military funding, as were the abominations. But after the pro-humanists successfully lobbied against his human classification, our research funding dried up. DARPA—the Defense Advanced Research Projects Agency—stepped in at that point, and after reviewing our early work on the abominations and Galahad, they agreed to fund our research."

"Why?"

Michael Cochran inhaled deeply, his eyes in turmoil. "Because they were convinced we were on the right path to building super soldiers. We had created the abominations with accelerated regeneration capabilities, superhuman strength, and speed. With Galahad, we abandoned our attempts to create him with similar traits since—for whatever reason—the sum of the effects were—" he glanced at the abominations. "Less than stellar. Instead we opted for an extended lifespan and enhanced awareness."

"Kinesthetic foresight," Zara murmured. It explained Galahad's exceptional reflexes and hand-to-hand fighting prowess.

"Yes," Michael confirmed. "We...I...wanted the abominations put down. They're dangerous and can't be controlled, but DARPA overruled. They thought we could learn more from them, and from Galahad. That's why we did all those experiments on you." He looked at Galahad, his expression apologetic, even guilty. "They wanted to know your capabilities, your limitations, the likelihood of your cracking under pressure. They want to use you as the genetic template—as the starting point—for a breed of super-soldiers, though they wanted to add a few minor modifications."

Confusion flicked across Galahad's face. "Such as?"

"They concluded that you were too intelligent, too strong-willed. They're trying to breed sergeants, not four-star generals."

"That kind of attitude certainly goes a long way toward explaining why we're in danger of losing our status as a military superpower," Zara remarked caustically but calmly. Nothing in her voice betrayed her sense of heightened urgency. "We're out of time. Let's go."

Galahad gritted his teeth. "One last question: which one of you called the military in?"

Silence. Michael and Roland exchanged accusatory glances, but no one said anything.

Galahad nodded and then turned to follow Zara as she climbed back out over the broken window. He glanced back over his shoulder and saw the abominations lumbering rapidly after him. "We can't take your car. There's not enough time to make a clean break. We'll be arrested if we pass them, and there's only one road in and out of Pioneer Labs for about two miles."

"I know." She ran toward the only gate in the high electric fence that surrounded the compound. "We'll lie low till they pass us, then head down to the town of Boonsboro and snag a car there." She slipped out through the open gate and veered right, racing for the densely wooded area. Just past a sharp dip in the terrain, she threw herself flat against the ground. Seconds later, Galahad joined her.

They were not a moment too soon. Five seconds later, the first APC in the military convoy turned the corner, permitting the occupants of the vehicle their first full view of Pioneer Labs and of the five abominations lumbering toward them. Cries of alarm, even panic, carried down the line as the soldiers opened fire.

Zara glanced briefly at Galahad's flawless profile and saw anguish flicker through the dark eyes before he closed them and turned his face away from her. He inhaled deeply and then breathed out, a jagged and unsteady sound.

"Let's keep moving," he murmured, his voice barely audible over the snarls of the abominations and the screams of the dying soldiers. Inching down the hill, he was well out of sight of the road when he finally pushed to his feet. He glanced back toward the road. The sounds were muted now, deflected by the dense tree line, but still audible.

"I'm sorry," Zara said simply. She laid a gentle hand on his shoulder.

"I know." Galahad's voice was steady, but his eyes were dark with emotions she could not easily decipher.

She said nothing else; she couldn't find the words. Instead, she slipped her hand into his, and was surprised when he squeezed her hand lightly in acknowledgement. It took him a few more moments to come to terms with some inner turmoil, but finally he said, "Let's go."

Twenty minutes later, they reached the little town of Boonsboro. The residents were in an uproar over the military convoy that had passed through its main street. Zara and Galahad's pace dropped to a casual stroll as they entered the more populated areas. Zara slipped her arm through Galahad's, a simple gesture that lent them an appearance of normality as they walked down a street filled with people who had gathered to express concern and outrage against Pioneer Labs and the military.

"That one." Zara nodded toward a florist's delivery truck idling on a side street. Boonsboro was a quiet backwater town in rural Maryland, after all. No one thought of locking doors there. She slipped into the driver's seat, waited until Galahad was seated, and then easily navigated through narrow side streets back onto the main street. She did not pick up speed until they were out of town. "I think we're about an hour from Leesburg."

He nodded and then glanced briefly at her. "Would you have made a different decision if you'd known I was a military experiment?" he asked, his voice very quiet.

"No." Her wickedly mischievous grin flashed. "But I would have gotten you out of the country a hell of a lot sooner."

"Where are we going now?"

"Leesburg Executive Airport. Lucien said he'd have a plane there for us."

"And then?"

She shrugged. "We'll have to make up a plan as we go. I know a couple of places where we can hide out for a while to sort through our options. I have some resources, and Lucien has even more. We'll find a way to get through this as long as we can make it past the initial dragnet." She inhaled deeply and glanced out the rearview mirror. They were not followed, at least not yet.

Safety was an hour away. For them, it was practically a lifetime away.

~*~

It was a massacre of gigantic proportions. The narrow two-way road leading into Pioneer Labs was a bottleneck, trapping the military convoy one vehicle behind the other. The abominations that would otherwise have been outnumbered clawed and tore through the unprepared crew of each APC one at a time.

It took over a half hour to bring the precarious situation back under control. By then, more than fifty soldiers had been killed and twice that number injured. Most of them would not survive the trip to the hospital.

Major General John Hayes, head of the Genetics Division of the Defense Advanced Research Projects Agency, was in a decidedly foul mood by the time his adjunct informed him that the abominations had been neutralized and the way to Pioneer Labs was clear. He climbed out of his car at the very end of the military convoy and strode briskly past injured soldiers lying in neat rows on the roadside. His smooth jaw was twitching noticeably by the time he arrived at the gate of Pioneer Labs to find Michael Cochran and Roland Rakehell, together with a younger man he did not recognize, waiting for him.

"Where is Galahad?" General Hayes demanded tersely without so much as pausing for the standard courtesies.

"He had returned here with the abominations, but fled again in the company of a mercenary, Zara Itani, who abducted him two nights ago from Pioneer Labs," Roland said, his tone strident. "I'm guessing he managed to sneak past your elite military teams?"

Hayes's teeth clenched. "My elite military teams just had their guts ripped out by your monsters."

Michael's eyes narrowed. "I warned you that they were dangerous, even deadly, but for years, you ignored my requests to euthanize them." He glanced toward the crumpled forms of four abominations, finally subdued and defeated in death, and then up at the last abomination—the first one created—he recalled vaguely, badly injured but very likely to survive. It snarled in vicious protest as it was herded into one of the rooms in the western wing with incessant prods of several electrical rods.

"Find him." Hayes gestured sharply to his adjunct, who stepped away to issue orders for the retrieval of Galahad.

Michael asked, "How did you even find out that they were here?"

"We have our sources," Hayes replied obliquely, his lips curling into a sneer. "Is your research compromised?"

"Compromised?" Michael echoed, his voice incredulous. "Have you been watching the news? The whole world now knows that we created and kept abominations."

"And Galahad's genetic code?"

"Irreparably compromised. It's out there now. It's gone."

"So anyone can recreate Galahad?"

"If they choose to defy the guidelines established by the International Research and Ethics Council twenty years ago, then yes, they can recreate Galahad."

"What about the work with live transfusions?"

"Well, all those research files are still secure but—" Michael's voice trailed into silence. He looked at Roland, his brown eyes wide, stunned with disbelief mixed with growing horror.

"What is it?" Hayes demanded.

"Nothing. I—" Michael began, but Roland stepped between him and General Hayes.

"None of this is beyond salvage," Roland interjected coolly. He would have only one chance at this; he had to make it count. "The abominations have been neutralized. Galahad will be located and retrieved. There is one more loose end though. One of the templates used to create Galahad now knows that his genetic code was used without his permission to create Galahad."

Hayes's eyes reflected his disbelief. "Do you have any good news for me at all?"

"Well, we know where he is now, and in the interests of national security, I strongly suggest that he be neutralized."

"Neutralized, as in killed?"

"Father." The young man who had been standing behind Roland and who had thus far been willing to listen in silence objected sharply, "You can't do that."

Michael looked similarly aghast, but Roland held up his hand. "He knows he is pivotal in this, and if he ever decides to take his information to the media, the public backlash would shut down the Galahad project immediately."

"Why? So you borrowed his genes without asking. So what?"

"Because he is an alpha mutant. His name is Danyael Sabre."

"Damn. Wasn't there anyone else you could have used as a template? Why a goddamned alpha mutant? Which of his genes did you use?"

"Physical appearance."

"The easiest thing in the world to prove. Did any of his mutant powers transfer?"

"No," Roland insisted sharply.

Hayes merely looked toward Michael, who shook his head. "We don't think so. It's never easy to say for sure with an alpha, because their mutations are usually very complex, but our best guess at this time is no."

"First good news I've had all day." Hayes growled. "I agree that he's a security risk but silencing him won't be simple. He's under the jurisdiction of the Mutant Advisory Council, and they can get real touchy when we off their people without consent. Especially alphas."

"So what can we do?"

"There are other ways to silence people without killing them. We issue a code red emergency, which will allow us sufficient authority to take a mutant into custody. We can then order a memory wipe," Hayes suggested, his demeanor brooding. "Net net, the effect will be the same. He will know nothing. The security risk is effectively eliminated."

Roland nodded. He seemed grimly pleased. "I'll oversee it personally. I want to make sure it is done right."

"All right. Let me call the Mutant Assault Group. I'll need their people." Hayes glanced back over his shoulder at another aide. "Set up a command center, and connect me with General Kieran Howard."

Twenty minutes later, he finally got in touch with the commander of the Mutant Assault Group. "What can I do for you, General?" General Kieran Howard's tone was all cool politeness.

Hayes struggled to contain his distaste for the man he had only met twice, but who had unnerved him both times. "We've identified a security risk, an alpha mutant, and we're ordering a memory wipe."

"On an alpha?" The disembodied voice sounded only mildly interested. "I will need more information from you to assess the risk associated with trying to contain an alpha."

"That information is beyond your security clearance, General Howard."

"And containing an alpha mutant is well beyond your capabilities, General Hayes. I believe you need me at this point. I'd recommend a demonstration of basic courtesy on your part."

Hayes ground his teeth together. "The alpha mutant in question was used as one of many genetic templates for Galahad."

"The one whose escape is causing such a furor? Were the mutated genes incorporated into Galahad?"

"We do not believe so," Hayes replied frostily, insulted by the condescending tone.

"Ah, what a shame. He would likely have been a great deal more perfect than he is now, had the genes been incorporated. Who, may I ask, is the alpha?"

"His name is Danyael Sabre."

There was a long silence on the other end.

Confused and more than a little concerned, Hayes finally prompted, "General Howard, are you still there?"

"Yes, I am. Where should I send my team to rendezvous with you?"

"We're at Pioneer Labs at Boonsboro."

"Very well. They will be there within twenty minutes."

There was a sharp click. General John Hayes pulled the receiver away from his ear and stared at it as if it were a snake. Something had been put in motion, and he was not entirely sure if he liked it, or if he even knew what it was.

~*~

General Kieran Howard's day had started out very poorly. The president had ignored his explicit request to allow the Mutant Assault Group to restore order to Washington D.C. That rejection had seared his pride, but things were definitely starting to look up.

Comfortable in jeans and a black sweater, the general leaned back in his chair and stared thoughtfully at the large screen on the far wall, covered with the faces of the alpha mutants he had been monitoring, carefully watching for the faintest crack in their fragile grasp on normality. Among them was Danyael Sabre, golden-haired, dark-eyed. He was more fragile than most, yet far out of the general's reach because he was also stronger than most. The alpha empath was stunningly resilient, and worse, determined to keep a low profile and play by all the rules of the council.

Playing by the rules set by pitiful humans kept Danyael out of the general's grasp, but by God, he *wanted* Danyael. There were no empaths who were Danyael's equal. Not in the United States. Not in the world. Now it appeared that circumstances were conspiring to drive Danyael into his arms. General Howard smiled contemplatively, the action so unnatural, so rare that the muscles in his cheek strained at the effort.

"Whom should we send?" his aide asked carefully, trying to assess his boss' mood.

"Tim Brown. Assign a human squad to him and make sure they're protected."

"Yes, sir." The aide hesitated. "Sir, are you sure that this is the right thing to do? An alpha empath without memories would be unstable."

"Exactly. I want Danyael destabilized. He is council-trained, but when his world is crushed by the will and decision of humans, he'll realize that the only way to protect himself is to ally with mutants. And not just any mutant group. Certainly not with the pacifist council that considers itself a supporter of the administration. He will turn to *us*."

"Yes, sir."

"Make sure Tim is aware of how important this is." The general's tone was contemplative now. "Among the alphas, empaths are the rarest because their powers tend to get them killed long before they learn how to control them. Danyael is exceptional because he has survived and thrived in spite of his mutant powers. And combined with his healing capabilities, there is simply no one like him. I want Danyael. We *need* him."

General Kieran Howard pushed to his feet, feeling immensely pleased with himself. He had much to plan. It was far more than an intellectual exercise now. How much pressure could he possibly put on Danyael Sabre before the alpha empath snapped?

EIGHTEEN

Dr. Seth Copper, alpha telepath and the leading expert on mutant physiology, looked down at his latest patient. Danyael Sabre was deeply unconscious, the extreme blood loss taking a severe toll on an exhausted body that had been pushed past the limits of human endurance. The empath appeared shockingly pale against the white sheets, but his breathing was steady. IV bags pumped fluids into one arm, and blood into the other. Seth glanced at the equipment that monitored Danyael's vital statistics. Danyael was in no danger. He would make it; it was just a matter of giving him enough time to regain his strength.

Gently he ran a finger over the faint bruises on the inside of Danyael's elbows, the discoloration merging with the faint blue-green tint of the veins beneath his skin. If Danyael had not struggled, the needles would have left no marks. If the off switch had worked, if Danyael had remained unconscious as he usually did through the procedure, he would still be utterly ignorant.

Now that Danyael was aware of the live blood transfusions, he would be a far more dangerous target, but Seth could not bring himself to fully regret the change in his previously safe indulgence. There had been something compelling about Danyael's anguish and torment as he had attempted to pull away from Seth's touch just two evenings earlier in the plane ride from New York City to Washington, D.C.

Change. Change was inevitable, and good.

Seth sighed, a satisfied sound that matched the smile on his lips. Sixteen years prior, he had met Danyael Sabre for the first time. The boy had been absolutely exquisite even then—young, brutally damaged, impossibly fragile, yet unbroken.

Because Seth had been a different man then, because he had actually cared, the boy's hopeless plight had moved him to help.

Over the years, Seth had inevitably lost the innocent altruism of that feeling, but he still clung to the memory. He had wanted nothing more than to help the boy gain control over his unchecked empathic powers. Merely trying to teach Danyael had not helped. The boy had been too deeply traumatized to trust the functioning of his mind and his powers to another. In desperation and frustration, Seth had deliberately stepped outside the boundaries of accepted science. Live blood transfusion had been the answer; it had allowed him to slowly cultivate Danyael's ability to create strong psychic shields, the hallmark of a defense-class alpha telepath. Those shields were the key to Danyael's ability to function normally.

How could he have known that Danyael's blood would be as intoxicating as his physical beauty, that the rush of energy, of power, that suffused him would be so addictive? That it would change him as surely as it had changed Danyael?

Seth stripped each piece of clothing from the unconscious mutant until Danyael lay naked on the bed. Seth dipped a clean towel into a bowl of warm water and then washed Danyael's body, cleaning off the blood that had caked on his skin. He smiled as he trailed the towel down the length of Danyael's body. The intimate act of cleaning Danyael's body was nothing compared to the intimacy they had already enjoyed for sixteen years through the sharing of blood.

You see, Danyael. You can't escape. Even where you think you are safest, there is no one to protect you from me.

~*~

Lucien looked up at the building before him. The Mutant Advisory Council occupied a nondescript three-story office building in Alexandria, Virginia, overlooking the Potomac. Nothing about the dull gray-brick structure hinted that it might be the powerbase of the only non-military government-sanctioned mutant organization in the United States. There was hardly any security to speak of, but when most of the people in that place were effectively armies of one, Lucien supposed the council would not need much security anyway.

He had been there many times when Danyael was younger and still struggling to control his emphatic powers. The last time was many years before though, Lucien recalled as he parked his car in the crowded parking lot and then entered the building. Little had changed. The furniture in the small reception area had been spruced up, but not significantly. The décor still screamed "frugal government" instead of "lavish corporate."

Lucien saw Xin waiting for him and released the breath he had not even realized he had been holding. She stood up and smiled at him as he walked in. Stepping gracefully up to him, she slipped her small hand into his. She said nothing, but then again, she did not have to. She was there, and just then, it was all that mattered.

The motherly gray haired receptionist at the front desk smiled as Lucien and Xin approached. "You're expected, Mr. Winter." Her voice was welcoming though raspy from a lifetime of smoking cigarettes. "You and Ms. Xin are welcome to take the elevator to the third floor. Mr. Saunders is waiting for you in room three-oh-one."

"Thank you," Lucien responded. He took a few steps toward the elevator and then tossed a quick glance back over his shoulder. "Is the council the only organization that employs telepaths instead of computer systems to verify the identity of visitors?"

The receptionist flashed a quick smile that made her seem younger, brighter, and prettier. "Identification can be faked, Mr. Winter, but no one can lie to me. Have a good day, sir."

Xin chuckled softly as they walked down the linoleum-tiled corridor toward the elevators. "Mutants can certainly keep you on your toes."

"Yeah, no kidding," Lucien said, easily recalling the first few weeks, heck, the first few months when he had first taken Danyael under his protection. Every day had been a series of one barely averted disaster after another. Danyael's empathic powers had been out of control, and Lucien did not dare leave his side, for fear that someone would come along and hurt him. The memories that had receded into Lucien's distant past returned vividly. He knew exactly why. He feared for Danyael's sanity, for Danyael's peace of mind. An unstable alpha empath was a natural disaster looking for a place to happen; he knew it better than most, and he also knew just how thin the line that separated Danyael's flawless emotional control from the madness of an emotional maelstrom.

The elevator doors opened onto a third floor that was several tiers of luxury removed from the dull reception area; Persian rug runners decorated burnished hardwood paneled floors, and expensive art was displayed on smooth cream walls. The temperature was cool and comfortable. The air was subtly scented with pine and cinnamon, and soft Christmas music piped through invisible speakers. "Maybe redecorating downstairs just didn't make it into this year's budget," Xin remarked smoothly.

"They're not big on visitors, and most people don't make it past reception," Lucien said, amused as always at the stark difference between the façade people saw and the real face of the Mutant Advisory Council. "The director general's office is down this way, if I recall."

"Do you know Alex Saunders?"

"We met once before some sixteen or so years ago, when the former director general introduced the team that would be working with Danyael to teach him to control his powers. Alex Saunders was a part of that team. Their sessions were private, so I never saw Alex again after that first introduction. He's done well since; I think he was promoted to director general about three years ago." He nodded toward an open door. "The office is this way."

Looking in, he saw Alex on the phone, standing behind his desk. Lucien stepped back to give Alex the privacy to complete his call, but Alex held up a hand, asking him to wait. "Be right with you," he mouthed. He nodded, "Yes, sir, I understand. We'd be happy to assist in bringing the situation back under control…Thank you, Mr. President. I'm honored by your trust in us. We'll deploy immediately and keep you apprised of the situation." He hung up the phone. "Please come in and have a seat. I know you're eager to see Danyael. This will be just another minute." He raised his voice and shouted across the hall. "Jake!"

The brown-haired, nerdish-looking mutant who had been part of the team that had followed Alex Saunders to Pioneer Laboratories earlier that day popped his head into the office. "What is it?"

"The president has decided that he doesn't want tanks and APCs, even if they're American-made, rolling through the streets of D.C. Get a team organized and bring the city back under control. No civilian deaths, not even accidental ones. Apparently the Mutant Assault Group requested permission to restore order to the city, but he turned them down because he didn't trust them not to hurt civilians. I don't want to hear the words *collateral damage* or *property damage*. This has to be subtle," he emphasized.

Jake used an index finger to poke his glasses a little higher on the bridge of his nose and then rolled his eyes. "If you want subtle, we'll need an empath. Most of the other people I can think of off the top of my head don't even know how to spell subtle."

"Find ones with better spelling skills then," Alex countered. "The only alpha empath who has the capacity for large crowd control is Danyael Sabre, and he's a little indisposed right now."

Jake sighed. "Fine, we'll figure out something else that doesn't involve too much bleeding on anyone's part. How long do we have to make them sit down and behave?"

"How about close of business today? That gives you about eight hours to do it right. Send your hourly updates in to Sasha; she'll know when to involve me."

"Right." Jake flipped Alex a jaunty salute, waved at both Lucien and Xin, and then turned around, striding briskly down the corridor.

"You're here to see Danyael, of course." Alex waved them toward the door. "I'll take you to him right away."

Lucien shook his head. "We need to talk. The military showed up at Pioneer Labs just after I left."

"What?" Alex looked at him sharply. "Sit, please. Tell me what you know." He gestured toward the comfortable leather couches at a small lounge area in a corner of his expansive office.

Lucien did not sit. His restlessness, his anxiety for Zara and Galahad, would not permit it. "It was a convoy of twenty, maybe twenty-five vehicles. Army, as far I could tell, but no other markings."

"And where is Galahad?"

"With Zara, on their way to Leesburg. I've a plane waiting there for them. Zara called to confirm that they managed to sneak past the convoy, at least as far as the town of Boonsboro itself. According to her, the abominations probably didn't make it." Lucien's jaw tensed. "I'm guessing a lot of good men died too."

"The president expressly said he didn't want the military involved." Alex's expression was unreadable, but one thing was clear; he wasn't happy.

"Maybe they forgot to tell him they wanted to play as well," Lucien said sardonically. "Why are you so concerned about the military, beyond the fact that they're disobeying their commander in chief?"

"Call it a power struggle. We have had some run-ins before with the military, most of them unpleasant, as we squabble over exactly who is authorized to take down rogue mutants. They have their own teams of mutants, and they tend to deploy them before they fully understand the background, the situation, or the capabilities of the mutant they're going after. On more than one occasion, their overzealousness created an even larger problem than the one they were trying to prevent."

A young woman looked into the office. "Alex." The calmness in her voice belied the tension in her eyes. "Three military vehicles, including a containment unit, just passed checkpoint three."

He inhaled sharply, his eyes suddenly bleak. "They're probably coming for Danyael. Get Miriya in here."

The young woman nodded and then disappeared. Lucien gritted his teeth, his jaw tense. His concern for Danyael immediately outweighed the anxiety he had felt for Zara and Galahad. "I can get him out of here," he said.

"With all due respect, you can't protect him. The military has no respect for the power that wealth and influence accord, and whatever they want to happen to Danyael will happen, even if all of them lose their jobs after that. Miriya." Alex looked up as she walked into his office in a fresh change of clothes, her hair still damp from her shower. "A military containment unit is on its way here."

"Danyael?" her eyes widened with alarm.

"Probably. Get him out of here," Alex ordered. "Lucien has a plane waiting at Leesburg; Zara and Galahad are on their way there too. Take him out of the country and keep him safe until we sort this out. Lucien, you and Xin are welcome to wait in one of our suites when I meet the military. If we're lucky, I can talk them out of whatever insanity they're planning. Otherwise, I'll have to escalate this to the chairman of the Joint Chiefs of Staff."

"Right." Miriya nodded, turned, and then sprinted through the hallway and down a curving staircase toward the sanatorium on the second floor. She burst into the room without knocking.

Dr. Seth Copper looked up calmly from the tablet into which he was inscribing Danyael's medical notes.

Without so much as a hello, Miriya blasted a psychic bolt into Danyael's brain with surgical precision, jerking him awake.

Danyael gasped as sleep violently ripped from him. An instinctive gasp of terror bubbled up in his throat, arrested only when he saw Miriya's face.

"Get moving," she ordered, sending him a rush of telepathic images to bring him quickly up to speed on what was happening.

He inhaled sharply at the images that blasted through his mind. Crap. Danyael nodded slowly and swallowed hard as he tasted bile in his throat. Nausea and weakness dragged him down, but he clenched his teeth and tried to rise. His physical limitations barely skimmed the surface of the sum of his problems. The emotions he had absorbed from his father and brother tangled in with his own emotions, creating a cacophony of self-doubt and self-hatred that ricocheted through an already fragile psyche.

"He's too weak to move," Seth Copper insisted, moving quickly to Danyael's side and supporting him. "He had a class three hemorrhage; I estimate he lost close to forty percent of the blood in his body. I've transfused two pints, but he could really use a third."

"He's out of time," Miriya said. "Get those IVs out." She eyed the discarded pile of bloodstained clothes in a corner of the room and then left the room, only to return a minute later with clean clothes in Danyael's size.

As quickly as his limited strength would allow, Danyael dressed, grabbed his black leather jacket off the floor, and then reached for his personal belongings, which had been placed in a tray by the bedside. He inhaled deeply, testing his physical strength while desperately trying to block out the crippling heartache, the emotional bleeding.

Just one step at a time. Segment. Separate. Your own pain doesn't matter. Not right now. Perhaps never. Don't think, just move. Don't stop moving or the pain will catch up with you.

The crisis made it easier to focus on something other than the swirling chaos of his emotions and the emotions he had absorbed. He struggled to keep pace with Miriya as she raced down hidden corridors and brightly lit underground tunnels to a building two streets south that ostensibly belonged to a package delivery company. His lungs burned from the effort. Green and black dancing circles tinted his vision as his head throbbed painfully. *Light headed. Not enough blood. And low blood glucose levels.* The sum total of his meals over the prior sixty hours had consisted of two meager breakfasts. *Need to take better care of myself, or I'll die of simple negligence before my enemies can kill me.*

Miriya chuckled. "You just don't know when to quit, and that's a good thing sometimes. This way." She led the way up the stairs, which opened into a small office tucked into the back of the store. "I need car keys."

The middle-aged man seated at the desk seemed to be expecting her. He shook his head and instead tossed her and Danyael each a set of keys, nodding in approval as Danyael snatched it out of the air. "Take the two bikes."

Miriya's eyes narrowed as she bent down to pick up the keys that hit her in the chest before falling onto the carpet. "Danyael can barely stand. He can't ride his own bike."

"Never argue with a pre-cog." The man smiled thinly. "Get moving."

"How good are you with a bike?" Miriya asked as she led the way to the garage.

"Good enough," Danyael said, swinging a leg over the seat of a black Ducati Superbike, and pulled a helmet over his head. He exuded enough easy, unconscious confidence to assuage Miriya's primary concerns that Danyael would crash and burn on a viciously fast speed machine. Miriya climbed onto a red Ducati, pulled on a matching helmet, and then accelerated out of the garage, ducking beneath the slowly rising garage door.

Danyael was right behind her, the powerful machine perfectly under control as they raced down the back alley and then shot out onto the main thoroughfare. He heard Miriya's voice through the microphone in his helmet. "You holding up okay, Danyael?"

"I'll be all right."

"I intensely dislike it when you use the future tense. I want to know that you're okay right now."

Danyael laughed softly. "I won't pass out on you." *I hope.*

I heard that.

~*~

"Where is Luke?" Roland Rakehell asked.

Alex Saunders looked up, calmly assessing the four men who stood in the doorway of his office. "Welcome to the council headquarters, Mr. Rakehell," he said mildly. "I hadn't expected to see you again after this morning."

Roland's lower lip twisted into a sneer. "You'll find I'm a lot harder to discount, dismiss, or dispose of than you would like, Saunders. Where is he?"

Alex ignored the question as his gaze shifted to the thin, anxious-looking man in military fatigues standing beside Roland. "Tim, it's good to see you again, though I wish it wasn't under these circumstances."

"Good to see you too, Mr. Saunders, sir," Tim Brown responded, the quickness of his speech betraying his nervousness. He swallowed hard, his Adam's apple bobbing noticeably when Roland scowled, obviously disapproving of the small courtesy he paid to the director general of the Mutant Advisory Council.

Alex looked back at Roland. "Danyael's resting. I'd be happy to show you to his room when he wakes. I'm sure he'd like to see his father."

"I'm not here for a goddamned reunion, Saunders. Luke has been classified a national security risk, and I have a code-red authorization to take him into custody." He slammed a thin tablet down on the table.

Alex calmly picked up the tablet, reviewed the information displayed on the screen, and then nodded once, thoughtfully. "What is the interest of the military in this matter?"

"It's none of your business."

Alex stood up. "Anything and everything that involves a mutant—especially an alpha mutant—is my business." His voice was calm, but firm. "You may very well have the authorization to take Danyael into custody, but let me remind you that you are not an employee of the US government; hence, you are not protected by its privacy laws. Your mind may be protected behind shields, but that temporary inconvenience is quickly rectified. We have several alpha telepaths in this building. It's no hardship for me to summon them to smash through those shields to painfully extract the answers I want. Your choice, Rakehell. We can do this the easy way or the hard way." He paused to let his words sink in. "Once again, I ask, what is the interest of the military in this matter?"

Tim answered after casting a nervous glance at Roland Rakehell. "Sir, the Galahad project is funded by DARPA."

Alex's eyes narrowed. "That explains quite a great deal, Tim. Thank you," he said. "But that doesn't explain DARPA's interest in Danyael."

"He's a national security risk," Roland said. "That's all you need to know."

Alex tilted his head to one side and gazed thoughtfully at Roland. "That branch of the military has no interest in Danyael, but you obviously consider him a risk to your reputation, to your career, perhaps? Before you take Danyael into custody, you should know that Danyael has enough pride and strength to walk away without looking back, if you told him that you want nothing to do with him."

"Luke is an alpha empath. He needs love, craves attention—"

"He just wants to be left alone," Alex corrected firmly. "You didn't know him, even when he lived under your roof. It's been a quarter of a century or more since he 'left' home. Please grant that you may not know everything there is to know about him."

"I want him gone forever. I want to be sure that he'll never come begging at my door, demanding compensation or recognition."

"On his behalf, I will make you that promise. There is no need for you to take Danyael into custody."

"We won't keep him for long, just long enough to wipe his memory and make sure he'll never be able to speak of what happened in the past few days."

"You're going to wipe his memory?" Alex's calm composure slipped. His brown eyes widened with alarm. "You can't do that."

"Of course we can." Roland tapped on the tablet. "We have the authority right here."

Alex shook his head sharply. "Danyael has just absorbed a host of extremely negative emotions from you and your son. He will need those memories to give context to what he feels; otherwise there's no telling how he'll process them. He typically demonstrates exquisite control over his powers, but we need to be circumspect about the emotional demands placed on an alpha empath. It's always safer to err on the side of less rather than more. Anything that potentially jeopardizes his ability to maintain the internal shields that control the full extent of his pain must be avoided. Anything that adds to the pain should also be avoided, although I'd be the first to point out that it's a little late for that warning. Our only line of defense is his emotional shields; people die when those shields come down."

Roland laughed out loud. "You're good at weaving fairy tales to protect your mutants, Saunders. Save them for children who still believe in trolls under their beds."

"Fairy tales? You obviously have no idea how close you were to dying this morning."

"Enough of this bullshit, Saunders. We have the authorization to take him into custody. And as you said before, we can do this the easy way or the hard way. Where is Luke?"

Alex pushed to his feet, a hard, cold light in his eyes. "This way." He led the way silently down the corridors to the second floor sanatorium, pushing open the door to the room that Danyael had occupied. He stepped in, allowing Roland, Tim, and the other two soldiers to enter behind him.

"Where is Luke?" Roland demanded of the man dressed in a white doctor's coat who was powering down the equipment in the room.

"You just missed him," the doctor said calmly.

Roland turned on Alex with a snarl of contempt. "Nice try, but not good enough. We'll find him. Turn on that tracker. Hunt him down." He nodded toward the scanner-shaped gadget that one of the soldiers held. It was the latest in anti-mutant technology—a portable super-sensor capable of picking up trace power signatures, especially those of alpha mutants, even when they were not actively exercising their mutant capabilities. The machine activated with a low hum. Two red dots blinked briefly in the center of the screen, and then suddenly, the small screen exploded into a furious scatter of bright colors—mostly reds, oranges, and yellows.

"Having trouble pinpointing Danyael's power signature?" Alex inquired politely.

"It'll clear up once we leave the building," the soldier assured Roland quickly. "It's picking up on too many mutants in here."

Roland's jaw tensed, but he turned and strode away without another word. Tim and the two soldiers kept pace with him easily.

Alex shook his head. "He's a piece of work."

"Indeed. What will you do now?" Seth asked.

"Give Lucien a quick debrief, and then I need to talk to the head of DARPA—remind him pointedly where his jurisdiction ends and mine begins." Alex turned away, but paused at the door and looked back over his shoulder, "Seth, if I may, a favor please?"

"Certainly."

"Make that two favors. First, we've got lots of mutants camping out in here since we ordered the lockdown. Tell them they're free to go, and send them in the approximate direction of Leesburg. Let's dump as much interference as we possibly can on that sensor."

Seth grinned wickedly. "Happy to do that. What's the next favor?"

"You were the doctor assigned to Danyael when he first came to us here at the council, weren't you?"

He nodded. "That was a good while ago. Fifteen years? Sixteen?"

"Would you be willing to provide care for him? Regardless of how this fiasco with his father turns out, I suspect Danyael will need a fair degree of attention to recover physically, and I'd rather place him with someone he already trusts."

"I'd be happy to help in any way I can."

"Thank you, Seth." Alex smiled, relieved. "I'll keep you informed on his whereabouts, once I figure it out myself." He turned and left the room, immensely relieved that Danyael would be in safe hands. Returning to the third floor, he stopped by one of the guest suites and tapped softly on the door. Lucien opened it immediately. "May I come in?" Alex asked.

Lucien stepped aside. "Of course. What happened?"

Alex walked into the room and inclined his head to Xin who was seated at the desk, her two tablets connected to the mainframe. "It was his father. Apparently the Galahad project is sponsored by the military, specifically DARPA, and somehow Roland has convinced them that Danyael is a national security risk."

"That makes no sense. That would make all of us national security risks. Danyael doesn't know any more than any of us do."

"But in concept, Danyael has more to gain."

Lucien stared at Alex in bewilderment. "Exactly what does he have to gain?"

"Money, perhaps?"

"Danyael doesn't want money. I can't get him to take a penny from me."

"Or a family?"

"Roland and Jason?" Lucien almost laughed out loud. He sat in one of the comfortable leather chairs by the window and looked up at Alex, amusement glittering in his eyes. "Danyael would slit his wrists before going back to them."

"Will he?" Alex did not agree immediately with Lucien. "We know that he cares, deeply, what happens to them." He sat down on the edge of the queen-sized bed, his expression thoughtful, contemplative. "What he did back at the lab, for them…those were not the actions of a man who doesn't care. Danyael, like most of us, needs love. He's learned to avoid it, or at least he's learned to avoid attention, and apparently prefers to live without it, but I cannot believe he has stopped craving it."

"What's your point, Alex?"

"My point is that we can't easily disentangle Danyael from his family. He would walk away, never return, if that's what they told him to do, but he'd never stop hurting from their rejection."

"Danyael has put up with a lot of crap. What his family is doing to him right now is nothing compared to what he endured as a child."

"You're underestimating the impact his family has on him and the extremity of the emotions he's just absorbed from them. You'll need to be prepared for the possibility that what happened to Danyael will permanently scar his psyche." He paused briefly, searching for the right words, and then realized, regretfully, that there were none. "Roland has secured sufficient authorization to take Danyael into custody. He wants Danyael's memory wiped."

"What?" Lucien shot to his feet. His blue eyes flashed. "That's crazy! He can't do that to Danyael!"

"That was my original instinct too," Alex confirmed, his tone deliberately measured and calm. "Danyael needs memories to understand and separate out what he absorbed from his own emotions. But that's in the short term. In the long term though, it may actually be more merciful to allow Danyael to forget that his family rejected him for the second time."

"Spit it out, Alex. You're hedging, and I hate that. What are you really trying to say?"

"We're doing everything we can to keep Danyael out of his father's grasp, but should the worst happen, and if Danyael is taken and his memory is erased, I strongly urge you to respect that and leave him be. Don't try to fill the gaps. It may just give the military another excuse to take Danyael away permanently or subject him to another memory wipe. The process, by the way, is excruciating. And, as I said, in the long run, it may be more merciful to allow him to forget what his family has done to him."

Lucien's eyes narrowed into dangerous sapphire slits. "That's bullshit."

"Yes," Alex agreed without hesitation, "but it's with Danyael's best interest at heart. The Mutant Assault Group, a branch of the military, has been eyeing Danyael for the longest time. They believe that an alpha empath on the front lines can alter morale meaningfully enough to change the outcome of an entire battle. I'm not going to give them any excuse to take him permanently into their custody, so if it means we have to play along with them, we do so for now."

"Where is he now?"

"With Miriya. She'll take good care of him. As soon as they come safely to ground, I'll send Dr. Seth Copper out to them, to keep an eye on Danyael. He'll know what to do for him. Meanwhile, I'm going to talk to General John Hayes, the head of that branch of DARPA, and point out that he knows too little about the capabilities of individual mutants to make good decisions about them. With some luck, we can get him to withdraw his support from Roland."

"And what do we do?" Xin asked, speaking up for the first time.

Alex looked over at her and shrugged. "Just wait, hope, and pray."

NINETEEN

Zara glanced up at the rearview mirror, releasing her breath in a quiet sigh of relief when it was apparent that she and Galahad were not followed. She had been checking every few seconds, slowly counting down the miles to Leesburg. They were at least fifteen minutes away from Leesburg, and their luck was holding so far, though it was too early to get complacent. She would not be able to relax until they were out of American airspace.

She looked over at Galahad. He was gazing out the window, his expression distracted. "How are you doing?" she asked.

"I'm fine," Galahad said. He looked back toward her. A faint smile curved his lips, but did not light his dark eyes. "Just thinking."

"What about?"

"Danyael."

"Why?"

He looked puzzled. "Why not?"

She could think of so many reasons why not, not the least of which was the fact that the merest thought of Danyael turned her stomach. There were so many reasons. His cowardice. His unwillingness to face up to his past, never mind the present or even the future. His inability to contribute anything meaningful to a conversation, let alone a fight. His failure to come through for Carlos when his mutant powers had been most desperately needed to make a difference between life and death, which had been unforgivable.

Instead of answering, she turned the question back on Galahad. "Why do you think he's worth the time and mental energy? You went back for him. You risked capture, even death, to free him. Why?"

"Shouldn't I have?"

"For Danyael? No. You need to weigh the risks and rewards. Your life—your freedom—is far more precious than his. There is nothing you could have risked for him that would have been worth the reward of keeping him alive."

"He's a powerful ally."

"Danyael, a powerful ally? You're kidding yourself. He's wasted his life. Done nothing with it." *And when you need him most, he'll fail to come through for you.* "He's an alpha empath, a healer. He has powers most people only dream about. And what does he do? Work crappy hours for pathetic pay in a free clinic that hires the worst doctors. He's an insult to the rest of us who started out with far fewer advantages and have worked insanely hard to make something of our lives."

"I don't think he considers his empathic powers an advantage. At least it's one he'd have preferred to do without."

The flicker of compassion that flashed through her was promptly quashed, steamrolled under rampaging emotions that she could not fully explain or control. She felt off center and unbalanced every time she thought of Danyael. The quiet voice of rationality that pleaded for moderation was muted, unheard over the screaming, deeply negative emotions that could not be calmed or redirected. "True enough," she said reluctantly, "but that was a long time ago. He's had sixteen years to face up to it and move on, but he hasn't. Instead, he's stupidly chosen to live under the same rules and in the same society that wrecked his life all those years ago. He could have relocated to another country, could have lived somewhere else where mutants are welcomed with open arms, but he's still here." Her eyes narrowed into violet slits. "If you're going to consciously choose to live under a regime without attempting to change it, then you shouldn't cry foul when it turns around and bites you, as it most certainly will."

"*Can* he change it? Can anyone?"

"Perhaps, but not that he would know. He hasn't even tried. And he won't. He's too afraid to change the way things are. He thinks he has so much, but he's wrong. He has so little, and even that, he's so afraid to risk. Other people dream and dare. He just sits and cowers. What the hell could he possibly be afraid of?"

"Himself," Galahad said, his voice pitched low. He turned his head to gaze out the window as the van sped past a suburban landscape that was lightly dusted with the snow that had fallen overnight. The snow was already melting and would be gone in a few hours. No winter wonderland here, just another bland, featureless suburb under threatening, gray skies. "He's afraid of himself."

"That's absurd. Why on earth would he be afraid of himself, when there's so much more crap in the world to be afraid of?"

"Is there?" Galahad looked back at her. She tore her attention off the road long enough to see the question and uncertainty in his eyes. "Miriya implied that there were few alpha empaths of Danyael's caliber, and when it finally comes down to it, empaths may actually be more powerful than telepaths. Change the emotion, and the thought processes and actions will align accordingly. I think Danyael is afraid of himself, of what he can do, and of what he carries inside him."

"And what is that, exactly?"

"Emotions powerful enough to kill."

Zara snorted dismissively. "You and I have both racked up a decently high body count over the past few days. I'd go so far as to say that it's even part of my job description. But we don't obsess about it. We do what needs to be done and then move on. Dead is dead, whether it's from a blade, a bullet, or voodoo magic. There's no possible reason under heaven for Danyael to be preoccupied and self-absorbed over what he can do to people, when anyone with a gun and a halfway decent aim can do the same."

"It's no wonder you can't stand him. You're a hard-headed realist, and Danyael, despite all appearances to the contrary, is a dreamer. He wants something more than he can have."

"The only thing that ever stands between what you have and what you want is ambition, or the lack thereof. The difference between us is that I dared to make my dreams a reality. Danyael is apparently content to let his dreams—whatever they are—drift just beyond his fingertips. He is a spineless, spiritless coward." Her eyes glittered, cold and hard. "Everything that is happening to him he has fully deserved. Thank God you are nothing like him."

"Even if I were anything like him, you wouldn't recognize it."

For the first time, something akin to uncertainty crept into her tone. "What do you mean?"

"His psychic shield gets in the way of people perceiving him as he really is."

Uncertainty transformed into incredulity. "Are you saying that he's messing around with the way I feel?"

"Yes. As I understand it, he does it with everyone."

Her eyes narrowed. "Why?"

"He never really explained that, other than to say that he didn't want the attention."

"So how much of what I feel is real?"

"I don't know. I don't think you can trust anything you feel about Danyael, or for that matter anything you feel about anything else when you're around him."

A momentary silence, pregnant with disbelief and coiling tension, passed. "The son of a bitch." She finally spit the words out, a cold and controlled fury in her tone.

A flash of dull green in her rearview mirror drew her attention back to the fact that their lives were still very much in danger. Four military APCs. She slammed her foot down on the accelerator, abandoning any pretense that they were just another white van cruising down quiet suburban streets on the morning of Christmas Eve. "They've found us," she said softly. "Time to make a run for it."

~*~

Danyael and Miriya were ten minutes out from Leesburg Executive Airport when Danyael first caught sight of trouble. "Check out the action on the overhead pass," he murmured into the microphone.

Miriya glanced up and saw a clunky, ungraceful white truck pursued by four military APCs. "Why didn't they steal something faster?" she commented critically.

"I think they were hoping to pass unnoticed." Danyael accelerated past Miriya and led the way around a few sharp turns and onto the overhead pass. They weaved through the thin traffic and caught up easily with the trailing APC. "Can you stop them?"

"Possibly, but I'll need to see the person I'm targeting if I'm making contact for the first time. The visibility sucks here. They've got darkened windows. Your powers diffuse better. Can you do it?"

Danyael glanced to the side as he shot past the APC and caught a glimpse of a slightly open rear window. His empathic powers surged, precise and targeted, transforming anxiety into fear and fear into terror. Within the APC, trained soldiers were seized by terror that wrapped like a shroud around their faces, by panic so real they could almost taste it. The APC screeched to a halt, and the sudden braking made worse by a panicked twist of the steering wheel swung the vehicle in a wide arc. It slammed into another APC, disabling both.

"Nice one."

Danyael grimaced, gritting his teeth. "I hope no one was too badly hurt."

"Those things are built to withstand more than just bad driving," Miriya assured him. She glanced back over her shoulder. "We've got a few more incoming, and they're faster." Two cars with military markings and a containment vehicle—specially designed for use in transporting dangerous criminals, or rogue mutants—chased them.

Danyael winced at the image that Miriya tossed his way. "They've found us. It's going to come down to a race to the plane, and there's no guarantee they won't shoot it down. Can you tell Zara and Galahad to get out of that van? We'll be faster on the bike."

"Damn pre-cog was right about taking two bikes. I hate it when they're right."

"Miriya, there's a reason Ralph's an alpha pre-cognitive. He's almost always right."

The white van swerved abruptly to the left and swung in a full circle. The APC that had been right behind it braked in a desperate attempt to avoid an accident, but the tail end of the van smashed right into the APC driver's seat, seconds before the second APC barreled into the side of the first APC.

Danyael's eyes narrowed. He twisted his bike sharply toward the left to avoid joining the three-vehicle pileup. "Where the hell did she learn to drive?"

"I told her to get out. I wasn't too specific on how." Miriya swung to the right, mirroring Danyael's actions as she stopped by the passenger door, waiting until Galahad was securely seated behind her before revving the motorcycle back into high speed. Danyael, with Zara behind him, shot past her on his bike, weaving through traffic with the ease of an expert. "Where did you learn to ride a bike?" she asked into the microphone.

"I'm not completely incompetent, Miriya, despite what Zara may think of me. Lucien has lots of expensive toys, and I grew up around him. I can ride a motorbike, fly a plane, and I even know my way around yachts and sailboats." His shoulders moved in a shrug, partly to alleviate the tension of Zara's emotions slamming into him. *Don't need this now.*

"Tell her to get a grip on her emotions," Miriya said.

"She can feel whatever the hell she wants. My reaction to her emotions is my problem, not hers." The voices of his instructors had merged into his voice; their morality was now his responsibility. His training—all-consuming, life-transforming—demanded that he defend all humans, including Zara, instinctively, in spite of the costs to himself.

He inhaled unsteadily, the insight into her emotions twisting like a knife in his gut. On top of everything else he had absorbed, her emotions were purest torture, salt against open, still bleeding wounds. Her highly critical animosity toward him simmered, waiting for the faintest reason, any excuse at all, to boil over. She was coiled like a tiger, waiting, watching. Did she want him to fail so she could revel in knowing that she was right about him?

The only relief from the onslaught of her emotions came from his awareness of her feelings toward Galahad, a blanket of protection, white, safe, surprisingly gentle. It went a long way toward softening his opinion of her. *She's not incapable of feeling, of caring for others. We're not actually too different from each other. We're both just hiding behind facades of strength.*

"Danyael!" Miriya said sharply, drawing his attention to the cacophony of sirens. He heard the tension race through her voice. "Cop cars—four of them. Incoming from the left about five hundred feet behind us. This race is going to come down to seconds."

Danyael gritted his teeth. They were desperately short on options. He glanced briefly at Galahad, seated behind Miriya on the red Ducati, his physical mirror image, but vastly different from him on many levels. Galahad was perfect and whole. The genetic code he carried was priceless. There was no one like Galahad in the entire world.

In contrast, Danyael knew he himself was, if not completely broken, then at least deeply flawed.

He knew he was not thinking clearly through the muddy swirl, the virtual quicksand of destructive emotions he had absorbed from his brother and father, but even so, the choice seemed perfectly obvious to him.

The decision, once made, wrenched at his soul. "It doesn't have to end like this," he said. He reached down, took Zara's hand from around his waist, and guided it to the handlebars of the motorcycle. Understanding him immediately, she reached past him with her other hand as well, taking control of the bike. "Tell Galahad to look this way and get ready to catch."

"Catch what?" Miriya asked, but Galahad glanced over a moment later and nodded, his pale blond hair streaming in the wind.

The two bikes curved smoothly around a sharp turn, momentarily ensuring that they were not visible to their pursuers. Leaning with the motion, Danyael reached for his wallet and then pulled off his helmet. He placed the thin leather wallet, worn with age, in the helmet and then tossed the helmet easily to Galahad, who caught it effortlessly.

What the hell are you doing? Miriya shouted into his mind now that she could no longer shout into the microphone in his helmet.

Too much pursuit. He took back control of the motorcycle from Zara. *We can't all make it. Tell Galahad to put on the helmet. He's got my wallet; ID's in it. Take him to Dulles, put him on a commercial flight out of the country. My ID identifies me as a mutant, which will exempt him from the genetic security screen, and I'm cleared for international travel. Zara and I will try to get to Leesburg.*

They're looking for you too, damn it!

There are rules on how to treat a mutant. There are none on how to treat a non-human. Galahad is in far more danger than I am.

But you're hoping they believe you're Galahad.

And a genetic screen will prove that I'm not.

Yeah, well, I hope before they beat the shit out of you. Miriya snarled a nasty curse word at Danyael, but she twisted her bike sharply, taking a right turn toward Dulles International Airport.

Danyael slowed down just enough to tempt the pursuing vehicles with a glimpse of him and Zara, both faces clearly visible. Zara shouted something at him, but the words were whisked away by the wind as he accelerated. He spared a quick glance back over his shoulder, relieved when the three military vehicles and the four cop cars followed them toward Leesburg Executive Airport.

They had all of a two-minute head start when he abandoned the motorcycle at the entrance of the airport and then raced into the building, Zara right on his heels. He gasped and stumbled against the wall. Zara's emotions scalded him fractions of a second before she grabbed his hand. "Move, damn it," she demanded.

Danyael gritted his teeth, fighting nausea and on the edge of blackout. He had been able to ride the bike without too much difficulty, but actual physical effort was more than his desperately weakened, starved body would allow. "I can't keep up," he confessed, flinching when her anger and disgust slapped him. "Just go. Hide. They're after me, not you. I'll..." His teeth clenched again, and he closed his eyes briefly. Resignation passed over the flawless features. "I'll be all right."

Zara ran, but did not go far. She was watching from a bookstore, her long dark hair bundled beneath a baseball cap she had just purchased, when fifteen or more uniformed men—some police, some army—pushed past startled passengers to grab Danyael, who had just made it through the doors leading out to the tarmac where Lucien's private jet was waiting.

He fought them with the ferocity of a trapped wildcat, surprising her with the taut strength in his body, but the outcome was inevitable. He was brutally beaten and then slammed facedown into the ground. His hands were pulled roughly back, his wrists bound with electrical cuffs. She saw him wince, saw the flash of pain that surged through his eyes as the cuffs sent bursts of electrical pulses through his skin, stunning his nerve endings into numbness and incapacitating movement from his fingertips up to his shoulders.

He was then hauled back to his feet. His dark eyes widened with alarm when one of the military personnel stepped forward, an electrical collar in his hand. Danyael struggled futilely when the collar was locked around his neck, then he convulsed, doubling over in agony as the collar was activated. The first flash of electricity was always the worst, shocking mind and body into submission. Subsequent pulses, less intense but constant, kept mind and body docile, helpless to resist. The ability to speak was stolen; it was impossible to form words with the jolts of electricity directly piercing his throat.

Zara winced, biting down on her lower lip as an odd sense of pity warred against her instinctive dislike of him. Safely concealed among gawking crowds, she watched Roland Rakehell stride through the airport. Roland looked steadily at Danyael, twisted his head sharply to the side, and scrutinized the almost invisible scar that marred the right side of Danyael's face. "It's just the fucking template," he snapped.

She saw the exact moment when Roland crushed his younger son with five simple words. The mutant could not speak. He would have collapsed from exhaustion and from the constant surge of electricity through his body if the soldiers were not holding him up, but he did not need to speak. Danyael's expressive dark eyes flooded with quiet, heartbroken misery a fraction of a second before he dropped his gaze to the ground, trying desperately to conceal his pain.

Roland looked at Lucien's private jet, silver and glistening in the sunlight. "It might as well be good for something." He glanced back over his shoulder at a thin man dressed in military fatigues. "Wipe his memory as we discussed and put him on the plane back to New York."

"Here, sir?" The man looked around the public airport with an expression of consternation. "That's not a good idea, sir. He's an alpha empath, and I'll need to get through his shields to shatter his memories. An alpha empath without shields is just...not a good idea. The containment vehicle is right outside. It'll be safer to do it there; his powers will be contained while we—"

"Do it right here, right now," Roland ordered, his eyes narrowing. "Humiliate him in public. He was going to embarrass me. This is nothing less than he deserves."

The man swallowed nervously and then nodded toward the soldiers. "Hold him down." He squatted on the tarmac and looked down into the terrified dark eyes. "I'm Tim Brown. I need to take two days of your memories," he said quietly, with an odd sort of compassion in his voice. "To be precise, I don't erase them. I shatter them in a way that no longer allows you to make any sense of them. You may recall fragments in dreams or flashbacks, but those would be the exception rather than the norm. I'm very good at what I do, and the memory fragments will be so small as to be largely passed over by both your conscious and unconscious mind."

Danyael shook his head weakly. He was desperately afraid. Even at that distance, Zara could see the growing terror in his eyes.

"It'll be all right," Tim promised, his voice softly coaxing. "You have to drop your shields, let me in. And you'll have to control your own emotions, or everyone else will be affected by what you feel. Come on," he urged gently. "Drop them, or I'll have to force my way through. The outcome is inevitable in any case. Save your strength for the aftermath because you'll need it."

Tim was briefly silent as he waited in vain for Danyael to comply, and then with genuine regret in his brown eyes, he looked back over his shoulder at the lieutenant holding the controls for the electrical collar. If Danyael was not going to lower his shields voluntarily, then the only way to break through was to subject him to excruciating pain, and then use the physical distraction—though the term was inadequate in view of the kind of pain that would entail—to smash through his shields. "Punch it," he ordered quietly. The lieutenant obeyed without question, flicking a switch that sent intense currents of electricity surging through Danyael's body.

The empath jerked violently as his dark eyes flashed open wide, unseeing. Brutalized by the pain ripping mercilessly through him, he opened his mouth and a silent scream tore from his throat. This was the only opportunity Tim would ever have. The alpha telepath inhaled deeply and then spiked his power like a lance straight into Danyael's mind, plowing through his psychic shields.

Zara knew Danyael's screams were silenced, but she did not need to hear his screams to know that he was in extreme agony. His body arched and writhed in pain as his head tossed from side to side. She watched transfixed and admired the slender line of his throat as he threw his head back, struggling to breathe. She smiled as Danyael's dark eyes glistened; shimmering and sparkling with unshed tears.

She was caught completely off guard by the jolt of lust that clawed at her gut. *Danyael?*

The mood of the crowd transformed.

Struggling to maintain her shaky grip on her emotions, she looked around and saw the vicious gleams in the eyes of the people around her as they closed in on Danyael, drawn as she was to his pain. Enjoying it. Loving it. Wanting more. He was so beautiful, so fragile, stunningly exquisite in his sheer vulnerability. She wanted—they wanted—to hear him scream, wanted to make him cry. *Good God.* She breathed, trying to cling on to the fact that she *knew* she hated him, that she did not want to be around him. The man standing next to her was actually sweating, breathing heavily as he reached down to adjust and massage his crotch. *What is happening to me? To all of us?*

What the hell is happening to Danyael?

The first spike of raw power would have bludgeoned Danyael to his knees had he been standing. It was unforgiving in its brutality, inescapably intense. His unshielded mind and the memories they protected crumbled before the assault as Tim's powers tore like lion's claws through fallen prey. Only Tim heard Danyael's anguished silent screams and sensed the terror and panic that Danyael kept clamped under control as his memories were shattered and crushed beneath the staggering force of Tim's mind.

Danyael's torment felt endless. Time was utterly meaningless. He was cast adrift, awash in an ocean of pain without any chance of reaching the shore on his own. He could only endure, watching helplessly as his memories were stripped from him, as the void in front of him grew dark and monstrous, threatening to engulf his sanity.

Far worse were the emotions that bombarded him from the outside, lust so potent it bordered on insanity. Without psychic shields, his unchecked empathic powers were once again driving people around him insane. The terrified memories of his childhood rose up, engulfed him. *No...Please, I can't go through this again. I can't.*

It's okay, Danyael, Tim soothed. A memory flashed through their linked minds. A ten-year-old child sobbing in panic and terror, his beaten body throbbing in pain as he was violently assaulted by a gang of teenagers. Tim flinched, gritting his teeth against Danyael's tormented memories. *It's okay. I'll protect you. I won't let them hurt you. Relax...you're making this harder than it has to be.*

Danyael bit back a silent sob, shuddered violently under Tim's touch.

We're almost there, Danyael. We're almost there. He glanced over his shoulder. The crowd was on the verge of turning into a mob, driven mad, compelled into insanity by the pain and suffering of an alpha empath. "Form around me," he ordered his team of ten men, grateful that as humans assigned to support the Mutant Assault Group, their minds were protected and they were not susceptible to the tidal wave of Danyael's unshielded emotions. "I want a fifteen-foot perimeter. Anyone breaks through that, you cripple them. If they keep moving forward, you shoot to kill."

"Yes, sir," the lieutenant confirmed and formed his team around Tim and Danyael. The sight of machine guns, braced against shoulders, dashed cold water against the rising heat of the crowd. The minutes ticked by and the crowd jostled restlessly, craning for a glimpse of Danyael through the wall of military fatigues. Finally, one man, his eyes gleaming with the madness of frustrated lust, surged forward.

Tim jolted, shocked by the sharp retort of a gun. A man screamed. Seconds later, the gun fired again, and then there was silence. The telepath grimaced. So stupid and unnecessary. If Roland Rakehell had allowed him to wipe Danyael's memories in a private room, all the insanity could have been avoided. Nothing good came out of humans interfering in mutant affairs. The humans knew nothing, and worse, cared for nothing. Driven by greed and fear, they clung desperately to the fragments of authority still available to them, even though it was clear that their time for leadership was long past.

Tim scanned Danyael's memories before crushing them. He finally understood Roland's insistence on destroying Danyael's—*his son's*—memories. Roland was driven by selfish ambition that cared nothing for the lives trampled underfoot. He was a human embarrassed and ashamed of a mutant son, a human who regarded mutants as rubbish to be discarded when they no longer served a purpose.

Tim checked his surging anger, unwilling to add to Danyael's suffering. Danyael had endured enough. He had endured too much. The alpha empath was today's sacrifice to human paranoia. There would be others tomorrow, more the day after, and it would never end, unless the mutants rose to claim the world according to the same rules that the humans had once used to stake their claim. Survival of the fittest.

General Kieran Howard was right. Tim's jaw set determinedly. It was long past time for mutant ascendancy, and it would begin with the Mutant Assault Group.

Done. It had taken longer than he had expected—a little more than an hour, far too long for anyone to have to endure that kind of pain because of a human's selfish whim. *I'm sorry, Danyael.* Tim sat back, his expression weary, removed the electrical handcuffs and collar, and then carefully helped Danyael rise to a sitting position. "My name is Tim Brown," he reintroduced himself. "I'm with the Mutant Assault Group. You've lost two days of your memories."

Danyael reached up with a trembling hand to cover his eyes and touched his face, checking for tears. Relief passed over the beautiful features when his hand came away dry. Racking his mind, he searched for memories that had been left behind. He recalled—still cringed from—the memory of the live blood transfusion in the plane. He recalled the surprise of seeing Phillip Evans waiting by the car when he exited the plane, of learning that Lucien had sent for him.

After that, nothing, just a terrifying emptiness that taunted him with a barrage of crippling, destructive emotions, emotions for which he had no context, no memories.

Panic surged, but his exquisite training clamped down brutally on the nameless terror. Voices from his past ingrained in his subconscious took over: *Control. Your only choice in any circumstance is control. You're an alpha empath. For your own sake, you don't have the luxury of any other choice.*

He yanked his external shields back up, suffocating under the weight of emotions he did not understand. Emotions clawed at him like living things, trying to tear their way out of him. Self-hatred, so potent, so bitter that he could almost taste it on his tongue, ripped and shredded the little that he still recognized as himself. He stared down at his hands as they clenched and unclenched helplessly, involuntarily, the subtlest physical betrayal of nearly devastating emotional turmoil.

"Is it complete?" an older man, not dressed in uniform, asked sharply.

Danyael glanced at him and recoiled visibly, stunned by the extremity of the emotions emanating from him. The disgust, the hate; he searched the man's face, struggling, desperately grasping for a memory that was no longer there. Nothing. He lowered his gaze, unable to meet the scathing, penetrating dark gaze that raked him, left him feeling exposed, desperately vulnerable. *You know me. Who are you?* His mind pleaded for answers, but nothing passed his lips.

Tim nodded carefully, his expression distracted as he searched Danyael's mind. "It's done."

A smile of supreme satisfaction passed over the man's face. "Good. Get him out of my sight." His lip curled as if the very sight of Danyael disgusted him. "Put him on the plane and send him back to New York."

There was no point in fighting them, not when he no longer knew what he was fighting for, or against; not when he had bigger—far bigger—battles to fight.

The emotional maelstrom twisting through him demanded all his attention, all his strength, to keep under control, to keep from spilling past his exhausted psychic shields. He did not resist when the soldiers dragged him to his feet and hauled him over to the plane. He listened numbly as the pilots were ordered to deposit him in New York City. Home, he recalled vaguely.

The plane doors closed and the engines purred as the small, sleek passenger jet accelerated for takeoff. He stared at his subtly misshapen left hand as he gently massaged it. It ached. It always hurt, some days worse than others. That day, it was excruciating, sharp shards of pain shooting up and down his wrist. There was nothing he could do about it, nothing he could ever do about his own pain.

He inhaled unsteadily and then raised his gaze to stare unseeingly out the window. His dark eyes were inscrutable, distant with ancient pain.

The tears remained locked in his heart.

TWENTY

"They got him," Lucien said grimly as he hung up the cell phone.

Xin twisted around in the chair to look at him. "Who? Danyael?"

Lucien stood by the bay windows in his study, gazing out at the lush landscaping. His employees were hard at work both in and outside the house, repairing the damage caused by the pro-humanists and preparing for the Christmas Eve party, which would start in two hours. He saw none of the activity, even though it swirled all around him. Lucien swallowed hard, painfully, a tight, crushing feeling in his chest, somewhere in the vicinity of his heart. "It appears that his father and the military caught up with him at the airport. They wiped his memory, put him on my plane, and told the pilots to take him back to New York."

"And Miriya?"

"No sign of her, nor of Zara or Galahad. Did you try to call Zara?"

"She's not picking up, but she switched her signal."

"Signal?" Lucien turned to look at her.

"It's just something she'd worked out with her employees to let us know when she was on a case and wasn't taking calls. She's probably trying to keep her cell from being traced. What are you going to do?"

"Call Alex, let him know Danyael is back in New York, and then I'll fly out to New York as soon as I can—probably tomorrow morning. I need to see him, make sure he's all right."

"It's Christmas tomorrow."

"All the more important for Danyael not to spend it alone," Lucien retorted.

Xin dropped her gaze at the implicit rebuke.

Immediately Lucien checked his temper, inhaling sharply, and then releasing his breath in a soft sigh. "I'm sorry. I shouldn't be taking it out on you." He raked his fingers through his dark hair. "There are problems money can't solve, and it galls me to admit it. Unfortunately, most of Danyael's problems fall into that category."

"You can't solve the world's problems, Lucien."

"I'm not trying to solve the world's problems. Just one friend's, and my success rate has been highly questionable as of late."

"You care a great deal for him."

Lucien shook his head, a faint frown on his lips. "The real problem is that no one else cares enough for him. His damn psychic shield repels people; if he got run over by a car, no one would stop to help him. He goes through life expecting to be treated like crap, or at the very best ignored, gets what he expects, and then we all wonder why he's so screwed up."

"I don't think he's screwed up."

"Zara does."

"Why do you care what Zara thinks of him?"

The question made him pause, hesitate. "I don't know," he admitted finally. "Maybe because it bothers me to see how he tenses every time they're in the room together. She hates him, and she doesn't even have to say a single word to hurt him."

"As a mutant, he's probably used to that."

"Which doesn't make it right," Lucien countered with a wry half smile. He glanced at the flat-screen television mounted on the far wall of his study. A male reporter standing in front of the White House recapped the highlights of the president's short speech, which included an affirmation that the riots had ended. Order and peace had been restored to the city. People were encouraged to go about their lives as usual.

There was absolutely no mention of the mutants or the enforcers from the council who had made it all possible.

It seemed as if America was determined to use mutants when necessary, but deny them the credit and any acknowledgment of their efforts. No wonder Danyael kept such a low profile, trying to conceal from as many people as possible the fact that he was a mutant. Humans bristled with intolerance for the derivatives, for those who were most like them, the clones and in vitros. In that world, there was no room for mutants whose capabilities set them above the humans.

There was certainly no room for Galahad.

"Will Zara be all right?" Lucien asked.

"She's resourceful, and she'll get word to me if she wants me to find her. As soon as I hear anything at all, you'll be the first to know."

"Good. Danyael's my priority, but I'm not going to lose sight of Galahad. I couldn't protect Danyael." His smile was bitter. "Let's see if I can do a better job with Galahad."

"The responsibility isn't yours to bear alone."

"No one else seems interested in the job description."

She smiled faintly. "I'll help."

"Won't that get you in trouble? As far as we know, the government wants *both* of them."

"I wasn't planning on telling them that I'm helping." She shrugged, chuckling softly. "What I do in my free time is my business, even if it is with government resources, and I can cover my tracks."

Lucien eased into a faint smile, the first real smile he had enjoyed in hours. He looked away briefly and then back again at Xin, directly meeting her gaze. His smile transformed unexpectedly into a grin, became hopeful. "You're staying for the party, aren't you?"

She blinked in surprise. "What party?"

~*~

Miriya turned her head to stare out of the window. The sky stretched out in a limitless horizon before her, but she saw nothing. She swallowed hard against the lump in her throat and then reached up absently to swipe a single teardrop before it rolled down her cheek.

"Miriya?" A gentle hand wrapped around hers.

She closed her eyes against the heartache that resonated through her. The voice was his voice, and yet it was not. She might never hear him speak her name again.

"They took his memory." She kept her voice low. There were few passengers in the first-class section of the plane, but this was a private conversation on an intensely personal topic. Her mind was still connected to Danyael's, the telepathic link so deeply buried that he was unaware of it. Even Tim Brown had not picked up on it. "He doesn't know us anymore. He doesn't remember me or you or Zara, though that's probably a mercy."

"Why? Why would they take his memory?"

"I don't really know. Roland Rakehell commanded the Mutant Assault Group officials who arrested him. He said something about Danyael embarrassing him." She shook her head and inhaled deeply. The extremity of Roland's decision stunned her. If all parents erased the memories of the children who embarrassed them, the world would be full of amnesiacs. "I don't know what he meant, though he got what he wanted. Danyael doesn't remember him now either."

"Miriya, why did he give me his identification?" Galahad asked softly, voicing the question that had been at the top of his mind ever since he stared in disbelief at the thin black wallet safely nestled in the motorcycle helmet he had caught from Danyael.

Miriya shrugged. "Because he thought you deserved a chance, and he was the only one who could give it to you."

"In spite of the cost."

"Danyael doesn't really count the cost, in large part because he undervalues what he brings to the table."

"Why?"

"Because when enough people look down on you and your life's choices, you eventually start to believe them."

"But—"

She shook her head and tried to change the topic. "I don't understand Danyael much, honestly. He's council-trained—"

"Aren't you as well?"

"Council-trained? No, I work for the council but I joined them as an adult. The council-trained are the young alphas who were raised—and some would say, *shaped*—by the council. There aren't many of them, but they all have two traits in common. They're all extremely talented, and they're all very highly placed in positions of authority and influence."

"Including Danyael?"

Miriya smiled thinly at the doubt she heard in Galahad's voice. "Yes, including Danyael. Danyael's one core failing is that as an empath, his self-image and sense of self-worth are far too dependent on what people feel about him. His psychic shield repels people, so it becomes a vicious, self-reinforcing downward cycle. Nevertheless, there is a profound disconnect between Danyael's self-image and who he really is. He may have a dead-end job in a poverty-stricken Brooklyn neighborhood, but he is unquestionably one of the most powerful alpha empaths alive. In addition, Lucien commands one of the largest private fortunes in the world, and as of right now, Danyael is the sole beneficiary in Lucien's will."

"But why would the fact that Danyael is council-trained matter?"

"Because they're different. They see the world differently from most mutants, and even from people like me—mutants who work for the council. Some say that council-trained serve the council's highest purpose, or its secret agenda. Those two terms are used interchangeably, though it has never been clear to me if they're one and the same."

"And that would be?"

"Officially? A peaceful coexistence between humans and mutants, and everything in between. The cynical might say the continued dominance of humans in spite of the genetic superiority of human derivatives and mutants."

"And you don't agree?"

"I work for the council. Of course I believe, on some level, in a peaceful coexistence, but the human domination part I can do without. Still, the council takes care of its own, especially the alphas. They'll take care of Danyael, but it's probably just as well we separated the two of you. Together you're too big a target to resist. America hates you for your perfection, him for his mutation. Getting out of the country was absolutely the right thing to do."

She heard the thoughts he did not give voice to. *But what good are power and influence if you're not even going to use them to defend yourself? That's insane. Why didn't he fight back? Why does he allow humans to treat him like that?* "And what will we do now?" he asked, the simple question standing out in stark contrast to the swirl of confusion, even distress, racing through his thoughts.

Miriya hesitated and then decided not to preemptively address the questions Galahad had not spoken aloud. Privacy was hard enough to come by these days; there was no need for her to dispel his illusions of personal space so quickly. "We'll lay low for a while. Contact Lucien and tap into his vast resources in Brazil. Maybe he can find a way for us to get out to an even safer country."

"Like Singapore?"

"Singapore has its own issues, but at least it's open to the genetic revolution." She glanced over at him. "The real question is what *you* want to do, Galahad."

The question stretched out before him, as limitless as the horizon. *Zara was right. I won't be like Danyael. I will not be taken again, and I won't be trapped. I will not live my life, like Danyael does, under the control and influence of those who fear and hate me.* "I want a chance to live up to my potential," he said quietly. His dark eyes were intent, focused, and serious. "My *full* potential."

A shiver raced down her spine as her telepathic powers gleaned the extent of the determination behind those simple words and assessed the depth of ambition that would drive the most perfect selection of genes available to humanity.

Shit, she concluded. *The world is seriously screwed.*

~*~

It was going to be a beautiful Christmas, Seth Copper concluded with a faint smile of relish. The recent infusion of Danyael's blood surged through his veins. He would enjoy the rush of energy, of vitality for several more weeks. More intoxicating was the rush of power. How much of it was Danyael's mutant powers and how much of it simply the psychological rush of being able to dominate someone as amazing as Danyael, he did not know.

The phone on his mahogany desk rang, interrupting his reverie. He glanced at the number on the caller ID display and decided to pick it up. That conversation was long overdue anyway. "Yes, what is it?" He paused, listening to the rush of words on the other end, the stammer in the man's typically smooth, relaxed voice.

Seth chuckled. The man was terrified of him. Seth enjoyed power in all forms. His current target was far less interesting, but until he had Danyael back again, it would have to do. "Yes, I'm well aware that Danyael has returned to New York."

He paused, frowning, as the man continued. His eyes narrowed, his brow furrowing slightly. "Are you backing out of our agreement?" His tone was cool, dangerous.

There was another rush of words as the man on the other end hastened to appease him.

"No, certainly not, Phillip," he cut off the conversation before it wasted more of his precious time. "I am aware that Lucien is similarly invested in Galahad, and that if anyone can find out where he is, it is you. However, Galahad and Danyael are not interchangeable. There is more to beauty than the physical appearance and so much more to power than perfect genes. Danyael's true beauty and power is in how his soul shimmers when you hold it to the light, stunningly vulnerable and impossibly fragile, yet perfectly whole. There is no substitute for him. Or for his blood."

He listened. The frantic stammer on the other end assured him that the idiotic suggestion had been a random idea, that his allegiance was unaltered, his loyalty still secure. He did not believe a word of it, but now that the off switch in Danyael's brain no longer worked reliably, Phillip Evans was something of a necessity. For the time being, he could stay close to Danyael publicly, since Alex had so conveniently asked him to care for the empath. Over the longer term, Phillip was far better positioned to keep track of Danyael's movements and to identify opportunities such as the one he had enjoyed just days before. Especially if Danyael put up a fight, any attempt to snatch him out from under Lucien Winter's watchful gaze would need a great deal more planning and subtlety. Phillip Evans was instrumental to that end.

"And one last thing, Phillip. Killing yourself will not solve the problem. Your family will pay the ultimate price, regardless, if you do not provide me with continued access to Danyael." Seth paused, unsurprised by the silence on the other end. The pace of Phillip Evans's breathing had accelerated. No question, the man was in a state of near panic.

Seth was mildly amused, but ultimately, the conversation wearied him. He wanted peace and quiet; he wanted to return to his ever-evolving fantasy of what he would do to Danyael the next time. Would Danyael resist, or would he be able to catch Danyael unawares? The game had become a great deal more engaging. Chuckling to himself, he said one last thing before hanging up the phone. "Merry Christmas."

~*~

This was not how she had envisioned spending Christmas Eve, Xin decided as she sipped slowly from a glass of champagne. It was even better. She scanned the room, recognizing many business and political leaders as well as key media personalities. She was content to watch unobtrusively from the sidelines as the rich and the powerful mingled in Lucien's magnificent home, now perfectly restored after the pro-humanist attack. Lucien's father and mother hosted the Christmas Eve event, as they did every year. Their divorce notwithstanding, they appeared happy and comfortable together as they circulated around the room chatting with their guests, their arms loosely linked in familiar intimacy.

Lucien, who wore a tuxedo with as much ease and comfort as he did jeans and a sweater, was at home in his surroundings, handling the inevitable attention with good humor and natural grace. There was a blonde in an exquisite and much-too-revealing violet dress who lingered close to him for several long minutes until Lucien introduced her to another guest and smoothly handed her off. The blonde was still blinking in surprise as the other man proudly escorted her toward the decorated buffet tables, probably wondering how she had managed to lose her grip on Lucien.

Xin stifled a giggle and was still smiling when Lucien weaved his way toward her. It took awhile. He was inevitably stopped by well-meaning guests along the way, people who wanted a moment of his time to talk to him and offer him their best wishes for the Christmas season and the New Year. "Something funny?" he inquired as he stepped up to her.

"I noticed how elegantly you pushed her onto someone else." She chuckled, her gaze shifting back toward the blonde.

"Ah." Lucien followed her gaze and grinned too. "Someone else who is more likely to appreciate her, I might add."

"She's beautiful."

"I suppose," Lucien replied. "Are you all right? I'm afraid I've been terribly remiss in my duties as a host, seeing how I've left you here on your own."

"Oh, no, I'm quite all right." She waved off his concern. "People-watching is one of my favorite pastimes, and there are so many people to watch here." She saw Phillip Evans step back into the room through the patio doors, a deeply worried expression on his face as he slipped a cell phone back into his pocket. It took him several seconds to regain his composure, and even then, his practiced smile was distinctly shaky as he turned to greet a guest. "He doesn't look happy," she observed, with a nod of her head toward Phillip.

"He's been distracted recently," Lucien agreed with a faint frown. "I'll check in with him when things settle down. Any word from Zara?"

"Not yet. I do have something interesting for you though, which I found when I had a spare moment in between scrambling home to get ready for your party and then rushing back here. According to a passenger dispatch, Miriya Templeton and Danyael Sabre boarded a Varig flight to Rio de Janeiro three hours ago."

"Danyael?" Lucien's eyes widened and then narrowed into thin slits. "Galahad."

"Right. I confess I didn't see that coming, but it looks like Galahad is safely on his way out of the country under Miriya's protection."

"How did they pull off the switch?"

"I don't know, but if they indeed did switch, then Zara may be with Danyael right now."

"That's not very consoling."

Xin laughed quietly. "I know, but it's better than his being alone."

"That's highly debatable. We know she wasn't on the flight with him back to New York, or the pilots would have mentioned it to me when they called."

"Zara's ingenious enough to get to New York in other ways that do not require showing her official identification. I'm fairly sure she carries multiple backup IDs on her at all times. Do you think Danyael will call you?"

"I know he will. The only question is when. If I don't like the way he sounds, I'll head out to New York." There was nothing he could do now, except wait. He released his breath, the soft sigh edged with frustration and self-condemnation. "I don't know what exactly the hell I accomplished by calling Danyael when this whole mess started. He's far worse off now than he was two days ago."

"I'd contend that he didn't have any chance of staying out of it. His father dragged him into this mess twenty-five years ago, not you. As for what we got out of it, the threat of the abominations has been neutralized and Galahad is safely out of the country." She kept her voice low. "By the way, I deleted his name and Miriya's from the Varig passenger manifest, and in about six hours, I plan to hack into the Brazilian immigration department and delete their names from the record of people entering the country as well. Unless someone found their names on the flight manifest before I did, they're effectively untraceable."

"You're a terror behind a computer, aren't you?"

She smiled winsomely. "Technology likes me, that's all."

"Unfortunately, none of Danyael's problems can be solved by money or technology," Lucien said, his blue eyes fractionally darkening as they always did when he was troubled.

"You're brooding again," Xin chided gently, her voice soothing. "Danyael's problems can be solved only by people, and I think you've found that he has friends. The council appears willing to protect and defend him. Danyael has powerful allies, Lucien, and he has more friends than he knows."

"And what does that give him?"

"Hope," Xin replied simply.

Lucien inhaled deeply, feeling oddly absolved of the vague sense of guilt that had been hounding him ever since he summoned Danyael from New York. Xin had a way of putting things in perspective with her calm, flawless logic. She was a blast of icy-cold fresh air compared to the heated swirl of complex emotions that simmered beneath Zara's seemingly cool façade.

Xin was good for him. The random thought that flickered through his mind caught him off guard, but he smoothed the frown of puzzlement before it had time to register on his face. Lucien glanced briefly at his watch and then turned back to Xin. "Come with me."

She arched a brow at him. "What?"

"Come mingle with me." He flashed a smile that for sheer impact almost rivaled Danyael's and Galahad's immaculate beauty. "If I have to endure this, then the least you could do is keep me company." He held out an arm to her and waited until she slipped her arm through the crook of his elbow.

Xin allowed Lucien to lead her back into the heart of the festivities. She smiled with easy, natural grace up at him, unaware of how radiantly beautiful she was just then or that Lucien's breath had caught in his throat. "If I forget to tell you later, Lucien, I had a wonderful time tonight. Merry Christmas."

~*~

"Danyael Sabre is back in New York City."

General Kieran Howard, sipping slowly from a glass of bourbon, swiveled around in his leather seat. "What is your assessment of Danyael?"

"He's impressive," Tim Brown said, standing at ease in front of his commanding officer. "He has stronger psychic shields than many defense-class alpha telepaths and—"

"He didn't lose control, did he?" Kieran interrupted. "Of course, he didn't. It would take a great deal more than a memory wipe to push Danyael over the edge."

"Sir, it would be dangerous to push Danyael too hard."

"Are the cracks already showing? Do you recall, Tim, the incident at Kivisuo, Finland, some twenty years ago? An entire village—two hundred and fifty-seven people—died under mysterious circumstances. The Finnish government clamped down on reports of the incident, but rumors leaked anyway. Fredrik Virtanen, the first confirmed alpha empath, had lost his mind and his unleashed empathic powers killed everyone within a two-mile radius."

"Sir, Danyael is believed to be a great deal more powerful than Virtanen ever was."

"Exactly. I want him for the assault group, Tim. I want him to turn to us. To do so, we'll have to drive him past his breaking point. Danyael has three anchors: the solace he finds in his calling as a healer, his faith in the council, and his friendship with Lucien. When we destroy each of his anchors, he'll realize that he has no one to turn to, but us."

"It's a dangerous game you're playing, sir."

"Yes, but Danyael Sabre is worth the price. Keep him under close surveillance, Tim. Our chance will come, soon. I don't want to miss it." Kieran relaxed in his chair, immensely pleased with the turn of events. "I know exactly what we need to do next. Danyael will be ours in under a month."

~*~

Zara Itani strode through LaGuardia Airport, indifferent to the attention she drew. She took her attractiveness for granted most of the time and did not realize how irritation and frustration made her violet eyes glitter, sparkling as they caught the light. With a single careless tug, waves of long blue-black hair cascaded from a loose knot that she had piled on top of her head. Men stared. Women loftily looked away. She did not notice or care as she shrugged into her long leather coat and stepped out onto the street.

She pulled out a pocket-sized electronic tablet as she slipped into a cab. The rarely used device was registered under the name of a fourteen-year-old boy in Wisconsin. No one had yet noticed that the device tended to access public records that no fourteen-year-old boy from Wisconsin would logically be interested in.

As she expected, Danyael Sabre was listed in the New York City public directory. Many mutants—especially those with secure day jobs—did not opt out of public records. They wanted to blend into the population, not give their critics additional ammunition against them by insisting that they had something to hide. Danyael fell into that category. She gave the cab driver his address in Brooklyn and then leaned back against the PVC-covered car seat.

She looked out of the window as the city flashed by. She hated New York City and had never been able to pinpoint exactly why. The unending crush of humanity packed into the filth and squalor of many of the poorer neighborhoods in Brooklyn and the Bronx were certainly among the driving reasons. Unfortunately, that was where Danyael lived and where she was headed.

On Christmas Eve, no less.

She ground her teeth in frustration and damned him for making her make a trip into one of the worst neighborhoods in Brooklyn for—what? To make sure he was all right? Danyael was an alpha mutant. He was powerful, gifted with abilities humans could only dream of. He did not need, would not want any help from her.

She did not want to help. The merest thought of him made her skin crawl in revulsion. She did not want to be anywhere near him, so why was she here, in a city she hated, on Christmas Eve, in a cab of questionable cleanliness, trying to locate a single person she despised in a city of ten million people?

She had lost her mind. No question about it.

How much of what I feel is real?

The cab deposited her outside a converted warehouse in Brownsville, Brooklyn. The brick façade was grimy, dark from pollution. Just wonderful, she noted sardonically, paying the cab driver and then stepping out of the cab.

No security; heck, the main entrance was not even locked. This wasn't a place where locks did any good, she suspected. The only defense was not to have anything worth stealing.

She took the stairs—there was no elevator—to the fifth floor, and then walked down dimly lit corridors, naked bulbs swinging from ancient electrical connections, to Danyael's apartment. She heard the sound of laughter coming from one of the adjacent apartments, probably a family celebrating Christmas, apparently happy in spite of living in a dump. She knocked briskly, absently noting the peeling paint on the door. No answer. She hesitated for only two seconds. The corridor was empty, so she picked the lock with easy expertise and pushed open the door.

He wasn't there.

Her eyes narrowed. He had at least an hour's head start on her. He should have been home. She stepped into his tiny studio apartment, closing the door behind her, and flicked on the light switch by the door.

So this was his home. Clean—she had not expected that—but in spite of that, downright depressing. The narrow, poorly lit entryway was dismal. The tiled bathroom had ancient fixtures, and the shower was so tiny that it was almost claustrophobic. The kitchen was small, with barely enough space for a two-burner stove, a refrigerator that looked at least twenty years old, an equally old microwave, and a small sink. A few dishes and cutlery lay in a drying rack next to the sink; an empty pot and frying pan sat on the stove. The attached dining area was large enough for a square table and two chairs. A light blinked on the phone that had been placed on the table announcing voicemails. She ignored it and proceeded to explore the rest of Danyael's pitiful home.

Two steps led up to a marginally larger room with exposed brickwork on the exterior wall. There wasn't much in that room, just a folded full-sized futon on a wooden frame, a tall bookshelf that held books on two of the top shelves and neatly folded clothes on the lower three shelves, and a laptop on the small coffee table next to the futon. Two pillows and a folded comforter, somewhat threadbare, lay on the futon. A book on the coffee table had a white tag on its spine, indicating that it had been borrowed from a library. The single radiator in the apartment was cool to the touch.

Life lived on the cheap, and ugly.

There were no carpets to break up the monotony or absorb the chill of the gray cement floors, other than the rug outside the bathroom near the entryway to the studio. No pictures. No photographs. Nothing transformed the studio from merely a place to eat and sleep, to a home.

It was as colorless and as bland as the personality of the man who lived there.

It was where she was apparently spending the night.

Scowling, she searched the kitchen, and within five minutes, she settled down on the futon—the only semi-comfortable chair in the apartment, and that wasn't saying much—with a ham sandwich and a glass of milk. Poor fare for Christmas Eve, but there wasn't much else in Danyael's home, and she was reluctant to leave the apartment when she did not know when he would return. She wanted to be there when he walked in.

She would give him a piece of her mind and rake him over hot coals. It was the least he deserved for dragging her away from family and friends on Christmas Eve.

Then maybe, *just maybe*, she would consider thanking him for what he had done for Galahad.

~*~

It was almost nine at night when Danyael slowly made his way out of the terminal of Teterboro Airport in New Jersey. Lucien's private jet had landed several hours earlier, and Danyael had managed to get off the plane only to have his fading strength give out on him as he made it to the terminal. He spent a few hours curled up on an uncomfortable chair in a corner of the waiting area, struggling—and largely failing—to work through the pain on his own. Passengers moving briskly through the airport took him for a homeless vagrant and ignored him. Finally a bored security officer told him to get moving, and he complied, leaving the terminal and getting into the only cab waiting at the curb.

"Where to?" the cab driver demanded impatiently.

"I—" he searched the pocket of his jeans, of his jacket, found keys and cell phone, but no wallet, no ID, no credit card, and no money. He squeezed his eyes shut and swallowed hard, a flicker of bitter resignation twisting his features. *Not this, not now. So tired.*

He needed to get home, needed to rest. More than anything, he desperately needed a break in his run of bad luck. "I'm sorry, I'm just going to walk."

"Don't fucking waste my time, man." The driver cursed at him as Danyael stepped out of the cab.

Danyael exhaled shakily and then raised his face to the cold night air that cut right through the minimal warmth afforded by his old leather jacket. The icy fingers of the wind caressed his face, and he welcomed the physical discomfort as a desperately needed distraction from the emotional torment.

He turned and started down the street. It would take hours to walk back to his home in Brooklyn, but he did not have anywhere else to be, anyway. His psychic shields were so tightly locked in place that it actually hurt to breathe. *Take one step at a time.* He stared down at his feet, feeling the cold of the freezing rain through his sneakers.

He felt cold, sick and hungry. He could barely think past the shafts of pain pounding through his skull or the deep, raw ache in his heart. He flinched when he caught a glimpse of his reflection in a store window, his bleak eyes haunted by a dark and wrenching pain that no amount of control or willpower could conceal.

He fought down the waves of revulsion that churned deep in the pit of his stomach. Where had it come from? How could he hate himself so viciously and with such fierce desperation?

Wrapping his arms around his cramping stomach to hold himself together, Danyael ground down on his teeth as if it would hold the pain in, pain that made him want to curl up on the sidewalk and pound his fists into the earth until they bled. Desperate to talk to the only friend he had, he reached into his jacket pocket for his cell phone. The battery indicator flashed red, perhaps enough for one call, if that.

The call went straight to voicemail. Danyael closed his eyes as he heard Lucien's familiar voice asking the caller to leave a message. What could he say? How could he say what was truly on his mind and in his heart? *What happened? You sent for me. What the hell did you do to me?*

Two days of unexplained hell warred against sixteen years of friendship. For a single tormented moment, their friendship and their future hung in the balance.

Ultimately, friendship won. Faith won.

Danyael inhaled deeply and then breathed out a shaky, almost sobbing sigh. "Hi, Luce." The familiar childhood name calmed him enough to blurt out the words before he changed his mind. "I…just called to wish you a Merry Christmas."

He disconnected the call and shoved the cell phone back into the pocket of his frayed denim jeans. Hunched against the freezing night wind, he walked slowly past groups of revelers celebrating Christmas Eve with friends and family. He tried to staunch the emotional bleeding as he watched love and laughter flow freely all around him, flow past him.

I'll be all right.

Still, it was going to be a long way home.

The sequel to Perfection Unleashed
October 2012

PERFECT BETRAYAL

Danyael Sabre fought a losing battle against fatigue and the wet chill of a New York winter storm. As the minutes ticked by slowly, he slipped past extreme exhaustion into mindless automation. The neighborhood deteriorated, the deeper he traveled into Brooklyn. The icy drizzle could not mask or wash away the stench of cheap alcohol and urine in the streets. He paused at the pollution-stained façade of an apartment complex. It was a welcome sight; home, at last.

Danyael unlocked the door of his apartment, slipped in, and quietly shut it behind him. He leaned his head against the door and closed his eyes. His shoulders sagged. He was alone; he could relax. With a soft sigh, he lowered his psychic shields. The suffocating weight of emotions he did not understand and could not remember flowed out of him.

A woman's shriek of panic ripped through the silence of the apartment and shattered his lethargy. His dark eyes flashed open. *I'm not alone!*

She hurled herself at him. Instinctively, he caught her wrists as she clawed at his face. The swirl of long dark hair, swaying wildly, concealed most of her face, but he caught a glimpse of unreasoning terror in her eyes, terror he had put in there.

He struggled to contain the emotions he had released. The effort plowed through him, a punch to his stomach. It tore the breath out of his lungs. He convulsed, doubling over, the strain too much for a body pushed to its limits. His grip on her wrists loosened. She lunged away from him and raced to the kitchen.

"No, wait." He grabbed her before her fingers wrapped around the hilt of the knife in the drying rack. His empathic powers surged, irresistible as the tides. They snaked, graceful tendrils of living vines, through her psyche and siphoned out the emotions he had unwittingly forced on her. To his relief, rationality seeped into her wide violet eyes. He started to ask if she was all right, but before he could utter a single word, scorching pain ripped down his spine.

Only his training suppressed the scream of agony. He flung himself away from her and crashed into the sink. Violent shudders wracked his body. He gripped hard on the countertop to brace against the spasms of pain.

What the hell?

He gritted his teeth and tasted blood in his mouth. He had not been prepared for *her* roiling emotions. Targeted at him, her emotions sliced through his defenses with devastating precision, anger and hate, vitally alive, scalding hot. They flared when he touched them, punished him when he tried to absorb them from her. He had to work through them. There was no other way. The alternative—returning the emotions to her—was not an option.

His eyes closed. Trembling, he focused on each breath burning in his lungs. As he shakily exhaled, he unclenched his fists. *Release the pain.*

Most of the time, the technique worked flawlessly. He had years of practice.

That day, it nearly didn't.

Minutes passed before the red haze of pain obscuring his vision thinned and eventually wafted away. He looked up to find her staring steadily at him, the passion and fury he had briefly witnessed now perfectly regulated beneath an icy-cold façade.

"Are you all right?" he asked hoarsely.

Her eyes narrowed. She tilted her head but did not answer. She merely looked at him as if he were insane for asking the question.

"Are you all right?" Danyael asked again. He leaned against the old fridge. His quiet tone concealed his exhaustion. A quick empathic probe confirmed she was calm and rational, but her lack of response worried him. He thought he had reabsorbed the poisonous brew of his emotions before they sank into her psyche, but perhaps he had not been fast enough. Had he hurt her?

"I'm sorry. I know you've had a shock. Would you like to sit?" He paused; the aloof distance in her demeanor caused him to hesitate. He tried for a smile, though fatigue limited it to a faint curve on the edges of his lips. "I'm Danyael Sabre."

"Zara." Her answer was brusque. She did not offer a last name.

The name toyed on the edge of his consciousness, as if he had heard it before, but he was certain he did not know her. There was no way he could have forgotten someone as attractive as she was.

His mind mocked him. Who was to say what he could have forgotten? After all, he had no memories of the prior two days.